MW00772021

Indigenous Studies Series

The Indigenous Studies Series builds on the successes of the past and is inspired by recent critical conversations about Indigenous epistemological frameworks. Recognizing the need to encourage burgeoning scholarship, the series welcomes manuscripts drawing upon Indigenous intellectual traditions and philosophies, particularly in discussions situated within the Humanities.

Map of Indigenous Nations of Turtle Island. There are over sixteen hundred nations on Turtle Island, or North America. In this volume, we are able to represent only a small selection of these Nations. For a more complete map, please visit www.tribalrelationships.com. (*Credit*: Aaron R. Carapella and Tribal Nations Maps)

READ • LISTEN • TELL

INDIGENOUS STORIES FROM TURTLE ISLAND

Sophie McCall, Deanna Reder, David Gaertner,
and Gabrielle L'Hirondelle Hill, editors

WILFRID LAURIER
UNIVERSITY PRESS

Wilfrid Laurier University Press acknowledges the support of the Canada Council for the Arts for our publishing program. We acknowledge the financial support of the Government of Canada through the Canada Book Fund for our publishing activities. This work was supported by the Research Support Fund.

Library and Archives Canada Cataloguing in Publication
  Read, listen, tell : indigenous stories from Turtle Island / Sophie McCall, Deanna Reder, David Gaertner, and Gabrielle L'Hirondelle Hill, editors.

(Indigenous studies series)
Includes bibliographical references and index.
Issued in print and electronic formats.
ISBN 978-1-77112-300-6 (softcover).—ISBN 978-1-77112-301-3 (PDF).—
ISBN 978-1-77112-302-0 (EPUB)

  1. Indians of North America—Literary collections. 2. Canadian literature (English)—Indian authors. 3. American literature—Indian authors. I. McCall, Sophie, 1969–, editor II. Reder, Deanna, 1963–, editor III. Gaertner, David, 1979–, editor IV. Hill, Gabrielle L'Hirondelle, 1979–, editor V. Series: Indigenous studies series

PS8235.I6R43 2017   C810.8'0897   C2017-900404-2
                                                            C2017-900405-0

Cover image by Sonny Assu, *The Paradise Syndrome, Voyage #32* (2016; archival pigment print, 21 x 36"). Courtesy of the artist. sonnyassu.com. Cover design by Angela Booth Malleau, designbooth.ca. Frontispiece: map by Aaron R. Carapella and Tribal Nations Maps. Interior design by Angela Booth Malleau.

TABLES OF CONTENTS

I. Table of Contents by Theme

The goal of *Read, Listen, Tell* is not only to share with readers an incredibly diverse collection of Indigenous stories, but also to transform methods of reading by bringing into the forefront practices in interpreting texts that are grounded in Indigenous knowledges and scholarship. Each of the chapters offers particular strategies for reading the stories in multiple ways, encouraging readers to expand the scope of the short story by including a broad range of story forms. The chapters consist of five to seven stories, accompanied by a critical essay that helps contextualize some of the questions and issues the stories raise.

1. "The Truth about Stories Is ... Stories Are All That We Are"

For Thomas King, stories not only *contribute* to our sense of who we are—stories are *who we are*. The stories in this chapter invite readers to think not only about the profound role that stories play in shaping the world, but also about our responsibilities to those stories as readers and critics. Reading and sharing stories is not simply a pastime; it is the most primary means for us to engage with and make sense of the world around us.

2. Land, Homeland, Territory

The interrelationship between land, story, and community plays a vital role in many of the works by Indigenous writers and storytellers. Looking closely at the way a story represents place can reveal a lot about human relationships and different ways of understanding place and land. How can we read a variety of settings—rural, urban, interior, exterior, reserve, bush—as enriching our understanding of the way the characters relate to their surroundings?

3. "Reinventing the Enemy's Language"

The stories in this section explore the distinct values and knowledges contained within Indigenous languages. Not only are the authors making intentional word choices to influence the tone, mood, and shape of their narratives; they are also alternating between Indigenous languages and various forms of English. This deliberate use of language suggests that languages hold specific ideas, cultural values, and specific knowledges that are worthwhile to stay connected to.

4. Cree Knowledge Embedded in Stories

One way of approaching Indigenous stories is to understand them in light of tribal ways of knowing. In this chapter, you will learn how to approach Cree literature as a body of work influenced by the intellectual, cultural and spiritual traditions that preceded the arrival of Europeans. You will also learn how to read these stories in reference to longstanding stories and storytelling styles.

5. "Each Word Has a Story of Its Own": Story Arcs and Story Cycles

Indigenous stories that might be categorized as "traditional" are often part of a larger story cycle—that is, the particular story is only one small part of a series of connected stories. Reading stories as part of a story cycle, and paying close attention to the interrelationships between stories, encourages us as readers to look for meaning beyond the confines of just one story.

6. Community, Self, Transformation

How do we understand the self in relation to others—not only human but those belonging to the wider living world? A recurring theme of transformation in these stories reminds us to respect the inter-relatedness of all beings—human, animal, and elemental.

7. Shifting Perspectives

Students and scholars of literature often are trained to identify and analyse how ideology functions within texts, but these readers sometimes overlook the ideologies that they themselves bring to the texts. Shifts in perspective and the juxtaposition of different points of view encourage readers to examine their own assumptions, and to consider how ideology influences the way we understand stories.

8. **Indigenous Fantasy and SF**

Indigenous authors have composed stories in any number of genres, including (but not limited to) fantasy, science fiction, erotica and horror. Indigenous writers are shaping, adapting and indigenizing well-known literary genres to create some of the most innovative, provocative and fun-to-read short fiction available.

II. Table of Contents by Decade of Publication

2000s

ACKNOWLEDGEMENTS

FIRST AND FOREMOST we extend our deepest appreciation to the contributors to *Read, Listen, Tell*—the amazing Indigenous writers and artists from far and wide who so generously shared their work, answered our many questions, and who have brought so much richness to this world through their words, stories, and images. The late Jo-Ann Episkenew, much missed friend and colleague, whose work we are honoured to include in this book, is first on the list to hail and thank. Thanks to the editors and the publishers who supported the works of these writers in their publications, and who granted us permission to reprint them in this volume.

In designing *Read, Listen, Tell* over the course of several years, we consulted with many friends and colleagues, and we are grateful to all who offered us invaluable advice. Thanks especially to all the participants at the workshop, Approaching Indigenous Literatures in the 21st Century: How Shall We Teach These?, co-organized by Deanna Reder and Linda Morra (Simon Fraser University, February 2014). The discussions at this event helped us completely overhaul the conceptual framework of the critical reader, ultimately making it a much stronger book. One of the participants at this gathering was another dearly missed friend and fiercely passionate reader of Indigenous literatures, the late Renate Eigenbrod. Along with Renate we thank Warren Cariou, Margery Fee, Michele Lacombe, Hartmut Lutz, Keavy Martin, Linda Morra, Dory Nason, June Scudeler, and Chris Teuton. Thanks to those who helped suggest some of the best stories from Turtle Island: Grace L. Dillon, Maurizio Gatti, Sarah Henzi, Daniel Heath Justice, Heather Macfarlane, Armand Ruffo, Paul Seesequasis, Isabelle St-Amand, and Richard Van Camp. Huge thanks to Christine Stewart, who taught an earlier version of *Read, Listen, Tell* in the Transition Year Program (TYP) at the University of Alberta in Fall 2014, and to the twenty-two Indigenous students enrolled in the class, for offering invaluable feedback. Sophie would also like to thank her graduate students in the MATE program (Spring 2014 and Spring 2017) and her undergraduate students in English 453W (Spring 2013 and Fall 2014) for their incisive discussions around the politics of anthology-making and for their feedback on the selection of the stories.

Many thanks to Kenn Harper for some key information on Joe Panipakuttuk, and thanks to Keavy Martin for getting us in touch. Thank you to Vicki White, daughter of Snuneymuxw Elder and writer, Ellen Rice White, for communicating with us on behalf of her mother. Thanks to Donald Frischmann, co-editor of *Words of the True Peoples/Palabras de los Seres Verdaderos*, for coordinating with us on behalf of the writers, Joel Torres Sánchez and Isaías Hernández Isidro, and Christian H. Rasmussen, co-editor of *Relatos del centro del mundo*, for helping us properly acknowledge the author, Sixto Canul, of the story "The Son Who Came Back from the United States." Many thanks to Cherokee researcher and cartographer Aaron Carapella for the extraordinary map of Turtle Island featuring the nations of the writers contained in this volume. Thank you, Aaron Leon, for photographing Tania Willard's work. Many thanks to Rachel Taylor (Iñupiat) for taking care of the enormous task of securing copyright and for copy-editing the completed manuscript. Thanks to Cameron Duder for an early copy-edit, to Valerie Ahwee for her own copy-editing, and to Ann McCall for careful proofreading.

Many thanks to the authors who devoted their time and energy in interviews associated with this critical reader: Jeannette Armstrong, Lisa Bird-Wilson, Tomson Highway, Daniel Heath Justice, Lee Maracle, Eden Robinson, Michael Nicoll Yahgulanaas, and Greg Younging. A special thanks is due to Omushkego Cree Elder and storyteller Louis Bird, who came to Vancouver and taught us so much about the importance of stories and performance in February 2017. Much appreciation to SFU Creative Studios, to Natalie Knight (Yurok/Navajo) for stepping in as an interviewer, as well as to independent videographers Alex Muir, Rachel Ward, and Ian Barbour.

Many thanks to Lisa Quinn and Siobhan McMenemy at Wilfrid Laurier University Press for supporting our vision for this project, and to the two anonymous readers of the manuscript for their excellent suggestions. Thank you to the entire team at WLUP for designing and preparing the manuscript so beautifully. Thanks especially to Sonny Assu (Kwakwaka'wakw) for the cover image and to Mike Bechthold for his input on the cover design.

We gratefully acknowledge financial support from the Social Sciences and Humanities Research Council of Canada. The grants associated with this project enabled us to hire the best research assistants anyone could wish for, including Alix Shield, Rachel Taylor, and Natalie Knight. Many thanks to Simon Fraser University for the University Publications Fund's Single Event

Publication Grant, and a teaching grant from the Institute for the Study of Teaching & Learning in the Disciplines. Thank you to the Griffin Foundation for help with some of the costs associated with copyright. We would also like to acknowledge ongoing and generous support from SFU's English Department and First Nations Studies Department, as well as the University of British Columbia's Institute for Critical Indigenous Studies.

Last but far from least, we would like to express our heartfelt thanks to our friends and families. Sophie sends her love and gratitude to her parents, and to David, Maya, and Skye Chariandy. Deanna would like to thank Mischa, Eli, Mili, Sam, Sophy, and especially Eric Davis. David would like to thank Oliver and Eloise for sharing so many stories with him, and Kathy for her love and support. Gabrielle would like to thank her families, both blood and chosen, for their constant and strengthening love and support.

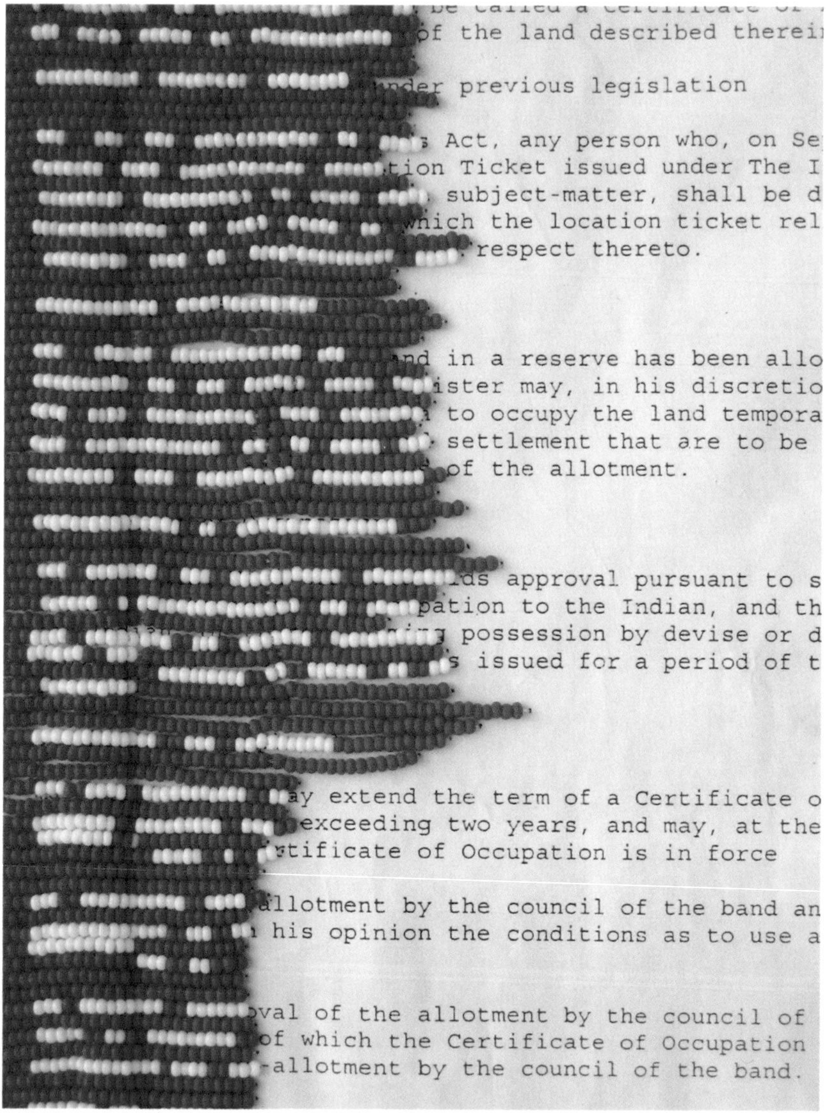

Figure 1 Nadia Myre, *Indian Act*, 1999–2002. Glass beads, stroud cloth, thread, and copies of the text of the *Indian Act*. (*Credit:* Nadia Myre and Art Mûr Gallery)

CENTRING INDIGENOUS
INTELLECTUAL TRADITIONS
Introducing *Read, Listen, Tell*

THE IMAGE IN FIGURE 1 is Nadia Myre's *Indian Act*, a series of beaded pages on which each letter, word, and sentence of the fifty-six pages of the Government of Canada's Indian Act is beaded over in white and red. Myre describes how and why she took on this project: "My mother was orphaned and through the experience of reclaiming our Native Status in 1997 as Algonquins and members of the Kitigan Zibi reserve in Maniwaki, Quebec, the exploration of my identity has become a major theme in my work" ("Nadia Myre: Indian Act"). We chose this piece to introduce our book because it is an exceptional example of the struggle for reclamation that many Indigenous artists and writers are engaged with through their creative practices; we also were drawn to the image because of the questions it poses to the viewer about how to *read, listen,* and *tell*. Why has Myre both referenced and transformed the text of the Indian Act? What alternative "Act" does Myre suggest in this work—especially through the extraordinary collective process she used in gathering together over 230 friends, colleagues, and strangers to help her bead? While Myre's *Indian Act* is meant to resemble a text, it is one that cannot, strictly speaking, be read. "Written" entirely in beads, the work suggests other forms of literacy and other ways of interpreting stories, such as through memory, alternative knowledges, and collective reasoning. It demands that you, its viewer, think carefully about the complex relationships between writing and reading, storytelling and image-making—relationships at the heart of the stories and the interpretive approaches in *Read, Listen, Tell.*

Read, Listen, Tell is, first and foremost, an acknowledgement of the many stories that have inspired us as students, teachers, and readers of Indigenous narrative texts. It is the first critical reader of its kind that spans Turtle Island or North America, including Canada, the United States, and Mexico, thereby contesting how Indigenous writing is often sectioned off by post-contact borders. Its goal is to transform methods of reading and interpreting texts in ways that respect and honour Indigenous histories and peoples of these lands. *Read, Listen, Tell* was conceived of by a team of Indigenous and settler scholars who saw the need for a critical reader that challenges the canon and prioritizes Indigenous methods, practices, and approaches. In these efforts, we have been inspired by many scholars and writers who have not only questioned the extent to which Western literary theory can adequately embrace the wealth of knowledge and complexity offered by Indigenous stories, but who have also created new analyses grounded in Indigenous thought and theory.

We have taken our lead from these new forms of analysis and have organized the material in this book in ways that address core concepts and concerns at the heart of Indigenous studies, such as the relationships between story, land, language, identity, and community; the politics of genre and narrative form; the relationship between word and image in comic books, graphic novels, and illustrated stories; the continuities between oral and written forms of expression; and the role of nation-specific critical approaches. Even as we model methods of reading that are based in the central concerns of Indigenous literary studies, we recognize that the term "literature" is at once too narrow (relying on Eurocentric literary categories) and too broad (since *Read, Listen, Tell* does not include poetry or drama). Indigenous stories profoundly challenge mainstream notions of literary value. The stories *resist* categorization and highlight other ways of knowing. Our goal is to challenge the false duality that sometimes is assumed between "stories" and "literature," particularly in the context of university study, which confers greater prestige on "literature." For this reason we prefer to use the more inclusive terms, "story" or "narrative," over "literature." While Indigenous writers often work within literary institutions that include the academy, their creative production both enhances and obscures that institutional frame to assert that there are other systems of narrative that work differently. Our goal, then, is to make visible that colonial frame as a first step in moving to a decolonial understanding of Indigenous narrative forms.

Indigenous-Centred Methods of Reading

The term "Indigenous literatures" covers (up) a vast range of writing and storytelling, by writers from many hundreds of communities and individuals, each of whom brings particular knowledges and perspectives to the table. Tension across points of view, not agreement, is an important part of what shapes this area of study, and what makes it such a dynamic and exciting field. Furthermore, Indigenous writers often move fluidly between the personal, the historical, the supernatural, and the theoretical in ways that confound expected conventions of the Western realist short story. Rather than offering a stable definition of what Indigenous literatures "are," definitions that risk excluding and silencing voices, this collection enacts a set of practices of critical reading that prioritizes the perspectives of a wide range of Indigenous critics, authors, and storytellers in interpreting the stories.

Two decades ago, Creek author Craig Womack's innovative study, *Red on Red: Native American Literary Separatism* (1999), advocated for an approach to interpreting texts that emphasized Indigenous literary sovereignty. His goal was, and continues to be, to reorient literary method away from one governed by Western European traditions toward one self-determined by Indigenous peoples and rooted in traditional and local knowledges. "Native viewpoints are necessary," Womack writes, "because the 'mental means of production' in regards to analyzing Indian cultures have been owned, almost exclusively, by non-Indians" (*Red* 5). This critical reader is about putting the means of production back in the hands of Indigenous storytellers, writers, and thinkers and giving you, as readers, students, and teachers, the skills to engage *with* those writers and *against* naturalized colonial world views and hermeneutic tools.

In order to facilitate an approach to reading stories that prioritizes the perspectives of a diverse range of Indigenous narrative artists, each chapter of *Read, Listen, Tell* presents a thematic or framework through which the reader can begin to interpret the stories. For example, the introduction to Chapter 4 by Deanna Reder, Cree-Métis scholar and co-editor of this text, offers insights into Cree texts grounded in Cree narrative traditions. At the heart of this chapter is the essay on Cree knowledge by the acclaimed writer and intellectual, Harold Cardinal. This chapter demonstrates a practice of *literary nationalism*, an approach to understanding Indigenous stories that considers the specific historical, political, social, and intellectual context of an author's Indigenous nation. Leslie Marmon Silko's essay in Chapter 5 also considers tribally specific knowledge, in this case Pueblo linguistic and literary structures. In Chapter 5, however, we encourage readers to see what Silko's offering of a Pueblo intellectual discourse can illuminate about a broad range of stories, ideas, and knowledges outside of tribal or national boundaries. Whether tribally specific, pan-national, or trans-Indigenous in orientation, readers will find that each chapter centres Indigenous scholarship and intellectual traditions and encourages doing research *with* Indigenous authors, as opposed to doing research *on* them. We demonstrate ways that readers can approach the stories through Indigenous contexts, epistemologies, and ways of knowing, all the while appreciating that there is no one way to interpret a story.

Centring Indigenous scholarship and intellectual traditions also means following good protocol and locating oneself, Indigenous or non-Indigenous, in relation to a text. Before you begin reading, ask yourself: Who am I, how have my experiences shaped what I know, and what do I need to learn? As co-editors, we ourselves have asked these questions, and you can read our answers in "About the Editors" near the back of the book (383–85). Reading and interpreting varies enormously depending on how much background information and knowledge you as a reader bring to the page. We do not read from a so-called neutral, omniscient perspective from which we can understand everything; instead, we read from particular positions that can include both insights and blind spots, positions that change as we learn more about a particular context or consider the perspectives of others. Embedded in the notion of positionality is the recognition that we are interconnected with those around us. How we establish relationships with one another, and how we might share rather than impose knowledges across cultures, languages, and social spaces, is shaped by our positionality. According to the Creek author Joy Harjo, the foundation of good protocol in Creek territories is self-identification. She writes: "protocol is a key to assuming sovereignty. It's simple. When we name ourselves ... we are acknowledging the existence of our nations, their intimate purpose, ensure their continuation" (118–19). In naming ourselves and our histories, we acknowledge the strengths of our readings and the limits of our knowledges; we recognize our relationships to each other and are reminded to behave respectfully; and we also acknowledge the sovereignty of the territory—in this case the story—that we are reading. Locating oneself is an act of continuance that pushes back against claims to universality and the assimilative drive of colonialism.

In a place and time when Indigenous peoples constantly have to contend with representations that marginalize their concerns and devalue their intellectual and cultural heritage, this collection proclaims the diversity, vitality, and depth of contemporary Indigenous writing. We aim to broaden students' complement of critical skills to include a sustained exploration of Indigenous perspectives, guided by the powerful stories and essays contained in this book.

What It Means to Read, Listen, Tell

The title of this book, *Read, Listen, Tell*, reflects both what we see the stories contained in this volume doing, and what we hope you, our readers, will take away from this collection. On the one hand, the stories in this reader initiate a conversation, a means of communicating knowledges and cultures. According to Cree scholar and poet Neal McLeod, the telling, listening, and retelling of stories is a way of coming home: "stories act as the vehicles of cultural transmission by linking one generation to the next. There are many levels to the stories and many functions to them: they link the past to the present, and allow the possibility of cultural transmission and of 'coming home'" (31). In their connections to home, the stories within these pages also hold within them a certain claim on the reader's sense of accountability. Inasmuch as stories are connected to homes, sharing them is an act of hospitality, and we, as "reader-guests," have a certain responsibility to read and listen carefully, to let the stories speak while remaining aware of our biases and preconceptions, and to share what we have learned—thus continuing the chain of cultural transmission. Thomas King reminds his readers, both Indigenous and non-Indigenous, of the responsibility that readers hold once they have listened to a story. He cautions: "Don't say in the years to come that you would have lived your life differently if only you had heard this story. You've heard it now" ("'You'll Never Believe'" 77). King is suggesting that once you have read a story it becomes a part of you, and it continues to shape the way you move forward in the world. Ultimately what the title of this reader refers to is the sacred power of words to alter not only our own thoughts, but also the world around us. Words and stories live: they help to keep other beings alive, and they reinforce the bonds between ourselves and "all our relations," to invoke a key phrase in many Indigenous cultures, languages, and world views, as well as in Indigenous studies. We ask you as readers to take this responsibility seriously, which is why we emphasize "telling" in the title. Yes, read these stories carefully, listen to what the stories have to say, enjoy them, analyze them, but share what you find here and remember that they are a part of your own story now too: *Read, Listen, Tell.*

Reading Stories, Essays, and Images Together

Included in each chapter are short pieces that may read more like essays than stories. These texts are meant to complement the other stories in the chapter, provide context, and demonstrate Indigenous-centred methods of reading. Some authors elected to write a commentary to accompany their story; we chose to publish these original commentaries alongside the authors' stories as they offer important guidelines on how to approach the interpretation of the story. For example, Inuit writer Alexina Kublu acknowledges in her "Introduction" where and from whom she first heard the stories she has written down, as well as those who carried the stories before that. In addition, she acknowledges how the social positions she occupies—teacher, scholar, and Language Commissioner for Nunavut—have influenced her choices as a writer (199–200). These roles connect Kublu to her relations, underline her responsibilities to her community, and demonstrate to the readers that there is no "neutral" position from which to write.

Rather than see these essay-like works as belonging to a separate genre or class of writing, we encourage you to notice the way that they contain—or are—stories themselves, and conversely, the way that the more conventional short stories function to teach, transmit knowledge, and theorize. Writers and scholars have pointed out that it is important to deconstruct the concept of genre for many reasons. To begin with, attending to generic binaries such as fiction/non-fiction or fantasy/realism can often lead to a devaluation of Indigenous stories that assert spiritual or supernatural events as real, true, or factual. Additionally, Indigenous knowledge in the fields of biology, botany, geography, political philosophy, and history, to name a few, can be obscured when stories are read within the restrictive genre of fiction. As Leslie Marmon Silko writes in "Language and Literature from a Pueblo Indian Perspective," included in Chapter 5 of this collection, stories from her community hold many types of information in them. The story about the little girl and the yashtoah that she relays in this essay contains biographical information about the teller, geographical data, and a recipe. Information is not "separated out and categorized" in this story; as Silko points out, "all things are brought together" ("Language" 241). Similarly, Anishinaabe literary critic Grace Dillon has argued that Western notions of genre do not apply to Indigenous texts: "[M]any Indigenous cultures do not classify discourse genres, making 'storytelling' the singular means of passing all knowledge from generation to generation" ("Global" 377). This is not to say that *all* Indigenous literary and storytelling traditions deny any form of genre—indeed, Chapter 4 discusses different Cree classifications of stories, including âtayôhkêwina, or sacred stories. Rather, in including works of writing that range from classic short fiction, textualized oral stories, orature, bilingual traditional stories, comic books, illustrated stories, and essays, and asking our readers to read through and beyond the limits of genre, we hope to inspire a critical approach to the stories, one that acknowledges genre as dynamic, shifting, limiting, and a potent medium for political critique.

It is important to recognize that even when Indigenous writers are producing short stories and short-story collections aimed at mainstream readers, they often connect their work to larger cycles of traditional stories. Readers will notice that some stories invoke a powerful connection between written and oral forms of expression, either by rewriting traditional stories, or by recording oral performances. We have included several variations of the "as-told-to" narrative in this book, such as Solomon Ratt's "I'm Not an Indian," which was told by Ratt in the Cree language, and transcribed by Jacyntha Laviolette as part of a morphology course taught by linguist and translator, Arok Wolvengrey. Another example is Alexina Kublu's "Uinigumasuittuq / She Who Never Wants to Get Married," an interlinear text in both Inuktitut and English. This story is not exactly a "transcription": Kublu wrote down the story from memory of her father's multiple tellings over the course of several years. Her father's version is part of a larger cycle of Inuit narratives about Uinigumasuittuq, or Sedna, who is also featured in Alootook Ipellie's "Summit with Sedna." These multiple variations allow you as a reader to see the difference between more fixed short stories and always-travelling traditional stories.

There are other stories that raise important questions regarding "transcriptions" of oral stories, showing how the multiple processes involved in recording, transcribing, translating, and editing stories often are disavowed by the various mediators involved in publishing the story in written form. For example, "The Son Who Came Back from the United States" was originally told in the Maya language by Sixto Canul, and indeed the word play in the story depends upon hearing the story aloud. The story was hastily written down by the anthropologists Silvia Terán and Christian H. Rasmussen, who were not initially interested in the stories as stories; rather, they wanted to learn more about traditional agriculture in maize fields. The story was then transcribed and translated, first into Spanish and then into English, by several different translators at later dates. It might be tempting to assume there is a kind of "textual colonization" at work when non-Indigenous *writers* record, translate, transcribe, and edit the work of Indigenous *storytellers*. But the stories in this book show that the processes of appropriation and transformation are two-way streets in which power is volatile and negotiable. For example, Tania Willard's "Coyote and the People Killer" was originally told by her great-grandfather, Isaac (Ike) Willard, and written down by the anthropologists, Randy Bouchard and Dorothy Kennedy in the 1970s. Willard's repositioning of the published version of the story as an interface with her artwork is arguably a kind of repatriation of the story.

Our inclusion of visually impactful graphic stories provides yet another good example of how this critical reader aims to emphasize the scope, not the limits, of what constitutes a "story." Texts by author/artists such as Alootook Ipellie, Michael Nicoll Yahgulanaas, Steven Keewatin Sanderson, Gord Hill, Walter Scott, and Tania Willard work at the borderlines between word, image, and spoken word, raising important questions about representation, orality, material culture, and "textuality" in general. Graphic novels provide at least two planes of interpretation, image and text (with multiple points of intersection between the two), which readers must study carefully in relationship with one another in order to grasp the full complexity and depth of the storytelling taking place. For instance, Yahgulanaas's "Haida Manga" in *Red* (2004) combines the narratives, visual traditions, and design conventions from Indigenous Pacific Northwest and Asia. Yahgulanaas expands comic motifs by abandoning the traditional square paneling and speech bubbles of North

American comics, adopting instead a curving, dynamic "formline" strongly associated with Haida art.

When reading the graphic texts in this book, be attentive to the ways in which these writers and illustrators challenge a reader's sense of time and place through the sophisticated use of panels and transitions. Think about the author/artist's use of colour, shading, and facial expressions. Consider the use of negative space and contrasts between light and dark. Reflect on how the size and layout of panels on a page influences your reception of the content. "Reading" a graphic novel means paying close attention to the intersections between text, visuals, and layout.

The Creation of This Reader

This book was created in response to the need we felt for an accessible yet challenging collection that featured stories that we knew would work in first- and second-year undergraduate classrooms. While there are a number of excellent anthologies available, none is aimed specifically at students who are new to reading narrative texts by Indigenous writers. What we felt was missing was not another *anthology* per se, but a *critical reader* that prioritizes the integration of Indigenous perspectives with literary method. The aim of our book is to engage students in the complexities of discerning from a variety of possible approaches to reading, and it is organized and designed as a learning and teaching resource for students and teachers alike. Our goal is not to define or set limits on what Indigenous narrative production is, but to provide readers with the tools and confidence to read and reflect on some of the many important ideas, styles, perspectives, and politics in the field.

The heart of this book is the stories themselves, which have been carefully chosen for many reasons, including the quality of the writing and storytelling, their accessibility, their potential to challenge social norms or preconceptions, and their ability to capture the imagination. Another important consideration was geographic span and Indigenous national/cultural breadth. While compiling *Read, Listen, Tell*, we considered the ways in which anthologies of Indigenous literature can often be complicit in reproducing and reinforcing colonially imposed borders between lands and languages, omitting the work of Chicana/o and Aztecatl authors, for example, as well as writers from Indigenous nations south of the United States–Mexico border. As Margery Fee argues, anthologies do not neutrally provide space or dissemination; rather they are "a part of a system—a set of interconnected institutional practices—that construct ethnic and racial identity" (139). As a consequence, many Indigenous readers are denied a reflection or affirmation of themselves as Indigenous, perpetuating not only the deterritorialization of their people but also a political and social divide between nations that serves the process of colonialism. In choosing writers from Turtle Island, a geographical body of land that does not recognize the borders drawn by Mexico, Canada, or the United States, we have included works that often have been marginalized from the canon, such as French- and Spanish-language Indigenous authors; Indigenous authors from south of the Mexican border; Chicana/o authors; Indigenous-language authors; works in translation; and "lost" or underappreciated texts. In particular, we honour the voices of many intellectuals and activists—from the Brown Berets to Gloria Anzaldúa, to Aztlan Underground—who have long argued for the identification of Chicano and Mestizo people as Indigenous.

The stories that we have selected initiate a vital dialogue between Indigenous writers who often are not studied together. Comparing Indigenous writers across state borders in North America is surprisingly uncommon in Indigenous literary studies. As co-editors we undertook extensive research to find the most engaging, aesthetically interesting, and tribally diverse texts. Building a critical reader of this historical, geographical, and inter-tribal scope has resulted in extensive discussions to ensure the best possible arrangements of stories into chapters, with theoretically informed essays, providing essential context and suggestions for how to approach the stories, all the while encouraging readers to explore their own reactions and responses.

In the main table of contents, the stories are grouped into chapters based on themes and concerns central to Indigenous studies. Each chapter opens with a reflection on a particular theme. Chapter 1 borrows a line from one of King's essays—"[t]he truth about stories is that that's all we are" ("'You'll Never Believe'" 63)—in order to invite readers to think not only about the profound role that stories play in shaping the world, but also about our responsibilities to those stories as readers and critics. Chapter 2, "Land, Homeland, Territory," explores the vital relationship between land, story, and community in many Indigenous narratives. Chapter 3, "Reinventing the Enemy's Language," features writers who engage with the complexities of language, particularly in relation to knowledge, colonization, and decolonization. Chapter 4, "Cree Knowledge Embedded in Stories," models for students how to approach the stories in light of Cree generic and storytelling traditions. Chapter 5, "'Each Word Has a Story of Its Own': Story Arcs and Story Cycles," focuses on the concept of the story cycle, or the interrelationships between stories, and asks readers to look for meaning beyond the confines of just one story. Inspired in part by the writing of Snuneymuxw Elder Ellen Rice White, Chapter 6, "Community, Self, Transformation," explores the interrelatedness of all beings, human, animal, and elemental. Chapter 7, "Shifting Perspectives," encourages readers to examine their own assumptions and consider how ideology can influence the way we understand stories. Chapter 8, "Indigenous Fantasy

and SF," shows how Indigenous authors are shaping, adapting, and indigenizing well-known literary genres (such as fantasy, science fiction, erotica, and
horror) to create some of the most innovative, provocative, and fun-to-read
short fiction available. In addition to this thematic grouping, we have also
included an alternative table of contents, organized by the date of publication
of the works, demonstrating a small fraction of the rich variety of Indigenous
writing and storytelling in Turtle Island from the late nineteenth century to
the present day.

Story interpreted expansively rather than restrictively opens up produc-
tive points of discussion concerning both the expansive and particular role
of stories in a variety of cultural contexts. The stories in this collection are a
means of sharing information, of bearing witness to history, of entertaining,
healing, mourning, and politicizing. Let the stories, essays, commentaries,
illustrations, and graphic texts inform one another, and think critically about
the ways in which these authors bring creative and critical writing together
to speak to the past, present, and future. The texts in this reader are a part of
a conversation—a conversation that you are now a part of. To invoke Thomas
King once more, don't say you'd have lived your life differently if only you had
had this conversation. You've had it now.

———•———

As co-editors of this reader, we strongly believe that Indigenous-centred
methods of reading offer rich bodies of knowledge and critical insights into
literature, history, political theory, and beyond. We suggest that the analytical
approaches explored in this reader may be applied not only to Indigenous
writing but stories from many traditions. For example, the idea that stories
describe a relationship to land and other beings provides an important reading
of Indigenous texts; and yet this approach is also deeply illuminating when
applied to settler and post-colonial literatures. Indigenous critiques of genre
are not only useful when approaching Daniel Heath Justice's speculative fiction, or Ellen Rice White's "The Boys Who Became a Killer Whale," but are
also critical to thinking through how genre works to impose ideology and
hierarchies of "truth" in many texts. Furthermore, the Indigenous linguistic
theories shared by Leslie Marmon Silko and Jeannette Armstrong in this collection have much to teach us about how all languages work, and the relationships between languages, literatures, and communities. Ultimately, our goal as
editors in this volume is to insist upon Indigenous theoretical approaches to
Indigenous narrative production and to assert the value of these approaches
for literary studies at large.

As much as we are proud of including such a tremendous range of stories,
we also feel humbled by the process, which required choosing, ultimately,

only a small handful of stories relative to the tremendous number currently published. This collection, then, is only a sampling—but hopefully enough to encourage readers to continue seeking out more. Like each bead in Myre's *Indian Act*, each of the individual stories in *Read, Listen, Tell* is connected to an expansive web of stories and histories. There is always another bead to be sewn. As such, *Read, Listen, Tell* is not only the title of this critical reader; it is also a provocation for our readers to delve into the stories and to contribute to the rich tapestry of the field.

CHAPTER 1

"THE TRUTH ABOUT STORIES IS ... STORIES ARE ALL THAT WE ARE"

Dawn Dumont, "The Way of the Sword"

Craig Womack, "King of the Tie-snakes"

E. Pauline Johnson, "As It Was in the Beginning"

Paula Gunn Allen, "Deer Woman"

Thomas King, "'You'll Never Believe What Happened'
Is Always a Great Way to Start"

"THE TRUTH ABOUT STORIES is that that's all we are" ("'You'll Never Believe'" 63). For Thomas King, stories not only *contribute* to our sense of who we are—stories *are who we are*. The places we've known, the bodies we inhabit, the pasts we've inherited, the futures we have dreamed of—all of these building blocks of identity are known to us only through the stories that give them shape. If you think about it like that, listening to, reading, and sharing stories is not simply a pastime; it's the most primary means for us to engage with and make sense of the world around us. King's story included in this section, "'You'll Never Believe What Happened' Is Always a Great Way to Start," begins with the retelling of a story of the earth being created on the back of a turtle. This story has multiple origins, with variations from the storytelling traditions of different Indigenous nations in North America. As King points out, it's a story that has been told many times, and it changes each time it's shared. In King's version, it's not just one turtle, it's turtles piled on turtles, piled on turtles—"it's turtles all the way down" (63). Through this image of an uncountable number of turtles upon turtles he mischievously evokes the role of the writer or artist in creating new stories from old ones, and building on known stories to uncover new perspectives.

King's image of many, many turtles captures the idea that there is a multiplicity of meanings to every story. Like a hall of mirrors that reflects an image infinitely, "turtles all the way down" suggests that the significance of stories is never stable and permanent; stories shift and change according to what the reader brings to the story, and what she takes away from it. As you read through these stories, allow yourself to look through that hall of mirrors made up of stories and language, and ask yourself what possible meanings your own perspective adds to the story.

The stories in this chapter continue on this theme of the echoes and resonances between stories. Craig Womack's "King of the Tie-snakes" refers to a well-known Creek story associated with a water snake, and Paula Allen Gunn's "Deer Woman" is a retelling of a story with many variations from the southeastern United States about a spiritual being who takes on the shape of a beautiful woman and lures men away from family and community. Dawn Dumont's "The Way of the Sword" also references and reshapes a classic narrative, though not a traditional Indigenous one: the main character, also named Dawn, is an avid reader of Conan the Barbarian comics. For Dawn, Conan is not just a comic book character; he is a "way of life" whose stories "mirrored the story of Native people" and whose exploits made sense of her own life (16).

Negotiating identity and finding new ways to self-define, in the context of a mainstream society with often rigid notions of gender, sexuality, ethnicity, and cultural difference, is another common theme to the stories in this chapter; they all invoke the power of stories to create alternative realities as ways of reconfiguring restrictive social norms. When reading this chapter, think about how approaching stories from multiple angles and incorporating different interpretations into your own reading provide a good place to begin thinking about Indigenous texts and the complex levels of narrative they offer. If stories are all that we are—if we are made up of stories we tell ourselves—then stories also allow us to create and recreate who or what we are or strive to become.

⟶ *The Way of the Sword* ⟶
Dawn Dumont

Dawn Dumont is a Plains Cree comedian, actor, and writer born and raised in Saskatchewan, Canada. She says of her reservation, the Okanese First Nation, that it is "quite possibly the smallest reservation in the world but what it doesn't have in terms of land area, the people make up for in sheer head size" ("Dawn Dumont"). Trained as a lawyer, Dumont has said (in a tongue-in-cheek interview) that she decided to follow the talk show host Oprah's advice to "follow your bliss" and become a writer instead ("Dawn Dumont"). The story included in this anthology is from her collection of linked short stories, *Nobody Cries at Bingo* (2011). Three of Dumont's plays, *The Red Moon (Love Medicine)*, *Visiting Elliot*, and *The Trickster vs. Jesus Christ*, have been broadcast on CBC. She has also published a novel, *Rose's Run* (2014). In addition to her work as a writer, Dawn has performed as a comedian at comedy clubs across North America, including New York's Comic Strip, the New York Comedy Club, and the Improv.

Dumont has no trouble bringing her prodigious talents as a comedian to the page—while also using her sharp wit to make us think more deeply about serious issues, such as the legacy of residential schools, poverty, racism, bullying, and the stereotypical ways that Native people often are represented in books, films, and media. "The Way of the Sword" is a story about a young girl, also named Dawn, who obsessively reads Conan the Barbarian comics. Dawn loves Conan because, as she says, the story of his people "mirror[s] the story of Native people" (16). Finding her own experiences "mirrored" in Conan's stories sustains Dawn and helps her find a way to counter the stereotypes of Native people that she contends with on a daily basis. But when Dawn is confronted with a real-life challenge by a group of older, stronger girls, she needs to find a solution other than hand-to-hand combat.

When I was growing up my hero was Conan the Barbarian. He wasn't just a comic book character—Conan was a way of life, a very simple way of life. When Conan wanted something, he took it. When someone stood in his way, he slew them. There were no annoying grey areas when you were a barbarian.

Uncle Frank introduced me, my siblings and all my cousins to Conan. He arrived from Manitoba one day with a bag filled with clothes and a box full of comics. I was ten and had no idea who Uncle Frank was. "This is your uncle," Mom said pointing at the thin man with no hair sitting next to her at the table.

"Yeah, hi, okay," I said, breezing by as I polished an apple on my T-shirt.

I would have kept walking had I not overheard the words, "horse ranch." I stopped short, reversed and sat to my uncle's right as he laid out the plans for possibly the greatest single thing that has ever happened to the Okanese reserve—Uncle Frank's ranch.

Frank had no children but his interests in horses, comic books and candies guaranteed that they would always surround him. From the first day he arrived, all the kids within a three-kilometre radius spent all our free time at Uncle Frank's—a fact, which delighted our bingo-addicted mothers to no end. When the horses weren't available, or the weather was inclement or we had stuffed ourselves with too many cookies and potato chips, my cousins and I gathered in Uncle Frank's living room where we would leaf through his Conan collection. Each week, we'd fight over who got to read the latest issue, but it was just as easy to lose yourself in an old comic while a slow reader mumbled his way through the new one.

Uncle Frank had hundreds of Conan comics from various different series. You see, Conan led such a long and complex life that it had to be told from several different angles. There was Conan the Barbarian, Conan the King, Young Conan and the Savage Sword of Conan. The Savage Sword was my favourite because it was more of a graphic magazine than a comic book. On these pages, the artists took extra time and care to bring across Conan's heroic form, stylized muscles and the blood splatters of his foes. These stories were savoured; each word would be read, each panel would be studied, to achieve maximum Conan absorption.

Every time I opened a new comic, I read the italicized print above the first panel that described the world of Conan, "The proudest kingdom of the world was Aquilonia, reigning supreme in the dreaming west. Hither came Conan, the Cimmerian, black-haired, sullen-eyed, sword in hand, a thief, a reaver, a slayer, with gigantic melancholies and gigantic mirth, to tread the jewelled thrones of the Earth under his sandaled feet."

Through these magazines we learned all we needed to know about Conan and his life philosophies. There was a recipe for living in those comics: love those who love you and conquer those who don't. My cousins took this to heart and ran headlong into adventures like chasing down the bantam rooster until he turned on them and flew at their faces with his claws. They emerged from their adventures with bruises, scrapes and confident smiles. I always hung back, afraid of breaking a limb or scratching my smooth, plump skin. I knew I could be like Conan too, but in the distant future, far away from sharp claws and bad tempered chickens.

Part of the reason we loved Conan was we believed he was Native. The story of Conan mirrored the story of Native people. Conan was a descendent of the Cimmerians, a noble warrior people who made swords yet lived peaceably. They were attacked and annihilated by an imperial army who murdered the men and women and enslaved the children. Conan was one of those children and the only one to survive slavery (according to the movie). He was the last of his kind.

This was exactly like our lives! Well, except for the last of our kind business. We were very much alive and well even though others had made a concerted effort to kill us off. Later, I learned that throughout the world, people thought that Indians had been killed off by war, famine and disease. Chris Rock does a comedy bit about this point, claiming that you will never see an Indian family in a Red Lobster. This is a misconception: my family has gone to Red Lobster many times. (However, we are most comfortable at a Chinese buffet.)

In Saskatchewan, most non-Native people were very much aware that nearly a million Native people still existed, mainly to annoy them and steal their tax dollars.

But someone had tried to annihilate us and that was not something you got over quickly. It was too painful to look at it and accept; it was easier to examine attempted genocide indirectly. We could read about the Cimmerians and feel their pain; we could not acknowledge our own.

Once we had owned all of Canada and now we lived on tiny reserves. While reserves weren't as bad as, say, a slave labour camp run by Stygian priests, sometimes life was reduced to survival. Like Conan, all we had was our swords and our wits. And if we weren't allowed to bring our swords to school, then we would use our fists. There was an unspoken belief among the Native kids that we would fight to defend our people should anyone decide to annihilate us again. As Conan once said as he incited a group of slaves to overthrow their master, "I would rather die on my feet than live on my knees!" I think other people have also said this. Most notably, Mel Gibson in *Braveheart*.

—·—

My sister Celeste and I made swords out of tree branches and practiced our swordplay in the backyard.

"Today I'm Conan," she announced proudly.

"No you're the Evil Wizard," I replied. I refused to be the evil wizard because with my dark hair, brown skin and, well, evil personality, I worried about being typecast.

"You were Conan yesterday."

"That's because I'm bigger."

"No, just fatter."

Thunk! Our swords met and the resulting explosion reverberated up our arms. It did not matter that Conan was a man and we were girls; we were all Conan in spirit.

Besides, in the barbarian world, women were just as good fighters as men. Conan had several female sidekicks who fought alongside him (and who often became his lovers). These women usually had long hair, feisty spirits and exceptionally large breasts. Perhaps there was a connection between hefting a sword and breast growth?

The women were just as much heroes as the men. There was Valeria, who was Conan's first love. She figured prominently in the Conan the Barbarian movie where her purple prose helped to cover her co-star's poor English skills.

Then there was Red Sonja who could not be beaten by any man. A goddess gave Red Sonja her fighting powers and attached a powerful price: Red Sonja could never take a man as a lover unless he had bested her in battle first. Needless to say, this was quite a drag on Red Sonja's sex life. Only Conan connoisseurs will remember his lost loves: Tetra and Belit. Tetra made it through a couple of stories before she died and was reborn as an evil witch who tried to kill Conan. Somehow this experience did not sour Conan on women. He later fell in love with the Pirate Queen Belit. Belit had been a princess whose ship went down. She convinced a group of Kush pirates (who looked a lot like

Africans) that she was a goddess and became their leader. Unfortunately as a Goddess, it was tough for her to show her affection for Conan in front of her crew, as a goddess does not have "needs." I had such regard for Belit and Tetra that I ended up naming two horses after them.

All of Conan's girlfriends were warriors like him; he had no place in his life for skinny little chicks that didn't know how to defend themselves. Conan was very forward thinking for a man who lived in the time before the oceans swallowed Atlantis.

These warrior women were my role models because they reflected the women in my life. Native women were also warriors though not always by choice. They would show up at the band office on Mondays with black eyes, bruised faces and swollen knuckles and tell stories about heroic battles held the weekend before.

"Thought he could just come in and kick me around. Well, I showed him a thing or two."

"He'll think twice about bringing the party back to the house next time."

"Kicked him in the ass, right between the cheeks. Sure taught him a lesson!"

Then they would throw back their heads and laugh, sometimes stopping to cough up a little blood.

From what I could see, Native women were tough as nails. My mom worked anywhere from two to three jobs while looking after all of us plus whichever friend or cousin was staying with us. She changed her own tires and siphoned her own gas. Mom wasn't much of a warrior in the physical sense. She had a wry sense of humour that evolved from watching conflicts rather than from engaging in them. In her mind, it was better to mock the fools than to be one of them. As long as you could run faster than the fools, that is.

When my dad would come thundering home after a week long drinking binge, Mom would pack up quickly and stealthily escape through the other door. Then again, stealth is also part of being a warrior. Many were the times when Conan had to run away from an irate King after sleeping with the wrong Queen.

———

At school, Natives were assigned the role as the ass-kickers. Even if you were a girl, you were expected to be as tough as a boy. And if you grew up on a reserve, you were doubly tough. In grade one when the girls in the class decided to punish the boys, they enlisted my help as the only Native girl in the class. "You're tough, Dawn. Go beat up Matt; he's being mean to us," they cooed into my ear.

How did they know I was tough? I wondered. I'd never fought anyone in the class; I'd never fought anyone outside of my immediate family. Perhaps they could sense the Cimmerian blood pumping through my veins.

Or maybe it was just that they saw the way the older Native girls punished one another in the schoolyard. They would throw down their jackets and pull out their long, dangling earrings, and run at each other with abandon. We'd make a ring around them so that they could have their privacy. Then we'd chant "fight, fight, fight!" so that they had proper motivation. The fighters would punch, pull hair, scratch, whatever it took to get the other girl down to the ground. For boys, that might be enough. For these girls, the loser not only had to fall to the ground, she had to stay down. And unlike the boys, these fights didn't end with good-natured handshakes.

My first fight happened when I was ten years old. I was outside of a bingo hall with my brother and sister and older cousins. We were playing on the playground equipment when a thin Native girl and her thin brother claimed the swings next to us. The two groups warily watched each other, each labeling the other group as outsiders.

My cousins were a few years older than me and a lot more foolish. When the little boy started to throw rocks at us, they devised a special punishment for him. They instigated a fight between his sister and me. I knew that this was not a good idea. The girl had not done anything to me and I had done nothing to her. It offended my barbarian sense of justice.

Darren, my older cousin, took me by the shoulders and explained the reasons why the girl needed to be beat down. "It'll be fun!"

I didn't want to fight, but I had to. As a Cimmerian, you couldn't back down. At that time my motto for life was, "What would Conan do?"

The girl was taller than me and had long legs. I remember this quite clearly because she kicked me in the face about five times in quick succession. Whomp. Whomp. Whomp. Whomp. Whomp. Her long legs flashed as they rose up to meet my head.

She did not vanquish me. As she tattooed my face with the bottom of her shoe, I managed to keep moving forward, mostly out of confusion. Once I got close enough, I employed my natural hair-pulling ability. I was the hair-pulling champ of my family and I often bragged that I knew seventy-five different ways to pull hair.

We ended up getting pulled apart by a security guard. I was crying. My opponent was crying, although I couldn't understand why since I had clearly gotten my ass handed to me. I suppose even Conan cried after his first fight.

My cousins hurriedly escorted me to their house. They cheered my exploits and flattered my fighting style in the hopes that I wouldn't tell on them. They didn't have to worry; I had no intention of reliving the battle any time soon. I excused myself to the washroom and examined my battle scars. There was a little blood under my nose and my lip was puffy and had its own heartbeat.

As I washed the blood off my face, my hands shook. Even though I was no longer in danger, the memory of the fight hummed through my body. I could not relax and felt like puking. I never wanted to fight again. That desire was incompatible with my love of Conan and with being a Native woman. By Crom, I'd be coming to this bridge again and next time I would be prepared!

I vowed that from now until my next fight, I would train every day. Like when Conan was kidnapped from Cimmeria and sold as a slave to the gladiators, I would train to be a warrior. Every night, to increase my strength, I would do push-ups, wall-sits and take out the garbage. I would beg my parents to enroll me in martial arts classes where I would find a sensei who would mold me into an unstoppable force. I would watch kung fu movies and practice the moves on my siblings.

Several years passed, in which I did nothing to prepare for my next bloody entanglement except read more Conan magazines. My next fight occurred in the seventh grade. There were many bullies at my school that year: older girls who gave you the mean eye and who looked for reasons to exercise their already honed fighting skills, and younger girls looking to establish themselves as "toughs." There were even aspiring Don Kings who went about their day trying to promote fights among the girls.

One of the tough older girls decided that I had called her a bad name and she stalked me in the hallways for weeks. Her name was Crystal and she was three years older than me. She was a single mom bravely going back to school to make something of herself for her child. She kept getting distracted by her frequent smoke breaks, make out sessions with the bus driver and her love of terrorizing the younger girls.

Crystal wasn't extraordinarily big or muscular but she was rumoured to be a fierce and merciless fighter. She wore a lot of makeup and had a feathery haircut tailored to hide her acne-scarred forehead.

I became aware of her dislike for me gradually. It took me awhile to figure out that someone would distinguish me from my group of shy friends. So Crystal had to make it clear. When I walked past her and her group leaning against the lockers, she whispered to them and they erupted in laughter. When I offered a nervous smile in their direction, they laughed louder.

When my group walked outside the smoker's door to make our way downtown for lunch, she spat inches from my feet.

In the hallways she stepped past me and pushed me with her shoulder as she did. At first I thought she was just clumsy but when she knocked me into the wall and did not pause to see if I was okay or even say "excuse me," I suspected it was personal.

"Umm ... Crystal ... are you angry with me?" I asked her, one afternoon. I was nervous. Still I managed to keep my voice relatively normal. However, I had no idea what to do with my hands. They moved around me as I spoke, settling on my hips for a second before migrating towards my tummy.

Crystal pressed her chest up against mine. I took a step back, partly from fear, partly from a natural aversion to touching boobs with another woman.

"Yeah, I am. Got a problem with that?"

"No. Well, yes. I mean you can have a problem with me if you want to ..." Was that my voice sounding like I'd sucked back a litre of helium? I cleared my throat. "I guess I'm just wondering, what did I do?"

"You know," she snarled.

I looked around at the people watching our exchange. A crowd of teen-agers had gathered, attracted to the smell of conflict. Everyone seemed to be glaring and shaking his or her head at me. "Yes, she is exactly the type of person who would do something and then pretend like she didn't know," their accusatory eyes said.

I wondered whether or not more questions would help or hinder my case. I decided to try again.

"Don't take this the wrong way but I'm not sure what I did. Or didn't do."

She pressed her face closer to mine. Her nicotine-tinged breath warmed my face. "You. Called. Me. A. Bitch."

There was a collective gasp from the onlookers as well as from myself. Her accusation reminded me of the feeling when I set off shoplifting sensors in the mall—even if I had done nothing, I still felt guilty. I ran through my activities for the past few weeks: had I done it? Had I called her a name and then forgotten?

I wasn't one to censor myself that was true. My friends depended upon my unedited commentary for entertainment, but calling someone a name, particularly someone far stronger and meaner than myself? That seemed out of character for a cowardly type. I shook my head. "You must be mistaken, Crystal, I would never do that."

"So now I'm a liar?"

I had fallen down the rabbit hole into the nonsensical land of teenage fighting. There was no getting out now. Still I tried. I apologized. She refused to accept it. I stared at her with soft eyes. She glared at me. I backed away. She gave me the finger. We were enemies and there was nothing I could do about it.

My friends Trina and Lucy and I discussed the situation behind the school. Trina was not helpful. "Did she say if she was mad at me?"

"She was too busy hating me."

"She doesn't hate me, right?" asked Trina.

"I don't know."

"Because I always liked her. Maybe I should pass her a note. Is that Crystal with a C or a K?"

My friend Lucy was no more helpful as she described Crystal's frightening prowess as a fighter. "I hear she grew her nails extra-long so she could scar the faces of the girls she fights," Lucy intoned. "They say that none of the girls she's fought have ever been the same again. One girl nearly lost her eye. Now she has a scar right down the middle of her retina. Eye scars never heal completely. That's what they say."

I shuddered. Although I often cursed my greasy, pimpled skin, I also loved its soft plumpness. I stroked my cheeks protectively. "Nobody will ever hurt you," I promised.

That day we headed downtown for lunch. I had just ordered and paid for the single greatest creation known to man, a peanut buster parfait, when the she-devil strode into the Dairy Queen, smacking her gum and glaring at everyone that stood in her way.

This was one of the moments when Crom separates the girls from the Cimmerians. A true Cimmerian would throw the parfait in her face. Then, while she was blinded by caramel and chocolate sauce, would throw a kick at her abdomen all while uttering the deadliest war cry ever known to man.

I chose my plan of action from Column B (B for Bashful). In an attempt to avoid her, I slowed my steps. If this move was done correctly, I could avoid eye contact as well as stop myself from crossing in front of her. My shaking hands betrayed me and instead I dropped the tray in front of her and watched as my parfait scattered across the floor. She smirked and stepped over me.

I had no more money for a new parfait so I sat next to my friends who had witnessed the interaction. They did not mention the incident though neither of them of offered me any of their ice cream.

I had to find a non-violent solution to this problem. I turned to Ghandi. Somehow he brought the British to their knees without even skinning a knuckle. This appealed to me. I dove into his book hoping to find some techniques to use against my violent opponent. After I learned that he had done it mostly through starving himself, I put aside his book. I'd been starving myself since I became a teenager and it hadn't helped me conquer shit.

Out of desperation I turned to my parents. I knew my mom's philosophy about fighting, which consisted of running to my aunt's house in the middle of the night. That technique wasn't going to solve this problem. So I turned to my dad.

I think I have consulted my dad exactly once in my life. And this was that one time. When I approached, he was watching television in the big chair. I sat next to him on the couch and laid out the problem to him during a commercial break. Dad realized the import of the situation and turned down the TV.

He took a deep restful breath as he leaned back in his chair. "When I was at school there was a bully." He smiled as he often did whenever he thought about his childhood. "He was a big guy, a boxer."

My dad had attended a Residential school. He had been raised in it. He had started when he was seven years old and had been accelerated two grades by the time he finished his first year. He graduated at the age of seventeen and went to business college until his grandfather, the chief of the reserve, asked him to come home and manage the band's affairs. We knew this via my mother who always relayed everything about my dad. If we hadn't had her, we wouldn't know anything about the dark-haired man who ate all the bacon and insisted that we watch hockey on Saturday nights.

My dad continued his story with a glimmer of excitement in his eye. Though most of us would have dismissed his upbringing in the red-brick boarding school as Dickensian, my dad had enjoyed every minute of it. The friends he made there were still his friends and they still had the power to make his laugh echo through the house when they called.

"This guy had been a provincial champ a few years in a row. He got so good no one wanted to go into the ring with him anymore to practice. Then he started picking on the younger students. Every week he would choose a young kid to jump in the boxing ring with him. He'd beat the hell out of them. One day he came up to me in the hallway. He pointed his finger in my face and told me the date and the time. I looked at my friend Irvin. He'd been in the ring the week before and still had a black eye and a cut lip from the lickin' he got. I knew I had no chance of beating the boxer so I had to be smart about it. When the day came for the fight, I was the first one in the gym."

"I know how you like to be on time," I chimed in. My parents' punctuality was legendary.

"It was more than that. I had to be first in the ring for my plan to work. That day I laced up my gloves as fast as I could. They weren't even completely laced when I saw that the Boxer had climbed into the ring. His friend was still lacing his when I made my move. I ran across that ring, pulled back my arm and punched him right in the nose."

My dad sat back in triumph.

I was confused. "When did you beat him up?"

"I didn't. I threw off my gloves and ran out of the ring. The boxer's nose was bleeding so badly he had to go to the nurse." My dad threw back his head and laughed.

I couldn't help but notice that my dad was no Conan. He wasn't even Red Sonja. "Uh, Dad ... wasn't that a cowardly thing to do?"

My dad looked not a bit embarrassed. "It's not like I had a chance against him."

"You cheated."

"Let me tell you something. It doesn't matter if you beat a bully, you only have to let them know that you won't go down easily."

Now here was something that made sense. Don't go down easy. That was easier to do than win at all costs. Especially since winning at all costs might scar me for life.

I took my dad's advice to heart and resigned myself to fighting the bully, though not in a fair fight. I walked around with a loonie tucked in my hand and waited for Crystal to approach me and invite me outside. I decided this was very Cimmerian of me. After all Conan would not force an enemy's hand but rather would let the enemy come to him. She never did. I suspect that Crystal got her satisfaction from the peanut buster affair and decided, quite rightly, that I wasn't worth it.

———

A few years later, my sister and I were outside a bingo hall again when my next battle occurred. We were teenagers and had the teenage ability to walk through the middle of town without supervision, which suited my mom and us just fine. My sister and I had escaped from the front door of the bingo hall as three Native girls were going in. "Excuse me," I said politely.

"Why? Did you fart?" retorted one of the girls. It was an old diss, one that I had even used myself on occasion.

However instead of dismissing it as such, I rose to the bait. "Maybe you're smelling yourself," I shot back and kept walking.

My sister and I thought nothing of the encounter as we returned to our conversation, which I am sure was about boys.

We reached our destination, the local arcade. Celeste set up shop in front of a Pac Man game. Celeste was a better than average player and could spend an hour on a single quarter. I stood beside her; my lack of hand-eye coordination had forced me to give up on video games years before. Kimmy, a friend of ours, jogged over when she saw us. "Your mom at bingo?" she asked.

We nodded.

"Yeah, I've been here since this afternoon—it's laundry day." The laundromat was directly across from the bingo hall.

I made room for Kimmy next to the Pac Man machine. She easily slid between two video games. Like my sister, Kimmy was a long stripe of a girl.

When I walked between the two of them, it looked like two giraffes were being taken for a walk by a hobbit. Kimmy and I watched as Celeste decimated the ghost population of the Pac Man game.

Someone tapped me on the shoulder. I turned around and saw a young boy standing there.

"My sister wants to fight you," he pointed over his shoulder at a group of girls. My eyesight wasn't the best especially as I refused to wear glasses in an attempt to make my parents get me contact lenses. As a result, the group of girls could have been anywhere from four to twenty depending on their individual size and breadth. All I knew from gazing at their amorphous hateful mass was that they did not like me.

My heart immediately began to pound. It was the age-old fight or flight response kicking in. In my case, it was more flight than fight. I wanted to run out of the arcade back to the bingo hall and cower next to my mom. My pride and the tightness of my jeans prevented that.

I cleared my throat as it had suddenly become thickened with fear. "Tell her I am not afraid to face her on the field of battle; that I will not lie down and allow her bullish stock to rule the world; that here on earth there remain a precious few who will stand up for what is right, what is strong and what is pure."

He rolled his eyes at the tremor in my voice. "When?"

"Anytime, anyplace."

"Can you pick one?"

"She's the one who wants to fight. She can make the arrangements."

He sighed and returned to his sister's side. I turned back to the Pac Man game and pretended to be calm.

"What was that about?" Celeste asked.

"Some girl wants to fight me," I replied casually as if I fought every day, while inside, my colon and spine were melting. Celeste and Kimmy nodded as if they, too, were approached to fight every day of their lives.

My mind began to analyze the situation with military precision. Numbers? Unknown. Fighting arena? Unknown. Fighting strength? Limited. Courage? Too low to gauge. I looked at my two compatriots. "If this girl doesn't fight fair—and it isn't likely that she will—then I will need one or both of you to step in."

Celeste nodded nonchalantly as her Pac Man feasted on another ghost. Kimmy looked slightly less sure.

"I don't know if my mom would like me to fight."

I ignored this. "Can each of you handle two girls? I mean I can handle three, I'm bigger than you two."

Sure, they nodded. Their body language seemed to say that they were almost insulted to be asked that question. However, their eyes shifted back and forth as if they could escape from their heads and therefore from this situation.

I looked around the arcade. It was filled with fifty or so young people and a harried looking middle-aged man. Like me, he surveyed the youth and looked as though he was seriously reconsidering his life choices. Why an arcade? Why not just sell drugs? He shook his head and returned his gaze back to the TV where nubile women danced through music videos. I looked around at the youth, my colleagues and saw my future. Within this group, my future boyfriend, best friend or enemy could be standing in front of an arcade game. These were my peers and in these last few minutes I realized how lucky I was to have them. Fear had made me sentimental.

The boy returned. "She said she'll meet you outside in ten minutes."

"Whatever," I answered, as my heart rate went from zero to sixty. I looked at my back up.

Kimmy's eyes flashed towards the exit sign. "Maybe we need another person."

"There's no time," I replied. If it were possible to hold onto her sleeve and hold her in place, I would have done so. But experience had taught me that you could not restrain people into being your friends.

"My cousin might be at the laundromat." Then before I could stop her, Kimmy slid away from us and scurried out of the arcade.

My sister dragged her gaze away from the Pac Man game. Our shared glance communicated everything: we were fucked.

It was two against six or seven or even eight. I'd been in one other fight and Celeste had never fought anyone except for our younger brother and me. My hair pulling techniques were effective against my sister but how effective would they be against someone who didn't know the rule about not hitting in the face?

Celeste and I had no way of knowing how this battle might escalate. I knew that even if it was tough we could handle it. Now if only my hands would stop shaking and my bowels would stop gurgling.

Pregnant women have told me that the anticipation of pain is always the worst part. I mentally played out scenes from the Savage Sword of Conan. Conan fought men bigger than him all the time and he was never afraid. He jumped in with both feet and his meaty fists raised. I clenched my own fist. It was not meaty. In fact, I could see the blood vessels below the skin, the outline of my slender bones, and covering it all, my smooth, unscarred skin. Such beautiful skin.

My sister continued playing her game. Her self-possession was to be admired. I stood beside her wracking my brain for some way to fix this problem. I was a nerd in school; surely I could make my brain find a non-violent solution to this problem? My brain seemed to disagree.

Perhaps I could walk outside and juggle a few rocks. This would show them that not only was I talented, I was also funny. If only I'd learned to juggle!

Perhaps I could put my oration skills to the test: "Must we fight, my Native sister, when the world has been fighting us for so long?! I say, let us unite against the world." Somehow I knew that would invite a more vicious beating.

Perhaps I could pretend that I was a felon with dangerous fists. "I can't fight you. If I do, the police will lock me up and throw away the key. I'll kill you and not even notice. My fist is registered as a dangerous weapon on six different reserves. I can't tell you which, otherwise I'd have to kill you."

Ten minutes later, my sister and I looked at each other and walked towards the exit. Let it never be said that the Dumont girls were ever late for a fight. Our residential school grandparents had ingrained punctuality into us. Though they might fight over everything else, my parents were never late for anything.

Celeste and I stood on the sidewalk. My fists were already clenched in anticipation of the brawl. A group of girls stood twenty metres in front of us. I had trouble making out their features in the light cast by the dim neon lights of the arcade.

"How many girls are there? Six?" I asked Celeste, under my breath.

"There's eight," she replied.

"Eight!" my voice squeaked out.

Then one girl stepped out in front of the group. She was little more than a blur to me; I got the sense of long dark hair and square shoulders.

"You ready to fight?" my enemy drawled. Her voice came out loud and brash.

"I'm ready." My voice sounded thin and shaky, like it had been drawn through a hose.

The girl and her friends laughed. "You sound scared. You wanna call this off?"

This was my chance. I could back down now, make a silly joke and walk away as if nothing had ever happened. Yes, people would mock me but who cared what every teenager within a hundred kilometres of my house thought of me. It's not like I was Miss Popular. I could stay inside for the remainder of my teen years and then move to New York City when I turned eighteen where nobody knew that I had cowardly backed down from a fight.

But I couldn't walk away. I had ten years of Conan flowing through my veins. Each comic book, each violent storyline, each panel had laid out my future. I was a fighter and fighters fight.

"I want to fight," I said firmly. My voice was still high and reedy but at least my eyes were not tearing up.

The girl and her back up fighters approached Celeste and me. "Remember," I whispered to Celeste, "you have to let them hit you first otherwise you can be charged with assault." This was an urban legend currently circulating among teenagers.

"Fuck that. I'm kicking them as soon as they get close."

Celeste and I held our ground. If we were American history students, one of us would have whispered, "Not until we see the whites of their eyes." For myself, I was going to wait until the girl was within hair-pulling distance. Hopefully, this one would not know how to kick.

As the girls got closer, my heart rate began to slow as if readying itself for the battle that was ahead of us. It was almost as if my body knew what to do. I can do this, I thought to myself just as a deep voice rang through the air.

"Hey!"

Every eye turned towards the right. In the doorway of the laundromat there stood a tall, dark-haired woman. Her long black hair outlined a tough masculine face—it was as though a Cimmerian woman had been transported through space and time to the streets of this Saskatchewan valley-town.

"You girls want trouble?" She crossed the distance from the laundromat in two steps with her tree trunk legs. I had no idea which side she was on until she came to stand in front of my sister and me. She stared into the face of my enemy. My enemy stared back with widening eyes.

In a low, quiet voice our Cimmerian growled, "Which one of you has a problem with my cousin?"

It might have been the timbre of her voice, the muscles in her biceps or the confidence with which she held herself that made all eight girls take a step backwards.

The lead girl sought to save her dignity. "Not your cousin, just this girl," she said pointing at me. I had no idea what was going on. I wasn't even sure who this barbarian woman was. I hoped we were related.

"They're all my cousins," the Cimmerian shot back.

"Yeah, all right," my enemy nodded as if they had made a deal that was to her liking. She backed away into her crowd. They absorbed her and as a group they went back into the arcade.

My sister and I stared at our unknown hero. Kimmy skipped out of the laundromat. "This is my cousin, Freda."

What do you say to someone who has saved you from a beating? Who has saved your ego, personal dignity and facial skin—three things that are invaluable to teenage girls?

"Hey," I said awkwardly. Celeste hung back shyly.

Freda barely acknowledged us as she gave her cousin a quick lecture. "You girls shouldn't be fighting," she said as she wandered back into the laundromat to finish folding her laundry. I'm sure she had no idea of what she'd done for us. In her eyes, this was a silly, pre-teen drama, one of many that would play themselves out on that street that night.

It was life changing for me. I knew at that moment that I would never be a warrior. If there were girls like Freda out there, my fighting career was over before it had begun. Even having someone like Freda on your side was frightening. Perhaps you could learn to resemble a Cimmerian but that was nothing compared to actually being one.

My sister and I headed back to the bingo hall where we sat beside our mom and harassed her into buying us junk food. We never discussed our adventure. Not because we were secretive—I certainly wasn't. Relating my adventures to my mom was one of the highlights of my day. I couldn't tell her this story because there was no way of telling the story that would make me look good.

Perhaps Conan was not the right hero for me. Perhaps I needed a mentor who offered a peaceful alternative, someone who did not need to prove their worth by separating a man's limbs from his body or a woman's hair from her head. There was one epic character who was currently dominating my thoughts at this time: a man who fought, not with a sword, but with great stick-handling skills; a man who would not be drawn into battle, but would only skate faster than the men who sought to bring him down; a man who defeated his enemy with goals rather than with landed punches. Swiftly my mantra changed from what would Conan do, to what would Wayne Gretzky do? Now all I had to do was learn how to skate.

⟶ *King of the Tie-snakes* ⟵
Craig Womack

Craig S. Womack is a Muskogee Creek and Cherokee author and professor of Native American literature at Emory University. He received his PhD from the University of Oklahoma in 1995 and has taught both there and at the University of Lethbridge and the University of Nebraska. He is a leading figure in Native American literary studies, and among his published works is the widely influential *Red on Red: Native American Literary Separatism* (1999), as well as the critically acclaimed novel, *Drowning in Fire* (2001).

The protagonist in "King of the Tie-snakes" is Josh Henneha, a Muskogee Creek teenager growing up in Oklahoma in the 1970s. Josh enjoys reading, doesn't like sports, has a crush on the athletic and popular Jimmy, and is an outcast among the other boys in his small town. He passionately desires Jimmy's attention and fanta-sizes about communicating secretly with him. Woven through the story are Josh's memories of fishing with his grandfather, during which time his grandfather would tell him stories from his Creek heritage. The story about the king of the tie-snakes, a water snake with powers of transformation, provides a framework for Josh not only to resist homophobia and prejudice but also to embrace his cultural and sexual identities.

JOSH HENNEHA, EUFAULA, OKLAHOMA, 1972

I spent my days that Oklahoma summer fishing with my grandfather or traipsing after my cousin and his friends through hills covered with blackjacks and post oaks, cicadas humming in my ears, chiggers at my ankles, following as they scouted dark places to smoke their cigarettes and gather their secrets. My cousin, Lenny Henneha, barely tolerated me, the ties of blood hardly enough to admit a sissy into his circle. This resentful inclusion was a step up, actually, from school, where I spent my days on the edge of the playground, watching the scrabbling bodies weave in and out, frenetic blurs of girls jumping rope, clumps of boys playing soccer, bobbing up and down over a lake of asphalt. As for me, I waited for the misery to end when the bell would proclaim relief, when the teacher would call roll, singing out "Josh," and I would at least have the comfort of hiding behind a book back in class, its hard cover held before me like a Jesuit missionary's crucifix. But that was another world, and I had two more months left of sweating and barely being able to breathe the dripping Oklahoma air before returning to school in the fall.

"I can't swim out that far," Josh said, shaking while beads of water ran off his chin and dripped onto his chest. He had started out toward the raft and turned back, the other boys urging him on, already halfway out in the lake. He stood ankle deep in a mossy bed of lake weeds under a bright blue sky, his shoulders sunburned and peeling. He turned, climbed out of the weeds, and headed up the embankment in the direction of the dam.

"You fuckin' pussy," Sammy Barnhill hollered from the lake at Josh's retreating form as he made the blacktop road at the top of the hill.

"Come on, Josh," Lenny yelled in exasperation. "We ain't taking you anywhere else with us."

Josh shrugged and kept walking.

It was Jimmy Alexander's turn. "It ain't that far. Look, you can swim out on that intertube." Jimmy pointed at the boat dock where the black tube was swollen on the top of the hot concrete steps. Josh paused and considered Jimmy's advice. Before long he had the tube untied, dipped on both sides in the

water to cool it off, and he was kicking his way toward the others, the willow
trees leaning over the lakeshore becoming farther away each time he cast a
backward glance, the dam road at the top of the hill a distant blur, the Texaco
station in front of the dirt access road that led down to the lake now invisible
as he kicked through the water, the sun burning overhead.

He and the boys swam out toward the old raft anchored off the shore of
Lake Eufaula, racing to see who could get there first. Sammy pulled himself
over the moss-covered sides, and, one by one, as the boys tried to grab onto the
ladder and climb aboard, he kicked them back into the water. He announced,
"Let's play king of the raft." As Sammy defended the ladder, Jimmy swam to the
other side and hopped aboard. Josh, floating on his inner tube on the opposite
side, watched Jimmy coming up out of the water. As Jimmy pulled himself
aboard he seemed to rise out of the lake in an unending succession; his wiry
arms and upper body kept coming and coming, followed by his swimming
trunks and long legs, like a snake uncoiling. He was taller than the rest of them.
Jimmy's eyes met Josh's just before Jimmy stood fully erect on the slippery
wooden planks. Jimmy quickly turned away and snuck over to where Sammy
stood, occupied with kicking Lenny back into the water, and Jimmy shoved
Sammy into the lake. "New king," he said to Sammy, who came up spitting
water and calling Jimmy a motherfucker.

Jimmy grew tired of using his superior size to keep Sammy off the raft, and
he pretended not to notice Sammy mouthing off. Jimmy was shaking water out
of his ears when Sammy climbed back up. The raft pitched a little, and Jimmy
lost his balance, falling to his knees.

"Dumb nigger," Sammy taunted. Jimmy grabbed Sammy's ankles and sent
him sprawling on his ass. He landed with a loud *thunk*. Jimmy stood above
Sammy. Jimmy's short-cropped hair glistened in the sun, and he seemed to
Josh bathed in light after emerging from the murky lake. Jimmy was more
mature than the rest of the boys, the athlete of the bunch, a basketball player
obsessed with the Lakers and his hero, Kareem Abdul-Jabbar. Jimmy, like many
Creeks, had black blood and features, a fact the other boys held against him
and used to discredit him since he could beat them at sports. Josh pretended to
watch a ski boat passing by, back and forth, but he was using each opportunity
to check out Jimmy, who was now lying back, hands folded behind his head,
taking in the sun. The water was drying on Jimmy's chest in mottled streaks
that ran down his belly to his swimming trunks, an old pair that was missing
a button, pinned at the top instead.

Josh had secret words with special powers. Each time he followed the ski
boat's pass between the raft and the shore, and his eyes swept over Jimmy, Josh
sent out another message. The way it worked was that only the right person
would know he was receiving the thoughts that Josh had stored up inside his

head. Not very many people would know what the words meant. In the wrong hands the message could be deadly, or the recipient might turn on him. Josh watched Jimmy for a sign that the signals had registered, but nothing seemed to be happening.

Josh carefully unknotted a plastic bag, which contained inside it another knotted plastic bag, which he also undid, retrieving its contents.

"You brought a book with you?" Sammy said scornfully.

"Give him a break, man," Jimmy said. "What you reading, anyway?" Josh held up the cover. Jimmy squinted, reading the title, *The Happy Hollisters*, then laughed. "What do you get out of a story like that?" he asked. Josh couldn't explain that the Happy Hollisters were so far away, and he took comfort in that. Jimmy let it drop when Lenny interrupted by pointing out a school of crappie darting up to the raft's ladder.

Josh knew the sting of being last at everything. During school recess, Miss Manier, whom the boys all called Miss Manure, would have the kids line up to choose teams for kickball. Each day she would send one of the girls over to fetch Josh from his lone perch near the tetherball poles. Miss Manier began by saying, "Okay, children. Which one of you boys wants to volunteer for team captain?" One of the more athletic guys, usually Jimmy, would speak up first and stand there with his hand up in the air. But Miss Manier always picked a white boy to lead the teams. And next time Jimmy would volunteer again. Josh wondered why Jimmy didn't give up after a while. Didn't he get it?

Alone, Josh dreamed of advising Jimmy about the ways of Miss Manier, inviting Jimmy over to his house where Josh would take him up to his room. Jimmy would sit on Josh's bed, and Josh would sit at his desk and say, "Jimmy, what you wanna do is watch close while captains are being picked. You might notice that Raymond gets picked every time, and he hates being team captain. Wait until we get out on the field, and offer to be last up if Raymond will let you lead the team because Raymond lives to bat." Jimmy would clap Josh on the shoulder and say, "Thanks, buddy, I never thought of that." Maybe afterward they would lie on Josh's bed, and Josh would casually pull out a *Sports Illustrated* with Kareem on the cover, and Jimmy would pick it up and explain to Josh all the mysteries of basketball.

Or Jimmy would toss Josh a ball lying in the corner of the room. "Hold it like this," he'd say, walking over and standing behind Josh. "Here, put your middle finger over the air valve," he'd add while helping Josh position his hands, and they would both slowly raise the ball together, time and time again, until Josh had it down perfect.

Out on the playground, Josh wondered why Miss Manier didn't just have them number off and separate into teams, sparing them all the daily humiliation. What was her game? But she was a white lady, so who knows? Not only did Josh never get picked for team captain, since he was Indian, but he got chosen just after the last boy was picked and before the first girl, because he was the least athletic of the schoolboys. Miss Manier never did anything to stop the girls from being picked last, either. She pretended not to notice any of this. Or maybe she really didn't see it. Hard to say. She looked busy pushing her glasses farther up on her nose when she wanted not to hear or see things.

The boys called him faggot. All the time. Every day. It might be summer vacation, but there was no vacation from that, and it had become like a second name; "Josh faggot" was as familiar to him as "Josh Henneha." He couldn't understand their world, either, whether they hated him because he read books or because he "walked like a girl," which they chanted to him in singsong voices on the bus rides home. Would it be any better in seventh grade? On the playground, Josh liked playing the girls' games because he didn't have to endure the burning shame of choosing teams. The girls simply took turns playing hopscotch or tetherball, and he felt more comfortable apart from the boys' cutthroat competition. During recess, when the kids could play with whomever they wanted, he knew that none of them would choose him for their team anyway. So he either joined the girls or stood alone at the edge of the blacktop watching the others.

Jimmy took a lot of shit for sometimes putting up with Josh. When Sammy would see Jimmy talking to Josh, he would say, "Jimmy, now we know. You're one of them, too. We see you got a new little girlfriend." Occasionally, Jimmy would convince the boys to let Josh throw in with them, although they complained about having him in their presence. Josh would join them only after relentless teasing. "You pussy. Playing with the girls again? Want to borrow my sister's panties?"

Today, though, Josh had figured out a way of making himself useful to Jimmy. From the bread bag, Josh pulled out Jimmy's pack of cigarettes, which he'd tied inside with his book before they swam out. Josh handed the pack to Jimmy. Jimmy passed each member of the gang one of them, and he demonstrated his awe-inspiring ability to light up even on the windiest days by holding the match with his thumb and forefinger and cupping his hand around the burning flame. Smokes were important, and Josh had managed to get them out to the middle of Lake Eufaula, an accomplishment that no one on the raft could deny. He'd used his head, he thought, even if none of them would admit it.

Lenny spoke up. "Let's have a diving contest." The first one to bring up a rock from the bottom of the lake would win, he explained.

The boys argued about who would go first. Josh sat alone on the edge of the raft staring wistfully, trancelike, over the side, his feet dangling in the water. They chose the diving order. Sammy would take the first turn, of course, then Jimmy and Lenny. They all agreed that Josh would go last, since, as Sammy said all the time, "He ain't no count nohow." Josh said, "You go ahead. I don't feel like diving just now." They met his statement with the usual jeers describing Josh's mother, words about unmentionable acts performed on close kin and the family dog, comments about his female relatives' sexual activities with ancient white men in overalls who sat on the town bench in Eufaula by the old Palmers Grocery and spat long streams of tobacco juice, and concluded with the final touch, without which any string of insults lacked finality: "I bet you're chicken, faggot."

Josh had an idea. He thought, "I'll see if Jimmy can receive my messages from beneath the water. I'll count to three after he dives and begin transmitting. I'll call to him from on top of the raft; Jimmy will answer back from below the waves. Maybe if I can't send my thoughts when we're sitting so close together, what about when I'm above the surface, and he's below?" It could be that brain waves can only be sent from opposite worlds, and only received if Jimmy is underwater, cut off from air and sunlight, blindly making his way deeper and deeper toward the sunken realms where big cats and largemouth bass lay hidden in sinkholes under fallen submerged tree trunks. When Jimmy returned and opened his hand, the rock would be a sign.

Sammy began the ritual by giving a sermon on deep-diving techniques. "You have to blow all your air out," he said, "and make your ears pop." Then, plugging his nose like a sailor jumping from the heights of a sinking battleship, he leaped, penetrating the surface and sending out waves that lightly rocked the raft. Feet first, the wrong way, Josh thought, if you wanna reach bottom. But he didn't say anything. The boys peered down into the light reflecting off the surface of the lake and tensed as they waited for Sammy to come back up. Finally, a hand shot from beneath the water, and Sammy's clenched fist broke through the glassy film, projecting toward the blue sky.

Sammy, pale and shaking from barely having enough air to make it back up, climbed onto the raft and didn't say a word in spite of the others' questions. "Did you reach bottom?" they asked. After he caught his breath, Sammy slowly opened his fist and proclaimed that he had dropped the rock shortly before reaching the surface. This explanation burned in Josh's ears.

"I'm going next," Josh said suddenly. He looked like he had just awakened from a long sleep. The boys looked quizzically at one another, wondering why Josh, who usually responded only at the last minute to their dares, took it upon himself to be one of the first divers. But Josh just had to go now. When Jimmy entered the lake waters, Josh wanted to have his dive over with so he could devote all his concentration to transmitting his message to Jimmy rather than having to worry about whether or not he would be the one to emerge with the rock.

Josh had listened attentively to Sammy's sermon on diving, but he jumped headfirst into the lake, unlike Sammy, then he blew the air from his lungs and pushed as hard as he could with his legs, grabbing desperately at the water, pulling himself down farther. He would finally show them. Maybe he couldn't kick a ball over second base, but he would come back out of the water with that rock, and he pictured shooting above the surface with it in his hand as the boys stared in amazement. He would climb the ladder one-handed, all the while holding the prize above his head like he had just won a new world title. He wouldn't say anything, just set the rock in the center of the raft and step back and smirk like he thought nothing of retrieving rocks from twenty feet below. Leading the contest would allow him to insist that Jimmy go right after him, bringing them even closer to each other's secrets, ready for Josh's messages. Maybe he and Jimmy would be the only ones to make it from the lake's depths with something to show for themselves, and they'd be united as winners. His lungs burned for air as he pushed deeper and deeper through the murky water, but he kept the image of claiming his victory before his eyes, urging himself on because it was a test, and his messages to Jimmy depended on it.

His hand struck soft mud. He couldn't believe he'd actually made it when even Sammy hadn't been able to reach bottom. He felt around until he clutched a slimy, moss-covered rock. He held it to his chest with one hand, embracing it like a mother holding her child, and he began grabbing at the water with his free hand and kicking his feet.

He broke the surface and gasped, but his hand had struck something solid just above his head, and he heard the thump resound like the inside of a kettle drum. He pulled in mouthfuls of air, but they smelled of dank mold. When he opened his eyes, he saw darkness, and he felt confusion, like having awakened in the middle of the night not knowing where he was. He wanted to call out, but he knew that would make him look chicken and spoil the effect of having retrieved the stone. He began to hyperventilate and panic, and the thought of winning the contest left him, replaced with the fear of surfacing in this unexpected world, breathing in darkness. He heard the voices of the boys above, and, finally, it dawned on him. He had come up under the raft. The others were sitting one foot above him and didn't even know it. They must have been busy chattering and not heard his hand strike the raft's bottom. He felt his way to the edge, ready to duck under and surface on the other side to show the boys his rock and claim his rights as winner.

Then he stopped. A single thought flashed through his mind and seemed to come from somewhere outside himself. "What if I just stay here? For like five minutes? Then when I come up, with the rock in my hand, I'll have proven I can stay underwater longer than anyone, beyond anything Sammy can explain.

I won't tell them how I did it. And when I send Jimmy under, he'll be ready to believe my powers."

———

During those fishing trips with my grandfather at Lake Eufaula, I learned to row our old aluminum boat a little ways offshore and drop the cement coffee-can anchor while he got the poles ready. He was rigging up a pole he'd given my father for his birthday, but my father wasn't much to fish. "Don't tell Dad I never use this," my father had cautioned me when I left the house with the pole to go over to Grandpa's that morning. Grandpa would set things up in the boat before we got started. This arrangement seemed to work best since he easily became grouchy when he had to tell me which lures to try, how to work them in the water, and what to put on my line when I wasn't having any luck. The third time out he had snapped at me, "How many times I gotta tell you don't tie on a leader to that plastic worm." He spoke a kind of broken English I'd heard many of the old people use around there, especially on the days he complied with my grandma's prodding to go to the Indian Baptist church. At Grandma's church the deacon seated you in some kind of hierarchy I didn't quite understand, but it had to do with length of membership since the oldest people were in the front. The deacon would point his cane to the proper pew, directing men to one side, women to the other. The sermon was in Creek, little of which I understood, and afterward, when Grandma's friends came up to visit, they would speak English since I was from the younger generation. But I took it that Grandpa cared a good deal more for fishing than churchgoing.

After we got settled on the plank benches on our respective sides of the boat, he handed me my pole rigged with a bobber and minnow. He had given up teaching me how to jig the bass lure through the water and had given me over as a useless case, destined to use live bait forever. Which is the way most Indian guys fished anyway, my grandpa always complained, one hand on the pole, the other on the Budweiser. My grandpa, for some reason, had mastered all the nuances of bass fishing rather than just slinging a bobber with stink bait underneath it out into the lake. So I sat, elbow on knee, chin in hand, watching the red-and-white sphere appear and reappear in the waves of shimmering water, imagining it as a boat approaching a distant shore and I had stood years on the beach awaiting the return of someone on board. One day I had brought a book to read while I waited for a fish to strike, but Grandpa had glared at me with such disdain that I had timidly put it back in my lunch sack. I didn't say anything, but I pouted all morning. I was rereading all of C. S. Lewis's *Narnia* books and was completely taken with the notion of a wardrobe that was a closet on one side and a world of talking animals on the other, and the boy who could go get his brothers and sisters and bring them back with him, if only they'd believe.

Grandpa could cast his lure, send it singing in an arcing loop out across the lake, land it with a soft *ker-plop* over by a stump where he said the bass were, and reel it in, working it at the same speed with a gentle tugging motion that made it snake through the water. But what was really beyond belief was his ability to talk during these adroit maneuvers. When he spoke, all his words led up to a story; all conversation was a prelude. So I wasn't surprised when he said to me, "Hey, how 'bout it, this lake pretty big mess of water, ain't it?"

It was huge; even had we owned a motorboat, it would have taken hours, I imagined, or days, to boat all the way around it. "I used to farm right over yonder," he said, nodding toward the middle of the lake. "Before the dam went in. Built it in '63, I think it was. Started gathering water in '64. Now, water's all over. Little cotton, little corn, I growed some of everything, few hogs, too. Yep, had a house, right over thataway. Your daddy was borned there. Now you can't get nowhere around here on the same roads you used to. All covered up."

I was fascinated by the thought of underwater farms, barns, houses, pastures, and I could see kitchens with families of bass and crappie darting in and out the windows and under the legs of dining room tables.

"There is something white man has never saw or caught," he went on, "something in the water. Their head is shape like a deer. If you are by water it has a power and will pull you in. It don't pull just anyone in water, just certain people. If you ever see a whirling water in the river you better get out of there. It makes a sound like a big snake then rises up on a sheet of water. If you ever see the strange monster, someone dies. White man never did catch this tie-snake. They have horns like a deer and all kinds of color, kinda greenish and red. Long time ago, they old Indian medicine doctor use to make them things come out and catch them. When they catch them, they use to cut the ends off their horns and hunt with them. They would throw something doctored with Indian medicine, throw it in four times in the whirling water, and make tie-snake come out. One time my daddy said he went fishing and he kinda got a funny feeling by the river, like scared, and pretty soon he heard a growling sound in water and after a while it started bubbling so he got out of there fast. I heard he told about it. It was near Gaines Creek south of here."

Grandpa reeled his line in and tied on a new spinner. I had been dangling my arm over the side of the boat. I pulled it back in. Grandpa started back up. "One man name Curtis Goolman, kin of yours, he told me one time…."

———

"I bet he's got the rock in his hand right now," laughed Jimmy. Sammy threw in, "Naw, he's probably got something else in his hand." All the boys laughed. Thirty more seconds passed, and a smothering silence fell over them. The boys began to take deep drags on their cigarettes and looked down at their bare toes. They coughed nervously and listened to the water slapping the sides of the raft. Sammy tried to kill time by blowing smoke rings, but the wind swept them out over the water.

Finally, Lenny spoke. "What do y'all s'pose happened to him?"

"I think we ought to swim to shore," Sammy said coolly.

"We don't know for sure if he drowned. We can't just leave him here," said Jimmy. "We gotta at least stay until we know what happened."

"What are we gonna tell everybody when we get home?" said Sammy. "We better get our stories straight or his folks are liable to blame us. It ain't our fault the dickhead can't swim." The other boys looked over at Sammy and saw that they were supposed to laugh again.

Jimmy said, "I'm staying here for a spell. Not that I'm afraid of getting in trouble or anything. I just wanna see if maybe he comes back up." Lenny sided with Jimmy and decided to stay on the raft. Sammy said, "Well, while y'all are sitting here getting cold in the wind, I'll be stretched out in the sun on the bank." Sammy slid into the water, and swam for shore.

Baa-rump. Baa-rump. Baa-rump. Under the raft, Josh heard the buoy bumping against it up above, steady as a heartbeat, and thought that he had better come back up before he stretched his miraculous powers too thin and the boys went home, leaving him for drowned. Then he wouldn't get to test his secret messages to Jimmy.

Josh dived and ducked under the raft. Just before he broke the surface, he felt a sudden tug on his leg. A clump of fishing line had wrapped around his ankle, and when he swam up he had pulled all the slack out, binding the entangled mesh tightly. He felt with his hands, unable to see in the murky water. The other end of the line was twisted around the cable that anchored the raft to the bottom. He dropped the rock. Had it been a single strand of line, he could have broken it easily since fishermen used light test weights for the bass and crappie in the lake. But with the whole clump wound around itself, the strength of the line was greatly magnified. Each tug dug into the flesh of his ankle with a sharp little searing that he couldn't exactly call pain. He almost wanted to laugh, then, panic-stricken, he placed both feet against the cable and pulled with his hands.

Josh strained and jerked. "Oh God! No. Please. Let me get loose. I won't try another trick like this," he thought, as he pulled at the line. He started to cry out in terror and swallowed some water. He began to choke and cough, fighting to keep holding his breath. He cut his palms on the thin strands, and, in desperation, he felt around, sightless in the murky water, to locate the individual strands. He began breaking them one by one. He had torn apart five or six of them when something brushed past his chest. Josh felt his arms flailing in the water around him. He opened his eyes and saw the underwater city where he was tethered to the spokes of somebody's wagon wheel parked on the street in front of a building. A large channel catfish with a Fu Manchu mustache was swimming in place just between the top porch rail and the roof of the building, making underwater burbling noises that sounded like garbled words. The fish darted inside the front window, and Josh watched him enter. A painted sign above the door stoop read:

GRAYSON BROS

DEALERS

IN

GENERAL MERCHANDISE

Josh could hear the catfish inside the store singing a jingle about seed, harnesses, farm machinery, groceries, "not to mention," he sang, "traveler's supplies, prints, hosiery, boots, shoes, hats, caps, and all the etceteras requisite to a first-class Western business house."

Josh looked down at his leg. A balled-up coil of snakes had wrapped themselves around him, from ankle to knee, and they moved in and out of each other, swaying in the lake bottom current and weaving between the wagon spokes. Just when they felt like they had loosened their grip on him, he'd pull and they'd tighten back up. He had gone off to the underwater world, but he couldn't get back to his ... *the bathtub water drains slowly down and I feel my body grow heavier Lucy scrubs my back the warm water goes galump galump galump down the drain as she blows the smoke in my ear in the beginning we were covered we were covered we were covered don't go near swirling water they got horns that make powerful medicine the bubbles this is a trade I'm trading my air for water air for water water for air it's not fair that rhymes water is heavier than air but they are both free we were covered by a mighty fog in her lap kicking that ball clean over third base out over the chain-link fence off over the housetops and Jimmy cheering while I run those bases at a slow dogtrot and he makes hook shots from center court those slimy bastards will wish they would have picked me first look at the bubbles it's not a fair trade air for water breathing smoke into me covered by a mighty fog and hold on to each other so they don't get lost I'll hold on to Jimmy and maybe he'll wanna hold on to me too if he gets my message.*

On top of the raft, Jimmy shouted, "Oh my God. Look at all the bubbles coming up!" He jumped to his feet and pointed toward the water. He leaned over the raft and noticed the tugging was coming from beneath, not from the waves. "It looks like he's just below the surface." Jimmy dove headfirst toward the troubled water. Josh saw a snake, with horns, swimming toward him. Jimmy bumped into Josh after having just barely broken water. The giant snake was trying to wrap itself around Josh, and he was too weak to stop it. Jimmy placed both arms around Josh's chest and tried to swim back up, but he couldn't budge him. He followed the length of Josh's body with his hands, feeling everywhere until finally reaching the entangled mesh of line around Josh's ankle. Jimmy popped above the waves and pulled himself back on the raft, shakily grabbing a pocketknife they kept stuck in the wood planks for fishing. Jimmy dove back below, grabbing handfuls of knotted line, and he kept sawing through whole bunches of the mesh. Finally he felt Josh drifting away as he sawed through the last of it. He grabbed him again below the arms and swam toward the raft.

Josh was awkward and heavy, and his legs and arms flopped limply while Jimmy pushed him against the ladder, keeping him in place by standing on the bottom rung and holding him with one arm and pressing against him with his body. Lenny grabbed Josh's arms while Jimmy shoved from behind. They pulled him onto the middle of the raft, where Josh lay pale and motionless. Jimmy kneeled over him. He hoped Lenny wouldn't notice his hands shaking. He tried to control his voice, but he got dizzy and thought for a moment he might pass out. "You know how to do that mouth-to-mouth thing they taught us at school?"

"I ain't kissing no guy," Lenny said. "Let's just swim back and get help."

"He'll die, you fucking idiot," Jimmy said. "You're going to help me right now!" He grabbed Lenny by the shoulders and slammed him down by Josh's side. "Just help me keep his head tilted back," he said. Jimmy leaned over Josh, plugged his nose, and boosted his head up, then began breathing into him. Lenny stared in horror at Josh's strange, pallid hue. "What are we gonna do?" he whimpered. "I wish we had never swam out here. Oh, God, I hope this works."

Josh coughed, and his body began to twitch. He threw up all over himself, and he rolled over on his side and started spitting out mouthfuls of water. Jimmy and Lenny threw lake water on him to rinse him off. Josh just lay there and sucked in big gulps of air. The two boys stared down at him. The color started to come back to his flesh, his skin returning to brown. "Do you reckon he can talk? I never seen anyone drown before," Lenny said.

"I don't know," Jimmy said. "Josh. Say something."

"I had it. Dropped it. Really, I had it in my hand," he sputtered.

"Sure you did, buddy. You almost drowned. We thought you were a goner. Josh, can you swim back? Um, I mean me and Lenny could help you if you need us to," Jimmy said. Josh tried to stand, but his legs crumpled underneath him, and he sagged back down to the floor of the raft.

Lenny helped Josh stand up. He placed one arm around his side and slowly pulled him to his feet. Lenny draped Josh's arm over his shoulder and helped him stand while Jimmy climbed down the ladder and stood on the bottom rung in the water. They helped Josh over the side. Jimmy wrapped his arm around Josh and said, "We'll take turns swimming him to shore." Jimmy started out, holding Josh with one arm while swimming on his side. Josh felt strange, his arm draped around Jimmy's cold, wet neck, Jimmy's legs accidentally kicking him as he tried to convey Josh toward shore, their bodies shivering together in the cold water. Jimmy and Lenny kept trading off until they reached shore and climbed out on land.

———

My back was sore from sitting on the wooden plank, and I was getting bored and hot. After popping open a Coke, I reeled in, watching my bobber skip across the lake, planning to check my minnow, but my line was crossed over Grandpa's, and, when I pulled up my hook, I had his line in my hand, too. He glared at me and said, "Watch where you're casting that thing." The way he said "that thing" made it sound more like I had a gaffing hook and I was such a fishing disaster that I might jerk his head off his shoulders with my next cast.

"Anyway," he grunted, "your Uncle Curtis he told me all about that tie-snake. Me and your Uncle Glen, Lucy's husband, and Curtis was always drive over to Muskogee together and go bowling. Glen wore a floppy fishing hat all the time, even at the bowling alley. Now, there's a man could work a lure like nobody's business. Me and him hit every spot of water around here. Couldn't hardly bowl to save his life, though. Curtis always give him a bad time about his bowling. If Glen wasn't with us at the bowling alley, Curtis says you might as well just tell stories because they's no one to laugh at. Long time ago, Curtis says, two men out somewheres hunting together. Camping and hunting, out in the woods. So it gets time to go off to sleep, and the two lay down on opposite sides of the fire and after a while the one of them is sleeping hard but see that other old boy gets hungry, him, and he thinks how much he likes fish real good and how fish fry sound tasty 'bout now. Just then he notices water dripping from the top of the tree a-splashing down on the ground, just falling *ker-plunk* in a puddle from those stripped branches 'cause it's wintertime, no leaves. He waked up his friend who wasn't any too happy about leaving his snooze and says, 'Hey you ain't gonna b'lieve this nohow. Look yonder,' and his friend rubs his eyes. The man who like fish real good says, 'I go up and see what's causing all that commotion.' Up in the top of that tree he found some water and fishes swimming in it up there splashing every whichaways from dashing around.

"That ole boy get a big grin and says, 'How 'bout it, that's what I been wanting,' and throwed him down some of them catfishes to his buddy. Then he climbed down the tree and cleaned them up and getting ready to dip them in flour and cornmeal and fry them fishes when his friend says, 'There may be something bad wrong 'bout fish found way up in a tree thataway.' That old boy too hungry to worry, and he eats them fish all up so good even clean his teeth with the bones afterwards. His friend won't touch a one of them. So now he's full sure enough but not feeling so hot no mores thinking maybe he kinda overeat too much and he stretched out and said his bones ached little bit. His buddy says, 'Well, I told you they might be no good,' and they both finally go to sleeping on their sides of the fire.

"So this here one who ate the fish woke up in the middle of the night and couldn't b'lieve his eyes and shook his friend real hard and hollering, 'Look here what's the matter with me?' His friend looked and jumped back now seeings how his buddy's legs glued together. 'Well, I told you 'bout that fish. I don't reckon there's nothing we can do,' and he went back off to sleep, that other one. 'Bout the middle of the night he wakes him back up and now his body head down is tail of a snake. Come daybreak, he wakes up his friend one more time and saying to him, 'Look at me now,' and he's completely a snake then, laying there in a big coil.

"So the snake says—he could still talk—'Friend, you gonna have to leave me, but first could you take me over to the water hole?' The snake slithered off into the hole when his friend turned him loose on the bank and that hole commenced to cave in on itself and getting bigger and the water to whirlpool around right fast in the middle. Snake raise up his head out of that rush of water and says, 'Tell my parents and sisters come down here an' visit me.' So his friend brought back to the spot same place all them ones who is kin. They stood on the bank, and the snake showed himself in the middle of the pond. He come up there and crawled out, crawling over the laps of his parents and sisters where they sat on a log next to the bank, him shedding tears while he crawled. He couldn't talk no mores, so he wasn't able to tell them his story. Then he slid in the water, and they went back home."

I had sat down in the gunwale of the boat to rest my back against the bench, keeping one eye on my bobber, the other on Grandpa as he told his story. I had half a dozen questions, and often his stories ended like that, with no explanations. "How could water be in the top of a tree?" I asked him, "and how did the fish get there in the first place? What happened to the snake afterwards?"

Grandpa said, "Hush up, gotta little bite," and readied himself for the next strike. As I wondered if this was the real thing or an avoidance of my pesky curiosity, he jerked his pole back, and it bent over in a wide half-arc while he started steadily working the fish toward the boat.

———

When they climbed up on the bank, Sammy stood on top, laughing. He had watched the whole thing from shore. "I see the rat didn't drown after all. Hey, Jimmy, I didn't know you liked teaching little girls to swim. Yeah, I seen you lean over and kiss him on the raft. What's the matter, Jimmy? Ashamed of your new girlfriend?"

On solid ground, Jimmy suddenly realized the way he was standing with one arm around Josh's waist, helping him to remain on his feet. He looked down at his arm with revulsion and let go; Josh sagged to his hands and knees in the grass. Jimmy started talking fast. "I just thought I'd dive down and check. I mean he probably can't even swim, what the fuck? I couldn't just let him die." Jimmy spit out his words. "Do you think I liked watching him puke all over himself? I just didn't want to get in trouble. What do you think his folks would say if we left him there? Good thing I dived down when I did." Jimmy kept talking faster, all the while explaining, getting hoarser, looking into Sammy's eyes for some reassurance.

Josh quivered and pulled himself to his feet. His eyes burned from way back, and he snarled, "I didn't need your goddamn help. I almost had that line unwrapped myself. Anyway, I could of stayed down there another couple minutes. I knew how to swim before you were crawling around on the kitchen floor. I could have if I wanted to, goddammit. I was just about to get it untied when you messed me up and I…."

Josh began to weep as the words drifted away from him like smoke. The other boys turned away disgustedly and walked up the bank toward the road, Jimmy the last one to leave. Josh heard their voices, laughing, like the small rasps of a steel file against wood. As they moved up the grassy hill, playing and shoving each other back down, Josh felt himself float out over his own body. He could see his skinny brown frame; it looked no more than an outline, a wisp of smoke that could easily blow away out over the lake. The boys, joking from the hillside, sounded like their voices came from deep within the belly of a cave where words dripped down red-streaked walls and echoed through caverns full of meanings he could not grasp. Confusion washed over him.

He watched Sammy and Lenny walking down the road that led home. Jimmy paused for an instant and turned back toward the lake. He approached slowly, and he stood off from Josh, looking down at him from the top of the bank. He waited until Sammy and Lenny were out of earshot. He stared at his feet as he spoke. "You know the guys. They're just playing around." Josh did not reply. The waves patted the shore in rhythmic claps. "Well, you know how it is around them, don't you?" Jimmy coughed and lit a cigarette. He waited for Josh to say something. He looked out toward the raft. "I didn't really mean it. I just didn't want them to think, well, you know how they tease you if they think you like someone too much."

Josh couldn't find the right words for his rage. He felt all the words flaming up before his eyes and burning away like stubble before he could use them. In church he had heard Jesus' words to the centurion: Speak the Word and you shall be healed. He no longer believed. He wished he could pick up words like stones, rub them to make them smooth and polished, and put them in his pocket to save and use during moments like this one. He longed for the comfort of those stones. He wished he had collected all kinds of them—agate streaked with red lightning, hard quartz pounded into indissoluble rage, blood-red hematite formed around secrets, yellow amaranth rained down by tears. He would put all the rocks in his mouth and find his voice in their swirled streaks of sky, fire, water. But there were no such rocks and none of them contained secret messages and there was nobody to send them to even if they had.

Jimmy snuffed out his cigarette on a broken willow trunk, flicking the stub into the grass. "Well, I guess I'll be seeing you around," he said. He turned and walked off toward the road.

"Yeah, I guess," Josh said.

———

Lord of the losers that summer, I lived inside my imagination and often felt myself floating away, as others talked, into my private world of dreams. But not when Grandpa launched into his stories, which demanded some kind of listening akin to physical participation, and he cast his voice in such a way that drew you into the presences his words created. Bored on the boat with no place to go, bored with staring at my bobber ride up one hill of waves and down the slippery slope of another, bored with trying to will a fish into hunger for my minnow or dangling night crawler, Grandpa's stories were a welcome, if strange, respite. And if I wasn't fishing with him, my grandma would send me over to my cousins to "play with boys your own age instead of being locked up in that room with those books of yours."

Grandpa strung his bass on the stringer, running the clasp through its mouth and gill slit and closing it, then tossing the chain in the water, the only catch of the day. Maybe that very fish had been violently jerked out of its underwater home, from the barn or farmhouse my grandparents used to live in before the lake covered up their former residence. He settled back into the bench, and I saw his eyelids flutter and his head start to nod off. I couldn't believe it; even he was bored with fishing. Afraid that he might fall over, I said, loud enough to rouse him, yet tentatively, knowing how much a pain in the ass I was on fishing trips, "Hey, wake up."

"Ain't asleep," he muttered, and when he surfaced from his nap, he came up in the middle of another story as if he'd never stopped talking. He tied a bass plug onto his line while he spoke.

"A *micco* one time he send his son out with a message for another chief. Sent him out with that message in a clay pot so the chief would recognize him. His son stopped to play with some boys—he was carrying that clay pot you know—who were throwing stones into the water. Pitching and throwing. Making them rocks skip. Chief's son wanting to show off a little bit maybe he can do it better than all them other ones, so he throwed that vessel on the water, but it sank. Like this here."

Grandpa laid down his pole for a second and tossed an imaginary pot in an easy underhanded curve out into the lake. "That boy 'fraid to go to the neighbor chief without his father's message, more 'fraid to go back home and tell his father he lost him his pot. He jumped into that stream and got to the place where it sunk and dove down under there.

His playmates waited a long time round that creek for him to come back up but never did. They went back home and told everyone he died.

"Underneath that murky water tie-snake grabbed a-holt of him and drug him off to a cave where he lived. Inside, tie-snake says, 'See that platform over yonder? Get up on there, you.' Up on the platform was the king of the tie-snakes." Grandpa dropped his voice and sounded commanding when he imitated the tie-snake ordering the chief's son.

"The boy didn't like too good what he saw; that platform was a heap of crawling snakes. Oh, they was just crawling around. Slithering around. Sliding around. Weaving in and out of each other. And that king sitting big up on a ledge right over there on that platform.

"Well, this boy walked up there anyway trying to not let on how scared he was. Plumb frightened. He lifted his foot to get up on the platform, but, as he did, it just rose up higher. He tried again, same thing. And a third time. That tie-snake said again, 'Get up yonder, boy,' and on the fourth try he got up there. King invited him come sit down on that ledge next to him. 'Better than them wiggling snakes all round my feet,' the boy thinks. King says, 'Over yonder is a feather; it's yours,' pointing to a cluster of red tail feathers from a hawk. That boy went over and reached out and every time his fingers went to grabbing those feathers they disappeared. But on the fourth try he got it and held to it.

"He goes back over to tie-snake who says, 'That knife over yonder is yours.' Same thing again. It rose up on its own every time the chief's son raise up his hand. On the fourth time it didn't go nowheres, and he laid holt of it. The king said the boy could go back home after four days. King says, 'If your father asks where you been gone, say, I know what I know, but no matter what don't tell him what you know. When your father needs my help, walk toward the east and bow four times to the rising sun, and I will be there to help him.'

"Tie-snake took the boy back after four days, up to the surface where he first dived under and put the lost vessel back in his hands. The boy swam to the bank and went home to his father who was right happy to see him seeings how he thought he was dead.

"Boy told his father about tie-snake king and his offer to help, but he didn't tell his father what he knew. His father heard about enemies planning an attack, and he sent his boy off to get help. The chief's son put the feathered plume on his head, grabbed up his knife, headed towards the east. He bowed four times before the sunrise, and there stood tie-snake king in front of him.

"'What do you need?' he asked.

"'My father needs your help,' the boy answered.

"'Don't worry none,' tie-snake told him. 'They will attack but nobody get hurt. Go back and tell him I'll make it all right.'

"The boy went back and delivered the message. The enemy came and attacked the town but no one got hurt. It came nighttime, and there were their enemies on the edge of the village all caught up in a tangled mess of snakes."

Grandpa was pulling up the coffee-can cement anchor since it was starting to get dark out. Crickets were chirruping on shore, and fireflies flitted here and there over the water. I burned to know the boy's secret, what he withheld from his father, what lay buried beneath the shadowy water, but already Grandpa was set on rowing, rowing toward shore.

➤ *As It Was in the Beginning* ➤
E. Pauline Johnson

Emily Pauline Johnson (also known by her Mohawk name, Tekahionwake) was born on the Six Nations Reserve near Brantford, Ontario, in 1861. Her father was the late G. H. M. Johnson (Onwanonsyshon), Head Chief of the Six Nations Indians, and a descendant of one of the fifty noble families of Hiawatha's Confederation, founded four centuries ago. Her mother was Emily S. Howells, of Bristol, England. Johnson spent much of her life travelling throughout Canada, the United States, and England, drawing large numbers to her poetry recitals and storytelling performances. She was well known for wearing clothes inspired by her Mohawk heritage for the first half of her performance, later changing into English Victorian dress for the second half. In 1895, she published her first book of verse, *The White Wampum*, and in 1903, her second book appeared, *Canadian Born*. *Flint and Feather*, a collection that includes the works of her first two books, as well as new writings, was published in 1912. This book, which has been reprinted many times, continues to be one of the best-selling titles of Canadian poetry. Johnson retired from the stage in 1909, moved to Vancouver, British Columbia, and began writing mostly prose. Many of her stories were based on her friendship with Squamish Chief Joe Capilano (Su–á-pu-luck), whom she met in London in 1906, eventually leading to the publication of *Legends of Vancouver*, first published in 1911. While her literary reputation declined after her death, there has been renewed interest in her life and works since the later twentieth century.

The story "As It Was in the Beginning" is a great example of Johnson's dramatic writing confronting its audience with the injustices of the colonial system and the underappreciated value of First Nations cosmologies, values, and world views. The story revolves around Esther, a Cree woman who is taken from her family to be raised in the "mission school"—or what today is commonly referred to as a residential school. Johnson weaves together the story of Esther's betrayal by her white lover, the son of the missionary and childhood friend, with a forceful attack on white religious hypocrisy. The dramatic conclusion asks you as a reader to consider the ethical implications not only of Esther's actions, but also of those who purport to care for her and love her.

They account for it by the fact that I am a Redskin, but I am something else too—I am a woman.

I remember the first time I saw him. He came up the trail with some Hudson's Bay trappers, and they stopped at the door of my father's teepee. He seemed even then, fourteen years ago, an old man; his hair seemed just as thin and white, his hands just as trembling and fleshless as they were a month since, when I saw him for what I pray his God is the last time.

My father sat in the tepee, polishing buffalo horns and smoking; my mother wrapped in her blanket, crouched over her quill-work, on the buffalo-skin at his side; I was lounging at the doorway, idling, watching, as I always watched, the thin, distant line of sky and prairie; wondering, as I always wondered, what lay beyond it. Then he came, this gentle old man with his white hair and thin, pale face. He wore a long black coat, which I now know was the sign of his office, and he carried a black leather-covered book, which, in all the years I have known him, I have never seen him without.

The trappers explained to my father who he was, the Great Teacher, the heart's Medicine Man, the "Blackcoat" we had heard of, who brought peace where there was war, and the magic of whose black book brought greater things than all the Happy Hunting Grounds of our ancestors.

He told us many things that day, for he could speak the Cree tongue, and my father listened, and listened, and when at last they left us, my father said for him to come and sit within the tepee again.

He came, all the time he came, and my father welcomed him, but my mother always sat in silence at work with the quills; my mother never liked the Great "Blackcoat."

His stories fascinated me. I used to listen intently to the tale of the strange new place he called "heaven," of the gold crown, of the white dress, of the great music; and then he would tell of that other strange place—hell. My father and I hated it; we feared it, we dreamt of it, we trembled at it. Oh, if the "Blackcoat" would only cease to talk of it! Now I know he saw its effect upon us, and he used it as a whip to lash us into his new religion, but even then my mother must have known, for each time he left the tepee she would watch him going slowly away across prairie; then when he was disappearing into the far horizon she would laugh scornfully, and say:

"If the white man made this Blackcoat's hell, let him go to it. It is for the man who found it first. No hell for Indians, just Happy Hunting Grounds. Blackcoat can't scare me."

And then, after weeks had passed, one day as he stood at the tepee door he laid his white, old hand on my head and said to my father: "Give me this little girl, chief. Let me take her to the mission school; let me keep her, and teach her of the great God and His eternal heaven. She will grow to be a noble woman, and return perhaps to bring her people to the Christ."

My mother's eyes snapped. "No," she said. It was the first word she ever spoke to the "Blackcoat." My father sat and smoked. At the end of a half-hour he said:

"I am an old man, Blackcoat. I shall not leave the God of my fathers. I like not your strange God's ways—all of them. I like not His two new places for me when I am dead. Take the child, Blackcoat, and save her from hell."

The first grief of my life was when we reached the mission. They took my buckskin dress off, saying I was now a little Christian girl and must dress like all the white people at the mission. Oh, how I hated that stiff new calico dress and those leather shoes! But, little as I was, I said nothing, only thought of the time when I should be grown, and do as my mother did, and wear the buckskins and the blanket.

My next serious grief was when I began to speak the English, that they forbade me to use any Cree words whatever. The rule of the school was that any child heard using its native tongue must get a slight punishment. I never understood it, I cannot understand it now, why the use of my dear Cree tongue could be a matter for correction or an action deserving punishment.

She was strict, the matron of the school, but only justly so, for she had a heart and a face like her brother's, the "BIackcoat." I had long since ceased to call him that. The trappers at the post called him "St. Paul," because, they told me, of his self-sacrificing life, his kindly deeds, his rarely beautiful old face; so I, too, called him "St. Paul," though oftener "Father Paul," though he never liked the latter title, for he was a Protestant. But as I was his pet, his darling of the whole school, he let me speak of him as I would, knowing it was but my heart speaking in love. His sister was a widow, and mother to a laughing yellow-haired little boy of about my own age, who was my constant playmate and who taught me much of English in his own childish way. I used to be fond of this child, as I was fond of his mother and of his uncle, my "Father Paul," but as my girlhood passed away, as womanhood came upon me, I got strangely wearied of them all; I longed, oh, God, how I longed for the old wild life! It came with my womanhood, with my years.

What mattered it to me now that they had taught me all their ways?— their tricks of dress, their reading, their writing, their books. What mattered it that "Father Paul" loved me, that the traders at the post called me pretty, that I was a pet of all, from the factor to the poorest trapper in the service? I wanted my own people, my own old life, my blood called out for it, but they always said I must not return to my father's tepee. I heard them talk amongst themselves of keeping me away from pagan influences; they told each other that if I returned to the prairies, the tepees, I would degenerate, slip back to paganism, as other girls had done; marry, perhaps, with a pagan—and all their years of labour and teaching would be lost.

I said nothing, but I waited. And then one night the feeling overcame me. I was in the Hudson's Bay store when an Indian came in from the north with a large pack of buckskin. As they unrolled it a dash of its insinuating odour filled the store. I went over and leaned above the skins a second, then buried my face in them, swallowing, drinking the fragrance of them, that went to my head like wine. Oh, the wild wonder of that wood-smoked tan, the subtlety of it, the untamed smell of it! I drank it into my lungs, till my innermost being was saturated with it, till my mind reeled and my heart seemed twisted with a physical agony. My childhood recollections rushed upon me, devoured me. I left the store in a strange, calm frenzy, and going rapidly to the mission house I confronted my Father Paul and demanded to be allowed to go "home," if only for a day. He received the request with the same refusal and the same gentle sigh that I had so often been greeted with, but this time the desire, the smoke-tan, the heart-ache, never lessened.

Night after night I would steal away by myself and go to the border of the village to watch the sun set in the foothills, to gaze at the far line of sky and prairie, to long and long for my father's lodge. And Laurence—always Laurence—my fair-haired, laughing, child playmate, would come calling and calling for me: "Esther, where are you? We miss you; come in, Esther, come in with me." And if I did not turn at once to him and follow, he would come and place his strong hands on my shoulders and laugh into my eyes and say, "Truant, truant, Esther; can't *we* make you happy?"

My old child playmate had vanished years ago. He was a tall, slender young man now, handsome as a young chief, but with laughing blue eyes, and always those yellow curls about his temples. He was my solace in my half-exile, my comrade, my brother, until one night it was, "Esther, Esther, can't *I* make you happy?"

I did not answer him; only looked out across the plains and thought of the tepees. He came close, close. He locked his arms about me, and with my face pressed up to his throat he stood silent. I felt the blood from my heart sweep to my very finger-tips. I loved him. O God, how I loved him! In a wild, blind instant it all came, just because he held me so and was whispering brokenly, "Don't leave me, don't leave me, Esther, *my* Esther, my child-love, my playmate, my girl-comrade, my little Cree sweetheart, will you go away to your people, or stay, stay for me, for my arms, as I have you now?"

No more, no more the tepees; no more the wild stretch of prairie, the intoxicating fragrance of the smoke-tanned buckskin; no more of the bed of buffalo hide, the soft, silent moccasin; no more the dark faces of my people, the dulcet cadence of the sweet Cree tongue—only this man, this fair, proud, tender man who held me in his arms, in his heart. My soul prayed to his great white God, in that moment, that He let me have only this. It was twilight when we re-entered the mission gate. We were both excited, feverish. Father Paul was reading evening prayers in the large room beyond the hallway; his soft, saint-like voice stole beyond the doors, like a benediction upon us. I went noiselessly upstairs to my own room and sat there undisturbed for hours.

The clock downstairs struck one, startling me from my dreams of happiness, and at the same moment a flash of light attracted me. My room was in an angle of the building, and my window looked almost directly down into those of Father Paul's study, into which at that instant he was entering, carrying a lamp. "Why, Laurence," I heard him exclaim, "what are you doing here? I thought, my boy, you were in bed hours ago."

"No, uncle, not in bed, but in dreamland," replied Laurence, arising from the window, where evidently he, too, had spent the night hours as I had done.

Father Paul fumbled about a moment, found his large black book, which for once he seemed to have got separated from, and was turning to leave, when the curious circumstance of Laurence being there at so unusual an hour seemed to strike him anew. "Better go to sleep, my son," he said simply, then added curiously, "Has anything occurred to keep you up?"

Then Laurence spoke: "No, uncle, only—only, I'm happy, that's all."

Father Paul stood irresolute. Then: "It is—?"

"Esther," said Laurence quietly, but he was at the old man's side, his hand was on the bent old shoulder, his eyes proud and appealing.

Father Paul set the lamp on the table, but, as usual, one hand held that black book, the great text of his life. His face was paler than I had ever seen it—graver.

"Tell me of it," he requested.

I leaned far out of my window and watched them both. I listened with my very heart, for Laurence was telling him of me, of his love, of the new-found joy of that night.

"You have said nothing of marriage to her?" asked Father Paul.

"Well—no; but she surely understands that—"

"Did you speak of *marriage*?" repeated Father Paul, with a harsh ring in his voice that was new to me.

"No, uncle, but—"

"Very well, then; very well."

There was a brief silence. Laurence stood staring at the old man as though he were a stranger; he watched him push a large chair up to the table, slowly seat himself; then mechanically following his movements, he dropped onto a lounge. The old man's head bent low, but his eyes were bright and strangely fascinating. He began:

"Laurence, my boy, your future is the dearest thing to me of all earthly interests. Why, you *can't* marry this girl—no, no, sit, sit until I have finished," he added, with raised voice, as Laurence sprang up, remonstrating. "I have long since decided that you marry well; for instance, the Hudson's Bay factor's daughter."

Laurence broke into a fresh, rollicking laugh. "What, uncle," he said, "little Ida McIntosh? Marry that little yellow-haired fluff ball, that kitten, that pretty little dolly?"

"Stop," said Father Paul. Then, with a low, soft persuasiveness, "She is *white*, Laurence."

My lover started. "Why, uncle, what do you mean?" he faltered.

"Only this, my son: poor Esther comes of uncertain blood; would it do for you—the missionary's nephew, and adopted son, you might say—to marry the daughter of a pagan Indian? Her mother is hopelessly uncivilized; her father has a dash of French somewhere—half-breed, you know, my boy, half-breed." Then, with still lower tone and half-shut, crafty eyes, he added: "The blood is a bad, bad mixture, *you* know that; you know, too, that I am very fond of the girl, poor dear Esther. I have tried to separate her from evil pagan influences; she is the daughter of the Church; I want her to have no other parent; but you can never tell what lurks in *a caged animal that has once been wild.* My whole heart is with the Indian people, my son; my whole heart, my whole life, has been devoted to bringing them to Christ, *but it is a different thing to marry with one of them.*"

His small old eyes were riveted on Laurence like a hawk's on a rat. My heart lay like ice in my bosom.

Laurence, speechless and white, stared at him breathlessly.

"Go away somewhere," the old man was urging; "to Winnipeg, Toronto, Montreal; forget her, then come back to Ida McIntosh. A union of the Church and the Hudson's Bay will mean great things, and may ultimately result in my life's ambition, the civilization of this entire tribe, that we have worked so long to bring to God."

I listened, sitting like one frozen. Could those words have been uttered by my venerable teacher, by him whom I revered as I would one of the saints in his own black book? Ah, there was no mistaking it. My white father, my life-long friend who pretended to love me, to care for my happiness, was urging the man I worshipped to forget me, to marry with the factor's daughter—because of what? Of my red skin; my good, old, honest pagan mother; my confiding French-Indian father. In a second all the care, the hollow love he had given me since my childhood, were as things that never existed. I hated that old mission priest as I hated his white man's hell. I hated his long, white hair: I hated his thin, white hands; I hated his body, his soul, his voice, his black book—oh how I hated the very atmosphere of him!

Laurence sat motionless, his face buried in his hands, but the old man continued, "No, no; not the child of that pagan mother; you can't trust her, my son. What would you do with a wife who might at any day break from you to return to her prairies and her buckskins? *You can't trust her.*" His eyes grew smaller, more glittering, more fascinating then, and leaning with an odd, secret sort of movement towards Laurence, he almost whispered, "Think of her silent ways, her noiseless step; the girl glides about like an apparition; her quick fingers, her wild longings—I don't know why, but with all my fondness for her, she reminds me sometimes of a strange—snake."

Laurence shuddered, lifted his face, and said hoarsely: "You're right, uncle; perhaps I'd better not; I'll go away, I'll forget her, and then—well, then—yes, you are right, it *is* a different thing to marry one of them." The old man arose. His feeble fingers still clasped his black book; his soft white hair clung about his forehead like that of an Apostle; his eyes lost their peering, crafty expression; his bent shoulders resumed the dignity of a minister of the living God; he was the picture of what the traders called him—"St. Paul."

"Good-night, son," he said.

"Good-night, uncle, and thank you for bringing me to myself."

They were the last words I ever heard uttered by either that old arch-fiend or his weak, miserable kinsman. Father Paul turned and left the room. I watched his withered hand—the hand I had so often felt resting on my head in holy benedictions—clasp the door-knob, turn it slowly, then, with bowed head and his pale face wrapped in thought, he left the room—left it with the mad venom of my hate pursuing him like the very Evil One he taught me of.

What were his years of kindness and care now? What did I care for his God, his heaven, his hell? He had robbed me of my native faith, of my parents, of my people, of this last, this life of love that would have made a great, good woman of me. God! How I hated him!

I crept to the closet in my dark little room. I felt for a bundle I had not looked at for years—yes, it was there, the buckskin dress I had worn as a little child when they brought me to the mission. I tucked it under my arm and descended the stairs noiselessly. I would look into the study and speak good-bye to Laurence; then I would—

I pushed open the door. He was lying on the couch where a short time previously he had sat, white and speechless, listening to Father Paul, I moved towards him softly. God in heaven, he was already asleep. As I bent over him the fullness of his perfect beauty impressed me for the first time; his slender form, his curving mouth that almost laughed even in sleep, his fair, tossed hair, his smooth strong-pulsing throat. God! How I loved him!

Then there arose the picture of the factor's daughter. I hated her. I hated her baby face, her yellow hair, her whitish skin. "She shall not marry him," my soul said. "I will kill him first—kill his beautiful body, his lying, false, heart." Something in my heart seemed to speak; it said over and over again, "Kill him, kill him; she will never have him then. Kill him. It will break Father Paul's heart and blight his life. He has killed the best of you, of your womanhood; kill *his* best, his pride, his hope—his sister's son, his nephew Laurence." But how? how?

What had that terrible old man said I was like? A *strange snake*. A snake? The idea wound itself about me like the very coils of a serpent. What was this thing in the beaded bag of my buckskin dress? This little thing rolled in tan that my mother had given me at parting with the words, "Don't touch much, but some time maybe you want it!" Oh! I knew well enough what it was—a small flint arrow-head dipped in the venom of some *strange snake*.

I knelt beside him and laid my hot lips on his hand. I worshipped him, oh, how I worshipped him! Then again the vision of *her* baby face, *her* yellow hair—I scratched his wrist twice with the arrow-tip. A single drip of red blood oozed up; he stirred. I turned the lamp down and slipped out of the room—out of the house.

I dream nightly of the horrors of the white man's hell. Why did they teach me of it, only to fling me into it?

Last night as I crouched beside my mother on the buffalo-hide, Dan Henderson, the trapper, came in to smoke with my father. He said old Father Paul was bowed with grief, that with my disappearance I was suspected, but that there was no proof. Was it not merely a snake bite?

They account for it by the fact that I am a Redskin.

They seem to have forgotten I am a woman.

⤙ *Deer Woman* ⤚
Paula Gunn Allen

Paula Gunn Allen was a feminist poet, novelist, and critic. She was born in Cubero, New Mexico, to a Lebanese American father and a Laguna-Sioux mother, and grew up on the Laguna Pueblo reservation. She obtained her PhD at the University of New Mexico in 1976. Allen authored many books of fiction, poetry, and criticism in her lifetime, including *The Woman Who Owned the Shadows* (1983), *The Sacred Hoop: Recovering the Feminine in American Indian Traditions* (1986), and *Skins and Bones* (1988).

"Deer Woman" interweaves realist and mythic narrative lines to tell the story of two young men, Jackie and Ray, who "snag" or pick up two beautiful women, Junella and Linda, at a stomp dance. There are clues that the women are not as they seem—Ray thinks he catches a glimpse of deer feet before the women quickly hide them—but the men seem spellbound as they follow the women to their "old house," hidden in the mountain. Both men know, from the stories they have been told by their Cherokee relatives, that they should never speak of their experiences with spiritual beings (often referred to as the little people or *Yunwi Tsundi* in Cherokee stories). Jackie, however, tells things "he wasn't supposed to tell," and his fate, the story implies, is connected to his indiscretion. As you read, think about how and why Paula Gunn Allen attributes such power and responsibility to the reception and transmission of stories. Do stories determine realities? What responsibilities do storytellers, listeners, and readers have?

Two young men were out snagging[1] one afternoon. They rode around in their pickup, their Ind'in Cadillac, cruising up this road and down that one through steamy green countryside, stopping by friends' places here and there to lift a few beers. The day was sultry and searing as summer days in Oklahoma get, hot as a sweat lodge.

Long after dark they stopped at a tavern twenty or thirty miles outside of Anadarko, and joined some skins[2] gathered around several tables. After the muggy heat outside, the slowly turning fan inside felt cool. When they'd been there awhile, one of the men at their table asked them if they were headed to the stomp dance.[3] "Sure," they said, though truth to tell, they hadn't known there was a stomp dance that night in the area. The three headed out to the pickup.

They drove for some distance along narrow country roads, turning occasionally at unmarked crossings, bumping across cattle guards, until at length they saw the light of the bonfire, several unshaded lights hanging from small huts that ringed the danceground, and headlights from a couple of parking cars.

They pulled into a spot in the midst of a new Winnebago, a Dodge van, two Toyotas, and a small herd of more battered models, and made their way to the danceground. The dance was going strong, and the sound of turtle shell and aluminum can rattles and singing, mixed with occasional laughter and bits of talk, reached their ears.

"All right!" Ray, the taller and heavier of the two exclaimed, slapping his buddy's raised hand in glee.

"Gnarly!" his pal Jackie responded, and they grinned at each other in the unsteady light. Slapping the man who'd ridden along with them on the back, the taller one said, "Man, let's go find us some snags!"

They hung out all night, occasionally starting a conversation with one good-looking woman or another, but though the new brother who had accompanied them soon disappeared with a long-legged beauty named Lurine, the two anxious friends didn't score. They were not the sort to feel disheartened, though. They kept up their spirits, dancing well and singing even better. They didn't really care so much about snagging, but it gave them something to focus on while they filled the day and night with interesting activity. They were among their own, and they were satisfied with their lives and themselves.

Toward morning, though, Ray spotted two strikingly beautiful young women stepping onto the danceground. Their long hair flowed like black rivers down their backs. They were dressed out in traditional clothes, and something about them—something elusive—made Ray shiver with a feeling almost like recognition, and at the same time, like dread. "Who are they?" he asked his friend, but Jackie shrugged silently. Ray could see his eyes shining for a moment as the fire near them flared suddenly.

At the same moment, they both saw the young women looking at them out of the corners of their eyes as they danced modestly and almost gravely past. Jackie nudged Ray and let out a long, slow sigh. "All right," he said in a low, almost reverent voice. "All right!"

When the dance was ended, the young women made their way to where the two youths were standing, "Hey, dude," one of them said. "My friend and I need a ride to Anadarko, and they told us you were coming from there." As she said that she gestured with her chin over her left shoulder toward a vaguely visible group standing across the danceground.

"What's your friend's name?" Ray countered.

"Linda," the other woman said. "Hers is Junella."

"My friend's name's Jackie," Ray said, grinning. "When do you want to take off?"

"Whenever," Junella answered. She held his eyes with hers. "Where are you parked?"

They made their way to the pickup and got in. It was a tight fit, but nobody seemed to mind. Ray drove, backing the pickup carefully to thread among the haphazardly parked vehicles that had surrounded theirs while they were at the dance. As he did, he glanced down for a second, and thought he saw the feet of both women as deer hooves. Man, he thought. I gotta lay off the weed. He didn't remember he'd quit smoking it months before, and hadn't had a beer since they'd left the tavern hours before. The women tucked their feet under their bags, and in the darkness he didn't see them anymore. Besides, he had more soothing things on his mind.

They drove companionably for some time, joking around, telling a bit about themselves, their tastes in music, where they'd gone to school, when they'd graduated. Linda kept fiddling with the dial, reaching across Junella to get to the knob. Her taste seemed to run to hard-core country and western or what Ray privately thought of as "space" music.

Linda and Junella occasionally lapsed into what seemed like a private conversation, or joke; Ray couldn't be sure which. Then, as though remembering themselves, they'd laugh and engage the men in conversation again.

After they'd traveled for an hour or so, Linda suddenly pointed to a road that intersected the one they were on. "Take a left," she said, and Ray complied. He didn't even think about it, or protest that they were on the road to Anadarko already. A few hundred yards farther, she said, "Take a right." Again he complied, putting the brake on suddenly as he went into the turn, spilling Junella hard against him. He finished shifting quickly and put his arm around her. She leaned into him, saying nothing, and put her hand on his thigh.

The road they had turned onto soon became gravel, and by the time they'd gone less than a quarter of a mile, turned into hard-packed dirt. Ray could smell water, nearby. He saw some trees standing low on the horizon and realized it was coming light.

"Let's go to the water," Linda said. "Junella and I are kind of traditional, and we try to wash in fresh running water every morning."

"Yeah," Junella murmured. "We were raised by our mother's grandmother, and the old lady was real strict about some things. She always made sure we prayed to Long Man[4] every day. Hope it's okay."

Jackie and Ray climbed out of the truck, the women following. They made their way through the thickest of scrub oak and bushes and clambered down the short bank to the stream, the men leading the way. They stopped at the edge of the water, but the young women stepped right in, though still dressed in their dance clothes. They bent and splashed water on their faces, speaking the old tongue softly as they did so. The men removed their tennis shoes and followed suit, removing their caps and tucking them in the hip pockets of their jeans.

After a suitable silence, Junella pointed to the opposite bank with her uplifted chin. "See that path?" she asked the men. "I think it goes to our old house. Let's go up there and see."

"Yes," Linda said, "I thought it felt familiar around here. I bet it is our old place." When the women didn't move to cross the shallow river and go up the path, the men took the lead again. Ray briefly wondered at his untypical pliability, but banished the thought almost as it arose. He raised his head just as he reached the far bank and saw that the small trees and brush were backed by a stone bluff that rose steeply above them. As he tilted his head back to spot the top of the bluff, he had a flashing picture of the small round feet he'd thought he'd seen set against the floorboard of the truck. But as the image came into his mind, the sun rose brilliantly just over the bluff, and the thought faded as quickly as it had come, leaving him with a slightly dazed feeling and tingling that climbed rapidly up his spine. He put on his cap.

Jackie led the way through the thicket, walking as rapidly as the low branches would allow, bending almost double in places. Ray followed him, and the women came after. Shortly, they emerged from the trees onto a rocky area that ran along the foot of the bluff like a narrow path. When he reached it, Jackie stopped and waited while the others caught up. "Do you still think this is the old homestead?" he quipped. The women laughed sharply, then fell into animated conversation in the old language. Neither Ray nor Jackie could talk it, so they stood waiting, admiring the beauty of the morning, feeling the cool dawn air on their cheeks and the water still making their jeans cling to their ankles. At least their feet were dry, and so were the tennies they'd replaced after leaving the river.

After a few animated exchanges, the women started up the path, the men following. "She says it's this way," Linda said over her shoulder. "It can't be far." They trudged along for what seemed a long time, following the line of the bluff that seemed to grow even higher. After a time Junella turned into a narrow break in the rock and began to trudge up its gradual slope, which soon became a steep rise.

"I bet we're not going to Grandma's house," Jackie said in quiet tones to his friend.

"I didn't know this bluff was even here," Ray replied.

"It's not much farther," Junella said cheerfully. "What's the matter? You dudes out of shape or something?"

"Well, I used to say I'd walk a mile for a camel," Jackie said wryly, "but I didn't say anything about snags!" He and Ray laughed, perhaps more heartily than the joke warranted.

"This is the only time I've heard of Little Red Riding Hood leading the wolves to Grandma's," Ray muttered.

"Yah," Linda responded brightly. "And wait'll you see what I'm carrying in my basket of goodies." Both women laughed, the men abashedly joining in.

"Here's the little creek I was looking for," Junella said suddenly. "Let's walk in it for a while," Ray looked at Jackie quizzically.

"I don't want to walk in that," Jackie said quickly. "I just got dry from the last dip." The women were already in the water walking upstream.

"Not to worry," Junella said. "It's not wet; it's the path to the old house."

"Yeah, right," Ray mumbled, stepping into the water with a sigh. Jackie followed him, falling silent. But as they stepped into what they thought was a fast-running stream of water their feet touched down on soft grass. "Hey!" Ray exclaimed. "What's happening?" He stopped abruptly, and Jackie plowed into him.

"Watch it, man," the smaller man said. He brushed past Ray and made after the women, who were disappearing around a sharp turn.

Ray stood rooted a moment, then hurried after him. "Wait up," he called. His voice echoed loudly against the cliff.

As Ray turned the corner he saw Linda reaching upward along the cliff where a tall rock slab leaned against it. She grasped the edge of the slab and pulled. To the men's astonishment it swung open, for all the world like an ordinary door. The women stepped through.

Ray and Jackie regarded each other for long moments. Finally, Ray shrugged and Jackie gestured with his outspread arm at the opening in the cliff. They followed the women inside.

Within, they were greeted with an astonishing scene. Scores of people, perhaps upward of two hundred, stood or walked about a green land. Houses stood scattered in the near distance, and smoke arose from a few chimneys. There were tables spread under some large trees, sycamore or elm, Ray thought, and upon them, food in large quantities and tantalizing variety beckoned to the men. Suddenly aware they hadn't eaten since early the day before, they started forward. But before they'd taken more than a few steps, Linda and Junella took their arms and led them away from the feast toward the doorway of one of the houses. There sat a man who seemed ancient to the young men. His age wasn't so much in his hair, though it hung in waist-long white strands.

It wasn't even so much in his skin, wrinkled and weathered though it was beneath the tall-crowned hat he wore. It was just that he seemed to be age personified. He seemed to be older than the bluff, than the river, than even the sky.

Next to him lay two large mastiffs, their long, lean bodies relaxed, their heads raised, their eyes alert and full of intelligence. "So," the old one said to the women, "I see you've snagged two strong young men." He shot a half-amused glance at the young men's direction. "Go, get ready," he directed the women, and at his words they slipped into the house, closing the door softly behind themselves.

The young men stood uneasily beside the old man who, disregarding them completely, seemed lost in his own thoughts as he gazed steadily at some point directly before him.

After maybe half an hour had passed, the old man addressed the young men again. "It's a good thing you did," he mused, "following my nieces here. I wonder that you didn't give up or get lost along the way." He chuckled quietly as at a private joke. "Maybe you two are intelligent men." He turned his head suddenly and gave them an appraising look. Each of the young men shifted under that knowing gaze uncomfortably. From somewhere, the ground, the sky, they didn't feel sure, they heard thunder rumbling. "I have told everybody that they did well for themselves by bringing you here."

Seeing the surprised look on their faces, he smiled. "Yes, you didn't hear me, I know. I guess we talk different here than you're used to where you come from. Maybe you'll be here long enough to get used to it," he added. "That is, if you like my nieces well enough. We'll feed you soon," he said. "But first there are some games I want you to join in." He pointed with pursed lips in the direction of a low hill that rose just beyond the farthest dwelling. Again the thunder rumbled, louder than before.

A moment later the women appeared. Their long, flowing hair was gone, and their heads shone in the soft light that filled the area, allowing distant features to recede into its haze. The women wore soft clothing that completely covered their bodies, even their hands and feet. It seemed to be of a bright, gleaming cloth that reflected the light at the same intensity as their bald heads. Their dark eyes seemed huge and luminous against skin that somehow gave off a soft radiance. Seeing them, both men were nearly overcome with fear. They have no hair at all, Ray thought. Where is this place? He glanced over at Jackie, whose face mirrored his own unease. Jackie shook his head almost imperceptibly, slowly moving it from side to side in a gesture that seemed mournful, and at the same time, oddly resigned.

Linda and Junella moved to the young men, each taking the hand of one and drawing him toward the central area nearby. In a daze Ray and Jackie allowed themselves to be led into the center of the area ringed by heavily laden tables, barely aware that the old man had risen from his place and with his dogs was following behind them. They were joined by a number of other young men, all wearing caps like the ones Ray and Jackie wore. Two of the men carried bats, several wore gloves, and one was tossing a baseball in the air as he walked. Slowly the throng made their way past the tables and came to an open area where Jackie and Ray saw familiar shapes. They were bases, and the field that the soft light revealed to them was a baseball diamond.

The old man took his place behind first base, and one of the young men crouched before him as a loud peal of thunder crashed around them. "Play ball!" the old man shouted, and the men took up their places as the women retired to some benches at the edge of the field behind home plate where they sat.

The bewildered young men found their positions and the game was on. It was a hard-played game, lasting some time. At length, it reached a rowdy end, the team Jackie and Ray were on barely edging out the opposition in spite of a couple of questionable calls the old man made against them. Their victory was due in no small measure to a wiry young man's superb pitching. He'd pitched two no-hit innings and that had won them the game.

As they walked with the other players back toward the houses, the old man came up to them. Slapping each on the back a couple of times, he told them he thought they were good players. "Maybe that means you'll be ready for tomorrow's games," he said, watching Jackie sharply. "They're not what you're used to, I imagine, but you'll do alright."

They reached the tables and were helped to several large portions of food by people whose faces never seemed to come quite into focus but whose good-will seemed unquestionable. They ate amid much laughter and good-natured joshing, only belatedly realizing that neither Linda nor Junella was among the revelers. Ray made his way to Jackie and asked him if he'd seen either woman. Replying in the negative, Jackie offered to go look around for them.

They agreed to make a quick search and rendezvous at the large tree near the old man's house. But after a fruitless hour or so Ray went to the front of the house and waited for his friend, who didn't come. At last, growing bored, he made his way back to the tables where a group had set up a drum and was singing lustily. A few of the younger people had formed a tight circle around the drummers and were slowly stepping around in it, their arms about each others' waists and shoulders. All right! Ray thought, cheered. "49s."[5] He joined the circle between two women he hadn't seen before, who easily made way for him, and smoothly closed the circle about him again as each wrapped an arm around his waist. He forgot all about his friend.

When Ray awoke the sun was beating down on his head. He sat up, and realized he was lying near the river's edge, his legs in the thicket, his head and half-turned face unshielded from the sun. It was about a third of the way up in a clear sky. As he looked groggily around, he discovered Junella sitting quietly a few yards away on a large stone. "Hey," she said, smiling.

"How'd I get here?" Ray asked. He stood and stretched, surreptitiously feeling to see if everything worked. His memory seemed hesitant to return clearly, but he had half-formed impressions of a baseball game and eating and then the 49. He looked around. "Where's Jackie and, uh—"

"Linda?" Junella supplied as he paused.

"Yeah, Linda," he finished.

"Jackie is staying there," she told him calmly. She reached into her bag and brought out a man's wristwatch. "He said to give you this," she said, holding it out to him.

Ray felt suddenly dizzy. He swayed for a moment while strange images swept through him. Junella with no hair and that eerie light; the woman that was some pale tan but had spots or a pattern of soft gray dots that sort of fuzzed out at the edges to blend into the tan; the old man.

He took a step in her direction. "Hey," he began. "What the hell's—" but broke off. The rock where she sat was empty. On the ground next to it lay Jackie's watch.

———

When Ray told me the story, about fifteen months afterward, he had heard that Jackie had showed up at his folks' place. They lived out in the country, a mile or so beyond one of the numerous small towns that dot the Oklahoma landscape. The woman who told him about Jackie's return, Jackie's cousin Ruth Ann, said he had come home with a strange woman who was a real fox. At thirteen, Ruth Ann had developed an eye for good looks and thought herself quite a judge of women's appearance. They hadn't stayed long, he'd heard. Mainly they packed up some of Jackie's things and visited with his family. Ray had been in Tulsa and hadn't heard Jackie was back until later. None of their friends had seen him either. There had been a child with them, he said, maybe two years old, Ruth Ann had thought, because she could walk by herself.

"You know," Ray had said thoughtfully, turning a Calistoga slowly between his big hands, a gesture that made him seem very young and somehow vulnerable, "one of my grandma's brothers, old Jess, used to talk about the little people[6] a lot. He used to tell stories about strange things happening around the countryside here. I never paid much attention. You know how it is. I just thought he was putting me on, or maybe he was pining away for the old days.

He said that Deer Woman[7] would come to dances sometimes, and if you weren't careful she'd put her spell on you and take you inside the mountain to meet her uncle. He said her uncle was really Thunder, one of the old gods or supernaturals, whatever the traditionals call them."

He finished his drink in a couple of swallows and pushed away from the table we were sitting at. "I dunno," he said, and gave me a look that I still haven't forgotten, a look that was somehow wounded and yet with a kind of wild hope mixed in. "Maybe those old guys know something, eh?"

It was a few years before I saw him again. Then I ran into him unexpectedly in San Francisco a couple of years ago. We talked for a while, standing on the street near the Mission BART[8] station. He started to leave when my curiosity got the better of my manners. I asked if he'd ever found out what happened to Jackie.

Well, he said that he'd heard that Jackie came home off and on, but the woman—probably Linda, though he wasn't sure—was never with him. Then he'd heard that someone had run into Jackie, or a guy they thought was him, up in Seattle. He'd gone alcoholic. Later, they'd heard he'd died. "But you know," Ray said, "the weird thing is that he'd evidently been telling someone all about that time inside the mountain, and that he'd married her, and about some other stuff, stuff I guess he wasn't supposed to tell." Another guy down on his luck, he guessed. "Remember how I was telling you about my crazy uncle, the one who used to tell about Deer Woman? Until I heard about Jackie, I'd forgotten that the old man used to say that the ones who stayed there were never supposed to talk about it. If they did, they died in short order."

After that, there didn't seem to be much more to say. Last time I saw Ray, he was heading down the steps to catch BART. He was on his way to a meeting and he was running late.

— *"You'll Never Believe What Happened"* — *Is Always a Great Way to Start*
Thomas King

Thomas King was born in Roseville, California, in 1943. He is of Cherokee, German, and Greek descent. In 1980, he moved to Canada to work at the University of Lethbridge to teach literature and later to the University of Guelph to teach creative writing. In 2003, he became the first Indigenous person to deliver the annual Massey Lectures, a series of public talks delivered in cities across Canada, and broadcast on CBC Radio. This story is taken from the first lecture of the series, which is now available in print in a volume titled *The Truth about Stories*. To get a sense of his voice, style, and delivery, you can listen to his lectures on CD and on the CBC website.

King's work has delighted audiences around the world for its subversive wit, its many layers of irony, and its biting humour. "'You'll Never Believe What Happened' Is Always a Great Way to Start" demonstrates King's hallmark style, in which he combines his talents as an engaging storyteller with his acute perceptiveness as a cultural critic. King moves fluidly and compellingly between details about his life growing up in California, to a retelling of a well-known Cherokee creation story, sometimes referred to as The Woman Who Fell from the Sky, to cultural commentary on "how stories can control our lives" (67). In spite of his extraordinary success as a writer and storyteller, King remains awed by stories, how they are both "wondrous" and "dangerous" (67), and how telling and writing stories comes with certain responsibilities for both writer and reader. In the conclusion, he lays down his challenge to his audience: "don't say in the years to come that you would have lived your life differently if only you had heard this story. You've heard it now" (77). As you read this story and other stories in this anthology, think about your own reaction to King's challenge and what stories mean to you: you've heard it now, what will you do with it?

There is a story I know. It's about the earth and how it floats in space on the back of a turtle. I've heard this story many times, and each time someone tells the story, it changes. Sometimes the change is simply in the voice of the storyteller. Sometimes the change is in the details. Sometimes in the order of events. Other times it's the dialogue or the response of the audience. But in all the tellings of all the tellers, the world never leaves the turtle's back. And the turtle never swims away.

One time, it was in Prince Rupert I think, a young girl in the audience asked about the turtle and the earth. If the earth was on the back of a turtle, what was below the turtle? Another turtle, the storyteller told her. And below that turtle? Another turtle. And below that? Another turtle.

The girl began to laugh, enjoying the game, I imagine. So how many turtles are there? she wanted to know. The storyteller shrugged. No one knows for sure, he told her, but it's turtles all the way down.

The truth about stories is that that's all we are. The Okanagan storyteller Jeannette Armstrong tells us that "Through my language I understand I am being spoken to, I'm not the one speaking. The words are coming from many tongues and mouths of Okanagan people and the land around them. I am a listener to the language's stories, and when my words form I am merely retelling the same stories in different patterns" ("Land" 146)

When I was a kid, I was partial to stories about other worlds and interplanetary travel. I used to imagine that I could just gaze off into space and be whisked to another planet, much like John Carter in Edgar Rice Burroughs's Mars series. I'd like to tell you that I was interested in outer space or that the stars fascinated me or that I was curious about the shape and nature of the universe. Fact of the matter was I just wanted to get out of town. Wanted to get as far away from where I was as I could. At fifteen, Pluto looked good. Tiny, cold, lonely. As far from the sun as you could get.

I'm sure part of it was teenage angst, and part of it was being poor in a rich country, and part of it was knowing that white was more than just a colour. And part of it was seeing the world through my mother's eyes.

My mother raised my brother and me by herself, in an era when women were not welcome in the workforce, when their proper place was out of sight in the home. It was supposed to be a luxury granted women by men. But having misplaced her man, or more properly having had him misplace himself, she had no such luxury and was caught between what she was supposed to be—invisible and female—and what circumstances dictated she become—visible and, well, not male. Self-supporting perhaps. That was it. Visible and self-supporting.

As a child and as a young man, I watched her make her way from doing hair in a converted garage to designing tools for the aerospace industry. It was a long, slow journey. At Aerojet in California, she began as a filing clerk. By the end of the first year, she was doing drafting work, though she was still classified and paid as a filing clerk. By the end of the second year, with night school stuffed into the cracks, she was doing numerical-control engineering and was still classified and paid as a filing clerk.

It was, after all, a man's world, and each step she took had to be made as quietly as possible, each movement camouflaged against complaint. For over thirty years, she held to the shadows, stayed in the shade.

I knew the men she worked with. They were our neighbours and our friends. I listened to their stories about work and play, about their dreams and their disappointments. Your mother, they liked to tell me, is just one of the boys. But she wasn't. I knew it. She knew it better.

In 1963, my mother and five of her colleagues were recruited by the Boeing Company to come to Seattle, Washington, as part of a numerical-control team. Everyone was promised equal status, which, for my mother, meant being brought into Boeing as a fully fledged, salaried engineer.

So she went. It was more money, more prestige. And when she got there, she was told that, while everyone else would be salaried and would have engineer status, she would be an hourly employee and would have the same status as the other two women in the department, who were production assistants. So after selling everything in order to make the move, she found herself in a job where she made considerably less than the other members of the team, where she had to punch a time clock, and where she wasn't even eligible for benefits or a pension.

She objected. That wasn't the promise, she told her supervisor. You brought everyone else in as equals, why not me?

She didn't really have to ask that question. She knew the answer. You probably know it, too. The other five members of the team were men. She was the only woman. Don't worry, she was told, if your work is good, you'll get promoted at the end of the first year.

So she waited. There wasn't much she could do about it. And at the end of the first year, when the review of her work came back satisfactory, she was told she would have to wait another year. And when that year was up …

I told her she was crazy to allow people to treat her like that. But she knew the nature of the world in which she lived, and I did not. And yet she has lived her life with an optimism of the intellect and an optimism of the will. She understands the world is a good place where good deeds should beget good rewards. At eighty-one, she still believes that that world is possible, even though she will now admit she never found it, never even caught a glimpse of it.

My father is a different story. I didn't know him. He left when I was three or four. I have one memory of a man who took me to a small cafe that had wooden booths with high backs and a green parrot that pulled at my hair. I don't think this was my father. But it might have been.

For a long time I told my friends that my father had died, which was easier than explaining that he had left us. Then when I was nine, I think, my mother got a call from him asking if he could come home and start over. My mother said okay. I'll be home in three days, he told her.

And that was the last we ever heard from him.

My mother was sure that something had happened to him. Somewhere between Chicago and California. No one would call to say they were coming home and then not show up, unless they had been injured or killed. So she waited for him. So did I.

And then when I was fifty-six or fifty-seven, my brother called me. Sit down, Christopher said, I've got some news. I was living in Ontario, and I figured that if my brother was calling me all the way from California, telling me to sit down, it had to be bad news, something to do with my mother.

But it wasn't.

You'll never believe what happened, my brother said. That's always a good way to start a story, you know: you'll never believe what happened.

And he was right.

We found our father. That's exactly what he said. We found our father.

I had dreamed about such an occurrence. Finding my father. Not as a child, but as a grown man. One of my more persistent fictions was to catch up with him in a bar, sitting on a stool, having a beer. A dark, dank bar, stinking of sorrow, a bar where men who had deserted their families went to drink and die.

He wouldn't recognize me. I'd sit next to him, and after a while the two of us would strike up a conversation.

What do you do for a living? How do you like the new Ford? You believe those Blue Jays?

Guy talk. Short sentences. Lots of nodding.

You married? Any kids?

And then I'd give him a good look at me. A good, long look. And just as he began to remember, just as he began to realize who I might be, I'd leave. *Hasta la vista.* Toodle-oo. See you around. I wouldn't tell him about my life or what I had been able to accomplish, or how many grandchildren he had or how much I had missed not having a father in my life.

Screw him. I had better things to do than sit around with some old bastard and talk about life and responsibility.

So when my brother called to tell me that we had found our father, I ran through the bar scene one more time. So I'd be ready.

Here's what had happened. My father had two sisters. We didn't know them very well, and, when my father disappeared, we lost track of that side of the family. So we had no way of knowing that when my father left us, he vanished from his sisters' lives as well. I suppose they thought he was dead, too. But evidently his oldest sister wasn't sure, and, after she had retired and was getting on in years, she decided to make one last attempt to find out what had happened to him.

She was not a rich woman, but she spotted an advertisement in a local newspaper that offered the services of a detective who would find lost or missing relatives for $75. Flat rate. Satisfaction guaranteed.

My brother took a long time in telling this story, drawing out the details, repeating the good parts, making me wait.

The detective, it turned out, was a retired railroad employee who knew how to use a computer and a phone book. If Robert King was alive and if he hadn't changed his name, he'd have a phone and an address. If he was dead, there should be a death certificate floating around somewhere. The detective's name was Fred or George, I don't remember, and he was a bulldog.

It took him two days. Robert King was alive and well, in Illinois.

Christopher stopped at this point in the story to let me catch my breath. I was already making reservations to fly to Chicago, to rent a car, to find that bar.

That's the good news, my brother told me.

One of the tricks to storytelling is, never to tell everything at once, to make your audience wait, to keep everyone in suspense.

My father had married two more times. Christopher had all the details. Seven other children. Seven brothers and sisters we had never known about. Barbara, Robert, Kelly.

What's the bad news? I wanted to know.

Oh, that, said my brother. The bad news is he's dead.

Evidently, just after the railroad detective found him, my father slipped in a river, hit his head on a rock, and died in a hospital. My aunt, the one who had hired the detective, went to Illinois for the funeral and to meet her brother's other families for the first time.

You're going to like the next part, my brother told me.

I should warn you that my brother has a particular fondness for irony.

When my aunt got to the funeral, the oldest boy, Robert King Jr., evidently began a sentence with "I guess as the oldest boy …" Whereupon my aunt told the family about Christopher and me.

They knew about each other. The two families were actually close, but they had never heard about us. My father had never mentioned us. It was as though he had disposed of us somewhere along the way, dropped us in a trash can by the side of the road.

That's my family. These are their stories.

———

So what? I've heard worse stories. So have you. Open today's paper and you'll find two or three that make mine sound like a Disney trailer. Starvation. Land mines. Suicide bombings. Sectarian violence. Sexual abuse. Children stacked up like cordwood in refugee camps around the globe. So what makes my mother's sacrifice special? What makes my father's desertion unusual?

Absolutely nothing.

Matter of fact, the only people who have any interest in either of these stories are my brother and me. I tell the stories not to play on your sympathies but to suggest how stories can control our lives, for there is a part of me that has never been able to move past these stories, a part of me that will be chained to these stories as long as I live.

———

Stories are wondrous things. And they are dangerous. The Native novelist Leslie Silko, in her book *Ceremony*, tells how evil came into the world. It was witch people. Not Whites or Indians or Blacks or Asians or Hispanics. Witch people. Witch people from all over the world, way back when, and they all came together for a witches' conference. In a cave. Having a good time. A contest, actually. To see who could come up with the scariest thing. Some of them brewed up potions in pots. Some of them jumped in and out of animal skins. Some of them thought up charms and spells.

It must have been fun to watch.

Until finally there was only one witch left who hadn't done anything. No one knew where this witch came from or if the witch was male or female. And all this witch had was a story.

Unfortunately the story this witch told was an awful thing full of fear and slaughter, disease and blood. A story of murderous mischief. And when the telling was done, the other witches quickly agreed that this witch had won the prize.

"Okay you win," they said. "But what you said just now—it isn't so funny. It doesn't sound so good. We are doing okay without it. We can get along without that kind of thing. Take it back. Call that story back."

But, of course, it was too late. For once a story is told it cannot be called back. Once told, it is loose in the world.

———

So you have to be careful with the stories you tell. And you have to watch out for the stories that you are told. But if I ever get to Pluto, that's how I would like to begin. With a story. Maybe I'd tell the inhabitants of Pluto one of the stories I know. Maybe they'd tell me one of theirs. It wouldn't matter who went first. But which story? That's the real question. Personally, I'd want to hear a creation story, a story that recounts how the world was formed, how things came to be, for contained within creation stories are relationships that help to define the nature of the universe and how cultures understand the world in which they exist.

And, as luck would have it, I happen to know a few. But I have a favourite. It's about a woman who fell from the sky. And it goes like this.

———

Back at the beginning of imagination, the world we know as earth was nothing but water, while above the earth, somewhere in space, was a larger, more ancient world. And on that world was a woman.

A crazy woman.

Well, she wasn't exactly crazy. She was more nosy. Curious. The kind of curious that doesn't give up. The kind that follows you around. Now, we all know that being curious is healthy, but being *curious* can get you into trouble.

Don't be too curious, the Birds told her.

Okay, she said, I won't.

But you know what? That's right. She kept on being curious.

One day while she was bathing in the river, she happened to look at her feet and discovered that she had five toes on each foot. One big one and four smaller ones. They had been there all along, of course, but now that the woman noticed them for the first time, she wondered why she had five toes instead of three. Or eight. And she wondered if more toes were better than fewer toes.

So she asked her Toes. Hey, she said, how come there are only five of you?

You're being curious again, said her Toes.

Another day, the woman was walking through the forest and found a moose relaxing in the shade by a lake.

Hello, said the Moose. Aren't you that nosy woman?

Yes, I am, said the woman, and what I want to know is why you are so much larger than me.

That's easy, said the Moose, and he walked into the lake and disappeared.

Don't you love cryptic stories? I certainly do.

Now before we go any further, we should give this woman a name so we don't have to keep calling her "the woman." How about Blanche? Catherine? Thelma? Okay, I know expressing an opinion can be embarrassing. So let's do it the way we always do it and let someone else make the decision for us. Someone we trust. Someone who will promise to lower taxes. Someone like me.

I say we call her Charm. Don't worry. We can change it later on if we want to.

So one day the woman we've decided to call Charm went looking for something good to eat. She looked at the fish, but she was not in the mood for fish. She looked at the rabbit, but she didn't feel like eating rabbit either.

I've got this craving, said Charm.

What kind of craving? said Fish.

I want to eat something, but I don't know what it is.

Maybe you're pregnant, said Rabbit. Whenever I get pregnant, I get cravings.

Hmmmm, said Charm, maybe I am.

And you know what? She was.

What you need, Fish and Rabbit told Charm, is some Red Fern Foot.

Yes, said Charm, that sounds delicious. What is it?

It's a root, said Fish, and it only grows under the oldest trees. And it's the perfect thing for pregnant humans.

Now, you're probably thinking that this is getting pretty silly, what with chatty fish and friendly rabbits, with moose disappearing into lakes and talking toes. And you're probably wondering how in the world I expect you to believe any of this, given the fact that we live in a predominantly scientific, capitalistic, Judeo-Christian world governed by physical laws, economic imperatives, and spiritual precepts.

Is that what you're thinking?

It's okay. You won't hurt my feelings.

So Charm went looking for some Red Fern Foot. She dug around this tree and she dug around that tree, but she couldn't find any. Finally she came to the oldest tree in the forest and she began digging around its base. By now she was very hungry, and she was very keen on some Red Fern Foot, so she really got into the digging. And before long she had dug a rather deep hole.

Don't dig too deep, Badger told her.

Mind your own business, Charm told him.

Okay, said Badger, but don't blame me if you make a mistake.

You can probably guess what happened. That's right, Charm dug right through to the other side of the world.

That's curious, said Charm, and she stuck her head into that hole so she could get a better view.

That's very curious, she said again, and she stuck her head even farther into the hole.

Sometimes when I tell this story to children, I slow it down and have Charm stick her head into that hole by degrees. But most of you are adults and have already figured out that Charm is going to stick her head into that hole so far that she's either going to get stuck or she's going to fall through.

And sure enough, she fell through. Right through that hole and into the sky.

Uh-oh, Charm thought to herself. That wasn't too smart.

But she couldn't do much about it now. And she began to tumble through the sky, began to fall and fall and fall and fall. Spinning and turning, floating through the vast expanse of space.

And off in the distance, just on the edge of sight, was a small blue dot floating in the heavens. And as Charm tumbled down through the black sky, the dot got bigger and bigger.

You've probably figured this part out, too, but just so there's no question, this blue dot is the earth. Well, sort of. It's the earth when it was young. When there was nothing but water. When it was simply a water world.

And Charm was heading right for it.

In the meantime, on this water world, on earth, a bunch of water animals were swimming and floating around and diving and talking about how much fun water is.

Water, water, water, said the Ducks. There's nothing like water.

Yes, said the Muskrats, we certainly like being wet.

It's even better when you're under water, said the Sunfish.

Try jumping into it, said the Dolphins. And just as the Dolphins said this, they looked up into the sky.

Uh-oh, said the Dolphins, and everyone looked up in time to see Charm falling toward them. And as she came around the moon, the water animals were suddenly faced with four variables—mass, velocity, compression, and displacement—and with two problems.

The Ducks, who have great eyesight, could see that Charm weighed in at about 150 pounds. And the Beavers, who have a head for physics and math, knew that she was coming in fast. Accelerating at thirty-two feet per second to be precise (give or take a little for drag and atmospheric friction). And the Whales knew from many years of study that water does not compress, while the Dolphins could tell anyone who asked that while it won't compress, water will displace.

Which brought the animals to the first of the two problems. If Charm hit the water at full speed, it was going to create one very large tidal wave and ruin everyone's day.

So quick as they could, all the water birds flew up and formed a net with their bodies, and, as Charm came streaking down, the birds caught her, broke her fall, and brought her gently to the surface of the water.

Just in time.

To deal with the second of the two problems. Where to put her.

They could just dump her in the water, but it didn't take a pelican to see that Charm was not a water creature.

Can you swim? asked the Sharks.

Not very well, said Charm.

How about holding your breath for a long time? asked the Sea Horses.

Maybe for a minute or two, said Charm.

Floating? said the Seals. Can you float?

I don't know, said Charm. I never really tried floating.

So what are we going to do with you? said the Lobsters.

Hurry up, said the Birds, flapping their wings as hard as they could.

Perhaps you could put me on something large and flat, Charm told the water animals.

Well, as it turns out, the only place in this water world that was large and flat was the back of the Turtle.

Oh, okay, said Turtle. But if anyone else falls out of the sky, she's on her own.

So the water animals put Charm on the back of the Turtle, and everyone was happy. Well, at least for the next month or so. Until the animals noticed that Charm was going to have a baby.

It's going to get a little crowded, said the Muskrats.

What are we going to do? said the Geese.

It wouldn't be so crowded, Charm told the water animals, if we had some dry land.

Sure, agreed the water animals, even though they had no idea what dry land was.

Charm looked over the side of the Turtle, down into the water, and then she turned to the water animals.

Who's the best diver? she asked.

A contest! screamed the Ducks.

All right! shouted the Muskrats.

What do we have to do? asked the Eels.

It's easy, said Charm. One of you has to dive down to the bottom of the water and bring up some mud.

Sure, said all the water animals, even though they had no idea what mud was.

So, said Charm, who wants to try first?

Me! said Pelican, and he flew into the sky as high as he could and then dropped like a knife into the water. And he was gone for a long time. But when he floated to the surface, out of breath, he didn't have any mud.

It was real dark down there, said Pelican, and cold.

The next animal to try was Walrus.

I don't mind the dark, said Walrus, and my blubber will keep me warm. So down she went, and she was gone for much longer than Pelican, but when she came to the surface coughing up water, she didn't have any mud, either.

I don't think the water has a bottom, said Walrus. Sorry.

———

I'm sure you're beginning to wonder if there's a point to this story or if I'm just going to work my way through all the water animals one by one.

———

So one by one all the water animals tried to find the mud at the bottom of the ocean, and all of them failed until the only animal left was Otter. Otter, however, wasn't particularly interested in finding mud.

Is it fun to play with? asked Otter.

Not really, said Charm.

Is it good to eat? asked Otter.

Not really, said Charm.

Then why do you want to find it? said Otter.

For the magic, said Charm.

Oh, said Otter. I like magic.

So Otter took a deep breath and dove into the water. And she didn't come up. Day after day, Charm and the animals waited for Otter to come to the surface. Finally, on the morning of the fourth day, just as the sun was rising, Otter's body floated up out of the depths.

Oh, no, said all the animals, Otter has drowned trying to find the mud. And they hoisted Otter's body onto the back of the Turtle.

Now, when they hoisted Otter's body onto the back of the Turtle, they noticed that her little paws were clenched shut, and when they opened her paws, they discovered something dark and gooey that wasn't water.

Is this mud? asked the Ducks.

Yes, it is, said Charm. Otter has found the mud.

Of course I found the mud, whispered Otter, who wasn't so much dead as she was tired and out of breath. This magic better be worth it.

Charm set the lump of mud on the back of the Turtle, and she sang and she danced, and the animals sang and danced with her, and very slowly the lump of mud began to grow. It grew and grew and grew into a world, part water, part mud. That was a good trick, said the water animals. But now there's not enough room for all of us in the water. Some of us are going to have to live on land.

Not that anyone wanted to live on the land. It was nothing but mud. Mud as far as the eye could see. Great jumbled lumps of mud.

But before the animals could decide who was going to live where or what to do about the mud-lump world, Charm had her baby.

Or rather, she had her babies.

Twins.

A boy and a girl. One light, one dark. One right-handed, one left-handed.

Nice-looking babies, said the Cormorants. Hope they like mud.

And as it turned out, they did. The right-handed Twin smoothed all the mud lumps until the land was absolutely flat.

Wow! said all the animals. That was pretty clever. Now we can see in all directions.

But before the animals could get used to all the nice flat land, the left-handed Twin stomped around in the mud, piled it up, and created deep valleys and tall mountains.

Okay, said the animals, that could work.

And while the animals were admiring the new landscape, the Twins really got busy. The right-handed Twin dug nice straight trenches and filled them with water.

These are rivers, he told the animals, and I've made the water flow in both directions so that it'll be easy to come and go as you please.

That's handy, said the animals.

But as soon as her brother had finished, the left-handed Twin made the rivers crooked and put rocks in the water and made it flow in only one direction.

This is much more exciting, she told the animals.

Could you put in some waterfalls? said the animals. Everyone likes waterfalls.

Sure, said the left-handed Twin. And she did.

The right-handed Twin created forests with all the trees lined up so you could go into the woods and not get lost. The left-handed Twin came along and moved the trees around, so that some of the forest was dense and difficult, and other parts were open and easy.

How about some trees with nuts and fruit? said the animals. In case we get hungry.

That's a good idea, said the right-handed Twin. And he did.

The right-handed Twin created roses. The left-handed Twin put thorns on the stems. The right-handed Twin created summer. The left-handed Twin created winter. The right-handed Twin created sunshine. The left-handed Twin created shadows.

Have we forgotten anything? the Twins asked the animals.

What about human beings? said the animals. Do you think we need human beings?

Why not? said the Twins. And quick as they could the right-handed Twin created women, and the left-handed Twin created men.

They don't look too bright, said the animals. We hope they won't be a problem.

Don't worry, said the Twins, you guys are going to get along just fine.

The animals and the humans and the Twins and Charm looked around at the world that they had created. Boy, they said, this is as good as it gets. This is one beautiful world.

———

It's a neat story, isn't it? A little long, but different. Maybe even a little exotic. Sort of like the manure-fired pots or the hand-painted plates or the woven palm hats or the coconuts carved to look like monkey faces or the colourful T-shirts that we buy on vacation.

Souvenirs. Snapshots of a moment. And when the moment has passed, the hats are tossed into closets, the T-shirts are stuffed into drawers, the pots and plates and coconuts are left to gather dust on shelves. Eventually everything is shipped off to a garage sale or slipped into the trash.

As for stories such as the Woman Who Fell from the Sky, well, we listen to them and then we forget them, for amidst the thunder of Christian monologues, they have neither purchase nor place. After all, within the North American paradigm we have a perfectly serviceable creation story.

And it goes like this.

———

In the beginning God created the heaven and the earth. And the earth was without form, and void and darkness was upon the face of the deep. And the Spirit of God moved upon the face of the waters. And God said, let there be light, and there was light.

You can't beat the King James version of the Bible for the beauty of the language. But it's the story that captures the imagination. God creates night and day, the sun and the moon, all the creatures of the world, and finally, toward the end of his labours, he creates humans. Man first and then woman. Adam and Eve. And he places everything and everyone in a garden, a perfect world. No sickness, no death, no hate, no hunger.

And there's only one rule.

Of every tree of the garden thou mayest freely eat. But of the tree of the knowledge of good and evil, thou shalt not eat of it, for in the day that thou eatest thereof thou shalt surely die.

One rule. Don't break it.

But that's exactly what happens. Adam and Eve break the rule. Doesn't matter how it happens. If you like the orthodox version, you can blame Eve. She eats the apple and brings it back to Adam. Not that Adam says no. A less misogynist reading would blame them both, would chalk up the debacle that followed as an unavoidable mistake. A wrong step. Youthful enthusiasm. A misunderstanding. Wilfulness.

But whatever you wish to call it, the rule has been broken, and that is the end of the garden. God seals it off and places an angel with a fiery sword at the entrance and tosses Adam and Eve into a howling wilderness to fend for themselves, a wilderness in which sickness and death, hate and hunger are their constant companions.

———

Okay. Two creation stories. One Native, one Christian. The first thing you probably noticed was that I spent more time with the Woman Who Fell from the Sky than I did with Genesis. I'm assuming that most of you have heard of Adam and Eve, but few, I imagine, have ever met Charm. I also used different strategies in the telling of these stories. In the Native story, I tried to recreate an oral storytelling voice and craft the story in terms of a performance for a general audience. In the Christian story, I tried to maintain a sense of rhetorical distance and decorum while organizing the story for a knowledgeable gathering. These strategies colour the stories and suggest values that may be neither inherent nor warranted. In the Native story, the conversational voice tends to highlight the exuberance of the story but diminishes its authority, while the sober voice in the Christian story makes for a formal recitation but creates a sense of veracity.

Basil Johnston, the Anishinabe storyteller, in his essay "How Do We Learn Language?" describes the role of comedy and laughter in stories by reminding us that Native peoples have always loved to laugh: "It is precisely because our tribal stories are comical and evoke laughter that they have never been taken seriously outside the tribe.... But behind and beneath the comic characters and the comic situations exists the real meaning of the story ... what the tribe understood about human growth and development."

Of course, none of you would make the mistake of confusing storytelling strategies with the value or sophistication of a story. And we know enough about the complexities of cultures to avoid the error of imagining animism and polytheism to be no more than primitive versions of monotheism. Don't we?

Nonetheless, the talking animals are a problem.

A theologian might argue that these two creation stories are essentially the same. Each tells about the creation of the world and the appearance of human beings. But a storyteller would tell you that these two stories are quite different, for whether you read the Bible as sacred text or secular metaphor, the elements in Genesis create a particular universe governed by a series of hierarchies—God, man, animals, plants—that celebrate law, order, and good government, while in our Native story, the universe is governed by a series of co-operations—Charm, the Twins, animals, humans—that celebrate equality and balance.

In Genesis, all creative power is vested in a single deity who is omnipotent, omniscient, and omnipresent. The universe begins with his thought, and it is through his actions and only his actions that it comes into being. In the Earth Diver story, and in many other Native creation stories for that matter, deities are generally figures of limited power and persuasion, and the acts of creation and the decisions that affect the world are shared with other characters in the drama.

In Genesis, we begin with a perfect world, but after the Fall, while we gain knowledge, we lose the harmony and safety of the garden and are forced into a chaotic world of harsh landscapes and dangerous shadows.

In our Native story, we begin with water and mud, and, through the good offices of Charm, her twins, and the animals, move by degrees and adjustments from a formless, featureless world to a world that is rich in its diversity, a world that is complex and complete.

Finally, in Genesis, the post-garden world we inherit is decidedly martial in nature, a world at war—God vs. the Devil, humans vs. the elements. Or to put things into corporate parlance, competitive. In our Native story, the world is at peace, and the pivotal concern is not with the ascendancy of good over evil but with the issue of balance.

So here are our choices: a world in which creation is a solitary, individual act or a world in which creation is a shared activity; a world that begins in harmony and slides toward chaos or a world that begins in chaos and moves toward harmony; a world marked by competition or a world determined by co-operation.

And there's the problem.

If we see the world through Adam's eyes, we are necessarily blind to the world that Charm and the Twins and the animals help to create. If we believe one story to be sacred, we must see the other as secular.

You'll recognize this pairing as a dichotomy, the elemental structure of Western society. And cranky old Jacques Derrida notwithstanding, we do love our dichotomies. Rich/poor, white/black, strong/weak, right/wrong, culture/nature, male/female, written/oral, civilized/barbaric, success/failure, individual/communal.

We trust easy oppositions. We are suspicious of complexities, distrustful of contradictions, fearful of enigmas.

Enigmas like my father.

I have a couple of old black-and-white pictures of him holding a baby with my mother looking on. He looks young in those photos. And happy. I'm sure he didn't leave because he hated me, just as I'm sure that my mother didn't stay because she loved me. Yet this is the story I continue to tell myself, because it's easy and contains all my anger, and because, in all the years, in all the tellings, I've honed it sharp enough to cut bone.

———

It was Sir Isaac Newton who said, "To every action there is always opposed an equal reaction." Had he been a writer, he might have simply said, "To every action there is a story."

Take Charm's story, for instance. It's yours. Do with it what you will. Tell it to friends. Turn it into a television movie. Forget it. But don't say in the years to come that you would have lived your life differently if only you had heard this story.

You've heard it now.

CHAPTER 2

LAND, HOMELAND, TERRITORY

Kimberly Blaeser, "Like Some Old Story"

Thomas King, "Borders"

M. E. Wakamatsu, "Rita Hayworth Mexicana"

Warren Cariou, "An Athabasca Story"

Gord Hill, "The 'Oka Crisis'"

Lee Maracle, "Goodbye, Snauq"

EVERY STORY HAPPENS in at least one place. Looking at the way a story represents that place can reveal a lot about human relationships and the different ways we see, interact with, and understand place and land. This connection between story and place has long been a powerful theme in the work of Indigenous authors. In Jeannette Armstrong's essay "Land Speaking," included in Chapter 3 of this anthology, the author argues that a people form their language and stories from their experiences on the land. She writes that we survive by "listening intently" to the land's teachings, and "inventing human words to retell its stories to our succeeding generations" (142). Similarly Leslie Marmon Silko, in her essay in Chapter 5, explains the connection between land and story when she writes that "stories are, in a sense, maps" ("Language" 242). In other words, like maps, stories describe our knowledge, experience, and beliefs about a physical space, whether the setting is indoors, outdoors, rural, urban, or on an Indigenous reserve or reservation. Furthermore, as with all maps, the ways in which the stories describe that spatial relationship is connected to the ideologies or world views that drive the way we use, claim, and contest land and territory.

Both Thomas King's short story "Borders" and M. E. Wakamatsu's "Rita Hayworth Mexicana" depict characters navigating the legal and physical terrain of international borders. As you read, consider the differences and similarities in the ways that relationships to the border are described in each story. How do the protagonists feel about the authorities that guard the borders? Are there other "borders" in their lives that similarly impede or obstruct the characters? Similarly, when reading Warren Cariou's "An Athabasca Story," consider how the writer "maps" a very particular way of relating to the land. Is he asking us to imagine a better way of seeing and understanding the earth we live on?

In addition to describing how land might be used, traversed, and remembered, stories are also maps in the way that they function to lay claim to a territory. In fact, when we talk about the events of a story, we say it "takes place." As one can see in King and Wakamatsu's work, some stories and maps define and enforce the masses of land taken by Canada, the United States, and Mexico through the process of colonization. In *The Five Hundred Years of Resistance Comic Book*, Gord Hill challenges the narrative of conquest that usually governs the reciting of colonial history, from the Spanish invasion of the Americas (1492) to the Six Nations land reclamation (2006). Instead, he constructs an alternative story of resistance by which to understand the past five hundred years. Indigenous stories about the land are important because they describe a historical Indigenous occupation of the land that predates settler nation-states, and in this way, the stories assert a right to continue that occupation. For example, both Lee Maracle's "Goodbye, Snauq" and Kimberly Blaeser's "Like Some Old Story" include descriptions of what can easily be identified as "traditional" Indigenous land use. In "Goodbye, Snauq," Maracle describes harvesting clams and other seafood on territory now lost to her people, while the narrator in Blaeser's story learns about deer hunting from an Elder. In both these works, the authors detail landmarks and other physical aspects of their homeland, as well as the sites where events occurred. The settings of these stories are more than neutral backdrops but instead "take place" in locales that describe and affirm Indigenous relationships to land. While Maracle and Blaeser describe a different experience of land and territory than King, Wakamatsu, and Cariou, all the authors in this section "map" a political and personal connection between land, story, and Indigenous rights on Turtle Island.

— *Like Some Old Story* —
Kimberly Blaeser

Anishinaabe author Kimberly Blaeser, an enrolled member of the Minnesota Chippewa Tribe, of mixed German and Anishinaabe descent, grew up on the White Earth Reservation. After graduating from Mahnomen High School and the College of St. Benedict in Minnesota, she worked for two years as a journalist before attending the University of Notre Dame, where she earned her MA and PhD in English. She has published three volumes of poetry, including *Apprenticed to Justice* (2007), *Absentee Indians and Other Poems* (2002), and *Trailing You* (1994), which won the Native

Writers' Circle of the Americas First Book Award. Her poetry and prose have appeared in numerous anthologies and literary magazines. She is an associate professor of English at the University of Wisconsin–Milwaukee, where she teaches courses in Native American literature, creative writing, and American nature writing.

Blaeser's passion for both literature and nature comes through in the following work of short fiction, "Like Some Old Story." In this piece, Blaeser portrays a tight-knit community in which people work together to cook, hunt, teach, and care for one another. Their lives are so tied to the natural world around them that one character is described as knowing the land in his very body: "His hands remember that journey in the air. His chin, his lips, know the directions" (81). However, for Blaeser's characters, sustenance also comes from an additional and perhaps surprising source. Indeed, the narrator professes to hunt not just rabbit and deer, but stories themselves. In what ways do hunting and storytelling provide nourishment in this story? How are they linked to community survival and resurgence?

I

"We got that deer way up by Strawberry Mountain, skinned it, butchered it, and packed it out, all the way back to Twin Lakes. I remember thinking how much warmer I felt wrapped in that deer meat. But it weren't vury long 'fore it began to feel awfully heavy. Jeezus we was sure happy to get home that night. All youse little kids woke up and wanted to eat right then."

We sit at the old man's table. I trace the knife cuts in the oil cloth as he talks. His hands remember that journey in the air. His chin, his lips, know the directions. I see the dance in his cloudy eyes and hear him laugh at the memory of that feast. "How-wah, we sure took the wrinkle out of our bellies that night!"

We hunt this way together often now. We clean and oil the guns, sharpen the knives. He brings a new box of shells out of the kitchen cabinet. (Good thing about being a bachelor he always said—you can keep your bullets handy.) We make us a lunch. He shuffles around the trailer, breathing pretty hard as he gets dressed. I pretend not to notice the way he has to lift his bad leg with his hand to get it into the boot. We sit down to a cup of coffee before going out. It's still dark and too early anyway.

"Wonder if you could show me how to make snares."

He answers in that way that he has. Gesturing with his neck and chin, his head bopping slightly, a throaty series of ahhs, and then a long drawn out "Well, sure I kin show you. You know what pitcher wire is?" I bring him things from here and there about the trailer. He shows me each of his tools, remembers just what he used to use and how he came to get the ones he has now. By the time I get the hang of the cutting, the tying, the sun's been up a while.

"Well lookit that. Them deer musta wondered what heppened to us. Spose they're out there looking at their clocks saying, 'Where is that ole hunter?' Jeez, what kind of hunter you gonna make, if you forget all about going out? I spose you gonna hunt just like my girls—out of my freezer. Well we mighd's well eat these sandwiches. Heppened to Dad and me like this one time we was camping where that ole McDougall used to have his sugarbush. I remember it was raining jest hard …"

II

The boys came in looking kind of funny. Awfully quiet, too. No teasing. Just set themselves to cleaning up. Boiling water to wash, emptying their pockets of spare shells and the match sticks they always carried. Soon your dad went to get some tobacco and a kind of a mumbled argument was going on in the back room. Tried to keep it secret they did, but Mum and Dad wouldn't have it. Sent for one of the uncles. Sent us little kids upstairs to the loft. Then they got the story out.

It was that man-deer spirit that's said to come out when them graves have been disturbed. Happens every forty years or so. Someone forgets. Gets too cocky. Pretty soon it's there on the edge of the clearing, antlers catching the early evening light. It looks straight at you when you take aim. Some reason you pause. Get a chill, a funny feeling. Talk yourself out of it. And, just as you set your finger to the trigger, the thing stands up on its man legs. And then is gone. Don't seem it was really there. But you're shaking.

III

The short squat little man comes out from behind a tree, walks furtively across the little field to position himself on the edge of some small wetlands. He's wearing the classic camouflage clothes in browns and tans, and waders that are fastened now just below his knees. Perhaps it's the duck-hunting hat or the way that he wears it with the ear flaps down, but something seems a little comical in his appearance, reminiscent somehow of a cartoon character.

He doesn't wait long before two mallards fly over. Perhaps he hasn't gotten settled yet, because his aim is off and he misses—twice. The gunfire must be muffled somewhat by the morning dampness because the birds seem strangely unruffled as the shots ring out and they fly on easily out of sight. His next shot brings down a honker, but the fourth, at a low-flying goose, hits a tree and ricochets, cartoon fashion. Soon the hunter seems to have found his rhythm and he brings down four more of the birds, which arrive miraculously in swift succession.

Suddenly the action stops. But the little man seems satisfied. He walks about picking up the birds from where they have fallen, putting the ducks in the large pockets of his hunting jacket. Like a magician he produces a small square cloth which, with a single flourish, turns into a shoulder pack. Into this he deposits the geese. Then, his weapon pointed down like he was taught in gun safety class, he walks off in the opposite direction from which he had come. The wetland scene seems hardly disturbed by the episode.

Then the tempo of the music picks up and a clone of the first man emerges again from the right edge of the screen.

IV

It was when the women were cooking together that I'd hear the other side of those stories. Like the one about the year the two deer were stolen from that tree down in the hollow. You know who always got blamed for that, don't you? I wondered at first why Aunt Maggie let those boys take the blame. But then I thought, well it was true often enough and could just as well have been true this time, too. "Good enough for them," Maggie would have said. But I never did let on or ask her about it. Later I realized how it *was* good for them—you know, to realize what a reputation they had earned. So I never told.

You remember how it happened? The men were all at Gram's having the big dinner the women had cooked in between their card games that day. Those pies were on the cook stove, looking jest juicy and waiting to be cut into. I saw when that blue pickup went by 'cuz I was sitting on the steps outside the screen door, you know, just far enough away so they would forget I was around but close enough to hear the stories. Anyway, pretty soon someone was walking up the path from where Ron's house used to be. It was June Bug's uncle, I forget his real name, but us kids used to jest call him Antler 'cuz he had that funny bump on the side of his head and it was covered with pale soft hairs so it looked to us like an antler jest beginning to pop out in velvet.

He never said *boozhoo*[1] or nothing. "Somethin's after yer deer." Thems the only words I remember him saying as he stood outside on the steps looking in on those happy hunters. His nose was against the screen door when he spoke, but he jumped back pretty quick 'cuz the chairs started scraping inside and six guys came out in a real hurry. Not mad, yet, 'cuz they thought dogs or maybe a bear.

I was just about to run after them when my aunt showed up, coming from the other side of the house, wiping her hands on a rag. "Your ole man sure can tie 'em up tight. Thought sure I was going to get caught there. Then what would we have said?"

"You manage?" It was my mom asked that.

"Ayah. Got that Brown boy to haul 'em. Said he could have a hind quarter."

Plenty of kids would have tole, you know, right that night. But I was patient, even then. I knew if you wanted to find things out you had to wait.

Turns out I didn't have to wait long. Next day the women couldn't tell it enough, how they tricked their husbands into hunting for that halfblood woman Sarah Goes Lightening. She was a Sioux, you know, and had those five kids. Used to live out on the Snyder Lake road, way back. I guess the men had it in for Sarah 'cuz they thought she done wrong by one of their own, LeRoy Beaulieu. But the women thought differently. I'm still hunting that story, but it'll come along some day. I know how to wait for stories.

V

The old man is standing there just where he said we should pick him up. He has his gun and a stick about a yard long which he holds up when he sees us approach. "Looks like he got him one," Auntie says in the back.

"Wonder how long he's been waiting," my mom says. "Wish he wouldn't go out like that alone."

"You could go with." We all laugh at that. "This one ain't my hunter," Grandpa used to say about my mom. "Sure about that?" Grandma would ask. "That girl is gonna surprise you with what she brings home some day." I guess she did, too. Brought home my dad. But I don't think that's what Grandpa meant, although it might be what Grandma had in mind. Never could tell about that woman either.

He holds up his stick when we get out and lifts his head toward what's hanging on it—a deer heart pierced through. "Had to fight a great big animal to save this heart for youse girls." It takes him a long time to say this because his words are always surrounded by gestures and because certain sounds he draws out, moving them up and down in his throat. He laughs then at what he's said, but doesn't tell us the story until later, until we've managed between the four of us to drag a small buck out of the woods where he left it, until we've heaved it into my trunk onto the gunny sacks I've laid out to catch the blood drippings, until we've driven back into the little village and sit inside drinking coffee and getting ready to butcher.

"It was a little weasel. Come out and tried to steal that heart right off the stick. You know how them little buggers are. Tough. Sure was mad at me, and didn't want to give up his supper. So I cut him a little piece." He looks over at me. "Shoulda said, 'Do your own hunting.'" He knows I'll take the part of the weasel. We both pretend I have to convince him.

I dream about the weasel that night. He's a least weasel in my dream and he's old. He sits on a log in the sun watching the birds, thinking of the time he was quick enough to snatch a bird before it could launch itself out of his reach. Dreams always come that way from life and life from dreams, don't they? I saw a least weasel snatch its dinner just that way once, a bird twice its size, too. That time becomes this time when I sleep, but it's only the weasel's dream. He's too old now. He needs some help, too, just like any old hunter.

I wake up to deer meat frying and come out to find him cleaning his gun again at the table. "Thought you were gonna sleep all day." I look outside. It's still dark, maybe five a.m. I smile when he cranes his neck toward the stove. I take the cups from the counter where he's laid them, pour in some canned milk, take the hot pad, letting myself sniff its stale flour smell, before I reach for the coffee pot.

"Spose we could be out and back before them ladies even wake up," I say pretty casual-like when I put the cups and plates on the table, like this is part of something old we've always done.

He nods, pretending with me again. "There's some boots you kin wear behind that wood stove there. You gut gloves?"

We both begin to eat fast and hearty, as if we hadn't just stuffed ourselves last night. "Howah, pretty good stuff." We're laughing too loud and wake up my mom.

"What are you two doing?" she drawls between yawns.

"Going hunting," I say, dropping my voice like it's the last line in some old story—like someone is going to answer, "*Aho*."

— *Borders* —
Thomas King

Thomas King, who also has a story in Chapter 1 of this text, is one of Turtle Island's most celebrated authors. King and his brother were raised by their single mother in California. As a young man, he worked as a photojournalist in New Zealand and Australia. In 1986, he completed his PhD in English and American studies at the University of Utah. He has taught Native studies at the University of California and the University of Lethbridge, and creative writing at the University of Guelph. He has authored novels, short stories, criticism, and children's literature and was made a member of the Order of Canada in 2004. His most recent novel, *The Back of the Turtle*, won the 2014 Governor General's Literary Award for fiction.

In King's short story "Borders," the author describes a Blackfoot family's attempts to cross into the United States. Determined to visit a daughter who has left home to live on her own in Salt Lake City, the narrator's mother gets trapped between the U.S. and Canadian border when she refuses to claim citizenship to any nation but the Blackfoot nation. The Blackfoot characters assert Blackfoot identity no less than eleven times in the story. Throughout this story, King uses metaphor and wit to draw attention to the role of national borders in heightening tensions between Indigenous nations and the Canadian state, as well as raising issues of culture, growing up, and personal independence.

As you read, you might consider how the mother in the story helps her family navigate these multiple and overlapping areas of concern. What skills and values does she pass on as tools to help her children? How does place become important to the story? What is the significance of the no-man's land between borders? What role does the sky play?

When I was twelve, maybe thirteen, my mother announced that we were going to go to Salt Lake City to visit my sister who had left the reserve, moved across the line, and found a job. Laetitia had not left home with my mother's blessing, but over time my mother had come to be proud of the fact that Laetitia had done all of this on her own.

"She did real good," my mother would say.

Then there were the fine points to Laetitia's going. She had not, as my mother liked to tell Mrs. Manyfingers, gone floating after some man like a balloon on a string. She hadn't snuck out of the house, either, and gone to Vancouver or Edmonton or Toronto to chase rainbows down alleys. And she hadn't been pregnant.

"She did real good."

I was seven or eight when Laetitia left home. She was seventeen. Our father was from Rocky Boy on the American side.

"Dad's American," Laetitia told my mother, "so I can go and come as I please."

"Send us a postcard."

Laetitia packed her things, and we headed for the border. Just outside of Milk River, Laetitia told us to watch for the water tower.

"Over the next rise. It's the first thing you see."

"We got a water tower on the reserve," my mother said. "There's a big one in Lethbridge, too."

"You'll be able to see the tops of the flagpoles, too. That's where the border is."

When we got to Coutts, my mother stopped at the convenience store and bought her and Laetitia a cup of coffee. I got an Orange Crush.

"This is real lousy coffee."

"You're just angry because I want to see the world."

"It's the water. From here on down, they got lousy water."

"I can catch the bus from Sweetgrass. You don't have to lift a finger."

"You're going to have to buy your water in bottles if you want good coffee."

There was an old wooden building about a block away, with a tall sign in the yard that said "Museum." Most of the roof had been blown away. Mom told me to go and see when the place was open. There were boards over the windows and doors. You could tell that the place was closed, and I told Mom so, but she said to go and check anyway. Mom and Laetitia stayed by the car. Neither one of them moved. I sat down on the steps of the museum and watched them, and I don't know that they ever said anything to each other. Finally, Laetitia got her bag out of the trunk and gave Mom a hug.

I wandered back to the car. The wind had come up, and it blew Laetitia's hair across her face. Mom reached out and pulled the strands out of Laetitia's eyes, and Laetitia let her.

"You can still see the mountain from here," my mother told Laetitia in Blackfoot.

"Lots of mountains in Salt Lake," Laetitia told her in English.

"The place is closed," I said. "Just like I told you."

Laetitia tucked her hair into her jacket and dragged her bag down the road to the brick building with the American flag flapping on a pole. When she got to where the guards were waiting, she turned, put the bag down, and waved to us. We waved back. Then my mother turned the car around, and we came home.

We got postcards from Laetitia regular, and, if she wasn't spreading jelly on the truth, she was happy. She found a good job and rented an apartment with a pool.

"And she can't even swim," my mother told Mrs. Manyfingers.

Most of the postcards said we should come down and see the city, but whenever I mentioned this, my mother would stiffen up.

So I was surprised when she bought two new tires for the car and put on her blue dress with the green and yellow flowers. I had to dress up, too, for my mother did not want us crossing the border looking like Americans. We made sandwiches and put them in a big box with pop and potato chips and some apples and bananas and a big jar of water.

"But we can stop at one of those restaurants, too, right?"

"We maybe should take some blankets in case you get sleepy."

"But we can stop at one of those restaurants, too, right?"

The border was actually two towns, though neither one was big enough to amount to anything. Coutts was on the Canadian side and consisted of the convenience store and gas station, the museum that was closed and boarded up, and a motel. Sweetgrass was on the American side, but all you could see was an overpass that arched across the highway and disappeared into the prairies. Just hearing the names of these towns, you would expect that Sweetgrass, which is a nice name and sounds like it is related to other places such as Medicine Hat and Moose Jaw and Kicking Horse Pass, would be on the Canadian side, and that Coutts, which sounds abrupt and rude, would be on the American side. But this was not the case.

Between the two borders was a duty-free shop where you could buy cigarettes and liquor and flags. Stuff like that.

We left the reserve in the morning and drove until we got to Coutts.

"Last time we stopped here," my mother said, "you had an Orange Crush. You remember that?"

"Sure," I said. "That was when Laetitia took off."

"You want another Orange Crush?"

"That means we're not going to stop at a restaurant, right?"

My mother got a coffee at the convenience store, and we stood around and watched the prairies move in the sunlight. Then we climbed back in the car. My mother straightened the dress across her thighs, leaned against the wheel, and drove all the way to the border in first gear, slowly, as if she were trying to see through a bad storm or riding high on black ice.

The border guard was an old guy. As he walked to the car, he swayed from side to side, his feet set wide apart, the holster on his hip pitching up and down. He leaned into the window, looked into the back seat, and looked at my mother and me.

"Morning, ma'am."

"Good morning."

"Where you heading?"

"Salt Lake City."

"Purpose of your visit?"

"Visit my daughter."

"Citizenship?"

"Blackfoot," my mother told him.

"Ma'am?"

"Blackfoot," my mother repeated.

"Canadian?"

"Blackfoot."

It would have been easier if my mother had just said "Canadian" and been done with it, but I could see she wasn't going to do that. The guard wasn't angry or anything. He smiled and looked towards the building. Then he turned back and nodded.

"Morning, ma'am."

"Good morning."

"Any firearms or tobacco?"

"No."

"Citizenship?"

"Blackfoot."

He told us to sit in the car and wait, and we did. In about five minutes, another guard came out with the first man. They were talking as they came, both men swaying back and forth like two cowboys headed for a bar or a gunfight.

"Morning, ma'am."

"Good morning."

"Cecil tells me you and the boy are Blackfoot."

"That's right."

"Now, I know that we got Blackfeet on the American side and the Canadians got Blackfeet on their side. Just so we can keep our records straight, what side do you come from?"

I knew exactly what my mother was going to say, and I could have told them if they had asked me.

"Canadian side or American side?" asked the guard.

"Blackfoot side," she said.

It didn't take them long to lose their sense of humor, I can tell you that. The one guard stopped smiling altogether and told us to park our car at the side of the building and come in.

We sat on a wood bench for about an hour before anyone came over to talk to us. This time it was a woman. She had a gun, too.

"Hi," she said. "I'm Inspector Pratt. I understand there is a little misunderstanding."

"I'm going to visit my daughter in Salt Lake City," my mother told her. "We don't have any guns or beer."

"It's a legal technicality, that's all."

"My daughter's Blackfoot, too."

The woman opened a briefcase and took out a couple of forms and began to write on one of them. "Everyone who crosses our border has to declare their citizenship. Even Americans. It helps us keep track of the visitors we get from the various countries."

She went on like that for maybe fifteen minutes, and a lot of the stuff she told us was interesting.

"I can understand how you feel about having to tell us your citizenship, and here's what I'll do. You tell me, and I won't put it down on the form. No-one will know but you and me."

Her gun was silver. There were several chips in the wood handle and the name "Stella" was scratched into the metal butt.

We were in the border office for about four hours, and we talked to almost everyone there. One of the men bought me a Coke. My mother brought a couple of sandwiches in from the car. I offered part of mine to Stella, but she said she wasn't hungry.

I told Stella that we were Blackfoot and Canadian, but she said that that didn't count because I was a minor. In the end, she told us that if my mother didn't declare her citizenship, we would have to go back to where we came from. My mother stood up and thanked Stella for her time. Then we got back in the car and drove to the Canadian border, which was only about a hundred yards away.

I was disappointed. I hadn't seen Laetitia for a long time, and I had never been to Salt Lake City. When she was still at home, Laetitia would go on and on about Salt Lake City. She had never been there, but her boyfriend Lester Tallbull had spent a year in Salt Lake at a technical school.

"It's a great place," Lester would say. "Nothing but blondes in the whole state."

Whenever he said that, Laetitia would slug him on his shoulder hard enough to make him flinch. He had some brochures on Salt Lake and some maps, and every so often the two of them would spread them out on the table.

"That's the temple. It's right downtown. You got to have a pass to get in."

"Charlotte says anyone can go in and look around."

"When was Charlotte in Salt Lake? Just when the hell was Charlotte in Salt Lake?"

"Last year."

"This is Liberty Park. It's got a zoo. There's good skiing in the mountains."

"Got all the skiing we can use," my mother would say. "People come from all over the world to ski at Banff. Cardston's got a temple, if you like those kinds of things."

"Oh, this one is real big," Lester would say. "They got armed guards and everything."

"Not what Charlotte says."

"What does she know?"

Lester and Laetitia broke up, but I guess the idea of Salt Lake stuck in her mind.

———

The Canadian border guard was a young woman, and she seemed happy to see us. "Hi," she said. "You folks sure have a great day for a trip. Where are you coming from?"

"Standoff."

"Is that in Montana?"

"No."

"Where are you going?"

"Standoff."

The woman's name was Carol and I don't guess she was any older than Laetitia. "Wow, you both Canadians?"

"Blackfoot."

"Really? I have a friend I went to school with who is Blackfoot. Do you know Mike Harley?"

"No."

"He went to school in Lethbridge, but he's really from Browning."

It was a nice conversation and there were no cars behind us, so there was no rush.

"You're not bringing any liquor back, are you?"

"No."

"Any cigarettes or plants or stuff like that?"

"No."

"Citizenship?"

"Blackfoot."

"I know," said the woman, "and I'd be proud of being Blackfoot if I were Blackfoot. But you have to be American or Canadian."

———

When Laetitia and Lester broke up, Lester took his brochures and maps with him, so Laetitia wrote to someone in Salt Lake City, and, about a month later, she got a big envelope of stuff. We sat at the table and opened up all the brochures, and Laetitia read each one out loud.

"Salt Lake City is the gateway to some of the world's most magnificent skiing.

"Salt Lake City is the home of one of the newest professional basketball franchises, the Utah Jazz.

"The Great Salt Lake is one of the natural wonders of the world."

It was kind of exciting seeing all those color brochures on the table and listening to Laetitia read all about how Salt Lake City was one of the best places in the entire world.

"That Salt Lake City place sounds too good to be true," my mother told her.

"It has everything."

"We got everything right here."

"It's boring here."

"People in Salt Lake City are probably sending away for brochures of Calgary and Lethbridge and Pincher Creek right now."

In the end, my mother would say that maybe Laetitia should go to Salt Lake City, and Laetitia would say that maybe she would.

We parked the car to the side of the building and Carol led us into a small room on the second floor. I found a comfortable spot on the couch and flipped through some back issues of *Saturday Night* and *Alberta Report*.

When I woke up, my mother was just coming out of another office. She didn't say a word to me. I followed her down the stairs and out to the car. I thought we were going home, but she turned the car around and drove back towards the American border, which made me think we were going to visit Laetitia in Salt Lake City after all. Instead she pulled into the parking lot of the duty-free store and stopped.

"We going to see Laetitia?"

"No."

"We going home?"

Pride is a good thing to have, you know. Laetitia had a lot of pride, and so did my mother. I figured that someday, I'd have it, too.

"So where are we going?"

Most of that day, we wandered around the duty-free store, which wasn't very large. The manager had a name tag with a tiny American flag on one side and a tiny Canadian flag on the other. His name was Mel. Towards evening, he began suggesting that we should be on our way. I told him we had nowhere to go, that neither the Americans nor the Canadians would let us in. He laughed at that and told us that we should buy something or leave.

The car was not very comfortable, but we did have all that food and it was April, so even if it did snow as it sometimes does on the prairies, we wouldn't freeze. The next morning my mother drove to the American border.

It was a different guard this time, but the questions were the same. We didn't spend as much time in the office as we had the day before. By noon, we were back at the Canadian border. By two we were back in the duty-free shop parking lot.

The second night in the car was not as much fun as the first, but my mother seemed in good spirits, and, all in all, it was as much an adventure as an inconvenience. There wasn't much food left and that was a problem, but we had lots of water as there was a faucet at the side of the duty-free shop.

One Sunday, Laetitia and I were watching television. Mom was over at Mrs. Manyfingers's. Right in the middle of the program, Laetitia turned off the set and said she was going to Salt Lake City, that life around here was too boring. I had wanted to see the rest of the program and really didn't care if Laetitia went to Salt Lake City or not. When Mom got home, I told her what Laetitia had said.

What surprised me was how angry Laetitia got when she found out that I had told Mom.

"You got a big mouth."

"That's what you said."

"What I said is none of your business."

"I didn't say anything."

"Well, I'm going for sure, now."

That weekend, Laetitia packed her bags, and we drove her to the border.

———

Mel turned out to be friendly. When he closed up for the night and found us still parked in the lot, he came over and asked us if our car was broken down or something. My mother thanked him for his concern and told him that we were fine, that things would get straightened out in the morning.

"You're kidding," said Mel. "You'd think they could handle the simple things."

"We got some apples and a banana," I said, "but we're all out of ham sandwiches."

"You know, you read about these things, but you just don't believe it. You just don't believe it."

"Hamburgers would be even better because they got more stuff for energy."

My mother slept in the back seat. I slept in the front because I was smaller and could lie under the steering wheel. Late that night, I heard my mother open the car door. I found her sitting on her blanket leaning against the bumper of the car.

"You see all those stars," she said. "When I was a little girl, my grand-mother used to take me and my sisters out on the prairies and tell us stories about all the stars."

"Do you think Mel is going to bring us any hamburgers?"

"Every one of those stars has a story. You see that bunch of stars over there that look like a fish?"

"He didn't say no."

"Coyote went fishing, one day. That's how it all started." We sat out under the stars that night, and my mother told me all sorts of stories. She was serious about it, too. She'd tell them slow, repeating parts as she went, as if she expected me to remember each one.

Early the next morning, the television vans began to arrive, and guys in suits and women in dresses came trotting over to us, dragging microphones and cameras and lights behind them. One of the vans had a table set up with orange juice and sandwiches and fruit. It was for the crew, but when I told them we hadn't eaten for a while, a really skinny blonde woman told us we could eat as much as we wanted.

They mostly talked to my mother. Every so often one of the reporters would come over and ask me questions about how it felt to be an Indian without a country. I told them we had a nice house on the reserve and that my cousins had a couple of horses we rode when we went fishing. Some of the television people went over to the American border, and then they went to the Canadian border.

Around noon, a good-looking guy in a dark blue suit and an orange tie with little ducks on it drove up in a fancy car. He talked to my mother for a while, and after they were done talking, my mother called me over, and we got into our car. Just as my mother started the engine, Mel came over and gave us a bag of peanut brittle and told us that justice was a damn hard thing to get, but that we shouldn't give up.

I would have preferred lemon drops, but it was nice of Mel anyway.

"Where are we going now?"

"Going to visit Laetitia."

The guard who came out to our car was all smiles. The television lights were so bright they hurt my eyes, and, if you tried to look through the windshield in certain directions, you couldn't see a thing.

"Morning, ma'am."

"Good morning."

"Where you heading?"

"Salt Lake City."

"Purpose of your visit?"

"Visit my daughter."

"Any tobacco, liquor, or firearms?"

"Don't smoke."

"Any plants or fruit?"

"Not any more."

"Citizenship?"

"Blackfoot."

The guard rocked back on his heels and jammed his thumbs into his gun belt. "Thank you," he said, his fingers patting the butt of the revolver. "Have a pleasant trip."

My mother rolled the car forward, and the television people had to scramble out of the way. They ran alongside the car as we pulled away from the border, and, when they couldn't run any farther, they stood in the middle of the highway and waved and waved and waved.

We got to Salt Lake City the next day. Laetitia was happy to see us, and, that first night, she took us out to a restaurant that made really good soups. The list of pies took up a whole page. I had cherry. Mom had chocolate. Laetitia said that she saw us on television the night before and, during the meal, she had us tell her the story over and over again.

Laetitia took us everywhere. We went to a fancy ski resort. We went to the temple. We got to go shopping in a couple of large malls, but they weren't as large as the one in Edmonton, and Mom said so.

After a week or so, I got bored and wasn't at all sad when my mother said we should be heading back home. Laetitia wanted us to stay longer, but Mom said no, that she had things to do back home and that, next time, Laetitia should come up and visit. Laetitia said she was thinking about moving back, and Mom told her to do as she pleased, and Laetitia said that she would.

On the way home, we stopped at the duty-free shop, and my mother gave Mel a green hat that said "Salt Lake" across the front. Mel was a funny guy. He took the hat and blew his nose and told my mother that she was an inspiration to us all. He gave us some more peanut brittle and came out into the parking lot and waved at us all the way to the Canadian border.

It was almost evening when we left Coutts. I watched the border through the rear window until all you could see were the tops of the flagpoles and the blue water tower, and then they rolled over a hill and disappeared.

— *Rita Hayworth Mexicana* —
M. E. Wakamatsu

Maria Elena Wakamatsu was born in the border town of San Luis R. C. Sonora, Mexico, to a Japanese father and a Mexican mother of Yaqui descent. Her father, Roberto Wakamatsu, was an agricultural worker and mechanic, and her mother, Cuca Gallego, was a storyteller and photographer. Wakamatsu was raised in Somerton, Arizona, but travelled across the border to Mexico routinely, visiting relatives in San Luis. Life on the border is an experience that she explores in much of her writing. Her poetry and prose, written from between cultures, between patterns of discourse, and between first and third worlds, appears in the journals *Drunken Boat*, *Cutthroat*, *Southwestern Women: New Voices*, and in the collection *Cantos al Sexto Sol: A Collection of Aztlanahuac Writing* (2002). She also has seven poems in *This Piece of Earth: Images and Words from Tumamoc Hill* (2014). Wakamatsu is part of Mujeres Que Escriben, a Latina writers' group in Tucson, Arizona, where she is a long-standing member of the writing community.

The following piece of short fiction, "Rita Hayworth Mexicana," tells the story of a young Sonoran woman in 1945 who must cross the border every day to her job in the United States and contend with "el Crane," the inspection officer. The author writes in both Spanish and English to illuminate the border as a space of tension, exchange, resilience, contradiction, and expropriation. While reading, consider how this short story maps the land. What kind of relationship to place does it describe? Does the story claim land? How and for whom?

In 1945, the U.S. was at war with Japan and that meant big business for Mexico. San Luis, Río Colorado, Sonora, a busy border town, exploded with greens and yellows and oranges that kept U.S. soldiers fed. El Golfo de Santa Clara just a few miles away teemed with totoaba y cahuama.[1] El Internacional kept soldiers on leave drunk and entertained. Las Vegas boomed. Jazz hit it big and Hollywood was born.

My mother, they called her Cuqui, was eighteen years old and as close to looking like Rita Hayworth as you can get. Preciosa, graciosa y dulce, she was everybody's doll. La mas alegre, la mas risueña con una voz de colibrí. La morena de los ojazos, she was the only one in San Luis who ordered from Chicago—the Spiegel Catalogue—and dressed for work like she were going to a Hollywood screening.

Every morning she walked the quarter mile through the desert from her home hasta la linea[2] to get to work en el otro lado.[3] You see, she was the only one of nine children her widowed mother had who could work in the U.S. She worked con el Señor Verdugo who owned the General Store and ran the Post Office. She did the mail, weighed the fish, stocked the store, did the payroll. Everything. She ran the place and everybody liked her. Always had a smile for everyone, sang while she worked—man, everybody loved her....

Even the Border Inspection guys. They say el Crane had a big crush on her. He worked the morning shift and got to stand there checking everybody's mica,[4] but not Cuqui's. You see, she was an American citizen. She'd been born in L.A. and Crane liked that. Even though she lived on the other side and he couldn't understand that, she wasn't really like the rest of those people, those Mexicans who came over here to work. She was a citizen.

So, he'd see her coming up the walk and his pulse would quicken just a bit.

"Damn, she looks like Rita Hayworth," he'd think and adjust himself and sit on the stool.

"Buenos días, Mr. Crane," she'd say.

"Buenos días," he'd respond in perfect Spanish. "Al trabajo tan temprano?" She would smile timidly.

"Como está el Señor Verdugo?" He could really care less about el Señor Verdugo or how much fish was coming in today or how big the totoaba was yesterday, but he had to try to prolong the formality of crossing from one country to another.

She'd stand there nervously for a while—her little purse clutched tight in both hands, shifting all of her one hundred pounds from one Spectator pump to the other. She couldn't just leave, you know … cut him off and go…. He was The Man—el Imigrante and although he would never question her citizenship, she knew she couldn't just leave.

He would have to give the sign and then she could go and walk the remaining block to the store while he watched on.

That day, she knew something was wrong when she approached. He was standing, tense not sitting on the stool as usual.

"Buenos días, Mr. Crane," she said.

"Dejeme ver sus papeles,[5] señorita," he responded. No buenos días. No smile. No chit chat. No flirting.

"Mis papeles? Cuales papeles?"

"Su acta de nacimiento."

"Mr. Crane, no la traigo. La tengo en la casa. Que hay algún problema?" She was scared. She was sure she was going to lose her job en el otro lado—her citizenship, everything. It's funny, she'd always felt the tension … that her days working here were numbered. That someone, someday would declare that U.S. citizens living in Mexico were not really citizens—not like the ones who lived here.

"Well, if you can't prove your citizenship," he said looking down and pulling the stool between his legs, "there is a problem." He sat, now, legs apart, arms crossed. "You can't proceed. That's the law."

His tone—flat, his face—frozen sour, his entire body once friendly, gentle even, now stiff exposed lo pinchi[6] que son los hombres.

"Pero, Mr. Crane, ustéd me conoce. Sabe quien soy, que tengo años cruzando, trabajando acá. Ustéd sabe que nací en Los Angeles …" she said, her voice trailing off becoming a futile plea.

"Lo siento, señorita, no puede pasar," he said opening his sunglass case carefully. He slipped them on slowly. He didn't see her now. He didn't hear her either. La Rita Hayworth Mexicana, you see, was really just like all these other Mexicans—no, worse. She was marrying a Japonés—a Nisei.[7] What a shame. What had he been thinking?

But she was invisible to him now … an irritant over which he had to look to see the viejita behind her.

"Señora, sus papeles?"

⤙ *An Athabasca Story* ⤚
Warren Cariou

Warren Cariou is a Métis writer, professor, documentary filmmaker, and Director of the Centre for Creative Writing and Oral Culture at the University of Manitoba. He was born in Meadow Lake, Saskatchewan, a place that continues to function as an important touchstone in his work. His books, films, photography, and scholarly research explore themes of community, environment, orality, and belonging. He is the author of *Exalted Company of Roadside Martyrs* (1999), a collection of short stories, and *Lake of the Prairies* (2003), a memoir that was nominated for the Charles Taylor Prize for Literary Nonfiction and won the Drainie-Taylor Prize for biography. He has also co-directed and co-produced two films about Aboriginal communities and tar sands development in western Canada: *Overburden* and *Land of Oil and Water* (2009). His work is particularly concerned with Indigenous rights and how Indigenous peoples are responding to corporate incursions into their land and their lives.

In "An Athabasca Story," Elder Brother is travelling in an alien landscape full of angry people and big yellow machines. That place may be recognizable to readers as the Athabasca tar sands. Taking his cue from the greedy world he finds himself in, Elder Brother, another name for the Cree figure Wîsahkêcâhk, tries to dig up his own pile of "magical dirt" with disastrous consequences. However, as Cariou writes, "perhaps not so luckily," Elder Brother cannot die, and indeed he doesn't in this story. In addition to paying attention to the relationship with land that this story describes, ask yourself what it might mean that Elder Brother survives. What does his continued existence serve to remind us of? Additionally, how might this open ending impact the way things turn out in the world Cariou describes, and our own?

One winter day Elder Brother was walking in the forest, walking cold and hungry and alone as usual, looking for a place to warm himself. His stomach was like the shrunken dried crop of a partridge. It rattled around inside him as he walked, and with each step he took the sound made him shiver even more.

Where will I find a place to warm myself? he wondered. Surely some relations will welcome me into their home, let me sit by the fire.

But he walked for a very long time and saw none of his relations. Eventually he traveled so far west that he didn't know the land anymore, and even the animals wouldn't dare to help him because they knew how hungry he was. They kept a safe distance. So he shivered and rattled his way farther and farther, without anything to guide him except the lengthening shadows and his unerring radar for trouble.

When he was nearly at the point of slumping down in a snowbank and giving up, Elder Brother thought he smelled something. It was smoke, almost certainly, though a kind of smoke he'd never encountered before. And though it was not a pleasant odour at all, not like the aromatic pine-fire he had been imagining, he knew that it meant warmth. So he quickened his frail pace and followed the scent, over one hill and then another and yet another. And eventually he came to the top of one more hill and he looked down across an empty valley and saw the source of the smoke.

A huge plume billowed from a gigantic house far in the distance, and between himself and the house there was a vast expanse of empty land. Empty of trees, of muskeg, of birds and animals. He had never seen anything like it. The only things moving on that vacant landscape were enormous yellow contraptions that clawed and bored and bit the dark earth and then hauled it away toward the big house. And the smell! It was worse than his most sulfurous farts, the ones he got when he ate moose guts and antlers. It was like being trapped in a bag with something dead.

Elder Brother knew he should turn away and get out of that smell as soon as he could. But that would mean spending the night by himself, freezing and chattering and rattling, and he couldn't bring himself to do it. There was warmth up there in the big house, he could see it floating away on the breeze. In places he could even see the heat rising in fine wiggly lines from the newly naked earth itself. So despite the smell he stepped forward and made his way out into that strange expanse.

The house was farther away than it had seemed. He walked and walked across the empty space, stepping over dark half-frozen puddles, holding his nose, following the tracks of the great yellow beasts. He attempted to stay far away from the beasts themselves because they didn't look the least bit hospitable. But by the time he got halfway across the open land, he strayed close enough to these creatures that he could see each of them giving off its own smaller stream of smoke. And as he stood there studying them, he realized something else: there were people inside.

Maybe they were houses, he thought. Warm, comfortable houses that by some magic were also capable of digging and hauling the earth. Certainly they were big enough to be houses. He got closer and watched again as one of them rumbled past, shaking the ground at his feet. The man inside was bare-armed, as if it was summer. And he was chewing on something.

Of course Elder Brother was scared by the noise and the smell and the shuddering earth. But his hunger and his shivering were stronger. When the next gigantic thing came rumbling down the track he bounded out in front of it and stood there, waving his right hand desperately while his left hand remained clamped on his nose.

The thing squealed and snorted and eventually came to a stop just before it touched him. A man immediately leaned out from a window near the top of it and shouted, Who in hell are you? Where's your machine?

Oh my brother, my dear relation, Elder Brother said. I'm very cold and hungry and I was hoping … to come and visit you in your house.

The man didn't say anything for quite a while. He scanned the blank horizon, as if looking for something. Finally he leaned further out the window and yelled, You're saying you're not with the company?

Uh, company.…

Are you Greenpeace?

I'm cold, Elder Brother said.

The man took off his strange yellow hat and gazed into it for a moment, placing one hand over his forehead as if to keep something from bursting out.

Well you'll be a lot worse than cold, the man said, if you don't get the hell out of my way and off this goddamn property.

Well, *that* was rude, Elder Brother thought, but he tried not to betray his disappointment. This man talked as if he had no relations at all.

Okay, he said to the man. I won't come visit you right now, but could I please ride along on the top of your house? I want to go to the big house over there, where I'm sure they'll let me come in and get warm.

The man laughed a little, and glanced up at the sky for a moment.

I don't know what you're on, buddy, the man said. But you need to snap out of it right this goddamn minute. Cause if you don't step aside I'm gonna call Security, see, and they're gonna come out here and throw your ass in the slammer with all those other yahoos from last month and the month before. I should've called them already. But on the other hand, I could save a little time if we just had a bit of an accident here. Nobody'd ever know it happened.

The man's house made a roaring sound that made Elder Brother step back.

Oh, there's no need for that! Elder Brother said. Don't worry, I'll move aside. But before I go, I just want to know one thing: what are you doing with all that earth?

We're burning it, the man said.

Burning. But earth doesn't—

This stuff does, the man interjected. You really are a moron, aren't you? It's very special dirt, this stuff. We dig it up and take it over to the big house, as you call it, and we mix it around in there and after a while it's ready to burn. Fuel to heat your house, if you have one which I doubt. Gas to power your car. Diesel to move this big rig here. All of it comes right out of the ground. You can tell that by the smell of the air around here. Just like napalm in the morning!

The man took a deep breath through his nostrils and then laughed, but his face turned sour when he saw that Elder Brother didn't understand.

Yeah, we got real big plans for this place, the man said. There's more of this special dirt here than anywhere else in the world. Everybody wants it, and we're happy to sell it to them of course. And all those people around the world are going to help us burn this very dirt that you see here, from under your feet all the way to the far horizon. We're gonna burn it, and burn it, and burn it, until we make so much heat that the winter never comes back! And then even you and the rest of your sorry kind won't be cold anymore. So how do you like that?

When will that be? Elder Brother asked, rubbing his hands together.

Fifty or sixty years. Maybe forty.

Oh. Not to complain, but I was hoping for something a little—

Elder Brother was interrupted by an explosion of noise from the front of the big yellow house-thing, and it lurched toward him with surprising speed. He was barely able to leap out of the way before it rolled right over his footprints.

Now get off this land! the man yelled as his house roared away. It doesn't belong to you. Go back to the bush or wherever it was you crawled out from. I'm calling Security right now!

Elder Brother stood there for a while and watched the house labouring over the hillocks and through the black puddles in its way. He was more than a little scared of this mysterious Security that would soon be coming after him, but he was also angry. How could this man tell him that the land wasn't his? How could this "company" keep all the magical dirt for itself? If there was so much of it, Elder Brother reasoned, there should be plenty to share with visitors.

Though he knew he should probably be running for his life, Elder Brother found himself unwilling to move. He was held there by an idea: if these people wouldn't give him any of this magical dirt, maybe he should take some for himself. Yes, what a fabulous plan! Since the man and his company were so rude, they deserved to have their precious dirt stolen. And the best part was that if Elder Brother gathered enough of this magic dirt for himself, he could burn it for years and keep warm until the winter was gone for good.

So instead of fleeing the empty land, Elder Brother began walking toward the place in the centre where the largest of the yellow contraptions were tearing away at the earth. The snow had all been cleared away there, and he could see how black this magical dirt really was. He watched the beasts moving this way and that, and he waited for his opportunity. Finally he saw an opening, and he darted between a couple of the great mobile houses toward a spot where the ground had recently been opened. It looked softer there, and warmer too. Yes, this was the place. He lifted his right hand and thrust it as hard as he could, right down into the soil, up to his elbow.

Ayah! a voice said. What are you doing, Elder Brother?

Sssshhhhhhhh, he answered. I'm taking what's mine.

And he reached deeper and deeper into the ground, spreading his fingers as wide as he could in order to hold the largest armload of dirt. A year's supply in one hand, he imagined! He reached so far that his cheek rested against the redolent earth itself. He nearly gagged at the smell but he didn't loosen his grip. He could already feel the warmth coming out of the soil and it made him a little stronger.

Elder Brother, you're hurting me! the voice cried out.

Not nearly so much as they are, he said, and with that he began reaching in with his other arm, tunneling in with his fingers, opening his arms wide in a desperate embrace. His nose was raw with the fumes, and particles of grit were getting in his mouth. He was about to heave the huge armload of dirt out right then and begin his run for the bush, but one thought stopped him. What if it wasn't enough? What if he ran out and then the winter came back?

So without another hesitation he kicked off his moccasin and began tunneling in with the toes of his right foot. He clasped and clawed until he was more than thigh-deep in the earth, and then he tilted his toes upward to hold as much as he could. Then quickly he kicked off his other moccasin and tunneled with that foot, squirming and worming until that leg too was embedded in the earth. Ass-deep and shoulder-deep in the magical soil! Surely this would be enough to last him for decades, until the winter had been vanquished for good.

You are a genius, Elder Brother, he said to himself. You deserve all the warmth you're going to get.

But when Elder Brother tried to lean back and lift the great clump of dirt out of its place, he discovered that he had no leverage. He pulled and pulled at the soil, flexing his arms and his legs all at once, but nothing moved. The only thing that happened was his limbs seemed to sink a little deeper into the ground. He grunted and panted, flexed again, shimmied his buttocks for extra oomph. However it didn't make a bit of difference.

Well, he thought, I guess I should just take a little less of this stuff, maybe make two trips. I'll just wiggle my legs out of these holes and settle for a nice big armload of magic dirt.

I imagine you can guess how that worked out. Right. It didn't. Elder Brother was stuck fast in that Athabasca tar. By this time he couldn't move a finger or a toe.

Instinctively he called out to the voice that had spoken to him earlier. Help me! I'm sorry I didn't listen to you. I'll leave now without taking anything at all.

But the voice didn't answer. And Elder Brother was stuck there in the ground all night, and all the next day and the following night. He howled to the voice, asking it for forgiveness. He yelled to any of his relations who might be in earshot. He even screamed to the men in the huge yellow creatures that, from their sound, seemed to be moving closer and closer to him. (Of course he couldn't see what was going on back there. All he could see was the clump of oily dirt that his nose was resting on.) If those men in the contraptions heard him, or saw him, they gave no sign of it.

Late in the afternoon of his second day of being stuck in the ground, the sound of the contraptions became much louder, and a dark shadow suddenly closed over Elder Brother. Then he was being lifted, along with his armload of dirt and a great deal more, and he felt himself falling with the thunderous sound of everything else falling around him. He cried out but he knew it was hopeless; no one would hear him over a cacophony like this. When he landed, the dirt closed over him. It pressed into his nostrils, his ears, his mouth, even into his clenched bum. The weight of it pushed down and down until he couldn't even move an eyelid. Soon the thing began to move, and it hauled him slowly across the wasteland, encased there in the tar as if he was a fossil. And eventually the truck reached the edge of the huge smoky refinery, where it dumped him and many tons of tar sand into the yawning hopper that was the beginning of the processing line. And inside the refinery he was made very warm indeed.

Of course Elder Brother can't die, luckily for him. Or perhaps not so luckily. He's still alive even now, after everything he's been through. It's true that people don't see him much anymore, but sometimes when you're driving your car and you press hard on the accelerator, you might hear a knocking, rattling sound down deep in the bowels of the machine. That's Elder Brother, trying to get your attention, begging you to let him out.

— *"The 'Oka Crisis'"* —
Gord Hill

Gord Hill is a member of the Kwakwaka'wakw nation, with Tlingit and Scottish ancestry. He has been involved in Indigenous, anti-colonial, and anti-capitalist social movements since his early years in Vancouver's punk scene. In the Preface to *The 500 Years
of Resistance Comic Book*, he writes: "Above all, I consider myself a warrior—one who
defends his people and territory" (5). Since 1988, he has participated in and written about many protests, occupations, and blockades. To date he has produced two
graphic novels: *The Anti-Capitalist Resistance* (2012) and *The 500 Years of Resistance*
(2010).

In *The 500 Years of Resistance*, through the medium of the comic book, Hill
strongly refutes what he calls the "false history" that too often is taught in the educational system. In many mainstream accounts, he argues, "our ancestors' resistance is
minimized, at best, or erased entirely" (5). While Hill directly illustrates the violence,
death, and destruction inflicted upon Indigenous communities by English, French,
and Spanish colonizers across present-day South America, Mexico, the United States,
and Canada, his aim is to focus his readers' attention on how Indigenous peoples have
always resisted colonialism. Within a brief sixty pages, Hill presents approximately 514
years of Indigenous history, with each major event being composed of anywhere from
two to ten pages, using precise and minimalist language and imagery. *The 500 Years
of Resistance* is a foundational contribution to Indigenous resurgence and an essential
counter-narrative to revisionist Western history. When reading and looking at this
excerpt from the comic book, which focuses on the "Oka Crisis" of 1990 (also known
as the standoff at Kanehsatake), think about how Hill uses the graphic novel form
to tell this particular story. How does a comic book disseminate history differently
than other media and what audiences does it reach? How do you think Hill's comics
supplement his work as an activist?

Figure 2.1 Gord Hill, "The 'Oka Crisis,'" from *The 500 Years of Resistance Comic Book.* (*Credit:* Gord Hill and Arsenal Pulp Press)

Figure 2.2   Gord Hill, "The 'Oka Crisis,'" from *The 500 Years of Resistance Comic Book.* (*Credit*: Gord Hill and Arsenal Pulp Press)

Figure 2.3   Gord Hill, "The 'Oka Crisis,'" from *The 500 Years of Resistance Comic Book.* (*Credit:* Gord Hill and Arsenal Pulp Press)

Figure 2.4 Gord Hill, "The 'Oka Crisis,'" from *The 500 Years of Resistance Comic Book.* (*Credit:* Gord Hill and Arsenal Pulp Press)

⟶ *Goodbye, Snauq* ⟵
Lee Maracle

Lee Maracle is a celebrated writer, poet, educator, storyteller, and performing artist. Among her best-known works, which span the genres of fiction, poetry, life narratives, short stories, and critical theory, are *Sojourner's Truth and Other Stories* (1990), *Oratory: Coming to Theory* (1990), *Ravensong* (1993), *I Am Woman: A Native Perspective on Sociology and Feminism* (1996), and *Celia's Song* (2014). She is a member of the Stó:lō Nation of British Columbia and a descendant of Mary Agnes Joe Capilano, known as the Princess of Peace of Capilano Reserve. Maracle has held numerous distinguished academic posts, including the Stanley Knowles Visiting Professor in Canadian Studies at the University of Waterloo, the Distinguished Professor of Canadian Culture at Western Washington University, Writer in Residence at the University of Guelph, and instructor at the University of Toronto.

In "Goodbye, Snauq," Maracle blends fact, fiction, history, and politics to make the story of the village site, Snauq, now known as False Creek in Vancouver, British Columbia, come alive for readers. Maracle's main character is a descendant of Squamish peoples, married into a Stó:lō community, and a graduate student studying Indigenous governance. As the woman mourns the loss of an important traditional gathering site, Snauq, to the Canadian government, she recalls the history of the place and her older relative, Khahtsahlano. It is important for readers to recognize the complex history and context of the land at stake in "Goodbye, Snauq." First, although the several First Nations who shared Snauq never legally ceded their land to the British Crown, the Squamish Nation now has no choice but to extinguish their claim for a monetary settlement. This means that, even though the court recognized their title to the land, continuing to occupy and use the land is not an option. Furthermore, as Maracle herself notes, Snauq is also part of the Musqueam and Tsleil Watuth nations' traditional territory; however, the Canadian courts recognize only the Squamish Nation as having title. This story is a good reminder that additional historical and political research not only enriches the reading of story, but also often is required in order to understand fully the subtleties involved.

Maracle's writing offers many avenues for thinking about and exploring issues related to land, story, and Indigenous stories. For example, this short story was one of the first publications to tell the Squamish history of the place known today as False Creek. Is this an unusual role for a fiction writer to take on? What benefits are there to reading history in the form of a short story? What is the role of both oral and written storytelling in preserving Indigenous claims to the land in this short story?

AUTHOR'S NOTE

Before 1800, "Downriver Halkomelem"-speaking peoples, my ancestors, inhabited the city of Vancouver. By 1812, the Halkomelem had endured three epidemics caught as a result of the east-west and north-south Indigenous trade routes. At that time, the Halkomelem were part of a group of five friendly tribes (according to court records in the case of *Mathias vs. the Queen*). Following the epidemics the Tsleil Watuth or Downriver Halkomelem were reduced to forty-one souls and invited the Squamish to occupy the Burrard Inlet. They did so. One group led by Khahtsahlanogh, from Lil'wat, occupied what is now False Creek. False Creek or Snauq (meaning sandbar), known to all the neighbouring friendly tribes as the "supermarket of the nation," became a reserve some fifty years after white settlement began. It was sold between 1913 and 1916, and Khahtsahlano, the son of Khahtsahlanogh, and his remaining members were forced to move. This sale was declared illegal in a court case at the turn of the millennium. Although the Tsleil Watuth and the Musqueam originally shared the territory, the courts ruled that the Squamish, because they were the only ones to permanently occupy the village, "owned" it. I am related to Khahtsahlano and the Tsleil Watuth people, and I had always wanted to write the story of Khahtsahlano. He was still alive when I was a child and was much respected by the Squamish, Musqueam, and Tsleil Watuth people as one of the founders of the Allied Tribes of B.C., a group that sought redress for the illegal land grabs by British Columbia in the decades following Confederation. There is still an unresolved ongoing court case involving the Canadian Pacific Railway station at Terminal Avenue and Main Street in False Creek and the Squamish Band.

Researching this story has been both painful and enlightening. For one thing, the formerly friendly tribes that once shared the territory are not quite so friendly with one another today. The Tsleil Watuth and the Musqueam sued the Squamish Band Council, all three claiming ownership of Snauq, and the Tsleil Watuth and the Musqueam lost. The case has convinced me that Canada must face its history through the eyes of those who have been excluded and disadvantaged as a result of it. Severely weakened by epidemic after epidemic and legally excluded from land purchases in the new nation of Canada, the First Nations peoples have had to make desperate and unfair decisions to assure their survival. The forfeiture of the right to Snauq is, hopefully, the last desperate measure we will need to take before we can be assured of our survival in Canada.

"GOODBYE, SNAUQ"

Raven has never left this place, but sometimes it feels like she has been neg-ligent, maybe even a little dense. Raven shaped us; we are built for trans-formation. Our stories prepare us for it. Find freedom in the context you inherit—every context is different: discover consequences and change from within, that is the challenge. Still, there is horror in having had change foisted upon you from outside. Raven did not prepare us for the past 150 years. She must have fallen asleep some time around the first smallpox epidemic, when the Tsleil Watuth Nation nearly perished, and I am not sure she ever woke up.

The halls of this institution are empty. The bright white fluorescent bulbs that dot the ceiling are hidden behind great long light fixtures dimming its length. Not unlike the dimness of a longhouse, but it doesn't feel the same. The dimness of the hallway isn't brightened by a fire in the centre nor warmed by the smell of cedar all around you. There are no electric lights in the longhouse, and so the dimness is natural. The presence of lights coupled with dimness makes the place seem eerie. I trudge down the dim hallway; my small hands clutch a bright white envelope. Generally, letters from "the Queen in right of Canada" are threateningly ensconced in brown envelopes, but this is from a new government—my own government, the Squamish First Nation govern-ment. Its colour is an irony. I received it yesterday, broke into a sweat and a bottle of white wine within five minutes of its receipt. It didn't help. I already knew the contents even before Canada Post managed to deliver it; Canadian mail is notoriously slow. The television and radio stations were so full of the news that there was no doubt in my mind that this was my government's offi-cial letter informing me that "a deal had been brokered." The Squamish Nation had won the Snauq lawsuit and surrendered any further claim for a fee. The numbers are staggering: $92 million. That is more than triple our total GNP, wages and businesses combined.

As I lay in my wine-soaked state, I thought about the future of the Squa-mish Nation: development dollars, cultural dollars, maybe even language dol-lars, healing dollars. I had no right to feel this depressed, to want to be this intoxicated, to want to remove myself from this decision, this moment, or this world. I had no right to want to curse the century in which I was born, the political times in which I live, and certainly I had no right to hate the decision makers, my elected officials, for having brokered the deal. In fact, until we vote on it, until we ratify it, it is a deal only in theory. While the wine sloshed its way through the veins in my body to the blood in my brain, pictures of Snauq rolled about. Snauq is now called False Creek. When the Squamish moved there to be closer to the colonial centre, the water was deeper and stretched from the sea to what is now Clark Drive in the east; it covered the current streets from

Second Avenue in the south to just below Dunsmuir in the north. There was a sandbar in the middle of it, hence the name Snauq.

I lay on my couch, Russell Wallace's CD *Tso'kam* blaring in the background—Christ, our songs are sad, even the happy ones. Tears rolled down my face. I joined the ranks of ancestors I was trying not to think about. Wine-soaked and howling out old Hank Williams crying songs, laughing in between, tears sloshing across the laughter lines. The '50s. My Ta'ah intervened. Eyes narrowed, she ended the party, cleared out the house, sending all those who had had a little too much to drink home. She confiscated keys from those who were drunk, making sure only the sober drove the block to the reserve. "None of my children are going to get pinched and end up in hoosegow."

My brain, addled with the memory, pulled up another drunken soirée, maybe the first one. A group of men gathered around a whisky keg, their children raped by settlers: they drank until they perished. It was our first run at suicide, and I wondered what inspired their descendants to want to participate in the new society in any way, shape, or form. "Find freedom in the context you inherit." From the shadows Khahtsahlano emerged, eyes dead blind and yet still twinkling, calling out, "Sweetheart, they were so hungry, so thirsty that they drank up almost the whole of Snauq with their dredging machines. They built mills at Yaletown and piled up garbage at the edges of our old supermarket—Snauq. False Creek was so dirty that eventually even the white mans became concerned." I have seen archival pictures of it. They dumped barrels of toxic chemical waste from sawmills, food waste from restaurants, taverns, and tea houses; thousands of metric tons of human sewage joined the other waste daily.

I was drunk. Drunk enough to apologize for my nation, so much good can come of this … So why the need for wine to stem the rage?

"The magic of the white man is that he can change everything, everywhere. He even changed the food we eat." Khahtsahlano faced False Creek from the edge of Burrard Inlet, holding his white cane delicately in his hand as he spoke to me. The inlet was almost a mile across at that time, but the dredging and draining of the water shrank it. Even after he died in 1967, the dredging and altering of our homeland was not over. The shoreline is gone; in its place are industries squatting where the sea once was. Lonsdale quay juts out into the tide and elsewhere cemented and land-filled structures occupy the inlet. The sea asparagus that grew in the sand along the shore is gone. There is no more of the camas we once ate. All the berries, medicines, and wild foods are gone. "The womans took of the food," he said. And now we go to schools like this one and then go to work in other schools, businesses, in band offices or anyplace that we can, so we can purchase food in modern supermarkets.

Khahtsahlano was about to say something else. "Go away," I hollered at his picture, and suddenly I was sober.

Snauq is in Musqueam territory, it occurred to me, just across the inlet from Tsleil Watuth, but the Squamish were the only ones to occupy it year-round—some say as early as 1821, others 1824, still others peg the date as somewhere around the 1850s. Before that it was a common garden shared by all the friendly tribes in the area. The fish swam there, taking a breather from their ocean playgrounds, ducks gathered, women cultivated camas fields and berries abounded. On the sandbar, Musqueam, Tsleil Watuth, and Squamish women tilled the oyster and clam beds to encourage reproduction. Wild cabbage, mushrooms, and other plants were tilled and hoed as well. Summer after summer the nations gathered to harvest, probably to plan marriages, play a few rounds of that old gambling game *lahal*.

Not long after the first smallpox epidemic all but decimated the Tsleil Watuth people, the Squamish people came down from their river homes where the snow fell deep all winter to establish a permanent home at False Creek. Chief George—Chipkaym—built the big longhouse. Khahtsahlanogh was a young man then. His son, Khahtsahlano, was born there. Khahtsahlano grew up and married Swanamia there. Their children were born there.

"Only three duffles' worth," the skipper of the barge was shouting at the villagers. Swanamia did her best to choke back the tears, fingering each garment, weighing its value, remembering the use of each, and choosing which one to bring and which to leave. Each spoon, handles lovingly carved by Khahtsahlano, each bowl, basket, and bent box had to be evaluated for size and affection. Each one required a decision. Her mind watched her husband's hand sharpening his adze, carving the tops of each piece of cutlery, every bowl and box. She remembered gathering cedar roots, pounding them for hours and weaving each basket. Then she decided to fill as many baskets as the duffles could hold and leave the rest.

Swanamia faced Burrard Inlet—she could not bear to look back. Her son winced. Khahtsahlano sat straight up. Several of the women suppressed a gasp as they looked back to see that Snauq's longhouses were on fire. The men who set the fires were cheering. Plumes of smoke affirmed that the settlers who kept coming in droves had crowded the Squamish out. This is an immigrant country. Over the next ten days the men stumbled about the Squamish reserve on the north shore, building homes and suppressing a terrible urge to return to Snauq to see the charred remains. Swanamia watched as the men in her house fought for an acceptable response. Some private part of her knew they wanted to grieve, but there is no ceremony to grieve the loss of a village. She had no reference post for this new world where the interests of the immigrants took precedence over the interests of Indigenous residents. She had no way to understand that the new people's right to declare us non-citizens unless we disenfranchised our right to be Squamish was inviolable. The burning of Snauq touched off a history of disentitlement and prohibition that was incomprehensible and impossible for Swanamia to manage.

We tried, though. From Snauq to Whidbey Island and Vancouver Island, from Port Angeles to Seattle, the Squamish along with the Lummi of Washington State operated a ferry system until the Black Ball ferry lines bought it out in the 1930s.

Khahtsahlano's head cocked to one side and he gave his wife a look that said, "No problem, we will think of something," as the barge carried them out to sea. We were reserved and declared immigrants, children in the eyes of the law, wards of the government to be treated the same as the infirm or the insane. Khahtsahlano determined to fight this insult. It consumed his life. We could not gain citizenship or manage our own affairs unless we relinquished who we were: Squamish, Tsleil Watuth, Musqueam, Cree, or whatever nation we came from. Some of us did disenfranchise. But most of us stayed, stubbornly clinging to our original identity, fighting to participate in the new social order as Squamish.

Khahtsahlano struggled to find ways for us to participate. In 1905, he and a group of stalwart men marched all over the province of British Columbia to create the first modern organization of Aboriginal people. The Allied Tribes mastered colonial law despite prohibition and land rights to secure and protect their position in this country. He familiarized himself with the colonial relations that Britain had with other countries. He was a serious rememberer who paid attention to the oracy of his past, the changing present, and the possibility of a future story. He stands there in this old photo just a little bent, his eyes exhibiting an endless sadness, handsomely dressed in the finest clothes Swanamia had made for him. A deep hope lingers underneath the sadness, softening the melancholy. In the photograph marking their departure, his son stands in front of him, straight-backed, shoulders squared with that little frown of sweet trepidation on his face, the same frown my sister wears when she is afraid and trying to find her courage. Khahtsahlano and his son faced the future with the same grim determination that the Squamish Nation Band Council now deploys.

The wine grabbed reality, slopped it back and forth across the swaying room that blurred, and my wanders through Snauq were over for another day.

The hallways intervene again; I head for my office, cubby really. I am a TA bucking for my master's degree. This is a prestigious institution with a prestigious MA program in Indigenous government. I am not a star student, nor a profound teaching assistant. Not much about me seems memorable. I pursue course after course. I comply day after day with research requirements, course requirements, marking requirements, and the odd seminar requirement, but nothing that I do, say, or write seems relevant. I feel absurdly obedient. The result of all this study seems oddly mundane. Did Khahtsahlano ever feel mundane as he trudged about speaking to one family head, then another, talking up the Allied Tribes with Andy Paull? Not likely; at the time he consciously opposed colonial authority. He too studied this new world but with a singular purpose in mind: recreating freedom in the context that I was to inherit. Maybe, while he spoke to his little sweetheart, enumerating each significant non-existent landmark, vegetable patch, berry field, elk warren, duck pond, and fish habitat that had been destroyed by the newcomers, he felt this way. To what end did he tell an eight-year-old of a past bounty that can never again be regained?

Opening the envelope begins to take on the sensation of treasonous behaviour. I set it aside and wonder about the coursework I chose during my school years. I am Squamish, descended from Squamish chieftains—no, that is only partly true. I am descended from chieftains and I have plenty of Squamish relatives, but I married a Sto:loh, so really I am Sto:loh. Identity can be so confusing. For a long time the Tsleil Watuth spoke mainly Squamish—somehow they were considered part of the Squamish Band, despite the fact that they never did amalgamate. It turns out they spoke "Downriver Halkomelem" before the first smallpox killed them, and later many began speaking Squamish. Some have gone back to speaking Halkomelem while others still speak Squamish. I am not sure who we really are collectively and I wonder why I did not choose to study this territory, its history, and the identity changes that this history has wrought on us all. The office closes in on me. The walls crawl toward me, slow and easy, crowding me; I want to run, to reach for another bottle of wine, but this here is the university and I must prepare for class—and there is no wine here, no false relief. I have only my wit, my will, and my sober nightmare. I look up: the same picture of Khahtsahlano and his son that adorns my office wall hangs in my living room at home. I must be obsessed with him. Why have I not noticed this obsession before?

I love this photo of him. I fell in love with the jackets of the two men, so much so that I learned to weave. I wanted to replicate that jacket. Khahtsahlano's jacket was among the first to be made from sheep's wool. His father's was made of dog and mountain goat hair. Coast Salish women bred a beautiful dog with long and curly hair for this purpose. Every summer the mountain goats left their hillside homes to shed their fur on the lowlands of what is now to be the Sea to Sky Highway. They rubbed their bodies against long thorns, and all the women had to do was collect it, spin the dog and goat together, and weave the clothes. The settlers shot dogs and goats until our dogs were extinct and the goats were an endangered species. The object: force the Natives to purchase

Hudson's Bay sheep's wool blankets. The northerners switched to the black and red Hudson's Bay blankets, but we carried on with our weaving, using sheep's wool for a time; then when cash was scarce we shopped at local second-hand shops or we went without. Swanamia put a lot of love into those jackets. She took the time to trim them with fur, feathers, shells, and fringe. She loved those two men. Some of the women took to knitting the Cowichan sweaters so popular among non-Indigenous people, but I could not choose knitting over weaving. I fell in love with the zigzag weft, the lightning strikes of those jackets, and for a time got lost in the process of weaving until my back gave out.

The injury inspired me to return to school to attend this university and to leave North Van. I took this old archive photo—photocopy, really—with me. Every now and then I speak to Khahtsahlano, promise him I will return.

My class tutorial is about current events. I must read the letter—keep abreast of new events—and prepare to teach. I detach, open, and read the notice of the agreement. I am informed that this information is a courtesy; being Sto:loh, I have no real claim to the agreement, but because ancestry is so important, all descendants of False Creek are hereby informed....

I look at the students and remember: this memory is for Chief George, Chief Khahtsahlano, and my Ta'ah, who never stopped dreaming of Snauq.

Song rolled out as the women picked berries near what is now John Hendry Park. In between songs they told old stories, many risqué and hilarious. Laughter punctuated the air; beside them were the biggest trees in the world, sixteen feet in diameter and averaging four hundred feet in height. Other women at Snauq tended the drying racks and smoke shacks in the village. Inside them clams, sturgeons, oolichans, sockeye, spring salmon were being cured for winter stock. Men from Squamish, Musqueam, and Tsleil Watuth joined the men at Snauq to hunt and trap ducks, geese, grouse, deer, and elk. Elk is the prettiest of all red meats. You have to see it roasted and thinly sliced to appreciate its beauty and the taste—the taste is extraordinary. The camas fields bloomed bounteous at Snauq, and every spring the women culled the white ones in favour of the blue and hoed them. Children clutched at their long woven skirts. There is no difference between a white camas and a blue, except that the blue flowers are so much more gorgeous. It is the kind of blue that adorns the sky when it teases just before a good rain. Khahtsahlano's father, Khahtsahlanogh, remembered those trees. On days when he carved out a new spoon, box, or bowl, he would stare sadly at the empty forest and resent the new houses in its place. Chief George, sweet and gentle Chief George—Chipkaym—chose Snauq for its proximity to the mills and because he was no stranger to the place.

By 1907, the end of Chief George's life, the trees had fallen, the villagers at Lumberman's Arch were dead, and the settlers had transformed the Snauq supermarket into a garbage dump. The newcomers were so strange. On the one hand, they erected sawmills that in disciplined and orderly fashion transformed trees into boards for the world market quickly, efficiently, and impressively. On the other hand, they threw things away in massive quantities. The Squamish came to watch. Many like Paddy George bought teams of horses and culled timber from the backwoods like the white man—well, not exactly like them; Paddy could not bring himself to kill the young ones. "Space logging," they call it now. But still some managed to eke out a living. Despite all the prohibition laws they found some freedom in the context they inherited.

"The settlers were a dry riverbed possessing a thirst that was never slaked." A film of tears filled Khahtsahlano's eyes and his voice softened as he spoke. "After the trees came down, houses went up, more mills, hotels, shantytowns until we were vastly outnumbered and pressured to leave. B.C. was so white then. So many places were forbidden to Indians, dogs, Blacks, Jews, and Chinamans." At one time Khahtsahlano could remember the names of the men that came, first a hundred, then a thousand; after that he stopped wanting to know who they were. "They were a strange lot—most of the men never brought womans to this place. The Yaletown men were CPR men, drifters, and squatters on the north shore of the creek. They helped drain one third of it, so that the railroad—the CPR—could build a station, but they didn't bring womans," he said as he stared longingly across the inlet at his beloved Snauq.

The students lean on their desks, barely awake. Almost half of them are First Nations. I call myself to attention: I have totally lost my professional distance from the subject; my discipline, my pretension to objectivity writhes on the floor in front of me and I realize we are not the same people any more. I am not in a longhouse. I am not a speaker. I am a TA in a western institution. Suddenly the fluorescent lights offend, the dry perfect room temperature insults, and the very space mocks. A wave of pain passes through me, and I nearly lunge forward fighting it. Get a grip. This is what you wanted. Get a grip. This is what you slogged through tons of insulting documents for: Superintendent of Indian Affairs, Melville … alternatives to solve the Indian problem, assassination, enslavement … disease, integration, boarding school, removal … I am staggering under my own weight. My eyes bulge, my muscles pulse, my saliva trickles out the side of my mouth. I am not like Khahtsahlano. I am not like Ta'ah. I was brought up in the same tradition of change, of love of transformation, of appreciation for what is new, but I was not there when Snauq was a garden. Now it is a series of bridge ramparts, an emptied False Creek, emptied of Squamish people and occupied by industry, apartment dwellings, the Granville Island tourist centre, and the Science centre. I was not there when Squamish men formed unions like white men, built mills like white men, worked like white men, and finally—unlike white men—were outlawed from full participation. I can't bear all this reality. I am soft like George but without whatever sweet thread of hope wove its way through his body to form some steely fabric.

I awake surrounded by my students, their tears drip onto my cheeks. Oh my Gawd, they love me.

"It's OK, I just fainted."

"You were saying you were not like Khahtsahlano, like Ta'ah. Who are are they?" The room opens up; the walls stop threatening. I know how Moses must have felt when he watched the sea part, the relief palpable, measurable, sweet, and welcome.

"That's just it. I thought I knew who I was. I know the dates. I know the events, but I don't know who they were, and I can't know who I am without knowing who they were, and I can't say goodbye to Snauq and I need to say goodbye. Oh Gawd, help me."

"Well, I am not real sure that clears things up," Terese responds, her blond hair hanging close to my face. Some of the students look like they want to laugh: a couple of First Nations students go ahead and chuckle.

"Snauq is a village we just forfeited any claim to, and I must say goodbye."

"Doesn't that require some sort of ceremony?" Hilda asks. She is Nu'chalnuth, and although they are a different nation from mine, the ceremonial requirements are close.

"Yes," I answer.

"This is a cultural class—shouldn't we go with you?"

They lift me so tenderly I feel like a saint. This is the beginning of something. I need to know what is ending so that I can appreciate and identify with the beginning. Their apathetic stares have been replaced by a deep concern. Their apathy must have been a mask, a mask of professionalism, a mask covering fear, a mask to hide whatever dangers lurk in learning about the horrors of colonialism. The students must face themselves. I am their teacher. The goal of every adult among us is to face ourselves—our greatest enemy. I am responsible as their teacher to help them do that, but I am ill equipped. Still, Hilda is right. This is a cultural class and they ought to be there when I say goodbye. In some incomprehensible way it feels as though their presence would somehow ease the forfeiture and make it right.

I reconjure the stretch of trees to the west and south of Snauq for the class, the wind whispering songs of future to the residents. The Oblates arrived singing Gregorian chants of false promise. The millwrights arrived singing chants of profit and we bit, hook, line, and sinker. How could we anticipate that we would be excluded if our success exceeded the success of the white man? How could we know that they came homeless, poor, unsafe, and unprotected? Yaletowners accepted their designation as "squatters." This struck the Squamish at first as incredible. Chief George had no way of understanding squatting. It took some time for the younger men like Khahtsahlano to explain to Chief George the concept of "ownership" of the white man, the laws governing ownership, the business of property. Sometimes he resorted to English because the language did not suffice. "B.C. is Indian land, but the government regarded Snauq citizens as squatters until a reserve was established." Andy Paull explained the law, its hypocrisy, and its strangeness to old Chief George. "Not all white man were granted land and not all were granted the same amounts. But those who did purchase or receive land grants were white. The minimum land grant to white men during pre-emption was three hundred acres; for us, it was a maximum of ten acres per family."

"What has this got to do with Snauq and, more important, with this class?" someone asks. I have been speaking aloud.

"There is so much more to history than meets the eye. We need to know what happened, and what happened has nothing to do with the dates, the events, and the gentlemen involved, it has to do with impact." A sole student, eyes lifted slightly skyward, lips pursed innocent and inviting, strokes my arm.

They all pull their seats forward. "We need to finish this story." They nod, as if for the first time they seem to know what's going on. Even the white students nod, affirming that they too understand.

As I get ready to head for the ferry terminal, it dawns on me that no one in this country has to deal with ancestry in quite the way we must. The new immigrants of today come from independent countries, some wealthy, some poor, but all but a few have risen from under the yoke of colonialism. They have nations as origins. Their home countries belong to the United Nations or NATO or other such international organizations. We do not, and this court case indicates we never will. The United Nations is debating an "Indigenous right to self-government" declaration, but Indigenous people will never be able to acquire the place other nations hold. Canadians have to face that they are still classically colonized, that because settlement is a *fait accompli*, we can only negotiate the best real estate deal possible. Indigenous people must face this, while the eyes of our ancestors, who fought against colonial conquest and lost, glare down upon us.

"This is an immigrant nation," Prime Minister Chrétien said after the twin towers of the World Trade Center in New York were felled. "We will continue to be an immigrant nation." How do we deal with this, the non-immigrants who for more than a century were rendered foreigners, prohibited from participation? The money for Snauq will be put in trust. To access it, we must submit a plan of how we intend to spend it. The Squamish Nation gets to pick the trustees but, like our ancestors, we must have trustees independent of the nation. Our money is still one step removed from our control.

This story is somehow connected to another story, more important than the one going on now. Surrender or dig up the hatchet. The Squamish Nation has chosen surrender. Which way will my journey take me? Do I dare remember Snauq as a Squamish, Musqueam, Tsleil Watuth supermarket? Do I dare desire the restoration of the grand trees to the left and in the rear of Snauq? Do I dare say goodbye?

The ferry lunges from the berth. Students surround me. We are on a mission. We travel to Snauq, False Creek, and Vancouver to say goodbye. In one sense I have no choice; in another, I chose the people who made the deal. In our own cultural sensibility there is no choice. There are fifteen thousand non-Indigenous people living at Snauq, and we have never granted ourselves the right to remove people from their homes. We must say goodbye.

In this goodbye we will remember Snauq before the draining of False Creek. We will honour the dead: the stanchions of fir, spruce, and cedar and the gardens of Snauq. We will dream of the new False Creek, the dry lands, the new parks, and the acres of grass and houses. We will accept what Granville Island has become and honour Patty Rivard, the First Nations woman who was the first to forge a successful business in the heart of it. We will struggle to appreciate the little ferries that cross the creek. We will salute Chief George— Chipkaym—and Khahtsahlanogh, who embraced the vision of this burgeoning new nation. I will pray for my personal inability to fully commit to that vision.

The wind catches the tobacco as it floats to the water, lifts it, and as we watch it float, a lone Chinese woman crosses in front and smiles. I smile too. Li Ka Shing, a multibillionaire, rose as the owner and developer of False Creek. He is Chinese, and he didn't live here when he bought it. I don't know if he lives here now, but for whatever reason I love the sound of his name. "Everything begins with song," Ta'ah says. His name is a song. It rolls off the tongue, sweetens the palate before the sound hits the air. It is such an irony that the first "non-citizen immigrant residents" should now possess the power to determine the destiny of our beloved Snauq. I know it shouldn't, but somehow it makes me happy, like knowing that Black Indians now people the Long Island Reservation in New York State.

The Chinese were subjected to a head tax for decades. Until sixty years ago they were banned from living outside Chinatown, though I met Garrick Chu's mother, who grew up at the Musqueam Reserve. Their economic activity was restricted to laundry businesses and tea houses. Once white men burned Chinatown to the ground. For decades Chinese men could not bring their families from China to Canada. Periodic riots in the previous century killed some of them and terrorized all of them. Underneath some parts of Chinatown they built underground tunnels to hide in as protection against marauding white citizens, who were never punished for killing Chinese. Like the Squamish, they endured quietly until assuming citizenship in 1948. For one of them to become the owner of this choice piece of real estate is sweet irony. "It was sold for a song by Premier Vander Zalm," the court records read. That too is a piece of painful, yet poetic, justice. I want to attend the Chinese parade, celebrate Chinese New Year, not for Li Ka Shing but because one of life's ironies has given me hope. Five thousand miles from here, a group of Mi'kmaq bought land in Newfoundland and gained reservation rights. Another irony. They thought they had killed them all, and 350 years later, there they were, purchasing the land and setting up a reservation. There is hope in irony.

I am not through with Canada. I am not a partner in its construction, but neither am I its enemy. Canada has opened the door. Indigenous people are no longer "immigrants" to be disenfranchised, forbidden, prohibited, outlawed, or precluded from the protective laws of this country. But we are a long way from being participants. I am not eager to be a part of an environmentally offensive society that can preach "Thou shalt not kill" and then make war on people, plants, and animals to protect and advance financial gain. The hypocrisy marring Canada's behaviour toward us is still evident, but it struggles for maturity, and while it struggles for maturity I accord myself a place. This place is still at the bottom, as the last people to be afforded a place at the banquet table where the guests have been partaking for over five hundred years; but still there it is, the chair empty and hoping I will feel inclined to sit in it. The invitation is fraught with difficulties. Although today I must say goodbye, tomorrow I may just buy one of the townhouses slated for completion in 2010. Today I am entitled to dream. Khahtsahlano dreamed of being buried at Snauq. I dream of living there.

We move to the unfinished longhouse at the centre of Granville Island, a ragged group of students and their teacher. I break into song: Chief Dan George's prayer song. "Goodbye, Snauq," I boom out in as big a voice as I can muster. The passing crowd jerks to a split-second halt, gives us a bewildered glance, frowns, sidesteps us, and then moves on. The students laugh.

"Indians really will laugh at anything," I say as the tears stream across my face. The sun shines bright and turns the sky camas blue as we drift toward the Co-op restaurant to eat.

CHAPTER 3

"REINVENTING THE ENEMY'S LANGUAGE"

Sixto Canul, "The Son Who Came Back from the United States"

Gloria Anzaldúa, "Ghost Trap"

Joel Torres Sánchez, "I'm Not a Witch, I'm a Healer!"

Diane Glancy, "Aunt Parnetta's Electric Blisters"

Jeannette Armstrong, "Land Speaking"

THE STORIES IN THIS CHAPTER explore the distinct values and knowledges contained within Indigenous languages. Marlene Brant Castellano (Mohawk) calls language "the code for interpreting reality" (101) and Marie Battiste (Mi'kmaw) argues that language is an essential tool for "recovering the kinds of knowledges that come from within a culture" (qtd. in Coleman et al. 148). For example, in the original version of Joel Torres Sánchez's "I'm Not a Witch, I'm a Healer!," the author describes spiritual power with the Purépecha word "jurhenani." In the notes following the story, the translator writes that jurhenani means "to prepare oneself into knowledge." However, in the English translation, the word "jurhenani" is replaced with "gift." What does the disjuncture between "knowledge" and "gift" suggest about the imperfect process of translation, as well as the differences between the two languages?

In the following works, the authors have used language to craft meaning in their stories in many ways. Not only are they making intentional word choices to influence the tone, mood, and shape of their narratives, but they are also alternating between Indigenous languages and various forms of English in order to assert the validity and beauty of Indigenous languages, accents, and mother tongues. For example, Gloria Anzaldúa in "Ghost Trap" switches back and forth between English and Spanish languages. Some stories, like Diane Glancy's "Aunt Parnetta's Electric Blisters," are primarily written in English. In a conversation with her husband Filo about a broken refrigerator, Aunt Parnetta comments: "Weld, dernd … Could have goned longer til the frost cobered us" (137). In these sentences, Glancy uses a heavily accented English that not only plays with grammar rules but also, by extension, challenges the idea that standard English is the only "correct" way to speak or write. Switching between languages, or between different "Englishes," is called "code-switching" and suggests that different languages hold different ideas, cultural values, and specific knowledge that are worthwhile to stay connected to.

In fact, Okanagan author Jeannette Armstrong argues that a writer can resist the imperial force of English by writing Indigenous accents into their narrative texts—whether in an Indigenous language like her mother tongue, N'silxchn, or in English that is influenced by her first language. "I believe Rez English from any part of the country, if examined, will display the sound and syntax patterns of the Indigenous language of the area," writes Armstrong, "and subsequently the sounds that the landscape speaks" ("Land" 154). She uses the example of the rigidity of sequential time within the grammar of English that affects the conjugation of verbs based on tense. In contrast, storytellers on her territory insist on the fluidity of time, suggesting that the story they share might have happened in some past time while concurrently happening in the present and even the future.

⌐ *The Son Who Came Back from the United States* ⌐
Sixto Canul

Maya storyteller Sixto Canul was born in 1948 in the village of Xocén. He completed only a few years of primary school and worked most of his life as a maize grower. Along with several other maize workers, he was interviewed by the anthropologists Silvia Terán and Christian H. Rasmussen, who were conducting a study of traditional agriculture in maize fields. In response to Terán and Rasmussen's questions the workers often told stories and myths. It was not until later that Terán and Rasmussen "realized that the explanations contained in their stories and myths were indispensable to understanding the logic of the maize-field system" (Terán and Rasmussen, *Tales* 7). Terán and Rasmussen then compiled the stories into a Spanish-language collection, *Relatos del centro del mundo*, published in 1992.

The circumstances surrounding the performance, transcription, translation, compilation, and editing of the story are complex, involving numerous mediators over a period of time. According to Rasmussen and Terán, Sixto Canul told the story in Maya intermixed with Spanish, in the village of Xocén near Valladolid during the years of 1989 and 1991 (7). Often the stories were written down quickly, in a variety of difficult conditions, as the workers went about their day. Pedro Pablo Chuc Pech then transcribed and translated the story into Spanish. The version we include here is yet another translation by Alejandra García Quintanilla, a specialist in the Maya language, who prepared the text for the English-language anthology *In the Language of Kings*, co-edited by Miguel León-Portilla, Earl Shorris, and Sylvia S. Shorris. Fittingly, the story itself is rather like a puzzle, turning upon several word plays that draw attention to both differences and the uncanny echoes between words in the Spanish, Maya, and English languages. The story explores the ties between language, culture, and identity through the story of a young man who returns to his parents after studying abroad and refuses to speak Maya. How does the father of the family explain the language his son uses? How does his mother? What values are connected to speaking Maya in this story?

A gentleman sent his son to study and work in the United States. He was a Maya who was sent there in order to help the family prosper. As the gentleman had money, he was able to send his son to work and study English.

And his son studied there. He came back home after six years.

When the boy came home, he asked his father, "What's to eat? What are you going to have?"

Well, they were going to eat eggs. And the son said, "*All right. Yes.*"[1]

"What is my son saying? Surely, he is saying that he is accustomed to eating ten eggs."

And the father went to tell the boy's mother: "You have to cook ten eggs for my son, because he just told me '*awrait diez.*'" Later he went to tell his son that the ten eggs were ready.

And the son said again, "All right, yes."

"My God! you have to go buy another ten eggs," the father said to the mother of the boy who was accustomed to eating twenty eggs, the great glutton. "Since they have a lot of money in the United States, my son eats a lot. He wants to eat ten more eggs. You must get another ten eggs, because the boy said again, '*awrait diez.*'"

"Absolutely, absolutely," and the father was wondering if the twenty eggs were ready.

But the mother was getting angry with the boy [who had not eaten the first ten eggs]: "My son doesn't want to eat? What the devil! Let's keep the ten eggs. Tell the boy to come here so that I can talk to him."

The boy came, and his mother asked him if he was hungry or not and he said again, "*Awrait, diez,*" in English.

He was only pretending to be stupid; he did not want to speak in Maya, although he really speaks it.

The mother grabbed a stick to hit her son so that he would speak Maya. Then he spoke in Maya, and he did not go back to saying, "*Awrait, diez.*"

"I know that you spoke Maya and Spanish very well when you left," she said. The mother understood that he only spoke English because he believed it showed that he comes from the United States.

⚊ *Ghost Trap* ⚊
Gloria Anzaldúa

Gloria Anzaldúa, a self-described "chicana dyke-feminist, tejana patlache poet, writer, and cultural theorist," was born to sharecropper/field-worker parents in South Texas Rio Grande Valley. When she was fourteen, her father died, and Anzaldúa was obliged to continue working in the family fields throughout high school and college. She nevertheless continued to find time for her writing, reading, and schoolwork, earning a BA from Pan American University and an MA from the University of Texas. Her best-known work is *This Bridge Called My Back: Writings by Radical Women of Color* (1987), which won the Before Columbus Foundation American Book Award and the Sappho Award of Distinction. One of the first openly lesbian Chicana writers, Anzaldúa played a major role in redefining Chicana/o, queer, feminist, and female identities, and in developing inclusionary movements for social justice. Her theories of mestizaje, the borderlands, and the new mestiza, as well as her code-switching, have had an impact far beyond the field of Chicano/a studies.

In "Ghost Trap," Anzaldúa gives us the story of Ursula la Prieta, a widow who, through her grief and loneliness, conjures the ghostly presence of her husband. In this playful work of short fiction, the author uses language incisively. As with any story, it is important to look up words you do not know as you read. Consider carefully the implications of Anzaldúa's decision to write in a mixture of English and Spanish dialects as well as her choice of specific words. For example, what do words like "chismear" or "maldecir" bring to mind about the power of language? What social and historical weight do words like "alcahueta," "prieta," or "La Llorona" carry for women? What might Anzaldúa be trying to say with her choice of words about the confluence of language, power, gender, and race?

At first Ursula la Prieta had been devastated by the death of her husband. She had thrown her plump short body into the grave on top of his coffin shrieking, "¡Ay viejito! ¿Por qué me dejaste? Yo te quería tanto. I loved you so much!" Everyone else was dry-eyed. In between sobs she heard someone say, "Hasta que se lo llevó el diablo al miserable." Another said, "Let him burn in hell." She only wept louder. For days she wailed. People felt skeptical, then uneasy at the drama and started referring to Prieta's cries as "La Llorona."

"It's not like he treated you that good," her comadre reminded her.

Often she would wake in the middle de la noche in a sweat, the echo de su grito/llanto still throbbing in her throat and feeling like the atmosphere. Her house was not the same. She would turn to him to be consoled, not that he would soothe her with a calm voice—he had only paid attention to her cuando quería algo. But she missed cushioning his skinny body and his sharp hip bones and knees. The presence de otro cuerpo had been a source of comfort in the silence of the night. Upon opening her eyes, she would find the bed empty. She would pace from room to room at night thinking about him, feeling numb and decepcionada. Gradually her loneliness soured and her grief turned into anger. Why, why, why had he deserted her? Actually his liver had deserted her. Cirrhosis.

One night, two months after his death, a snoring woke her. Se despertó to find him, or rather his ghost, in bed with her. "¡Viejo!" she cried out, astounded. She smiled for the first time since his death. She reached for him, then suddenly drew back her hand and clutched her corazón.

Durante el día he would follow her around the house, only her steps creaked the floor boards. She was amazed at just how small her house had become. He dogged her steps or hovered nearby while she hoed up and down the rows and rows of corn, squash, and beans of her immense jardín. Still, he would never go beyond the front gate when she left to do her mandados. She began to spend more time in the homes of her comadres o se iba a pasear con ellas.

"Ay, Doña Ursula, you never used to spend time chismeando with us?" said one of her comadres.

"Sí, comadrita y ahora tú eres la alcahueta."

After a couple of weeks, as they were in the living room watching T.V. she asked him "Viejo, why do you keep coming back every night? Did you forget something? Did you leave something unfinished? Is there some business you want to complete? Tell me y yo te ayudo a hacerlo. If only you'd tell me what you want."

"Vieja, prietita linda, bring me clean clothes," his voice was thin as a trail of smoke.

"Bah, estás muerto, you're dead ¿pa' qué necesitas ropa?" she whispered back. He repeated his request, his voice getting louder and louder, finally driving her to the closet. Of course his clothes were missing, she'd given them away. Now she would have to go into the shop to buy men's things and face the look of censure on the shopkeeper's face at how fast she had replaced her marido can otro pelado.

"Vieja, vieja, fix me some dinner," he said in a harsh mutter. Le guisó carnitas, his favorite dish, and set it on the table. But a ghost can't eat, so the comida sat on the table gathering moscas. "Vieja, viejita linda, tráeme una cerveza." Off she would go to la tiendita de la esquina to get the beer. La gente de la colonia began to talk about how her grief had driven her to drink. She would pull the tab and place the can of beer en la mesa by "his" chair. "You know I only drink

Tecate," he growled. But a ghost can't drink. The beer would go flat. She was tempted to drink his cerveza to alleviate her increasing irritation.

Instead, she thought of all the cositas she would make with popsicle sticks. She would give them away as gifts or sell during fiesta days. She would make altar pieces, frames to hold photos of dead ancestors. She would paint them with bright colors.

Tending to his ghost seemed to take all of her time. She began to resent the time she had spent washing and cooking and trimming his hair and toe-nails when el pelado had been alive. She realized that she missed her solitude. Hadn't he made her feel wanted and protected? Well, now his constant pres-ence stifled her. Just when she thought herself free, el pendejo was back and even more trouble than when he was alive. Her only consolation was that she didn't have to wash his smelly calcetines and dirty underwear. She had been two weeks without him. Pero su nueva vida de dos semanas sin él ya no era suya. She wanted her new life back. Yes, now that she was free of taking care of others, now that she lived alone, now that she had time to get together with las comadres things were different. Now, how was she going to stop her marido muerto from returning?

One day inspiration brought a smile to her face. She made a little model of her house with popsicle sticks and glue and placed it in a safe spot half-way between his grave in the nearby camposanto and her home. One of her comadres had told her that ghosts have no sense of perspective. Her chair creaked on the porch as she waited and rocked, hoping el espanto would enter the model house thinking it was hers.

That night nothing woke her. In the morning cuando despertó she turned towards the side where su viejo had been sleeping the past thirty years. His ghost was not there, nor was it there the following night. While she didn't want it to return, she had a feeling it would come back and waited all nerviosa for it to appear. But suppose someone found la casita and accidentally opened the door and let the ghost out. Some element of nature—a strong wind or a fire—could destroy the flimsy cage and her dead husband would get out. The tiny house was too fragile to be buried—the earth would crush it and the ghost would escape. She went to where she had left la casita and barred the door with a popsicle stick. Now she had to put it somewhere safe and out of the reach of others.

After several days of deliberation, she carefully carried the ghost trap into her house and placed it under the bed where mischievous nietos would not find it.

That night a voice woke her. It called out, no longer at a whisper, "Vieja, vieja todavía estás buenísima. Ándale, déjame probar ese cuerpazo. Let me touch ese cuerpo exquisito." El pelado chiflado was back. She thought she felt his body stirring under the bedcovers. Half dreaming, half awake, she pushed him away, saying "Vete viejo aguado." But he kept climbing on top of her.

"I wish you were alive so I could wring your neck." Both were surprised by the sharpness in her voice.

"You shouldn't talk to me like that."

"Why not? You've always said mean things to me."

All night she refused to open her legs to him.

The next morning she woke with deep grooves down the corners of her mouth and bruises on her breasts, arms, and inner thighs. She peered under la cama and saw that the mattress had squished the cage, forcing the door to crack open. She walked from room to room looking for el pinche desgraciado and muttering to herself. "¡Ya me voy a deshacer de ese cabrón!" She considered going to the local curandera and asking her to drive his soul into el pozo, better yet, al infierno. Huh, or she could look through the yellow pages to find an hechicera.

Ah, no, if my loneliness has summoned him, my anger will drive him away. I'll do it myself, she said to herself. "Afuera desgraciado. Get out of here. Be gone you ghost. If you don't leave te voy a maldecir."

Just in case her words failed, she plugged in the vacuum cleaner and put it by her bed. To make it harder for his hands to reach her body, she tugged on two of her sturdiest corsets, several pairs of pants, and three shirts, turned off the lights, and got into bed. Almost immediately she jumped out of bed to fetch her heavy sartén just in case he'd taken on more substance than the vacuum could handle. But if the suction wouldn't get him maybe the noise would drive him back to the cemetery and into the other world. She hid it under las cobijas. "Come on cabrón, hijo de la chingada, vente pendejo," she said under her breath. "Viejito, viejito lindo, come into my bed. I'm waiting for you," dijo con voz de sirenita.

She saw his ghostly body edge cautiously into the room. "¿No estás enojada, viejita?" he asked softly.

"¡Apurate viejo! que te quiero dar algo."

Translations

marido, *husband*

Ay viejito ¿por qué me dejaste? Yo te quería tanto, *Why did you leave me old man? I loved you so much*

La Llorona, *the weeping woman*

decepsionada, *disillusioned, disenchanted, disappointed*

despertó, *she woke up*

viejo, *old man*

corazón, *heart*

Durante el día, *during the day*

jardín, *garden*

mandados, *errands*

comadres, *co-mothers, very good female friends*

o se iba a pasear con ellas, *or she'd go for a ride with them*

chismeando, *gossiping*

y ahora tú eres la alcahueta, *and now you're the instigator*

y yo te ayudo a hacerlo, *and I'll help you do it*

Vieja, prietita linda, *woman, sweet lady (Prietita is the diminutive of Prieta, the dark one)*

Bah, estás muerto, ¿pa' qué necesitas ropa? *Agh, you're dead. What do you need clothes for?*

marido can otro hombre, *husband with another man*

Le guisó carnitas, *She cooked him beef seasoned with spices*

comida, *food*

moscas, *flies*

traéme una cerveza, *bring me a beer*

la tiendita de la esquina, *the little corner store*

La gente, *People (began to talk)*

en la mesa, *on the table*

cositas, *small things*

el pelado, *the good-for-nothing*

el pendejo, *the stupid asshole*

calcetines, *socks*

pero su nueva vida de dos semanas sin él ya no era suya, *but her new two-week-old life without him was not hers anymore*

marido muerto, *dead husband*

camposanto, *graveyard*

el espanto, *ghost*

cuando despertó, *when she woke up*

nerviosa, *nervous*

nietos, *grandchildren*

Vieja, vieja todavía estás buenísima. Ándale, déjame probar ese cuerpazo, *You're still really hot. Come on, let me have a taste of that big, beautiful body.*

ese cuerpo exquisito, *that exquisite body*

El pelado chiflado, *the scoundrel*

Vete viejo aguado, *go, get away from me you flabby old man (one with flabby genitals, i.e., who is sexually wasted or worn out)*

la cama, *the bed*

el pinche desgraciado, *that no good son of a bitch*

Ya me voy a deshacer de ese cabrón, *I'm going to rid myself of that stubborn man*

curandera, *healer, medicine woman*

el pozo, *hole*

al infierno, *to hell*

hechicera, *female sorcerer*

afuera desgraciado, *get out you damned man*

te voy a maldecir, *I'm going to curse you*

sartén, *iron skillet*

cobijas, *bed covers*

cabrón, hijo de la chingada, vente pendejo, *go you old goat, son of a bitch, come here stupid*

viejito lindo, *sweet old man*

dijo con voz de sirenita, *she said with a siren's voice*

"¿No estás enojada, viejita?" *You aren't angry, are you, old lady?*

"¡Apúrate viejo! que te quiero dar algo." *Hurry up, old man, I want to give you something*

⊶ I'm Not a Witch, I'm a Healer! ⊷
Joel Torres Sánchez

Joel Torres Sánchez was born in San Jerónimo Purenchécuaro, Michoacán. He is a graduate of the Rural Teacher Training School in La Huerta, Michoacán, and the Autonomous University of Tlaxcala. In both his academic work and his writing, Torres Sánchez is dedicated to the teaching and spreading of his maternal language, Purépecha. Torres Sánchez's writings have appeared in various newspapers and magazines across Mexico, as well as in *P'urhepecha Uandatskuecha/Narrativa P'urehepecha* (2001). The story included here comes from Montemayor and Frischmann's anthology, *Words of the True Peoples/Palabras de los Seres Verdaderos: Anthology of Contemporary Mexican Indigenous-Language Writers* (2007).

In "I'm Not a Witch, I'm a Healer!" Torres Sánchez tells the story of Nana Delfina, a woman who transforms into a coyote each night to hunt for game for the people who live in her small town. Torres Sánchez originally wrote "I'm Not a Witch, I'm a Healer!" in Purépecha, and the story has been published elsewhere in Spanish. Translation—between languages, ideas, and cultures—is a compelling theme in this work. For example, the title points to the importance of words, and the world views attached to them, in relation to spirituality, Indigeneity, and gender. Note that in both the English and Purépecha versions, Spanish terms pepper the author's writing. Make sure to read the notes that accompany these words; you will find that many of them stem from words in Indigenous languages in Mexico, including Purépecha, Nahuatl, and Taino. In choosing these words, what might Torres Sánchez have been trying to say about language? What might he be saying about Indigenous cultures and ideas in Mexico today? What influence might they exert on Mexican culture and knowledge production?

Translated from the Purépecha language.[1]

As they worked, Delfina noticed that with each passing day her grandmother grew more and more weary; she was no longer steady on her feet; she no longer ate well; she spent a lot of time looking at her granddaughter and making numerous recommendations regarding what she should do once she had left this world.

One day her grandmother spoke to her very early and said: "I want you to bathe me. Then comb my hair and dress me in my black *nahuas*,[2] my cross-stitched *huanengo*[3] with purple flowers, my engraved sash—the one the woman from Purenchécuaro gave me—the woman who wanted to know where her son was. How happy she was when we located him! I also want to put on the apron I embroidered just as my mother taught me; and please look for the black striped *rebozo*[4] they brought me from Ahuirán."[5]

"Why do you want to dress up as if there were a fiesta?" asked Delfina.

"Because there is going to be a fiesta," answered her grandmother.

"When?" Delfina asked.

"This afternoon a high-ranking woman is going to come, and I want her to find me well dressed; she gets angry when the person she goes to visit is dirty and complaining. On the other hand, when she finds one smiling, in fresh clothing and without fear, she treats one better. That is why I want to be prepared; do you understand me?"

"Well, if that is what it is about, then I will do everything you want," Delfina responded to her grandmother.

Delfina took care of everything that her grandmother had ordered. When she was ready, she sat her in the center of her *choza*.[6] As Father Sun was about to depart, Nana[7] Simona received the visit of Lady Death, who carried away her soul, leaving upon her face a smile full of satisfaction.

She was buried the following day; and despite the ongoing dispute between "those from up above" and "those from down below,"[8] people from both groups showed up at the burial. They decided that out of gratitude for the *señora*[9] who had healed so many, it was proper that there be no fighting much less killing that day, out of respect for her memory.

In the graveyard, Delfina was virtually promoted; as they were leaving, everyone who approached to give her the "hug of consolation" added "Cha"[10] to her name, which in our language is a symbol of respect. From that day on, she became "Cha Nana Delfina."[11]

Nevertheless, the town conflict was growing, and the desire for revenge was on the rise. Nana Delfina also began to feel pressure from her husband, who admitted that he already had learned some things but wanted to know more and constantly observed her in everything she did.

Due to the scarcity of food in town, many people called on Nana Delfina to give them something to eat. They did not know how, but she always had some meat: rabbit, squirrel, mutton, and at times even deer; they appeared on her fence always in the morning, with puncture wounds on their necks.

One day her husband said that he could wait no longer: she had to share her knowledge with him. He often had seen her get up at night, leave the house wrapped in a black tunic with her hair untied, and head for a place at the foot of the hill, where she would roll about in the loose dirt. He would then see a cloud of dust rise, from which an enormous she-coyote would emerge and run off into the dark of night. The same animal would later return and leave on their fence the animals, which Delfina would begin to clean early the next day. They would eat only a little of those animals, and she would give most of the meat to the people who came begging. Her husband assured her that she need not worry: everything was fine; he just wanted to learn more, and since he was her husband she had the obligation to teach him.

Nana Delfina told him that he needed time to learn those things and that not everyone possessed the "gift";[12] those who desired to learn needed much patience and had to be able to concentrate and clear their mind. They could not be motivated by envy or the desire to harm others but only by need or the desire to help.

The husband kept on insisting until one day Nana Delfina told him she would teach him. She was not confident, however, that he would learn well because she did not see the "gift" in his eyes. She also feared he would use his newly acquired knowledge—along with the little that he already possessed—to cause harm.

Once he had promised to use what he would learn to do good, Nana Delfina began to teach him. She then realized that the man did not pay proper attention, was not steadfast, and often forgot things. Despite it all, the night arrived when they made their first trip to the hill together. Beginning that afternoon, she prepared her husband with her final suggestions; she repeated several times to him the words to pronounce in the beginning; what to do immediately following; then the words and actions he had to remember to recover his normal shape. At nightfall, when he said he was ready, they left for the place of loose earth.

Everything went well at the beginning and in collecting the animals that would provide them with meat and hide; but in the early morning something went wrong. The man could not recover his form no matter how hard he struggled, even with Nana Delfina's advice. When Señor Sun awoke, she told her husband to hide inside the house so that no one would see him, and they would await nightfall to fix the problem.

That day, more people than usual went to visit Nana Delfina; some of them were followed by their dogs, who, when they approached the place, barked and encircled the house. In a laughing tone, one person said: "What do you have hidden inside, Nana Delfina? My dog is barking and running about as if he sensed a coyote."

"It must be the animals' blood," she answered with a smile.

"And your husband?"

"Ah! He decided to go to the hill for firewood today."

Day became night, and when it reached its mid-point, the attempts began once again for the husband to recover his form; but they could not achieve their objective: neither she with her advice nor he through his struggling.

Having made an effort for several nights, they realized that they would accomplish nothing; therefore, she told him to resign himself to his fate and to go off to the hill and live his life.

Days later, when someone would ask about her husband, she would simply say that he had grown tired of being there and had gone back to his home town. But from then on, many people would see an enormous coyote in the afternoons or very early in the day. It would approach Nana Delfina's house to leave a rabbit, a squirrel, or, mistakenly, a hen that had foolishly gotten lost right in town. "How foolish!" Nana Delfina would say.

Father Time continued his journey, and with it things began to change in town. After nine years the government, "the big law" as they called it, finally decided to intervene to halt the conflict; arresting the leaders of each group imposed order. At some other time, I will tell how these truly unique events transpired. The important thing is that, little by little, the division among the people came to an end. Outsiders once again were coming to town, and merchants brought the first automobiles ever seen there. They would bring many new things; that was when we saw the first battery-powered radios. I remember how Tata[13] Nacho Ramos wanted to "kill" a radio with his pistol because it would not repeat a song it had just played. It was very difficult to make him understand that those who were singing were not inside the radio but rather in a transmitting station in Zacapu. Once he was convinced, my papá and I took him to see the radio station.

In mid-1959 work began to bring electricity to town. Once the posts were up, they began to hang the wires on them. The first men to head to the hill early one day saw something out of the ordinary. One of them went to notify the teacher who was serving as secretary of land tenure, who headed out to tend to the matter along with his ten-year-old son: me.

What we saw was astonishing indeed: stuck up among the four electric wires was Nana Delfina, whose only article of clothing consisted of pieces of an old *petate*.[14] She asked us to get her down. I was requested to step back; two of the men went to get a ladder to help her get down. Someone loaned her an overcoat; and, wrapped up in it, she headed off toward her house without saying a word. That was the first time I saw her, since she passed near where I was standing. I knew of her existence because I often had heard tell of her, but I had never seen her up close. She was elderly, and that was why my eye was drawn to her hair: very long, black, and shiny. I then approached my papá, who was talking with the men and some women who had come around. Everyone was asking each other just how, and why, she had gotten up there.

Then a very confident man said: "The thing is, Nana Delfina is much older now; she knows more; she now travels further; she goes off to other towns to see people who request favors. Now at night she turns into a *tecolote*[15] and flies everywhere. Therefore, as she was returning, she forgot they had just put up the wires and she got stuck."

A younger man, more modern, more skeptical, said: "No, the thing is that she has already lost a lot of people, and many no longer visit her; with someone's help she climbed up there so that we would think what this man just said. But I do not believe it is true that she can fly."

My papá ended the discussion: "Well, it is getting late: let us get back to our chores and later on we shall see. Let us go!"

I followed my papá while thinking and thinking. From that day on, I have not been able to find a reasonable explanation. Did she really get stuck while flying? That is hard to believe. Or did she allow someone to help her get up among the wires? That is even harder to believe; she did not possess, as we would say today, the need for publicity. It is even less likely that she would decide to climb up there naked; besides, at her age, it was difficult to endure who knows how many hours in such an uncomfortable position. Well, the truth still eludes my scant knowledge.

— *Aunt Parnetta's Electric Blisters* —
Diane Glancy

Diane Glancy is a Cherokee poet, short-story writer, playwright, essayist, and educator, born in 1941 in Kansas City, Missouri. She obtained an MA from Central State University in 1983 and an MFA from the University of Iowa in 1988, before taking a position as an assistant professor of English at Macalester College in St. Paul, Minnesota. She is known for works in which she uses realistic language and vivid imagery to address subjects such as spirituality, family ties, and her identity as a mixed-blood person. Among her most notable and critically acclaimed prose works are *Claiming Breath* (1992), *Pushing the Bear: A Novel of the Trail of Tears* (1996), *Flutie* (1999), and *Stone Heart: A Novel of Sacajawea* (2003). She has also written ten collections of poetry, many of which have won prestigious awards.

In Glancy's "Aunt Parnetta's Electric Blisters," the narrator is an elderly woman who must contend with a troublesome fridge that reminds her of the people she knows: "Filled with our own workings, not doint what we shulb" (138). Of course, the fridge is not the only thing in this short story that doesn't work how it should; the roof leaks, the truck is broken, and the words on the page certainly don't behave the way one might expect. Rife with misspellings, Cherokee words, and elusive grammar, Glancy's writing style challenges readers to reconsider whether language and narrative are "working," for whom, and whether her own writing has fixed or broken them further.

Some stories can be told only in winter
This is not one of them
because the fridge is for Parnetta
where it's always winter.

Hey chekta! All this and now the refrigerator broke. Uncle Filo scratched the long gray hairs that hung in a tattered braid on his back. All that foot stomping and fancy dancing. Old warriors still at it.

"But when did it help?" Aunt Parnetta asked. The fridge ran all through the cold winter when she could have set the milk and eggs in the snow. The fish and meat from the last hunt. The fridge had walked through the spring when she had her quilt and beading money. Now her penny jar was empty, and it was hot, and the glossy white box broke. The coffin! If Grandpa died, they could put him in it with his war ax and tomahawk. His old dog even. But how would she get a new fridge?

The repairman said he couldn't repair it. Whu chutah! Filo loaded his rifle and sent a bullet right through it. Well, he said, a man had to take revenge. Had to stand against civilization. He watched the summer sky for change as though the stars were white leaves across the hill. Would the stars fall? Would Filo have to rake them when cool weather came again? Filo coughed and scratched his shirt pocket as though something crawled deep within his breastbone. His heart maybe, if he ever found it. Aunt Parnetta stood at the sink, soaking the sheets before she washed them.

"Dern't nothin' we dude ever work?" Parnetta asked, poking the sheets with her stick.

"We bought that ferge back twenty yars," Filo told her. "And it nerked since then."

"Weld, dernd," she answered. "Could have goned longer til the frost cobered us. Culb ha' set the milk ertside. But nowd. It weren't werk that far."

"Nope," Filo commented. "It weren't."

Parnetta looked at her beadwork. Her hands flopped at her sides. She couldn't have it done for a long time. She looked at the white patent-leathery box. Big enough for the both of them. For the cow if it died.

"Set it out in the backyard with the last one we had."

They drove to Tahlequah that afternoon, Filo's truck squirting dust and pinging rocks.

They parked in front of the hardware store on Muskogee Street. The regiments of stoves, fridges, washers, dryers, stood like white soldiers. The Yellow

Hair Custer was there to command them. Little Big Horn. Whu chutah! The prices! Three hundred crackers.

"Some mord than thad," Filo surmised, his flannel shirt-collar tucked under itself, his braid sideways like a rattler on his back.

"Filo, I dern't think we shulb decide terday."

"No," the immediate answer stummed from his mouth like a roach from under the baseboard in the kitchen.

"We're just lookin'."

"Of course," said Custer.

They walked to the door leaving the stoves, washers, dryers, the televisions all blaring together, and the fridges lined up for battle.

Filo lifted his hand from the rattled truck.

"Surrender," Parnetta said. "Izend thad the way id always iz?"

The truck spurted and spattered and shook Filo and Aunt Parnetta before Filo got it backed into the street. The forward gear didn't buck as much as the backward.

When they got home, Filo took the back off the fridge and looked at the motor. It could move a load of hay up the road if it had wheels. Could freeze half the fish in the pond. The minute coils, the twisting intestines of the fridge like the hog he butchered last winter, also with a bullet hole in its head.

"Nothin we dude nerks." Parnetta watched him from the kitchen window. "Everythin' against uz," she grumbled to herself.

Filo got his war feather from the shed, put it in his crooked braid. He stomped his feet, hooted. Filo, the medicine man, transcended to the spirit world for the refrigerator. He shook each kink and bolt. The spirit of cold itself. He whooped and warred in the yard for nearly half an hour.

"Not with a bullet hole in it." Parnetta shook her head and wiped the sweat from her face.

He got his wrench and hacksaw, the ax and hammer. It was dead now for sure. Parnetta knew it at the sink. It was the thing that would be buried in the backyard. "Like most of us libed," Aunt Parnetta talked to herself. "Filled with our own workings, not doint what we shulb."

Parnetta hung the sheets in the yard, white and square as the fridge itself.

The new refrigerator came in a delivery truck. It stood in the kitchen. Bought on time at a bargain. Cheapest in the store. Filo made sure of it. The interest over five years would be as much as the fridge. Aunt Parnetta tried to explain it to him. The men set the fridge where Parnetta instructed them. They adjusted and leveled the little hog feet. They gave Parnetta the packet of information, the guarantee. Then drove off in victory. The new smell of the gleaming white inside as though cleansed by cedar from the Keetowah fire.

Aunt Parnetta had Filo take her to the grocery store on the old road to Tahlequah. She loaded the cart with milk and butter. Frozen waffles. Orange juice. Anything that had to be kept cool. The fridge made noise, she thought, she would get used to it. But in the night, she heard the fridge. It seemed to fill her dreams. She had trouble going to sleep, even on the clean white sheets, and she had trouble staying asleep. The fridge was like a giant hog in the kitchen. Rutting and snorting all night. She got up once and unplugged it. Waking early the next morn to plug it in again before the milk and eggs got warm.

"That ferge bother yeu, Filo?" she asked.

"Nord."

Aunt Parnetta peeled her potatoes outside. She mended Filo's shirts under the shade tree. She didn't soak anything in the kitchen sink anymore, not even the sheets or Filo's socks. There were things she just had to endure, she grumped. That's the way it was.

When the grandchildren visited, she had them run in the kitchen for whatever she needed. They picnicked on the old watermelon table in the back-yard. She put up the old teepee for them to sleep in.

"Late in the summer fer that?" Filo quizzed her.

"Nert. It waz nert to get homesick for the summer that's leabing us like the childurn." She gratified him with her keen sense. Parnetta could think up anything for what she wanted to do.

Several nights Filo returned to their bed, with its geese-in-flight-over-the-swamp pattern quilt, but Aunt Parnetta stayed in the teepee under the stars.

"We bined muried thurdy yars. Git in the house," Filo said one night under the white leaves of the stars.

"I can't sleep 'cause of that wild hog in the kitchen," Aunt Parnetta said. "I tald yeu that."

"Hey chekta!" Filo answered her. "Why didn't yeu teld me so I knowd whad yeu said." Filo covered the white box of the fridge with the geese quilt and an old Indian blanket he got from the shed. "Werd yeu stayed out thar all winder?"

"Til the beast we got in thar dies."

"Hawly gizard," Filo spurted. "Thard be anuther twendy yars!"

Aunt Parnetta was comforted by the bedroom that night. Old Filo's snore after he made his snorting love to her. The gray-and-blue-striped wallpaper with its watermarks. The stovepipe curling up to the wall like a hog tail. The bureau dresser with a little doily and her hairbrush. Pictures by their grand-children. A turquoise coyote and a ghostly figure the boy told her was Running Wind.

She fell into a light sleep where the white stars blew down from the sky, flapping like the white sheets on the line. She nudged Filo to get his rake. He turned sharply against her. Parnetta woke and sat on the edge of the bed.

"Yeu wand me to cuber the ferge wid something else?" Filo asked from his sleep.

"No," Aunt Parnetta answered him. "Nod unless id be the polar ice cap."

Now it was an old trip to Minnesota when she was a girl. Parnetta saw herself in a plaid shirt and braids. Had her hair been that dark? Now it was streaked with gray. Everything was like a child's drawing. Exaggerated. The way dreams were sometimes. A sun in the left corner of the picture. The trail of chimney smoke from the narrow house. It was cold. So cold that everything creaked. She heard cars running late into the night. Early mornings, steam growled out of the exhaust. The pane of window glass in the front door had been somewhere else. Old lettering showed up in the frost. Bones remembered their aches in the cold. Teeth, their hurt. The way Parnetta remembered every bad thing that happened. She dwelled on it.

The cold place was shriveled to the small upright rectangle in her chest, holding the fish her grandson caught in the river. That's where the cold place was. Right inside her heart. No longer pumping like the blinker lights she saw in town. She was the Minnesota winter she remembered as a child. The electricity it took to keep her cold! The energy. The moon over her like a ceiling light. Stars were holes where the rain came in. The dripping buckets. All of them like Parnetta. The *hurrrrrrrrr* of the fridge. Off. On. All night. That white box. Wild boar! Think of it. She didn't always know why she was disgruntled. She just was. She saw herself as the fridge. A frozen fish stiff as a brick. The Great Spirit had her pegged. Could she find her heart, maybe, if she looked somewhere in her chest?

Hurrrrrrrrr. Rat-tat-at-rat. Hurrr. The fridge came on again, and startled, she woke and teetered slightly on the edge of the bed while it growled.

But she was a stranger in this world. An Indian in a white man's land. "Even the ferge's whate," Parnetta told the Great Spirit.

"Wasn't everybody a stranger and pilgrim?" The Great Spirit seemed to speak to her, or it was her own thoughts wandering in her head from her dreams.

"No," Parnetta insisted. Some people were at home on this earth, moving with ease. She would ask the Great Spirit more about it later. When he finally yanked the life out of her like the pin in a grenade.

Suddenly Parnetta realized that she was always moaning like the fridge. Maybe she irritated the Great Spirit like the white box irritated her. Did she sound that way to anyone else? Was that the Spirit's revenge? She was stuck with the cheapest box in the store. In fact, in her fears, wasn't it a white boar which would tear into the room and eat her soon as she got good and asleep?

Hadn't she seen the worst in things? Didn't she weigh herself in the winter with her coat on? Sometimes wrapped in the blanket also?

"Filo?" She turned to him. But he was out cold. Farther away than Minnesota.

"No. Just think about it, Parnetta," her thoughts seemed to say. The Spirit had blessed her life. But inside the white refrigerator of herself—inside the coils, an ice river surged. A glacier mowed its way across a continent. Everything frozen for eons. In need of a Keetowah fire. Heat. The warmth of the Great Spirit. Filo was only a spark. He could not warm her. Even though he tried.

Maybe the Great Spirit had done her a favor. Hope like white sparks of stars glistened in her head. The electric blisters. *Temporary!* She could shut up. She belonged to the Spirit. He had just unplugged her a minute. Took his rifle right through her head.

The leaves growled and spewed white sparks in the sky. It was a volcano from the moon. Erupting in the heavens. Sending down its white sparks like the pinwheels Filo used to nail on trees. It was the bright sparks of the Keetowah fire, the holy bonfire from which smaller fires burned, spreading the purification of the Great Spirit into each house. Into each hard, old pinecone heart.

⟿ *Land Speaking* ⟾
Jeannette Armstrong

Okanagan author Jeannette Armstrong was born in 1948 and grew up on the Penticton Indian Reserve, part of the Okanagan Nation's territories, in British Columbia, Canada. Armstrong, the first published Indigenous woman novelist from Canada, is the grand-niece of Hum-Ishu-Ma (Mourning Dove, a.k.a. Christal Quintasket), the first Native American woman novelist. While growing up, Armstrong received a traditional education from Okanagan Elders and her family. From them, she learned the Okanagan language, and she is still a fluent speaker of the Okanagan (or N'silxchn) language today. In 1989, she helped to found the En'owkin School of International Writing, which is the first creative writing program in Canada that is run by and for Indigenous writers and editors. Her well-known and critically acclaimed works include the novels *Slash* (1985) and *Whispering in Shadows* (2000); a collection of poetry, *Breath Tracks* (1991); and the first collection of essays on Indigenous literature by Indigenous critics, *Looking at the Words of Our People: First Nations Analysis of Literature* (1993).

In this essay, Armstrong draws on ideas about linguistics held by Okanagan Elders who explain that as their nation migrated to the territory they now occupy, their language changed, reflecting the new knowledge given to them by the land. As an Okanagan writer, Armstrong explains, this connection between land, Indigenous knowledge, and language compels a "reinvention of the enemy's language" in her work (142).[1] In this spirit, Armstrong uses words carefully to communicate ideas that are often left out of writing in English. As you read the prose, fiction, and poetry contained in this essay, pay attention to the different ways of relating sound, time, and images that Armstrong offers. How do the shifts in genre impact your interpretation of the text as a whole?

I want to discuss the intensity of my experience as an Okanagan who is Indigenous to the land I live on and how that experience permeates my writing. It is my conviction that Okanagan, my original language, the language of my people, constitutes the most significant influence on my writing in English. I will discuss how my own experience of the land sources and arises in my poetry and prose and how the Okanagan language shapes that connection.

I want to comment on the underlying basis for how this occurs within my personal experience of the land as an Okanagan-speaking writer. I will emphasize the significance that original Native languages and their connection to our lands have in compelling the reinvention of the enemy's language for our perspectives as Indigenous writers.

As I understand it from my Okanagan ancestors, language was given to us by the land we live within. The land that is the Okanagan is part of the Great Columbia River Basin on the interior plateau of Washington State and British Columbia. The Okanagan language, called N'silxchn by us, is one of the Salishan languages. My ancestors say that N'silxchn is formed out of an older language, some words of which are still retained in our origin stories. I have heard elders explain that the language changed as we moved and spread over the land through time. My own father told me that it was the land that changed the language because there is special knowledge in each different place. All my elders say that it is land that holds all knowledge of life and death and is a constant teacher. It is said in Okanagan that the land constantly speaks. It is constantly communicating. Not to learn its language is to die. We survived and thrived by listening intently to its teachings—to its language—and then inventing human words to retell its stories to our succeeding generations. It is the land that speaks N'silxchn through the generations of our ancestors to us. It is N'silxchn, the old land/mother spirit of the Okanagan People, which surrounds me in its primal wordless state.

It is this N'silxchn which embraces me and permeates my experience of the Okanagan land and is a constant voice within me that yearns for human speech. I am claimed and owned by this land, this Okanagan. Voices that move within as my experience of existence do not awaken as words. Instead they move within as the colors, patterns, and movements of a beautiful, kind Okanagan landscape. They are the Grandmother voices which speak. The poem "Grandmothers" was written in N'silxchn and interpreted into English. The English term *grandmother* as a human experience is closest in meaning to the term *Tmixw* in Okanagan, meaning something like loving-ancestor-land-spirit.

GRANDMOTHERS
In the part of me that was always there
grandmothers
are speaking to me
the grandmothers in whose voices
I nestle
and draw nourishment from
voices speaking to me
in early morning light
glinting off water
speaking to me in fragile green
pushing upward
groping sun and warmth
pulling earth's breath
down and in
to join with porous stone
speaking to me
out of thick forest
in majestic rises to sheer
blue
in the straight slight mist
in twigs and fur
skin and blood
moon and movement
feathers stroking elegant curves against wind
silent unseen bits
in the torrent of blood
washing bone and flesh
earth's pieces
the joining of winds
to rock
igniting white fire
lighting dark places

and rousing the sleeping moment
caught in pollen
a waking of stars
inside
and when blue fire
slants to touch this water
I lift my eyes
and know I am seed
and shooting green
and words
in this hollow
I am
night glittering
the wind and silence
I am vastness stretching to the sun
I am this moment
earth mind
I can be nothing else
the joining of breath to sand
by water and fire
the mother body
and yet
I am small
a mote of dust
hardly here
unbearably without anything
to hold me
but the voices
of grandmothers (*Gatherings*, Volume III)

The language spoken by the land, which is interpreted by the Okanagan into words, carries parts of its ongoing reality. The land as language surrounds us completely, just like the physical reality of it surrounds us. Within that vast speaking, both externally and internally, we as human beings are an inextricable part—though a minute part—of the land language.

In this sense, all Indigenous peoples' languages are generated by a precise geography and arise from it. Over time and many generations of their people, it is their distinctive interaction with a precise geography which forms the way indigenous language is shaped and subsequently how the world is viewed, approached, and expressed verbally by its speakers.

I have felt within my own experience of travel to other lands of Salishan-speaking people an internal resonance of familiar language and familiar land. I can hear the N'silxchn parts in all Salishan languages. I have been

surprised by how unfamiliar sounds in those languages resemble and reso-
nate closely with the physical differences between their land and mine. The
language lets me feel the points where our past was one and lets me "recognize" teaching sites of our common ancestry. The poem "Ochre Lines" imitates
the way N'silxchn engages a constant layering of land and human experience
within its imagery.

OCHRE LINES
skins
drums
liquid beat fluttering under the breast
coursing long journeys
through blue
lifelines
joining body to body
primeval maps
drawn under
the
hide
deep
floating dreams past
history
surging forward
upward
through indigo passages
to move on the earth
to filigree into fantastic
gropings over the land
journeys marking
red trails
a slow
moving earth vision (*Gatherings*, Volume IV)

I experience land as a fluent speaker of Okanagan. N'silxchn, the Okanagan land language, is my first language, my Earth Mother language. When
I close my eyes and my thoughts travel, N'silxchn recreates the sounds, the
smells, the colors, the taste and texture precisely. N'silxchn emulates the land
and the sky in its unique flow around me. I feel its vast outer edges touching the
sky and the horizon in all that I experience as life. I feel it speaking the oldness
of earth, speaking to us. I have given English voice to this sense of N'silxchn
land presence in my grandmother landscape poems. The poem "Winds," from
that series, intertwines land presence through my human voice presence.

WINDS

```
Winds      moving                                clouds
past                    earth                    sky
are                     one                      moves
around     me          silent                   colors
drifting   sometimes   present                  dark
with       soft                     white
                                    flakes    touching
life                    rich        lacework  unknown
           hands                    twined    with care
a place    forever     still        tracing   quietly
a line     stretched   to a         horizon
fading                              with time and gently
ending                  breath
```
(Armstrong, *Breath Tracks*)

As it is spoken today, the Okanagan language carries meanings about a time that is no more. Its words speak of a world different in experience from this one. Its words whisper more than the retelling of the world. Through my language I understand I am being spoken to, I'm not the one speaking. The words are coming from many tongues and mouths of Okanagan people and the land around them. I am a listener to the language's stories, and when my words form I am merely retelling the same stories in different patterns. I have known this about my language since learning English as a second language. Learning English as a second language allowed me to "hear" the different stories in English words from those that N'silxchn brings forward from its origins. I now know this is true of any language. I hear words speak old stories. The poem "Words" emerged through an exercise in both languages to capture N'silxchn imagery interpretive of such an illusive and abstract concept as meaning.

WORDS
Words are memory
a window in the present
a coming to terms with meaning
history made into now
a surge in reclaiming
the enormity of the past
a piece in the collective experience of time
a sleep in which I try to awaken
the whispered echoes of voices
resting in each word
moving back into dark blue
voices of continuance

countless sound shapings which roll thunderous
over millions of tongues
to reach me
alive with meaning
a fertile ground
from which generations spring
out of the landscape of grandmother
the sharing
in what we select
to remember
the physical power in thought
carried inside silently
pushing forward in each breathing
meaning wished onto tongues transforming with each
utterance
the stuff of our lives
to travel on wind
on air
to bump wetly
against countless tiny drums
to become sound
spasms coursing upward into imagine
there to tum gray silence
into explosions of color
calling up the real
the physical
the excruciating sweetness of mouth on mouth
the feltness of the things of us
then settling soundless
colorless
into memory
to be hidden there
reaching ever forward into distances unknown
always linking to others
up to the last drum
vibrating into vast silence (Armstrong, *Breath Tracks* 17-18)

By speaking my Okanagan language, I have come to understand that whenever I speak, I step into vastness and move within it through a vocabulary of time and of memory. I move through the vastness into a new linking of time to the moment I speak. To speak is to create more than words, more than sounds retelling the world; it is to realize the potential for transformation of the world. To the Okanagan, speaking is a sacred act in that words contain spirit, a power waiting to become activated and become physical. Words do so upon being spoken and create cause and effect in human interaction. What we speak determines our interactions. Realization of the power in speaking is in the realization that words can change the future and in the realization that we each have that power. I am the word carrier, and I shape-change the world. The poem "Threads of Old Memory" was an inquiry in English-language imagery of the N'silxchn concept of speaking as a profound and sacred responsibility.

> **THREADS OF OLD MEMORY**
> Speaking to newcomers in their language is dangerous
> for when I speak
> history is a dreamer
> empowering thought
> from which I awaken the imaginings of the past
> bringing the sweep and surge of meaning
> coming from a place
> rooted in the memory of loss
> experienced in ceremonies
> wrenched from the minds of a people
> whose language spoke only harmony
> through a language
> meant to overpower
> to overtake
> in skillfully crafted words
> moving towards surrender
> leaving in its swirling wake
> only those songs hidden
> cherished
> protected
> the secret singing of which
> I glimpse through bewildered eyes
> an old lost world
> of astounding beauty
>
> When I speak
> I attempt to bring together
> with my hands
> gossamer thin threads of old memory
> thoughts from the underpinnings of understanding
> words steeped in age
> slim
> barely visible strands of harmony
> stretching across the chaos brought into this world

through words
shaped as sounds in air
meaning made physical
changers of the world
carriers into this place of things
from a place of magic
the underside of knowing
the origination place
a pure place
silent
wordless
from where thoughts I choose
silently transform into words
I speak and
powerfully become actions
becomes memory is someone
I become different memories to different people
different stories in the retelling of my place
I am the dreamer
the choice maker
the word speaker
I speak in a language of words formed of the actions of the
	past
words that become the sharing
the collective knowing
the links that become a people
the dreaming that becomes a history
the calling forth of voices
the sending forward of memory
I am the weaver of memory thread
twining past to future
I am the artist
the storyteller
the singer
from the known and familiar
pushing out into darkness
dreaming splinters together
the coming to knowing

When I speak
I sing a song called up through ages
of carefully crafted rhythm
of a purpose close to the wordless

in a coming to this world from the cold and hungry spaces
     in the heart
through the desolate and lost places of the mind
to this stark and windswept mountain top
I search for sacred words
spoken serenely in the gaps between memory
the lost places of history
pieces mislaid
forgotten or stolen
muffled by violence
splintered by evil
when languages collide in mid-air
when past and present explode in chaos
and the imaginings of the past
rip into the dreams of the future

When I speak
I choose the words gently
asking the whys
dangerous words
in the language of the newcomers
words releasing unspeakable grief
for all that is lost
dispelling lies in the retelling
I choose threads of truth
that in its telling cannot be hidden
and brings forward
old words that heal
moving to a place
where a new song begins
a new ceremony
through medicine eyes I glimpse a world
that cannot be stolen or lost
only shared
shaped by new words
joining precisely to form old patterns
a song of stars
glittering against an endless silence (Armstrong, *Breath Tracks* 58-60)

The Okanagan language, as I have come to understand it from my comparative examination with the English language, differs in significant ways from English. Linguists may differ from my opinion, arguing that the mechanics of grammar differ but the functional basis of the two languages does not. I will not argue. I will only say that I speak Okanagan and English fluently, and in so doing I perceive differences that have great influence on my worldview, my philosophy, my creative process, and subsequently my writing.

Okanagan is completely vocally rooted in that it has never been written down. It is a language devised solely for use by the human voice and the human body. The elements inherent in that are straightforward. A good example is the N'silxchn method of differentiating between the word for "this," *axa* (used only with something you can touch), and "that," *ixi* (used only with something near, as in a room), and "that over there," *yaxis* (used for something farther away but still only when you can point at it), the last with a voice stretching of the vowels to indicate far away. In a vocally rooted language, sound, with all its emotive qualities, determines how words are used and forms a backdrop in meaning, as do gesture, stance, and facial expression.

While this seems to impose limitations on what one has available for descriptive imagery in written languages, actually the opposite occurs. The range is broadened by the way the sounds in words can be combined and the way each sound can be used, in much the same way that classical music stretches the imagination by the various mathematically possible ways sound elements can be combined.

Over time, the Okanagan language has acquired a music-based sensitivity in the creation of meaning. The sound elements of tempo, beat, rhythm, volume, and pitch have a greater significance for comprehension than in languages that rely on visually based imagery. The language re-sounds patterns of action and movement as imagery. This is what the Okanagan people mean when they say that everything is a singing. Sounds solicit emotion even in babies; certain sounds cause sadness, and certain rhythms cause excitement. Sounds "speak" in particular ways of inner response. Music relies on such responses to communicate its message. In the same way, Okanagan, as a vocally based language, relies heavily on sounds and sound patterns to communicate meanings.

N'silxchn recreates sounds of the land in its utterance, but it also draws on the natural human emotional response to sound and rhythm to contain and express a philosophical or spiritual idea. The poem "Frogs Singing" is the result of a long discussion on our language and worldview with my sister Delphine, who spoke only Okanagan until age twelve. She pointed out that the stars and the frogs in the Okanagan summer nights have the same rhythm and that in saying it to recall the sound and the night filled with stars, the rhythm filled her soul and became hers.

FROGS SINGING
my sister did not dream this
she found this out when she walked
outside and looked up and star
rhythms sang to her pointing their spines of light
down into her and filled her body with star song
and all around her
frogs joined the star singing
they learned it
long ago (Armstrong, "Frogs Singing")

It has become apparent to me that, for the most part, English lacks this kind of musical coherence. For the most part, the "sounds" of the words and the rhythms created in their structure clearly are not constructed to draw a musical response. In fact, the language is deaf to music and only chances on it through the diligent work of writers. Perhaps this has to do with the loss of the body as the sole carrier of words. Perhaps literacy—with its marks on stone, wood, paper, and now in electronic impulses—silences the music that writers are able to retrieve.

Okanagan is a language guided by active components of reality. Syllables form base units that carry meaning in the language. Root syllables are where meanings reside rather than only in whole or complete words. Words are a combination of syllables, each of which carries meaning and contains function. Each word, when examined, can be broken down into root syllables, each of which has an active meaning and when combined activates a larger animated image.

An example is the Okanagan word for dog: *kekwep*. The word has two syllables. The first syllable, *kek*, is an action syllable meaning something like "happening upon a small (thing)," and the second syllable, *wep*, meaning something like "sprouting profusely (as in fur)." In English, the two together would not make specific sense. However, when these two syllables are combined in Okanagan, they immediately join together to become an activator of a larger image. They create an action together—fur growing on a little living thing—made familiar only by a connective experience.

When you say the Okanagan word for dog, you don't "see" a dog image, you summon an experience of a little furred life, the exactness of which is known only by its interaction with you or something. Each such little furred life is then significant in its own unique way. Although each dog bears the commonality of having fur and being little and particularly familiar, no kekwep can ever be just a dog.

Speaking the Okanagan word for dog as "an experience" is quite different semantically from reading the English word *dog*. The English word solicits an inanimate generic symbol for all dogs, independent of action and isolated from everything else, as though a dog without context and without anything to which it is connected could really exist. It must be a frightful experience to be a dog in English.

In Okanagan, then, language is a constant replay of tiny selected pieces of movement and action that solicit a larger active movement somehow connected to you by the context you arrange for it. Times, places, and things are all made into movement, surrounding you and connected to you like the waves of a liquid stretching outward. The following excerpt from my novel *Slash* gives an example of this sense of time and place merging into one through imagery in my prose.

> She came and knelt in front of me. She took my hands and spoke my Okanagan name softly. I had a strange feeling like I did when I heard the dance songs inside my head. I felt like I was made of mist or something and I melted into the scene around me. She said in our language, "We are now more than one. We have become three. Your son will be born in the springtime when the saskatoon flowers bloom. He will be named to your side of the family." I couldn't speak. All I could do was reach out and pull her to me and rock her while the feeling washed over us. I knew she felt it. Somewhere in my head, I saw us from another point of view, just a little above us, like through clear glass. I saw us kneeling and moving with the rhythm that flowed around us in shimmering waves, then we grew smaller and smaller until we were just a speck on top of that mountain and our land was vast and spread out around us, like a multicolored star quilt. (Armstrong, *Slash*)

In the Okanagan language, perception of the way reality occurs is very different from that solicited by the English language. Reality is very much like a story: it is easily changeable and transformative with each speaker. Reality in that way becomes very potent with animation and life. It is experienced as an always malleable reality within which you are like an attendant at a vast symphony surrounding you, a symphony in which, at times, you are the conductor.

Fluent speakers of both English and Indigenous languages sometimes experience a separation of the two realities. I have experienced this separation, and it has fascinated me since my formative years as a learning storyteller and later as an interpreter for my elders at ceremonial and political gatherings. My concern as a writer has been to find or construct bridges between the two realities.

In the use of English words, I attempt to construct a similar sense of movement and rhythm through sound patterns. I listen to sounds that words make in English and try to find the sounds that will move the image making, whether in poetry or prose, closer to the Okanagan reality. I try, as in the example below, to create the fluid movement of sounds together with images in a fashion that to me resembles closely the sounds of the Okanagan.

> Tonight, I sit up here at the Flint Rock and look down to the thousands of lights spread out in the distance where the town is creeping incessantly up the hillsides.
>   Across the Okanagan valley the sun begins to set. Blazes of mars-red tinged with deep purple and crimson brush silvery clouds and touch the mountain tops. The wind moans through the swaying pines as coyotes shrill their songs to each other the gathering dusk. Long, yellow grasses bend and whip their blades across cactus, sand and sage. (Armstrong, *Slash*)

In North American colloquial English, I have found some of the rhythms I search for. I find them more abundant in Rez English, so I often use Rez English in the prose I write, as in this example from "This Is a Story":

> Actually Kyoti himself was getting pretty sick and gaunt from eating stuff that didn't taste or look like food. Especially real food like fresh salmon. But the headman would just shake his head and say, "Get out of here, Kyoti. Your kind of talk is just bullshit. If you say them things, people will get riled up and they might start to raise hell. They might even try to do something stupid like break the dams." (Armstrong, "This Is a Story")

Okanagan Rez English has a structural quality syntactically and semantically closer to the way the Okanagan language is arranged. I believe that Rez English from any part of the country, if examined, will display the sound and syntax patterns of the Indigenous language of that area and subsequently the sounds that the landscape speaks. I believe it will also display, through its altered syntax, semantic differences reflecting the view of reality embedded in the culture.

An example is the Rez English semantic pattern that subverts and alters the rigid sequential time sense compelled by the way the English language grammatically isolates verb tense. Standard English structures a sentence like this: Trevor walked often to the spring to think and to be alone. Rez English would be more comfortable with a structure like this: Trevor's always walking to the spring for thinking and being alone. The Rez style creates a semantic difference that allows for a fluid movement between past, present, and future.

Another example is the way spoken Rez English often seeks to supplant a divisive disposition in human interaction revealed in English grammar through the designation of gender-based pronouns. Mother-tongue speakers of Okanagan experience great difficulty in the use of the gender-based pronouns. They most often seek to leave them out. An example of spoken Rez English that seeks a balance would be structured something like this: Mary was talking with Tommy about the balky car and then the talking was on how to fix it. In English this would be: Mary spoke to Tommy about the balky car, and then she talked with him about how it could be fixed.

In Okanagan storytelling, the ability to move the audience back and forth between the present reality and the story reality relies heavily on the fluidity of time sense that the language offers. In particular, stories that are used for teaching must be inclusive of the past, present, and future, as well as the current or contemporary moment and the story reality, without losing context and coherence while maintaining the drama. There must be no doubt that the story is about the present and the future and the past, and that the story was going on for a long time and is going on continuously, and that the words are only mirror-imaging it having happened and while it is happening.

I concern myself with how to capture and express that fluidity in my writing. I have found a serious lack of fluidity in English grammatical structure. Perhaps here may be found the root of the phenomenon that gives rise to the discussion about linear and nonlinear reality.

My writing in English is a continuous battle against the rigidity in English, and I revel in the discoveries I make in constructing new ways to circumvent such invasive imperialism upon my tongue.

CHAPTER 4

CREE KNOWLEDGE EMBEDDED IN STORIES

Tomson Highway, excerpt from *Kiss of the Fur Queen*

Steven Keewatin Sanderson, excerpt from *Darkness Calls*

Solomon Ratt, "I'm Not an Indian"

Paul Seesequasis, "The Republic of Tricksterism"

Lisa Bird-Wilson, "Delivery"

Louise Bernice Halfe, "Rolling Head's Grave Yard"

Harold Cardinal, excerpt from "Einew Kis-Kee-Tum-Awin
(Indigenous People's Knowledge)"

MANY MEMBERS OF DISPARATE INDIGENOUS nations across Turtle Island know what it is like to be isolated on reserves or reservations, often with substandard access to the necessities of life, or impoverished, removed from traditional territories, living in urban or suburban spaces with little access to the wealth of one's culture. While colonization experienced by Indigenous peoples is often used as a way to understand the themes in Indigenous studies, this focus can flatten out the analysis, giving more attention to the effects of colonization, which prioritizes the people's losses, rather than focusing on the persistence of specific world views and perspectives of each Indigenous nation or tribe.

An exclusive focus on colonization can also obscure the long-standing traditions and histories of Indigenous peoples that existed before contact. In the words of Cree intellectual Harold Cardinal, "[t]hroughout the eons of time preceding the arrival of the White man to our lands and territories, our people evolved, developed, maintained and sustained complex systems through which they continued the knowledge quest" ("Einew" 195). Indigenous intellectuals, like Okanagan writer Jeannette Armstrong in "Land Speaking" (Chapter 3), have insisted that these complex systems continue to persist in contemporary writing. In her 1993 introduction to *Looking at the Words of Our People*, Armstrong asserts that culture experts are essential to guide the study of Indigenous stories written in English because "the voices" embedded within these stories "are culture-specific voices" (Reder and Morra 230).

In this chapter, we do not consider Cree literature as a body of work that began when Cree people started learning English through contact with Christian missionaries and European-styled education systems. Rather, we approach Cree literature as a body of work influenced by the intellectual, cultural, and spiritual traditions that precede the arrival of Europeans. We examine the following writings in reference to long-standing stories and storytelling styles.

In traditional Cree orature, the two major genres in Cree storytelling are âtayôhkêwin, translated by linguist H. C. as "myth text or legendary text," and âcimowin, which is a "report" or an "account" (Wolfart, "Cree" 245–46). The first is marked by its setting in a world of legend, in a time when animals could talk and Wîsahkêcâhk, the Cree trickster, regularly transformed from one being to another. The second is set in historical time and is capacious enough to hold within it funny little stories, autobiography, and old-time stories that might feature exploits of battle or stories passed down through families. Wolfart clarifies: "That they contain magical experiences does not disturb their status as true stories" (Wolfart, Plains 12).

While the stories in this chapter easily fit into English generic categories of the novel, the vignette, short fiction, satire, graphic novel, academic address, and speech, reading these texts through the lens of Cree genres enables us to think about these stories in different ways. For example, consider the layers of protocol surrounding the telling of âtayôhkêwina, or legends. In the chapter from Tomson Highway's novel, The Kiss of the Fur Queen, when the Okimasis brothers piece together the fragments of a Wîsahkêcâhk legend while on a trip to the shopping mall, they reveal their lack of education about the dangers of telling these sacred stories out of season or without the proper respect. They don't recognize that the very act of this storytelling summons Wîsahkêcâhk, in the guise of the Cree-whispering mannequin.

Louise Bernice Halfe, on the other hand, recognizes the power of the ancient story she retells and demonstrates some of the various ways one might interpret key parts of the legend. She avoids equating Rolling Head with Eve and the serpent in the Christian origin story. Instead, she models for us the priority of Cree storytelling to evoke questions about the Rolling Head story rather than to provide answers. Likewise, the fight scene in Steven Keewatin Sanderson's graphic novel, Darkness Calls, has Wîsahkêcâhk battling Wetigo in order to save the vulnerable protagonist, Kyle. Yet the story does not end with either winning the day. Instead Kyle ignites his own power to save himself. Kyle models the way that the listener or reader has to take responsibility to make sense of Cree stories rather than to be saved by predictable endings.

But Cree storytelling is not just focused on legends. Solomon Ratt's story belongs to a sub-genre of âcimowina called wawiyatâcimowinisa, or funny little stories, which are contemporary stories or accounts. Consider its similarities to the story in Chapter 1 of this volume, "The Way of the Sword," by Plains Cree writer Dawn Dumont. Both focus on the humour in the actions of youngsters who take seriously the messages embedded in the culture around them. Just as the young boy in Ratt's story understands that to play the part of the Indian in a game against the Cowboys—and in the colonial hierarchy—is a no-win proposition, Dawn recognizes that her adoption of Conan as a hero leads her into trouble.

To what extent might Seesequasis's send-up of band politics and government legislation be read as an extension of wawiyatâcimowinisa? While he references Wesakaychuk and Rigoureau, the Cree and the Métis shape-shifters, Wetigo, the cannibal monster, and Pakakos, a dreaded spirit, these classic Cree characters simply populate the scene, with the real focus on the foolish antics of Tobe and Seesequasis's mother and her flatulent commentary. The author's depiction of himself as a "cross-breed mutt" is a distraction, for it isn't his mixed parentage that banishes him from his family's reserve, but rather the laws determining who gets to inherit the right to treaty benefits. By situating his story in a world full of Cree characters, Seesequasis is able to turn this loss into comedy and claim his Cree identity.

Harold Cardinal's speech, part reflection, part philosophy, might best be thought of as kakêskihkêmowin, or counselling text; in the entry to Cree Literature in the *Encyclopedia of Canadian Literature*, kakêskihkêmowin is defined as "deploring the present and extolling the past but also predicting the future and laying out ways of coping with it … a favourite focus of formal Cree rhetoric" (Wolfart, "Cree" 246). Rather than identify Cardinal as an exceptional individual, this identification of his work as kakêskihkêmowin recognizes him as one in an honoured long line of Cree intellectuals, intergenerational seekers of knowledge of the four worlds.

The short story by Lisa Bird-Wilson, however, does not seem to fit easily into any of the above Cree categories. Instead, it is an example of how Cree writers adopt and adapt other storytelling styles to the Cree imagination. Bird-Wilson, a Cree-Métis writer, situates her drama on a reserve. A woman who is about to go into labour does not receive the care and respect she needs, but rather is kept from medical attention and isolated from her mother, a trained midwife. Her desire to leave this place of peril and go home is likely literal, but also metaphorical—the desire to return to a place where she is loved and where she belongs.

Excerpt from *Kiss of the Fur Queen*
Tomson Highway

Tomson Highway was born into a Cree-speaking family in northwestern Manitoba in 1951. As a Status Indian—Highway is a member of Barren Lands First Nation near Brochet, Manitoba—he and his siblings were separated from their family and educated in residential schools in the southern half of the province, the experience of which inspired the storyline of his first novel, *Kiss of the Fur Queen*, published in 1998. Like Jeremiah, the elder of two brothers in the story, Highway studied classical piano at school and eventually became a playwright and director in the Toronto theatre scene. He won the Dora Mavor Moore Award for Best New Play in 1987 for *The Rez Sisters* and again in 1989 for *Dry Lips Oughta Move to Kapuskasing*. Highway has also received numerous other accolades over the years, including the Order of Canada in 1994 and the National Aboriginal Achievement Award in 2001.

In the following story, Jeremiah has been living in Winnipeg to attend high school. His younger brother Gabriel, now fourteen, having spent the summer at home with their parents, joins Jeremiah in the city. On a trip to buy Gabriel school clothes, the brothers interpret the typically humdrum setting of a city shopping mall through their experiences in Catholic school and in contrast to their much smaller remote home community. Overwhelmed by the number of shoppers and consumer goods, they are reminded of a traditional Cree story that they were forbidden to learn and barely remember. While underwear shopping they relate to each other the story in which culture hero Weesageechak transforms into a weasel and crawls up the anus of Weetigo, the cannibal monster, in order to chew out his intestines and kill him. As they slowly recount the events of this story, Jeremiah is not yet able to remember and articulate the damage caused by his experiences at residential school, nor is Gabriel able to understand his burgeoning sexuality. Still the brothers use their knowledge of Cree and their memories of stories to make sense of what they see. In what ways does the telling of Cree stories help the brothers? How can you interpret the telling of the story of "Weesageechak kills the Weetigo" (163)?

"*Tansi*"

Jeremiah stopped breathing. In the two years he had spent in this city so lonely that he regularly considered swallowing his current landlady's entire stock of angina pills, he had given up his native tongue to the roar of traffic.

"Say that again?"

"*Tansi*," repeated Gabriel. "Means hi, or how are you doing? Take your pick." He was smiling so hard that his face looked like it might burst. "Why? Cree a crime here, too?"

How strange Jeremiah looked. Clipped, his eyes like a page written in some foreign language. Even his clothes looked stilted, too new, too spick and span, as if lifted from a corpse in a coffin.

"It's … your voice. It's so … low." Jeremiah couldn't get over Gabriel's height, his breadth of shoulder, the six or seven black bristles sprouting from his chin. He didn't look fourteen going on fifteen, more like eighteen.

"Mom send me a jar of her legendary caribou *arababoo*?" Jeremiah chirped as they waltzed, arms over shoulders, out the station doors and into the white light of morning. Gabriel's navy blue windbreaker, his red plaid flannel shirt, his entire person sparked off microscopic waves of campfire smoke, of green spruce boughs, of dew-laden reindeer moss.

"Nah," said Gabriel. "She says city boys don't eat wild meat."

"Yeah, right." Jeremiah rolled his eyes. "So. Tell me. How's Eemanapiteepitat?"

"Annie Moostoos went and got killed by the airport outhouse door."

"Airport outhouse door? Yeah, right."

"*Tapwee!* We have an airport now. Uncle Kookoos helped clear the land for it last summer. Before you know it, he predicts, jet planes will be landing in Eemanapiteepitat like flies on dog shit."

"*Neee, nimantoom.*" Jeremiah laughed, light as a springtime killdeer. For two brown Indian boys—not one, but two—were dancing-skipping-floating down Broadway Avenue, tripping over each other's Cree, getting up and laughing, tripping over each other's Cree, getting up and laughing.

———

"The mall," said Jeremiah early next morning as he reached for the handle of the large glass door, "was invented in Winnipeg," his confidence in this stunning piece of information all the greater by reason of its being utterly unsubstantiated. If he was going to usher Gabriel into the rituals of urban life, then he was going to render the experience memorable, even if he had to stretch truth into myth.

Like a lukewarm summer wave, the silken strings of a hundred violins swept over them, the bulbs of twenty thousand fluorescent lights a blinding buzz. The chancel of a church for titans, the gleaming central promenade of the Polo Park Shopping Mall lay before them.

Gabriel gasped: at least three miles of stores if he was judging distance right. And the people! You could put fifty Eemanapiteepitats inside this chamber and still have room for a herd of caribou. And such an array of worldly wealth, a paradise on earth.

"Weeks," he whispered, his knees wobbly.

"Weeks what?" Jeremiah checked to see if the poor boy's eyeballs had jumped their sockets.

"Our shopping. It's gonna take weeks."

"Not when a hundred bucks is all *Sooni-eye-gimow* gives you for a clothing allowance."

"*Anee-i ma-a*?" Gabriel pointed through the glass at a pair of tan knee-high leather boots, the toes so pointed that one kick and the victim would be punctured grievously.

"You wanna look like an Italian gigolo?" Jeremiah sneered.

Shoppers labouring under piles of merchandise passed by, their reflections wriggling in the floor-to-ceiling windows like fat suckers in a reedy cove.

"What's a gigolo?" Innocent as a five-year-old, Gabriel scampered after Jeremiah, who had just walked up to the perfect store.

"A gigolo," the elder sibling proclaimed, as though from a pulpit, "is a man who sells a woman who wears shoes like these," pointing at multicoloured footwear with heels so sharp they could have roused the envy of a porcupine.

"You," Gabriel peered through the glass with grave suspicion, "can sell"— how could humans stand in such outlandish constructions—"a woman?"

"In cities," Jeremiah airily dismissed him, "it's done all the time, all the time. It's like selling meat. Come on, we gotta get you out of those rags. You look like you just crawled out of the bush."

"I didn't crawl," huffed Gabriel. "I took a plane. *And* a train." Grabbing Gabriel's sleeve, Jeremiah plunged deep into the entrails of the beast.

No-nonsense, flat-heeled oxfords winked at Gabriel, who rebuffed their gentlemanly advances as too no-nonsense, too business-like. If heels the height of coffee mugs came unrecommended—the price of cowboy boots, in any case, was prohibitive—then shoes of an athletic bent might be more to the point, with jazzy red or blue stripes down their side. Jeremiah pooh-poohed the idea as too informal; white high school classrooms were not "gymnasia."

"What, then," asked Gabriel in mounting exasperation, "do city boys wear on their feet?"

Whereupon Jeremiah announced that white boys lived in dark penny loafers with socks so white they looked like snow.

As, like Odyssean sirens on treacherous shoals, the hundred violins slid shamelessly into "Ave Maria," socks began to wave at Gabriel, in colours, weaves, and textures that made his heart strings fibrillate. He had never heard of argyle socks, for instance, and was scandalized to hear that Argyle was a Scottish earl who drank his enemies' blood on the battlefield and then went home to eat their children. So brutal was the tale that Gabriel threw a curse

at an entire rack of the lugubrious knitwear. He announced, instead, his pref-
erence for a six-pack of wool-polyester socks so white they looked like snow.
The tricoloured bands around their tops would not be seen, of course, but
knowing they were there would boost his confidence, Gabriel explained in
understated Cree. He insisted, moreover, that he wear a pair home with his
brand-new muskrat-coloured patent-leather penny loafers. Leaving his tar-
nished, near-soleless paratrooper boots and malodorous lumberjack socks
with the bouncy bleached-blond clerk, the brothers went tittering out the door
like Eemanapiteepitat housewives at a late-night bingo.

At Fischman's, they passed miles of somber suits that made them think of
priestly gatherings in Olympic-sized football stadiums. They mistook the *t* of
"Eaton's" for a crucifix, missed their elevator stop, and ended up scrumming
through racks of shift dresses waiting for nuns divorced from God. But for
the mannequin in white fox fur who whispered "*ooteesi*"—"this way"—the
brothers would have been suspected of transvestite tendencies.

By the time they entered Liberty's Fashions for the Discerning Man, the
lethargic mall air made Gabriel's head swim in circles, and the unkind lighting
overhead became so oppressive that he swore the underwear at Liberty's had
spirits of their own, that he could see their penumbra glowing like saintly
haloes.

Jeremiah, however, was wrestling with visions of his own. "Remember
Aunt Black-eyed Susan's story," he asked distractedly, his heart still palpitating
from their brush with the Cree-whispering mannequin, "about the weasel's
new fur coat?" A sudden swerve to Cree mythology might disarm such occult
phenomena.

"You mean where Weesageechak comes down to Earth disguised as a weasel?" Gabriel alighted on a manly pair of spirit-white Stanfield's, and examined
the Y-front with such rapacity that the bespectacled curmudgeon of a clerk,
smelling sabotage, flared his nostrils. "And the weasel crawls up the Weetigo's
bumhole?" Gabriel poked a finger through the opening.

"Yes …" Jeremiah, in spite of himself, exploded with jagged laughter. "In
order to kill the horrible monster."

"And comes back out with his white fur coat covered with shit?" laughed
Gabriel, dropping the Stanfields's on a pile of sky-blue boxers.

"You know," said Jeremiah, suddenly philosophical. "You could never get
away with a story like that in English."

Gabriel's voice swooped down to a conspiratorial undertone, "'Bumhole'
is a mortal sin in English. Father Lafleur told me in confession one time."

"He said the same thing about 'shit,'" said Jeremiah.

Gabriel dashed across the aisle to a selection of skin-hugging jockey-style
shorts—with no holes for the penis. The nearby rack of neckties launched into

"O Sole Mio" as Gabriel decided on three pairs of black jockeys designed by Alberto Bergazzi.

At Wrangler's, Gabriel wedged his lithe frame into a pair of blue jeans so tight that Jeremiah expressed concern. At Popeye's, the black patent-leather belt with a large silver buckle cost less than ten dollars. At Sanderson's, the red cotton shirt with pearl-white buttons became number one in Gabriel's heart. At Jack and Jill's it was the red, white, and blue silk baseball jacket with striped knit wrists and collar, to Jeremiah's puzzlement.

At every store, Gabriel virtually danced into each article of clothing and stood before the mirror not so much preening as plotting "his Winnipeg years." Like moulted skin, his old wardrobe accumulated in multicoloured shopping bags. At Aldo's Barbershop, once the deed was done—to his specifications, not Brother Stumbo's—his appearance had changed so dramatically that if Jeremiah had not witnessed the metamorphosis, he would have taken his sibling for a rock star with a tan.

Which is when they came across the belly of the beast—one hundred restaurants in a monstrous, seething clump. Never before had Gabriel seen so much food. Or so many people shovelling food in and chewing and swallowing and burping and shovelling and chewing and swallowing and burping, as at some apocalyptic communion. The world was one great, gaping mouth, devouring ketchup-dripping hamburgers, french fries glistening with grease, hot dogs, chicken chop suey, spaghetti with meatballs, Cheezies, Coca-Cola, root beer, 7-Up, ice cream, roast beef, mashed potatoes, and more hamburgers, french fries … The roar of mastication drowned out all other sound, so potent that, before the clock struck two, the brothers were gnawing away with the mob.

"Why did Weesageechak kill the Weetigo?" asked Gabriel, as he washed down a gob of bleeding beef with a torrent of Orange Crush.

"All I remember is that Weetigo had to be killed because he ate people," replied Jeremiah through a triangle of pizza. "Weesageechak chewed the Weetigo's entrails to smithereens from the inside out."

"Yuck!" feigned Gabriel, chomping into a wedge of Black Forest cake thick with cream.

They ate so much their bellies came near to bursting. They drank so much their bladders grew pendulous. Surely this place had a washroom hidden away somewhere. Gabriel went hunting.

There—glaring light, ice-white porcelain, the haunting sound of water dripping in distant corners—standing nearby was a man. Six feet, thin, large of bone, of joint, brown of hair, of eye, pale of skin. Standing there, transported by Gabriel Okimasis's cool beauty, holding in his hand a stalk of fireweed so pink, so mauve that Gabriel could not help but look and, seeing, desire. For

Ulysses' sirens had begun to sing "Love Me tender" and the Cree Adonis could taste, upon the buds that lined his tongue, warm honey.

——

The brothers Okimasis burst into the bronze light of late afternoon.

"My coat!" moaned the weasel. "My nice white coat is covered with shit!" Gabriel continued the story of Weesageechak, the image of a certain man aflame with fireweed clinging to his sense with pleasurable insistence.

"Feeling sorry for the hapless trickster," said Jeremiah circumspectly, "God dipped him in the river to clean his coat. But he held him by his tail, so its tip stayed dirty."

"And to this day," Gabriel took his brother's words away, "as Auntie would say, 'the weasel's coat is white but for the black tip of the tail.'" Exulting that they could still recall their wicked Aunt Black-eyed Susan's censored Cree legends, the brothers Okimasis danced onto the sidewalk.

Grey and soulless, the mall loomed behind them, the rear end of a beast that, having gorged itself, expels its detritus.

— Excerpt from *Darkness Calls* —
Steven Keewatin Sanderson

Steven Keewatin Sanderson is a Plains Cree artist and comic book creator. At seven feet tall, he names The Incredible Hulk as one of his childhood heroes. He has written several graphic novels for the Healthy Aboriginal Network, a publishing house that commissions stories on health issues to be released to Indigenous communities. Fifty thousand copies of *Darkness Calls*, a story that addresses youth suicide, were distributed across Canada. He also illustrates an animated series and designs computer games.

Sanderson credits the experiences of a young cousin as the inspiration for Kyle's story and draws Cree culture heroes as though they have been generated from the comic book universe. Traditional comic book heroes and villains are easily identifiable as polar opposites, as if good is necessarily the opposite of evil. In contrast, in Cree storytelling, as evidenced by Sanderson's depictions of the Cree trickster, Wîsahkêcâhk, and the cannibal monster, Wetigo, a more nuanced understanding of power, danger, and resolution is explored. While a traditional comic book story might recognize the cannibal monster as villain, Kyle has to fight against bigger demons. He has to assert his desire to live despite the disrespect shown to him by the school system and his unhappy family. While friends can reach out to him, or Wîsahkêcâhk, in the guise of a visiting Elder, might stop by to support him in this struggle, it is Kyle who has to realize his own power to oppose those who threaten him.

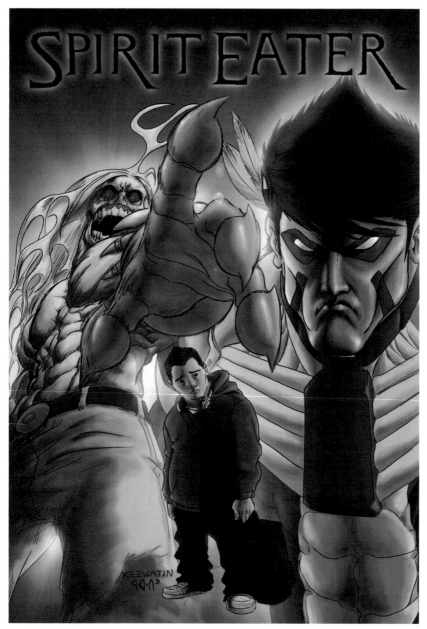

Figure 4.1   Cover of Steven Keewatin Sanderson's *Darkness Calls*. (*Credit:* Steven Keewatin Sanderson and Healthy Aboriginal Network)

Figure 4.2   Steven Keewatin Sanderson, from *Darkness Calls*. (*Credit*: Steven Keewatin Sanderson and Healthy Aboriginal Network)

Figure 4.3 Steven Keewatin Sanderson, from *Darkness Calls*. (*Credit*: Steven Keewatin Sanderson and Healthy Aboriginal Network)

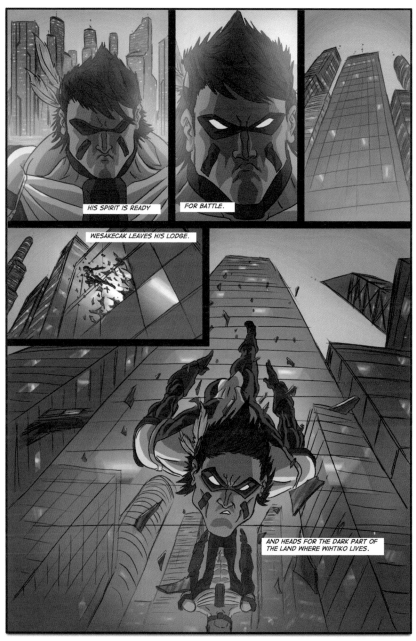

Figure 4.4 Steven Keewatin Sanderson, from *Darkness Calls*. (*Credit:* Steven Keewatin Sanderson and Healthy Aboriginal Network)

⟶ *mōtha nītha Indian / I'm Not an Indian* ⟵
Solomon Ratt

Solomon Ratt is a Woods Cree man from Stanley Mission, Saskatchewan, and a renowned language teacher who is the author of, among other texts, *Woods Cree Stories* (2014). In 2006, Ratt told this story in Cree to transcriber Jacyntha Laviolette as part of a morphology course taught by linguist Arok Wolvengrey. The story is an example of a traditional genre of storytelling, of funny little stories, called wawiyatāci-mowinisa, that are amusing, based on personal experience, and gently self-deprecating. While the genre is traditional, it is clear that the content can be contemporary. Ratt tells a story from his time at residential school, in which he was reluctant to take on the role of "Indian" in a game of "Cowboys and Indians." Residential schools, as part of a larger federal policy of cultural assimilation and genocide, aggressively prevented children from speaking their languages or identifying in any way with their Indigenous nations. Paradoxically, the school supervisor insists that the young Solomon call himself "Indian," the colonial misnomer indiscriminately applied to all Indigenous peoples in North America.

Examine the sentence structure in the story. What indications do you have that this story is told orally from one person to another? Look at the Cree version of the stories. What words were originally spoken in English, with no translation in Cree? Why is *Indian* not translated into Cree?

kayās māna kā-kī-awāsisīwiyān ōtī māna nikī-nitawi-ayamih-cikānān kistapinānihk ikotī māna ī-nitawi-kiskinwahamākosiyāhk. tahtw-āskiy māna takwāki-pī-sim kā-kī-mācihtāyāhk ī-kī-nita-wi-kāh-kiskinwahamākosiyāhk ikota ōma *residential schools* kā-kī-icikātīki, ikotī kā-kī-itohtīyān, āh, *Prince Albert Indian Student Residences* kī-isithihkātīw iyakw ānima. īkwa īkota māna mistahi māna awāsisak kī-kitimākisiwak mistahi māna kī-māh-mawīhkātīwak onīkihikowāwa.

Long ago when I was a child we used to go to school over here, over there in Prince Albert was where we attended school. Every year we'd start in September we'd go off to attend school there at the "residential schools" as they were called. That's where we went, it was called Prince Albert Indian Student Residences, that's what it was called. And while there the children used to be really desolate and they used to really cry for their parents, missing them a great deal.

aya, mīna mistahi mīna māna nikī-mōcikihtānān māna taht-wāw kā-mātinawi-kīsikāk, ikospī māna nikī-kanawāpahtīnān, āh, cikāstīpathihcikana, *picture shows* nikī-isithihkātīnān māna. iyakoni māna, mitoni māna nikī-māh-mōcikihtānān kā-ponī-wāpahtamāhk wīth āthisk māna ī-nitawi-mītawīyāhk wathaw ītimihk tāpiskōc māna nīthanān, āh, *Pirates* māna nikī-mītawānān ikwa mīna *Cowboys and Indians*. ikosi māna kā-kī-pī-is-ōh-pikiyāhk ōma mitoni māna, āh…,nikī-wīnīthimisonān, mōtha nīthanān nīhithawak ta-kī-isi-pimā-tisiyāhk ī-itikawiyāhk māna. ikosi māna kā-kī-is-ōhpikihikawiyāhk īkota kiskinwahamātowikamikohk.

māka piyakwāw ōma ī-kī-ni-tawi-kanawāpahtamāhk *Cowboys and Indians* cikāstīpathihcikan, *John Wayne* ikota mīna kā-kī-ayāt, ī-kī-nōkosit, nikī-cīhkinīn, iyakw ānima nikī-cīhkāpahtīn, nimithwīthihtīn ta-wāpahtamān, *John Wayne* ta-kanawāpamak. ikwa māna kā-kī-pōni-wāpahtamāhk iyakoni aya māna nikī-nitawi-mītawānān *Cowboys and Indians* māka māna ī-kī-māwasakonitoyāhk. āh, piyakwāyihk ita *Indians* īkwa piyakwāyihk kotak *Cowboys*; ikwa māna nītha kapī māna nītha iskwīyānihk kā-kī-otinikaw-iyān. ikwa kītahtawī ōma ōta piyak kīsikāw nikī-ati-otinikawin, *Indians* īsa nītha ta-ayāyān. āh, namōtha nikī-cīhkīthihtīn, namōtha nītha *Indian* nikī-nōhtī-itakison ikota.

Well, we also used to have a great deal of fun every time Saturday came around for at that time we used to watch, uh, movies, we used to call them "picture shows." Those were the ones, we really used to have fun when we finished watching them for we'd go and play outside just like we were, well, we used to play "Pirates" and also "Cowboys and Indians." That's how we used to play, and at that time as we were growing up we really used to, uh … we had a very poor opinion of ourselves. We used to be told that we shouldn't live like Cree people, that's the way we were raised there at that school.

But this one time we were going to watch this Cowboys and Indians movie, and it had John Wayne in it. I liked it, I really enjoyed watching those ones, I liked to watch those, to watch John Wayne. Then, when we had finished watching those ones, we used to go to play Cowboys and Indians and we'd gather ourselves together [choosing sides]. Ah, on one side were the Indians and on the other were the Cowboys. And I used to always be the one chosen last. Well, eventually on this one day I came to be chosen, and apparently I was supposed to be an Indian. Oh, I didn't like that, I really didn't want to be considered an Indian.

"mōtha nītha Indian," nikī-twān. "namōtha niwī-*Indian*iwin!" ī-itwīyān.

"ēy," itwīw ōta piyak nāpīw kā-kī-kanawīthimikoyāhk, *supervisor* kā-kī-itiht; "ēy, tāpwī kikitimākisin ikosi ī-itīthihtaman. *Indian* athisk ōma kītha ta-kī-itīthimisoyan ikos īsi ī-itakisoyan," nikī-itikawin.

    ikosi.

"I'm not an Indian," I said. "I'm not going to be an Indian." I was saying.

"Hey," said this one man who looked after us, he was called the "supervisor." "Hey you're really pitiful thinking that way. You should think of yourself as an Indian because that's what you are." I was told.

    That's all.

⟶ *"The Republic of Tricksterism"* ⟵
Paul Seesequasis

Paul Seesequasis is the first editor of *Aboriginal Voices* magazine, founded in 1993, and for several years was the editor at Theytus Press, the longest established Indigenous publishing house in Canada. He also worked for many years as a literary arts officer for the Canada Council. He released his first novella, *Tobacco Wars*, in 2010. Like the main character in his story, Seesequasis is the child of a Cree mother and Ukrainian-Canadian father, losing the inheritance promised him as a descendant of the signatories of Treaty Six because his Status Indian mother married a non-Status man. (The reverse would not have been true; had his father been Status and his mother non-Status, Seesequasis would have retained his legal identity as Indian.) Also like the main character in his story, Seesequasis qualified to regain his status under Bill-31, which was passed in 1985.

In this biting, humorous story, Seesequasis critiques the divisive effects of legislation upon his community and the misuse of the status card, issued to those registered as "Indians" in Canada under the Indian Act, as the measure of who is Indigenous and who is not. He demonstrates the gender disparity embedded in the Indian Act that from its inception in 1876 until 1985 allowed only men with status cards to be able to pass on status, including the right to live on reserve, to their wives and children. This means that women had the rights as Status Indians only if their fathers or husbands had status cards.

While the first-person narrator refers to himself as a "cross-breed mutt" (174), the author makes the point that some with status have similar bloodlines, although different legal identities. Chief Tobe, for example, is referred to as a "mixed-race pure blood" (173). Likewise, while the narrator refers to himself as an "urban mixed-blood" (173), he does not call himself Métis or Halfbreed, often considered to be a separate community with its own history of disinheritance. However, the main character celebrates Uncle Morris, modelled on the famous Métis leader and community organizer

Malcolm Norris, a trickster described as capable of transforming into a termite in order to undermine political structures. In what way does Seesequasis draw on the Cree story of the cannibal Wetigo to critique these same political structures? Why does he title this story "The Republic of Tricksterism"?

We were urban mixed-bloods. Shopping malls and beer parlours were our sacred grounds, reaching adolescence in the '70s, the Sex Pistols and the Clash provided the tribal drums. Fallen between the seams and exiled from the reserves we were the prisoners of bureaucratic apartheid, of red tape and parliamentary decrees.

Our tribal links were obscure, our colonial banishment confirmed by the Indian Act. White bureaucrats and tribal politicians alike were our oppressors. "We are heading toward self-government," proclaimed Tobe, the Grand Chief of the Fermentation of Saskatchewan Indian Nations (FSIN) as he shook the hand of then Saskatchewan Premier Allan Blakeney.

In his hands Tobe, the Grand Chief, held a paper promising tens of millions of dollars, but that money and power were destined only for a select few. The Grand Chief's vision was obscured by power and long-legged blondes. He denounced Indian women who married white men, while at the same time blond secretaries and assistants crossed their legs in his plush office at the FSIN.

Mary Seesequasis, a.k.a. Ogresko, was born on Beardy's Reserve on January 20, 1934. The first child of Sam Seesequasis, of Beardy's Reserve, and Mary Rose Nahtowenhow, of the Sturgeon Lake band. Sam, my *nimosom*, danced through life with gentleness and humour and became a leader in the community. Mary Rose, my *nohkom*, was large and became a bear when she laughed. She hunted rabbits, decapitated chickens, and farted in the direction of bureaucrats and posers.

They made love, had nine children, and seven lived to adulthood.

The grand-chief-to-be and his family lived downwind from my grandmother's farts. He was born the same day as my mother but their lives were destined to take far different paths. Tobe was born mixed-blood; his father Cree, his mother white. But the irony and humour of being mixed-race was lost on Tobe. He would grow up as a mixed-race pure-blood, purer than thou and given to exaggerating the quantity of his half-cup of tribal blood. Tobe lived in denial of his white parentage.

Being the same age, Tobe and my mother played together as children, they fell asleep infused with dreams of *Wesakaychuk* and *Pakakos*, they hid under the covers from the wetigoes and hairy hearts.

But The Indian Act enabled Tobe to imagine himself a pure-blood. With Indian father and white mother he was allowed to stay on the reserve. In 1950 my mother met and fell in love with a white man, Dennis Ogresko, and because she was in love with a white man and she was *hisqueau*, she had to leave the reserve.

The hairy hearts ran amuck in 1950s Saskatchewan. Cannibal spirits plagued the small towns and hid in grain elevators. It was open season on squaws, wagon-burners, and breeds. By courageously proclaiming brown-white love my parents challenged the humourless segregational values of the time.

Unable to hide on the reserve they weathered taunts and jeers with laughter. That love could exist between races offended all the pure-bred breeders; and in making love, Dennis and Mary parented two cross-breed mutts, my brother and I.

We experienced childhood between the seams, spending summers on the reserve, winters in the city. We played without leashes, without pedigree we learned to live with our genetic-mixture coats and our lack of papers. We lived in a no-man's land between Indian and white. At school we quickly learned to stick together to avoid the beatings of the pure-bred breeders. We found delight in the repulsion others felt for us. We pissed on the city trees, marked our traditional urban territories, and barked ferociously at the white poodles.

It was the 1960s and my mother, now a registered nurse, worked at the Community Clinic in Prince Albert, where she healed the urban orphans and mixed-bloods who were now entering the cities in increasing numbers.

Tobe, the mixed-blood/full-blood too had grown up. He became a tribal politician, a Chief of the reserve and a wearer of suits and ties. His hair was short and his speeches were long. He spoke of self-government and economic development but his mind was focused on attending conferences and getting laid in hotels.

With enthusiasm he joined Wild Jean's Indian Affairs Bandwagon and Wild West Show and with conferences here and there and blondes to his left and right, it was the modern-day chief's delight. Tobe sold his Pontiac—*the Poor Old Nechee'd thought it was a Cadillac*—and actually bought a real Cadillac, and a blond chauffeur. But while Tobe played the colonial game a revolution was brewing in Prince Albert.

Uncle Morris was a *rigoureau*, a mixed-blood shape-shifter. He often came to visit our home on the east side, the poor side, of the city. My uncle was a co-founder of the Metis Association of Alberta in the 1930s, and an urban activist who cut through the lies of white bureaucrats and tribal politicians alike. His mission was to liberate the urban reserves from the cannibal spirits and the hairy hearts. He told my mother of his vision and Mary laughed and agreed to help him. Uncle Morris wanted to take over the Prince Albert Friendship Centre and remove the metal detectors from the door. Those detectors beeped any time someone without a status card tried to walk in.

Morris spoke passionately about uniting all urban skins, mixed or full. "Burn your status cards!" he proclaimed, "and throw away your colonial pedigree papers. Don't let the white man define us. Let's define ourselves."

Uncle Morris knew how to respond to taunts and jeers with trickery. When he laughed he became a bear and his joyous chuckles reverberated from deep within. My mother would prepare dinner and then we would sit, expectantly, waiting to hear of his latest exploits.

As a *rigoureau* Morris was hated by the hairy hearts and the cannibal spirits. They envied his power, his ability to turn into a dog, a bear, or almost any kind of rodent he chose. I remember once his turning into a red squirrel, jumping from his chair and scurrying around the kitchen floor while my parents cried with laughter and said "Enough! Enough!"

From Morris I learned to see the evil spirits around me. I saw them in the frown and looks of scorn us mixed-bloods received on the streets. I felt the disapproving glares of the police, farmers, tribal politicians and store owners. They were everywhere in the city and their numbers were increasing.

———

The cannibal spirits and the hairy hearts ruled the cities and reserves. They fed on both Indians and whites. "There just aren't enough of us *rigoureaus* left to stop them," uncle once told me. "These evil spirits," he explained, "feed on souls that are empty, rub against their bodies and penetrate the skin. Sometimes a person can repel them if they are strong enough or if they can call on a *rigoureau* to drive the spirit away. But most people succumb and the cannibal spirits continue in their goal to create a world of hate. A world in which they can proliferate."

Morris would often go to the clinic where my mother worked to watch and to offer humour to those who were forgetting how to laugh. He played the compassionate trickster, upsetting the plans of the cannibal spirits, and frustrating the violent emotions of the hairy hearts. Many a body was purged of poison.

Then, one day, Uncle Morris went missing. Search parties were organized and the mixed-bloods and urban orphans looked everywhere, but it was the squirrels, the rodent friend of the *rigoureau*, who led us to him. He had been dumped into a grain chute and his body was badly beaten. We lowered ropes and a canvas stretcher. My mother was among those selected to gently retrieve his body from that dark cavern.

While the crows cawed mournfully and the stray dogs howled their lament, our procession carried Morris back to our house. He was laid in the guest room and a group of women healers worked with him. They washed his bruised body, set his broken bones, removed all the grains that had been shoved down his throat and nostrils, and after a few days, his heart began to beat again.

Time passed and Morris cracked a smile and we rejoiced, knowing he would live. "My spirit has tasted life again though parts of my body never will," he confessed. True he was now paralyzed from the waist down. We pooled our meagre resources and had made for him a cedar wood wheelchair with wheels of rounded stone. Being confined to a wheelchair didn't slow Morris down. Rather he called for a gathering of mixed-bloods and urban orphans.

———

I remember that day. We met at an old skating rink. Long benches had been set up for the occasion. The building was packed. Uncle Morris's life history was in that building and each person had a story to tell. Some kindness, some help from trouble, some funny story. There were trappers from the north, none more than three feet tall, with bristled faces and wooden pipes. I remember how they stamped their fur-covered feet in applause when Morris was wheeled into the arena. There were *kokums*, grandmothers, with shawls wrapped tightly around their heads and their aged but strong fingers beading leather. There were young street girls who took the day off from work. I recall the smell of perfume, their make-up, and the candy they gave to the children, who ran up and down the aisles. And there were nurses, construction workers, loggers, teachers, drunks, and others and they had all come to hear my uncle.

"The main cannibal spirit has arrived in town," Morris roared in his bear voice. There was silence in the hall. "He has come for me. I have frightened him and he seeks to destroy me with violence."

"Shame!" cried the audience.

"He has come in the guise of an Indian. A Chief. A person you know well. He is Chief Tobe, the plains warrior wearer of chokers and ties, the politician without humour. The one whose ideas are short and his speeches are long."

The crowd laughed.

"You remember Tobe. He speaks of purity and his heart is cold. He has chased the mixed-bloods from the reserves and he has created a world of urban orphans. I shall trick him with humour. With your help we will create a story. A myth. That is something that cannot be destroyed by violence. It will annoy him immensely because we will create a world he cannot shatter with hate, for it exists here," Morris said, pointing to his head.

Uncle told his plan to establish the Republic of Tricksterism, a place where humour rules and hatred is banished, where love's freedom to go anywhere is proclaimed. "Our headquarters will be the Indian Friendship Centre which, as you know, has been controlled by the hairy hearts. We don't seek permanence for our republic but a moment of time that lasts forever."

We cheered and with Morris's wheelchair at the head, we marched downtown on our mission of liberation. We marched into the Friendship Centre as the hairy hearts, panic-stricken, climbed out the back windows. They left in a rush, not having the time to shred their Indian Affairs hit list of their sacred status card membership rolls. We took their defining documents, turned them upside-down, and wallpapered the building. The children, myself included, were given crayons and told to draw freely. We created a world of merging colours, a world without paint-by-numbers.

The Republic of Tricksterism was proclaimed. All skins are equal was the first constitutional decree and a pair of red drawers became the new flag. Skins from the street came in to help the social workers heal themselves and tribal lawyers were deprogrammed.

Chief Tobe was soon in a fury. He roared with anger and dark clouds pelted the city with hail. He smashed his fists on the ground and the streets cracked and the sewers overflowed. He called loudly and the poisoned souls congregated outside the office of the Prince Albert Regional Tribal Council to hear his message of hate. The Tribal Council was in an uproar, they passed resolutions and sent ultimatums to the Republic of Tricksterism demanding they abdicate power. "We are the Chiefs!" they proclaimed. "The big white men in Ottawa say so." "Ah—go on," replied the Republic of Tricksterism. When even memos from the Minister of Indian Affairs failed to dislodge the trickster-upstarts, Tobe went into action.

A hundred tribal goons were summoned. They were armed with baseball bats, dog repellent and mace. "We shall disperse these mixed-bloods. These defilers of our traditions. These people without status!" The goons chanted their approval in unison. The Tribal Council Chiefs smiled, patted their beer bellies, and licked their fat lips in anticipation.

The assault came at dawn. Calling in the mounties, who in honour of the chiefs donned full regalia and did a musical ride, Tobe, the goons, and the mounties marched in a column toward the Friendship Centre. But the urban animals, the squirrels, raccoons, and foxes, ran out ahead of the approaching army and barked out a warning to the citizens of the Republic of Tricksterism.

"We must avert bloodshed," Morris observed to the citizens. "Violence is the tool of fools. It is with humour and irreverence that we urban animals must survive. Let them have their building back, let them issue their proclamations with dead trees, let them have their dubious titles like national chief, let them become the media stars. We'll find our humour back on the streets."

And so it came to be that Tobe and his goons recaptured the Prince Albert Friendship Centre without bloodshed. "These mixed-bloods are cowards," Tobe proclaimed, in disappointment.

Uncle Morris was captured by the tribal goons and brought before the Prince Albert Regional Tribal Council. "He must be punished as an example," proclaimed Tobe. "He has committed blasphemy and challenged our noble and sacred institutions."

"Spare him!" yelled the urban orphans and mixed-bloods but, as always, the chiefs were deaf to the sounds of the streets. On a Sunday, surrounded by a procession of goons, Morris was forced to wheel his chair to the highest hill in Prince Albert.

There he was nailed to a metal medicine wheel, his arms and legs spread in the four directions. Morris died soon after and his body was taken by the goons and buried in an unmarked grave. The mixed-bloods and urban orphans mourned. Crows flew high and cawed his name to the clouds. A wake was held and for four days the memory fires burned from street corner garbage cans. On the fifth day the crows told the people that my uncle had been resurrected but that he had come back as a termite.

The urban people rejoiced and Morris, in his new life form, moved into the regional Indian Affairs building and gnawed at the bureaucrats' desks until they dissolved into sawdust. Meanwhile Tobe, sporting the retaking of the Friendship Centre as another dishonourable feather in his war bonnet, ran for national leader of the FSIN and won the big chief position at that fermenting organization.

"Who better to speak the politicians' garble? Who better to hide the truth between platitudes of self-government and economic development than Tobe?" proclaimed the FSIN in their press release announcing his victory.

Then one day, despite the opposition of the FSIN, C-31 became law. At the stroke of a bureaucratic pen, status was restored to those long denied, a government decree pronouncing the end of a hundred years' damage. "Hallelujah, we're Indians," responded the mixed-bloods. Our hearts soared like drunken eagles. We donned our chicken feather headdresses, our squirrel-tail bustles, and fancy-danced around the Midtown Plaza.

My mother, a full-blood Cree woman, could only laugh at the gesture. Meanwhile in the FSIN offices Tobe, the mixed-blood/pure-blood, and his Indiancrats, were having a bad day. They grumbled, drank double shots of rye, and hit their blond secretaries.

But C-31 was only a temporary irritation for Tobe. He remained focused on careerism and playing the colonial card game. He wore blinkers whenever he entered the city to avoid seeing the urban orphans. He talked about first nations as if the cities did not exist. He became bloated with his power and gained weight by the hour. As the Honourable Heap Big Chief he increased his salary and his belly respectively. Mary Seesequasis moved to Saskatoon and worked at the 20th Street Community Clinic where she administered to the mixed-bloods: the whores, dykes, queers, street people, everyone. My uncle's words, "We are not victims. We are survivors," was the motto she lived by. Tobe also was a survivor, but in a more dangerous game. My mother saw the Indian Act as a bad joke. Tobe embraced it as a career. His sense of humour was lost in the shuffle of colonial cards and his heart was hardened by the cannibal spirits.

Meanwhile Uncle Morris, having completed his job in Prince Albert, found his way into a chief's pocket and made it to Ottawa. Rumour has it that even today he has led an army of termites into a certain national chief's organization where he is currently munching away at the legs of that chief's chair.

⟶ *Delivery* ⟶
Lisa Bird-Wilson

Cree-Métis author Lisa Bird-Wilson was born and raised in Saskatchewan and has worked for almost two decades for the Métis educational organization, the Gabriel Dumont Institute. Her first book of fiction, *Just Pretending* (2013), features poignant, disturbing stories in intimate settings. The collection has garnered several awards, including the 2013 Saskatchewan Book of the Year. She also published a book of poems, *The Red Files*, in 2016.

In this story Ruth Ann is alone and about to give birth. We soon learn that she needs more than just to have her baby delivered; she needs to be delivered from her violent partner and from a desperate situation. There are few markers in the story that designate the setting is in Cree territory; instead Ruth Ann, Ray, and her childhood friend Old Man, all live on "the Rez," on a turn-off from the highway. Reserves and reservations are spaces across Canada and the United States that were established in order to sequester "Indians" away from urban areas, making the settlement of the remaining lands and the establishment of largely white cities possible.

While there is a universal quality to the theme of family violence and its damage to the health of women and children, the fact that the setting is a "Rez" reminds readers of the history of colonization that has impoverished Indigenous nations. In particular, the story illustrates how colonial patriarchal governance systems on reserves have undermined the power of women. Even in the best circumstances, women who live on reserves often have inadequate access to doctors, midwives, and other forms of health care, and the infant mortality rate of Indigenous children remains nearly double that of the general population. While Bird-Wilson carefully demonstrates how vulnerable Ruth Ann and her daughter are, in what ways does she demonstrate Ruth Ann's strength and resourcefulness? What is the author trying to convey by creating Ruth Ann as a strong character who is unable to save herself?

Ruth Ann looks out the bedroom window and registers the shifting light through the grey drizzle. She wonders if Ray will come home soon. She imagines him sitting in his car on the shoulder of the highway, just before the turn off to the rez, chain-smoking and watching their house. She knows it's a test. He wants to see if she'll try to escape.

Her belly tightens and she rocks her hips in an effort to keep the contraction at bay. Ever since Ray pushed her down this morning, she's felt the cramping with more and more urgency. When he pushed her, she had the feeling of witnessing the event from outside her body, from a distance, as if she were a spectator. She remembers flying across the bathroom in a backward spin, her arms spiralling to try to catch her balance. She was brought up short as her legs caught the edge of the bathtub and she fell in. Her lower back smashed against the back of the tub and her head struck hard against the wall. The impact moved through her body like a wave, through her belly, through the baby, and into the thin air of the room.

The shock of the impact sharpened her senses and she searched her mind for the best move she could make. Her ears rang as she lay in the bathtub, perfectly still, except for placing her hands protectively over her belly. Experience told her not to show her pain, to put up the front that she wasn't vulnerable. She looked up and met his eyes as he stood over her. He was breathing hard, waiting.

"*What* are you doing?" she said, trying her best to keep her voice steady. She achieved a tone that seemed to imply this was a startling, singular event.

His pupils were so dilated his irises were like black saucers, the surrounding whites tinged a sickly yellow. In the back of her mind, she registered the yellow, associated it with a character flaw rather than the ill health it likely represented.

"You're not going," he said, then turned and walked out of the bathroom.

She struggled to get out of the tub, to regain her feet, and followed him into the bedroom in time to see him take the car keys from her purse.

"There." He tucked the keys into the front pocket of his jeans. His voice was flat, his eyes daring. "You're not going anywhere."

Another contraction, stronger and sooner than the last one, jars her from her memory of the morning's events. *This is it*, she thinks, *active labour*. She's seen enough babies born to know the second baby comes a lot faster than the first. Her mother's admonition to the women she midwifed: "You can't wait with the second baby. As soon as those contractions are coming regularly, or your water breaks, you call for me." She has no idea if Ray will be home in time to take her to the hospital.

Ruth Ann decides to call Old Man, beg him to come and get her. To hell with Ray and his stupid games watching the house. Old Man isn't afraid of Ray. In Ruth Ann's mind, he isn't afraid of anyone. She fumbles her cell phone out of her purse and picks out Old Man's number. "Come," she says just as a contraction builds to its crest. She clenches her jaw against it and says, through gritted teeth, "I need you." She's surprised by these words. She thought she was going to say "help"—*I need help*.

Old Man doesn't ask any questions. "Hang on," he says. His voice taking on an edge, a you-can-count-on-me edge, purposely reassuring. The sort of macho thing she might ordinarily find irritating. "I'm coming to get you."

She breathes deeply in and out, focused on riding the contraction to its end. She whimpers into the phone and hates herself for it.

"Don't panic," he says before he hangs up.

She drops the phone into her purse and thinks about Old Man, whom she's known all her life—her oldest friend. Maybe her only friend. Old Man is only a nickname—he's not old at all, same age as her. They went to boarding school together.

Three months ago, Old Man returned to the community. He'd been in the city, trying to work. "Got tired of it," he said when she asked why he came back. That was all, just tired of it. He didn't elaborate.

"What about you?" he asked then. "You doing okay?" And the tone of his voice combined with the look on his face told her he knew she wasn't. But she couldn't tell him how bad it was. Instead, she found ways—made excuses to see him, to be the same places he was. First, she volunteered to work the Tuesday bingo because his uncle ran the hall and she thought he might be there. When he didn't show up the first two times, she decided to look in town.

She parked to go to the grocery store further east on Main Street than was necessary. This was so she could walk past the café she knew he frequented.

As she approached the café door, her chest tightened. She told herself she was going in just to use the washroom and grab a quick cup of coffee. She would pretend she wasn't looking for him. The door jangled as she walked in and her face flushed. She was sure everyone was looking at her. She saw him at the counter and he smiled. "Howdy, stranger," he said, and she sank into the seat beside him, faint with relief. That was how it started. He was someone to talk to like they were familiar friends and they quickly found their old connection, eventually getting bold enough to talk on the telephone in stolen moments.

She knew it was risky. They both did. Old Man was the only person she trusted enough to tell about her plans to leave, her intention to go to her mother's and have the baby without Ray.

She leans on the bed to get through the next contraction. As it builds, she thinks about Ray, watching her, watching the house, and again has a thought she's had often—a semi ramming his parked car from behind, leaving him in a twisted metal wreck on the highway. The police at the door to tell her the bad news. *Fatal. He's gone.* She imagines their words. Or maybe a bar fight gone too far. He's such a prick when he drinks, this isn't hard to imagine—him picking a fight with the wrong person and getting beaten, maybe by a group of men, beaten to the ground and kicked again and again in the stomach, the ribs, the head. Maybe a call from the hospital to tell her he's in a coma. On life support. Dead. These sorts of things happen. Would solve everything, in some ways. But each time she has wished something like this, she regrets it when he shows her another side—a shift that suggests he might come around—the times when he gets better for a while. Full of a hundred promises, bargains— earnest in his resolve, he seems, to her, sincere. And so, once again, she allows herself to be tugged forward by hope until it all comes crashing down anew, as it did this morning.

When the pain subsides, she caresses her belly as she walks across the bedroom, opens the closet and takes out an old gym bag. She sets it on the bed and begins to pack, opening and closing her dresser drawers. She fills the bag with socks and underwear, leaving little room for the rest of her clothes. Then she returns most of the socks and underwear to the drawers and starts again.

She leans her forearms on the dresser as another contraction builds to its peak, a pair of socks gripped in both hands like a prayer. At the end of the contraction, she hastily puts a few more items into the bag and closes it, stroking her belly, wishing for her labour to slow down—for a clear-headed moment.

As the next strong contraction spikes and then passes, she feels an urgent need to pee. She closes the bathroom door, willing herself to stay alert to sounds of Ray entering the house. The door might as well be wide open for all the privacy or protection it gives, the useless lock long ago smashed by one strong kick with a heavy workboot. It's remained broken—a reminder that he won't be denied.

As she stands from the toilet, a thump deep inside her body is the only warning before her water bursts in a cascade down her legs. Her legs begin to shake as she grabs the towels from the towel bar and sinks to her knees on the floor. She tries to soak up the clear fluid pouring from her body.

Her chest tightens with renewed fear. After the last pregnancy, she read books about prolapsed cords and breaking water. She consulted endlessly with her mother, read as much as she could, paid special attention to those things that might go wrong. The last time, the first time, her baby had made it to full term. When he was born, he had a smooth, round face accented by a tiny mouth that looked as though it was waiting for a kiss. Silky black hair cupped a round skull that fit in her palm like a baseball, and he had long-lashed eyes that never opened. It was Ray's fault the baby was born still and lifeless. Her overdue placenta had been knocked from the wall of her uterus. Her baby had drowned.

She stays on her hands and knees on the bathroom floor, afraid that any downward pressure of the baby's head on the cord might cut off its oxygen. She's convinced that, again, her baby is dying, right this moment, inside of her. She can't think of what to do next. She leans her head against the edge of the tub while waves of contractions pound her body.

When she feels the baby shift downward in the birth canal, she fights a surge of panic, certain the baby is dying. She rolls onto her back, half of her on the towels, the other half on the cold tile floor. Immediately, another contraction rocks her body and she closes her eyes and wills herself through it. She's afraid to move because each time she does, the movement triggers another contraction. She gingerly stuffs another towel underneath her hips and takes quick, shallow breaths in an effort to stay focused.

She panics as another contraction rises. "Nooo," she begs, out loud. She rides the crest of pain to its peak and eases down the other side. More contractions follow quickly and tears spring to her eyes as she finally gives in, bearing down to let sound escape from her throat like hot steam. Her work is purposeful and she listens intently to her body as it guides her.

When the head is born, she cries out, relief washing her in a chill. She guides the baby from her body and quickly wipes mucus from its face, looking for signs of life. She lifts the floppy infant to her stomach, pulling at the corner of a towel to work it free, wiping at the baby's nose and mouth, desperate to clear its airway. She scoops mucus from its mouth with her finger while images of her lifeless first infant threaten to choke her. She lifts the baby to her face as though she's going to kiss it and bends her head forward to place her mouth over its innocent nose. She sucks out the mucus, spits it to the side and sucks again. She's rewarded by a sputter; the baby's face contorts with the effort. Then its chest moves, heaves, and it takes its first real live breath. It gives a small cry, first only sputtering, but as she rubs its body with the towel, the faltering sounds finally give way to a tiny bawl.

All at once, Ray is there. When she looks up into his eyes they aren't hard and suspicious, as she's come to expect. Instead, she reads concern.

"It's okay," Ruth Ann says. "Listen to her," she laughs, cupping the baby close. "She's alive. Look. She's a girl."

Ray reaches out to run a finger lightly over the baby's hair, ruffling it back. He looks intently at the infant, who lies wide-eyed and alert on Ruth Ann's chest. For an instant Ruth Ann is hopeful. Together they look into the mystery of those deep, fluid eyes.

"That's great, babe," he says.

Ruth Ann wants him to say more. She wants him to show some emotion, maybe cry; she wants him to be moved by this miracle. She watches him for a sign that he has empathy, for a sign that maybe she can trust him. She wants it to be different—a new start for all of them. And for just one moment, while she and Ray look at their new baby together and he tenderly touches her soft head, Ruth Ann believes that this new beginning might just be possible.

Ruth Ann's legs begin to shake. Ray leaves the room and is back within seconds with towels from the hall closet. He wraps her legs with them and places towels over the baby to keep her warm.

A sharp knock at the back door causes Ray's eyes to narrow and the line of his jaw tightens.

Ruth Ann's scalp prickles as Ray strides from the bathroom. She shuffles her hips, blood gushing as she moves, so she can see through the bathroom door—across the hallway into the kitchen, where she can just get a glimpse of Ray at the back door. He has it open, and she hears Old Man talking but can't see him. Ray steps forward and pushes Old Man with one hand, likely on Old Man's chest, from the angle of Ray's arm. Pushes him back firmly, but not violently, out the door. She hears Ray say, "No, she's not," as he closes the door on Old Man.

Ray returns to the bathroom and as Ruth Ann meets Ray's gaze, her face turns hot. She gives an involuntary shudder. She knows by his look that he'll make her pay for Old Man's presence. She knows Ray well enough to understand that he's calculating, now, just how to do this.

Finally, he curls his lips back and says, "Clean this mess." His gaze takes in the bloody and fluid-soaked towel; his look implies that this detritus from having the baby is something foul and obscene. He makes sure to only look at her and the surrounding scene in the bathroom—he purposely ignores the baby. He leaves the bathroom doorway and goes to the bedroom, where Ruth Ann can feel his presence, his keyed-up anger, radiating through the thin walls.

Her breath comes in panicky waves. *What now, what now?* she asks herself. She shifts, the baby still in her arms, trying to get up to her knees. As she rises, a strong contraction delivers the placenta. She feels the cramping pain in her stomach as hot blood rushes between her legs. She realizes that her bleeding is more than what's normal and lies back again, hopeful that reclining will help staunch the flow. Her muscles go weak and every bit of strength leaves her body.

"Ray," she calls out faintly. He should be able to hear her, even though her voice is small. "Ray, please. I need an ambulance," she tries again.

Another crisp knock at the back door brings Ray striding out of the bedroom and across the hallway. "That mother-fucking—I'll kill him," Ray barks at her as he stomps to the door. He grabs the doorknob and jerks the door open, ready to strike. But then his tense and sure body recoils.

Ruth Ann can only imagine what he sees on the other side of the door. Does Old Man have a weapon? Is he threatening Ray just outside of her sightline?

"What?" Ray demands, defiance in his voice.

Ruth Ann thinks about Ray's baseball bat, behind the speaker in the living room. She wants to warn Old Man. "Don't," she tries to call out, but there's no power in her voice.

There are loud male voices, more than one. She can't make out their words. Has Old Man brought friends? Her neck muscles are painfully tense as she strains to see and hear what is happening. Her trembling arms fall to her sides and she's too weak to raise them again, to protect the baby, still lying on her chest. The blood is thick, congealing on her legs but still moving in a steady stream from her uterus.

"… Some sort of problem," a male voice, closer now, cuts into the house.

Ray takes a step back as the back door is pushed open. Ruth Ann expects to see Old Man enter. Instead she sees a volley of blue and grey; a yellow stripe down a dark pant leg makes her think of the track uniforms the older kids wore in school. For a second, she wonders why Old Man would wear his old school tracksuit to her house. She closes her eyes for a moment.

"I have rights. I can say no," Ray says.

"No, sir. You can't." The male voice is firm.

She opens her eyes as the yellow stripe comes through the kitchen and across the hallway, toward her. The black boots look familiar but she can't quite place them. They're speckled with small, perfect raindrops. Ruth Ann desperately tries to raise her arm, to tell the person to take the baby to a safe place, but she's too weak.

She hears static and a beep, followed by a woman's radioed voice: "Unit twelve, we have confirmation." The radio crackles and clicks. A hand is raised to turn the volume low.

"Are you alright? Can you hear me?" the officer asks, standing over her, his hand still on the radio at his hip.

"I want to go home," Ruth Ann whispers. She closes her eyes and tries to listen. Through the ringing in her ears and the voices that make no sense to her now, Ruth Ann hears sirens, far away. Her mind drifts to a time when she was young, at home with her parents: warm amber light, a quilt made by her Kokum, and her father's strong, wide hands around a chipped mug of hot tea with honey. The baby's movements, its heartbeat next to her own, force Ruth Ann back to the present. The sirens seem closer now.

Almost there, she thinks, willing her spirit to stay strong.

She opens her eyes to see Old Man standing down by her side. He places one warm hand on her shoulder and the other on the baby's back. Almost there.

⇌ *"Rolling Head's Grave Yard"* ⇌
Louise Bernice Halfe (Skydancer)

Louise Bernice Halfe, also known as Skydancer, is a fluent Cree speaker and a member of Saddle Lake First Nation who attended Blue Quills Residential School as a child and who currently lives in Saskatoon, Saskatchewan. She is the author of several books of poetry, including *Bear Bones and Feathers* (1994), *Blue Marrow* (1998), *The Crooked Good* (2007), and *Burning in This Midnight Dream* (2016), all infused with Cree language, histories, and stories. She has been granted numerous awards, including the Saskatoon Book Award for *The Crooked Good*, and she served as Saskatchewan Poet Laureate for the years 2005–06.

The following retells one of the foundational stories in the Cree canon, the story of Rolling Head. Along with the story itself, Halfe provides ways to interpret several parts of the story, demonstrating its depth and complexity. Specifically, she highlights the importance of language in developing an interpretation of the story: "In the attempt to arrive at the interior I have had to delve deeper into the Cree language. Within the language lies the philosophy, the psychology, and the spirituality of our people" (187). What effect does Halfe's commentary have on your understanding of the Rolling Head story? How does the concluding poem add another layer of complexity to the interpretation of the story?

I grew up listening to stories. Books and the written word were not yet the flavour and never were for as long as both my parents lived. One of these stories was "The Creation Legend," a long and convoluted epic. "The Sacred Story of the Rolling Head" (*Cihcipistikwan-Atayohkewin*) is part of it, and the part I wish to discuss today.

This story is ancient. No one knows its origins, and no one knows how much of it has been framed to suit the needs of a society in transition. Unfortunately, Catholicism continues to wave its twisted tongue and confuse our stories and our beliefs.

I have made an effort to understand the depths of this story. In the attempt to arrive at the interior I have had to delve deeper into the Cree language. Within the language lies the philosophy, the psychology, and the spirituality of our people. I have also explored other snake ideologies. Perhaps all I can offer at this time is a whirlwind of Cree thought. Therefore, what I will share is only my version of "The Rolling Head": an exploration of a story told in many ways by many bands and in many families. In spite of the various ways of telling, there remain some constants and similar characteristics, none of which I want to examine or elaborate on at this time. However, for anyone who wishes to hear other variations of the story when the snow lies deep, I would recommend two books: James R. Stevens and Carl Ray's *Sacred Legends of the Sandy Lake Cree* (1971) and Leonard Bloomfield's *Sacred Stories of the Sweet Grass Cree* (1930).

Now the story and the discussion:

A man and a woman left the main camp with their two young boys. (One boy's name was wisahkecahkw, the other's mahihkan; however, this detail is not known at the onset of the story.) They travelled for a long, long time. Sometimes thick in the forest, at other times their thighs sucked deep by muskeg. Mosquitoes fell in hordes, and the young boys cried. In the pines they gathered blueberries, cranberries, and what the chickadees and sparrows left of dried saskatoons, chokecherries, and rosehips. Eventually they camped in a clearing surrounded by aspen, birch, and flowers. They were certain they'd find honey when the earth completed its turn. Not far away a brook sang. Before the sun rose the man left with his bow and arrows to stalk the woods for the offered game. He was a great hunter. However, each evening when he returned with food, supper was often late. He noticed that his boys hadn't gathered enough wood, and his wife hadn't tanned many hides.

The father asked the boys what their mother did all day. The boys wrestled with their tongues, and when the eldest spoke, butterflies fluttered. "After she feeds us and gives us our chores she instructs us never ever to follow her." Their mouths pointed to a light trail leading into the forest. For days the father followed his wife's every movement. He shadowed among the trees. One day he took his tobacco pouch, stone axe and arrows, and strung his bow with fresh sinew. He took his sons aside and gave them a sharp bone, a file, a flint, and a beaver tooth. He filled their heads with plans should he not return.

He watched his wife move among the trees like a deer. She sniffed, ensuring her moccasins were gentle where dew rolled off the grass. The plants, wise in their knowing, called the wind to bend their backs. She untied her raven braids till the freed strands kissed her cheeks. He followed, each movement watched. She sat on a large log and sang a song, fist drumming on the wood. A large snake slithered out, it stood tall on its tail as it swayed to and fro. It slowly slithered up her ankles, her waist, her shoulders and around her neck. The snake rubbed its head against her face, its sinuous body writhing against her. Small snakes crawled at her feet. Each squirmed at the delight of seeing her and feeling her warm hands on their cool long bodies. The man observed, his heart engorged with jealousy.

The following day the man went hunting as usual, though much, much earlier. He returned to the log and drummed it as his wife had done. As each snake slithered out the man chopped off their heads, till all lay scattered at his feet. He gathered the largest, returned home early and made a broth for his beloved. As she drank hungrily, commenting on the delightful flavour, he informed her of the destruction of her snake lover. The woman wept. Soon the tears turned into a burning rage and a roaring fight ensued. Bellows and screeches filled the air as the man and woman fought. He eventually severed her head from her body with his axe, and threw her torso into the sky. He too ascended into the heavens. There, in the night sky you see him, dressed in the golden fire of the morning star, while her torso is still pursuing him as the evening star, her gown a purple sun. However, her head remained on earth and began to roll where the grass bent.

In the distance the boys watched the sky. When they saw it turn blood red, and heard the thunder, they rechecked their bundles and ran.

The head wept, rolled and squeezed through the trails. Off in the distance the boys heard their mother's terrible cry. They ran. Their hearts raced ahead, wind cut their throats, bones bent and stretched. Their mother's breath was at their heels.

"Astum peke we. Come home. *I love you, my babies. My babies," she begged. But their father's wrath and words coiled inside their guts. With icy fingers the eldest son threw the sharp bone. Large stone hills with pointed peaks rose with crevices and valleys so deep that she would surely fall to her death. Like a*

frustrated wolf she bayed. The head rolled back and forth searching for a trail, foam filled her mouth.

A fox came by. His heart was touched by the rolling head's sorrowful wail and desperation. He led her through a pass. She rolled and rolled, hurrying only as a head could rush.

She continued her restless roll. She called and called. Still the boys ran. Again she begged her sons as with painful breath she sang, "Oh love, oh love … come home to your mother's hearth." Again the eldest boy threw one of his father's gifts, this time a sharp file. The brambles, burs and rosehip thorns awoke. Sharp-chewed poplar stumps arose and crowded the rolling head. Trees lay everywhere. The head had to roll under and around wherever she could. Her cheeks were torn and gouged. Blood sprung from her wounds. She crashed through this tangle a matted mess. Still she called her sons, her voice pitiful and filled with pain.

"Oh come sweet precious ones, my boys, my boys," the head sang. Her voice ebbed and flowed as the wind's breath tore through the tall grass. Still the boys ran. The eldest dug in his bundle and threw one more gift. The flint sprung from the eldest boy's hand and hit the pebbled rocks. Here the fire awoke. Unable to stop her frantic chase she burned her face. It blistered and the skin hung in shreds. She continued her wretched roll.

"My babies. My babies. My tired babies. Come home. Come home. Come home to your mother's heart." The boys bled too. Their moccasins were eaten by their travel, their bellies empty, eyes swollen with tears and fear. They limped as they ran. The eldest threw his last gift of a beaver's tooth. It fell as before between the head and the boys. A great lake formed, thick as red-blood honey. The waves roared. The boys knew this was their last hope. They walked the shore, afraid the head would find a way to reach them. They gave themselves to the night. A large water bird spread its wings and offered the head a lift, but only if the head kept still, for the bird's back suffered some lonesome bones. Any movement caused great pain.

The head clung to the slick feathers, but was unable to maintain its grip and it crashed against the bird's backbone. The bird screeched and flopped. In the middle of the lake the head fell, deep into the black depths. The boys travelled on.

Cihcipistikwan (The Rolling Head) conjures excitement, fear, mystery, and even anger. It sends shivers, with immediate images of beheaded women, violence, and a frantic chase. This fascination and ambivalence with women's power and their ultimate demonization has been with humankind since the beginning of time. Hence, my own bewitchment with this story began in childhood.

The Elders teach that "All life is related." The snake has been deemed evil by some and most feared. "Snakes bear symbolic connotations in many cultures, be they beneficent or ominous … for they combine in disturbing ways the comforting and familiar with the terrifying and repellent. Linking desire with fear, and attraction with repulsion, such images, often highly erotic, exercise a strong hold on the imagination" (Lapatin 76, 77, 79).

The command to take ownership over my fear of snakes came when I was quite young. I dangled a baby garter snake on a stick and ran after a man who made my skin crawl. That was the first time I sensed my power. In later years I tested my fear and wrapped pythons around my body and neck, and cradled their lovely heads on the palm of my hand. I thought of the Rolling Head as I explored their scaly reptilian bodies.

Snakes respond to sound, scent, and touch. Naturally when Ms. Rolling Head drummed on the log the snakes knew their beloved had arrived to give them affection. They would respond to the warmth of her hand and to her tenderness. They would know her scent and her familiarity. Perhaps they responded to her air of alienation or her loneliness. Her husband provided well, but apparently was unavailable otherwise. If you leave things or people to themselves they go elsewhere for nourishment. Hence the snakes reciprocated her affection and took pity upon her. Perhaps they rewarded her with medicines to heal her people, for snakes are closest to the earth. They feel the vibrations of the earth, hear her heartbeat, know her touch, know her sounds, and know her scents and medicines.

The story implies the large snake may have been Rolling Head's lover and the smaller snakes were the product of their union. Certainly the phallic imagery is not lost. The head is also round; both represent their respective genitalia.

The Rolling Head had every right to be outraged at the demise of her loved ones. Slaughtered and decapitated the snakes and the woman both "lost their heads." The snake's blood became a sacrificial offering to their caregiver. Perhaps this whole story has been misconstrued, however. Perhaps the woman's attachment to the snake-people was too great. They had much more medicine to offer in their death, but she could not bring herself to kill them. The sacrifice to gain their underworld for mankind's gifts was too great.

The gifts of the snake are powerful. My Grandmother was a healer. She used snake skins to heal those in need, yet she received more fear than respect in spite of the healing that occurred.

Often a woman is perceived to "lose her head" during her menstrual cycle, which is as cyclic as the shedding of the snake's skin. Unbeknownst, in the slaughter of the snake and in the ritualistic offering of the blood, the husband may have empowered his wife. Perhaps indeed he blessed her, but the power was not balanced.

Let us now examine the boys. The husband prepared the boys for their escape and gave them small, but nonetheless powerful, tools to protect themselves from their mother: a sharp bone, a file, a flint, and a beaver's tooth. These tools are filled with spirit, and they serve humankind. The tools were used to gouge flesh and pulverize it. The early inhabitants scraped the hide and pierced the skin to make clothing and shelter. Fire was used for warmth as well as for cooking and providing light. Further, it was used in hunting and as a weapon. These are also the Creator's tools. Mountains, forest, and underbrush, fire and water are given life and give form and shape to the earth.

In order for young boys to achieve manhood, the "umbilical cord must be cut." The woman's love for her offspring, as indicated in this story, has the potential to be destructive to young men. Therefore, it becomes necessary for the husband/father/man to help the young boys not only to grow up, but also to sever the maternal "bond or tie." However, to sever this tie too early in a child's life is detrimental. This is told further in the story, which you, the audience, will have to seek for yourself when winter comes. The father, in this case, is unable to accept the circumstances of his wife's affection for the snakes and speeds up this "severing" by "demonizing" his wife. He does not question his inability to nurture his relationships, focusing instead on being the great hunter and provider. He instills a tremendous amount of fear in the boys so that they can successfully flee for their lives. He is rewarded ultimately by ascending to the heavens. Only the woman's torso is sent to the heavens. Her head remains "grounded" to go "rolling," to explore, to adventure and face the dangers, to be willing to risk death and, yes, even to take on death. In death one gives birth. Rolling Head eventually drowns. However, the "head" has its own symbolic meanings. It houses the brain and hosts much of humankind's ability to make moral judgments, decisions, thoughts; to create, imagine, and dream. When she entered the underworld, she sank into the silent dark depths of the waters, where she created dreams for the visionary, the poet, the dreamer, the singer, and the painter. She became a muse, as "water flows through our memory" (Suzuki 53).

The Elders tell us that the longest and most arduous task that humans will ever undertake is the journey between the head and the heart. Perhaps this story reflects just how hard it is to seek and find one's heart's desire with simply the head.

On the other hand, perhaps she is the manifestation of the creatures that inhabit the deeper waters. If this is the case she is experienced in lakes and rivers as monsters. Whatever the case, "The Sacred Story of the Rolling Head" will continue to live in our imagination and puzzle those attempting to unravel her mystery.

My efforts to unravel the story's philosophy, its psychology and spirituality in my language did not lead me any closer to definitive truths. If anything, I am left with more questions. This, I believe, is the crux of an excellent story, which has conferred its longevity. I will be scratching "my head" and seeking to listen closely to "my heart" for a long, long time. The irony, as always, is that I am looking to the heavens for a part of myself, but only in death shall I be whole, unless the task of putting head and heart together can be achieved while the wind still breathes.

THE ROLLING HEAD'S PROMISE
In this death
I sing you this.

When your Big Heavens slumber
the lightning sears
and thunder caresses the prairie
I'll enter your sleep.
Not land, nor water, wind, nor fire
rock, nor bone, tooth, nor file,
not a fisherman's net, or dreamcatcher
can impede my good grace.

Some will say
But … I never dream.

I will be in their barren walls
wide-eyed or in folded sleep
I will be water-borne, the shadow
in your paradise, the fantasy
in your nightmares, the sorcerer
in your illusions, the magician
in your desire.

I will harvest your bed.

⌒ Excerpt from "Einew Kis-Kee-Tum-Awin (Indigenous People's Knowledge)"[1] ⌒
Harold Cardinal

Harold Cardinal, a member of the Sucker Creek Indian Band, now Sucker Creek Cree First Nation, was only in his early twenties when he rose to national prominence as the author of *The Unjust Society*, written in opposition to Pierre Trudeau's 1969 White Paper. The White Paper, introduced by then Minister of Indian Affairs Jean Chrétien, proposed the dismantling of the Indian Act and the termination of Indigenous rights in Canada. While a flawed document, the Indian Act remains the main piece of legislation that ensures that Status Indians can keep their inheritance based on agreements their ancestors made at the time of Confederation. Cardinal's work is credited with causing the government of the time to retract its proposed changes and for inspiring a new generation of Indigenous leaders, activists, and writers.

While Cardinal studied Canadian law, he spent his lifetime learning from Elders and bringing Cree concepts into his scholarly work. The following is an excerpt of one of the last speeches that Cardinal ever gave, in Vancouver in 2005, shortly before he passed away from lung cancer.[2] Note how Cardinal recreates the conversations with his Elder. What does this inclusion of conversations about Cree philosophy tell you about the search for knowledge? Why is the study of Cree important? What does his speech tell you about each human being's role in the pursuit of knowledge?

"Kis Kee Tum Awin" is a Cree term which means "Knowledge." It is a concept rooted in the language and conceptual framework of the Cree people. It is a term which incorporates many different, complex, and complicated, though inter-related terms and concepts, each originating from and rooted in the Cree language and Cree belief systems. Each of the Indigenous peoples had, and still has, within each of their respective languages, cultures, and traditions, complex and complicated systems for gathering, analyzing, distilling, testing, understanding, and transmitting "knowledge."

Any processes which seek to understand our respective Indigenous peoples' systems of education or Indigenous systems dedicated to the pursuit of "knowledge" can acquire that understanding *only to the extent* that persons working within those processes are fluent in and understand the languages of the people and the conceptual framework and spiritual belief systems utilized by the Indigenous peoples.

This principle lies at the core of "comparative principles and methodologies" utilized by various academic disciplines, be it in education, sociology, anthropology, history or law. These disciplines recognize that comparative research and study of a peoples coming from different linguistic, cultural nationalities can only be properly undertaken if there is an understanding of the language, cultural and conceptual framework of the peoples who are the subjects of the research of study. This is the only guarantee toward reaching a proper and accurate understanding of the differences or similarities in approaches used by peoples who are linguistically, culturally, and nationally different from one another.

We look to our own experiences for validation of some of these principles. An obvious example is how labelling has impacted upon our identities as peoples and the degree to which such labelling has and continues to skewer our understanding of who we are.

The citizens of the Cree nations are known as Neehiyowak in the Cree language. They are known by different terms in the English language. Sometime they are described as "Cree"; or as "Indian"; or as "Native" and more recently as "Aboriginal peoples." We are told that the English term "Cree" comes from a French term "Le Cri" that the French employed to describe the Cree people. Apparently when Cree Warriors went into battle with the French military, the Cree warriors challenged the French by "giving them what they called the War Whoop," a call indicating that they were not afraid to meet them in battle. So the French came to identify the Cree warriors as Le Cri or as "the People who give a War Whoop." The English anglicized the term to the English word Cree.

Federal law and other English sources described the Cree persons as "Indians." It is said that the White man was on his way to India, got lost and when he landed in the Americas thought that he had landed in India and therefore thought that the Indigenous peoples he saw were "Indians." Hence the label "Indian" which has been ascribed to us.

The Indian Act used the term Indian in another way. It used "Indian" as a term, which would deny our identity as "Cree People" more precisely as "Neehiyow." It also served as a convenient way of placing the Cree into a "melting pot" where the term was used to lump all "First Nation persons" as being the same irrespective of their linguistic or cultural background. It was a convenient way of denying all of us our respective identities.

As well we have been known as "Native" and more recently, we are coming to be know as "Aboriginal peoples." All of these labels were placed on us for a variety of reasons—the most common reason being the denial of our respective identities.

As we proceed to reassert control over our institutions and over our affairs, our people need to have a clear understanding—no matter how painful it may be for some—of the reason for and the rationale behind many of the laws and policies which were applied to our peoples.

Approaches which our people adopt, whether for the implementation of the Inherent Right to Self Government or the Implementation of our Treaty, must be based on, anchored in or rooted in the languages, cultures, traditions, and spiritual base of our respective Peoples.

Knowledge of our identity is crucial to any nation building exercise undertaken by our peoples. It is our Elders and it is our traditions which provide us with knowledge of the laws, values and principles, which must, at the core, support and sustain any institutions we create. I share with you an example of why I believe this to be the case.

Many years ago, a Cree elder asked me the following question: Awina Maga Kiya—who is it that you really are? I replied in Cree—Neehiyow Neyah—at that time I thought I was saying "I am an Indian." The Cree Elder then asked in Cree: Ta Ni Ki Maga Nee hi yow Kee Tig A Wee Yin? Tansi Ee Twee Maga? Why is it that you are called "Neehiyow"—what does that word mean? When the Elder realized that I did not fully understand the meaning of the word "Neehiyow," the Elder proceeded to explain. For the purposes of this presentation I will only provide the English translation of the Elder's explanation. The Elder said:

> The word "Neehiyow" comes from two words in our language: (1) Nee-woo—Four and (2) Yow—Body [World]. In the context in which I use the term it means: Four Worlds or Four Bodies. We believe that the Creator placed knowledge in each of the Four Worlds. These are the sources of knowledge, which our people must seek to understand so that both their spiritual and physical survival will grow and continue. When we say that "I am a Neehiyow," what I really am saying is that I come from "the people who seek the knowledge of the Four Worlds." In short when I apply the word "Neehiyow" to myself, what I am saying is that "I am a seeker of knowledge."

"Neehiyow" Elders recognized that the four worlds contained such enormous sources of knowledge that even a person's lifetime was not long enough in which to gather and understand the knowledge which was there. Hence they saw the pursuit of knowledge as an unending, continuous, inter-generational exercise in which one generation would pass onto the next generation, the knowledge which had been gathered and understood with the expectation that the subsequent generations would continue the inter-generational process of gathering and understanding knowledge.

Throughout the eons of time preceding the arrival of the White man to our lands and territories, our people evolved, developed, maintained and sustained complex systems through which they continued the knowledge quest.

Those systems that had to do with the health of our spirits concentrated on discovering and understanding the connection and relationship between our peoples and the creator and His creation. These in turn produced the values and teachings, which guided and still guide the lives and existence of our peoples. Other systems concentrated on knowledge relevant to the physical survival and prosperity of our peoples. These systems enabled our peoples to acquire the knowledge which was necessary to make a living from the lands and water within their territories; to discover the medicines and food needed for the health and well being of the people and the kinds of relationships which had to be nurtured between the land, the environment and the peoples. Many describe our systems of pursuing knowledge as "holistic" in the sense that our systems of knowledge did not isolate knowledge in a way, which separated the spiritual from the physical aspects of First Nations life.

This perspective and understanding of "knowledge" and the pursuit of knowledge is not peculiar to or particular to the Cree people. It is an understanding and perspective of knowledge and the pursuit of knowledge, which all other Indigenous peoples shared. This is the legacy of Education, the pursuit of knowledge, which our people shared prior to the arrival of the White man.

CHAPTER 5

"EACH WORD HAS A STORY OF ITS OWN"
Story Arcs and Story Cycles

Alexina Kublu, "Uinigumasuittuq / She Who Never Wants to Get Married"

Alootook Ipellie, "Summit with Sedna, the Mother of Sea Beasts"

Susan Power, "Beaded Soles"

Zitkala-Sa (Gertrude Bonnin), "The Devil"

Tania Willard, "Coyote and the People Killer"

Leslie Marmon Silko, "Language and Literature from
a Pueblo Indian Perspective"

THE STORIES INCLUDED in this section describe turns of events that may surprise or enthrall you: after all, this is one of the most compelling things about stories—finding out *what happens*. However, the narratives here may also leave you with more questions than answers. One way they do this is by referring to events that happen in other stories, outside of their own narrative arc. Leslie Marmon Silko discusses the concept of stories occurring within a web of other stories in her essay, "Language and Literature from a Pueblo Indian Perspective." Silko writes, "the idea that one story is only the beginning of many stories and the sense that stories never truly end … represents an important contribution of Native American cultures to the English language" (237). In the Laguna Pueblo language, Silko explains, "each word that one is speaking has a story of its own" (237). Stories in Silko's community are connected to many other stories, not only through the characters, who may go on to experience different events in multiple other tales, but also through the very words contained within the stories.

Indigenous stories that might be categorized as "traditional" are often part of a story cycle—that is, the particular tale told is only one small part of a series of connected events. Each narrative exists in relationship to—and in the context of—this larger web of stories. For example, in this chapter, Alexina Kublu's "Uinigumasuittuq / She Who Never Wants to Get Married" relates the story of the Sea Goddess, Uinigumasuittuq, or Sedna. Kublu's short text describes the origins of Sedna, how it is that she came to live in the depths of the ocean, and why she rules over the sea mammals. Alootook Ipellie's "Summit with Sedna" takes up this tale, painting a picture of Sedna's life in the author's signature psychedelic and surreal style. Reading both of these stories can help to fill in the narrative blanks that reading just one might leave you with. You can imagine that the more stories about Sedna you hear, the fuller a picture you will have of her. Of course, one could point out that all stories work this way, no matter what their narrative or cultural contexts. When we read a story about a princess in a castle, for example, we make sense of it in relation to all the other stories about princesses in castles we know. In fact, we form our idea of what a princess *is* by adding together all the things we have heard and seen about princesses. Much like how words in the Laguna Pueblo tradition have their own stories, words in English—like princess—have meaning through the stories connected to that word.

In story cycles, the action often begins before the first words of the story itself are uttered or written and extends past the "end" of the story. Of course, a story does not have to be a part of an identifiable cultural or narrative tradition to function as a story cycle. When reading these works, ask yourself what information you are provided with, and what information is implied in events outside of the narrative arc. For example, how can Zitkala-Sa's short story, "The Devil," be understood in relation to stories in the bible that she takes "revenge upon"? Furthermore, how is "The Devil" illuminated by the history of American Indian boarding schools or their Canadian counterpart, Indian residential schools? As critical readers, it is important to look outside of the texts in this anthology in order to find the histories and other stories that influence, connect to, and extend the narrative arc within them.

➤ "Uinigumasuittuq / She Who Never Wants to Get Married" ➤
Alexina Kublu

Alexina Kublu is an Inuk author and a certified Inuktitut–English translator who was born in Igloolik, in the Qikiqtaaluk region of Nunavut, Canada. Kublu has served as the chair of the Akitsiraq Law School Society and the language commissioner for Nunavut with the Federal Ministerial Task Force on Aboriginal Languages and Culture. Kublu has also held teaching positions in various Nunavut communities and has worked as an instructor in the Language and Culture Program at Nunavut Arctic College.

In Kublu's "Uinigumasuittuq/She Who Never Wants to Get Married," a young woman refuses many suitors until she finally accepts the attentions of the wrong man.

Kublu explains that the story of how Uinigumasuittuq, or Sedna, came to live on the ocean floor has been told many times, by many people. Her own telling is influenced by multiple factors, including her memories of her father's storytelling, her academic background, and her work as an Inuktitut language teacher. We have published the piece here in alternating lines of English and Inuktitut, also known as an interlinear text, just as Kublu originally wrote it. How does knowing that this story has been told many times and in various ways change the way you understand the story? To what extent do you think each telling is influenced by the context in which it is told? What historical contexts are referenced in this version that may not exist in other versions? What role might the reader have in giving the story meaning?

INTRODUCTION

This chapter contains several stories that have been passed down by Inuit from one generation to another. Besides the stories which I collected, the chapter also contains the story of the Earth eggs told to Marie Lucie Uvilluq by her father George Agiaq Kappianaq, the story of Taliillajuut told to Maaki Kakkik by her grandmother, Miali Tuttu, and Lumaaju told to Tapia Keenainak by an elder. The students' stories were collected in the first year of our collaboration with Jarich Oosten from the University of Leiden, the Netherlands.

The following are some of the many stories that I heard numerous times from my father as a child before I went off to the hospital in Montreal at the age of six. My mother would also tell us stories when my father was gone for an extended period of time and though they were the same ones that my father told they never had the same flavour.

My father Michel Kupaaq Piugattuk E5-456 (1925–96) was raised by his grandparents Augustine Ittuksaarjuat and Monica Ataguttaaluk. He learned the stories that he told to his own children as a child from his grandfather.

Even though I received these stories from my father the retelling is coloured by many influences. My father's stories were recorded by Bernard Saladin D'Anglure and transcribed by my late sister Elise Qunngaatalluriktuq and her husband Joe Attagutaluk. Those unaltered forms might be available through the department of anthropology at Laval University.

I first wrote these stories out to satisfy a course requirement while working on my Bachelor of Education degree; that was the deciding factor in the selection of these particular stories and was hence the first influence. The second influence is that I am an Inuktitut language teacher; that influences any retelling that I do. The third influence that shows up in my retellings is that although I am an Inuktitut language teacher and know the mechanics of the language almost impeccably I am not what in Inuktitut is considered to be an "*uqamminiq*" or someone who is linguistically nimble; therefore except for the "direct speech" the language is mine.

"*Uinigumasuittuq*" is I think the most well known of all Inuit stories. It is also known as Sedna, also as the story of the Sea Goddess. She is also known as *Nuliajuk* or *Takannaaluk*. I have always heard this myth told in the complete form as I have written it. Even though it is a story that is widely known throughout the Inuit world, the Iglulingmiut lay claim to the island that she was sent to with her dog. We say it was Puqtuniq. Originally, at the time of the story, Puqtuniq was a small island. The water receded, and Puqtuniq became a hill on the island of Qikiqtaarjuk. Today, after the water has further receded, even the island of Qikiqtaarjuk has become part of the main island of Iglulik. Even though I state that the origin of this myth is in the Iglulik area which is known to be rich in the walrus hunting traditions I do not include the walrus among the sea mammals created from her fingers. The creation of the walrus occurs in another story (not told here), that of the myth of "*Aakulugjuusi* and *Uummaarniittuq*," the first people.

I express my gratitude to my father in this publication. I hope that I let him be aware of my gratitude in some way, however minute, while he was alive.

"UINIGUMASUITTUQ / SHE WHO NEVER WANTS TO GET MARRIED"

arnaqtaqalauqsimavuq uinillualiraluarmat nulianiktuqtauvaktumik.
There was once a woman of marriageable age who was frequently wooed.

nulianiktuqtulimaaraaluit narrugivak&unigit.
She rejected all the suitors.

tikittuqarivuq suluvvautalingmik qajaqtuqtumik tuktunik annuraaqsimalluni
Then there arrived a man with his hair in a forehead topknot, a *qajaqer*, wearing caribou clothing.

sunauvva pangniq, ammailaak taanna narrugijaugilluni.
As it turned out, he was a bull caribou, and once again this one too was rejected.

taimanna nulianiktuqtauvassuujaq&uni uinigumasuittuluaraaluungmat
So, because she was wooed for a long time but never wanted to get married,

uinigumasuittuuniraqtauliq&uni.
they started calling her "She who never wants to get married."

ataatangata ninngautigamiuk uinigumasuittuuninganik
Her father became angry with her because of her unwillingness to get
married

qimmirminik uitaaquliq&uniuk qikiqtaliarutillunigiglu.
and told her to take her dog as a husband, taking them off to an island.

qimmiriik qikiqtamiissuujaliq&utik,
The woman and the dog were on the island for a long time.

niqairutijaraangamik qimmini nangmiuttiq&uniuk ataataminut
niqiisuqtippakpaa
Whenever they were out of food, she put a pack on her dog and sent it to
get food from her father.

qangannguqtillugu arnaq singailiq&uni. qimmirlakulungnik
irniuq&uni.
A long time went past; then the woman became pregnant, and gave birth
to little pups.

qimminga niqiisurajuksiluarmat ataatanga qajaqtuq&uni
takujaqtu&&upuq
Because the dog was now coming so often to get meat, her father came
by *qajaq* to see

qanuimmat niqiirujjalualiriaksanginnik.
why they ran out of meat so often.

qimmirlarasakulungnit unamajuktunit niuvviuqtaulluni.
He was greeted by all the fawning little pups.

qimmirlangnik irngutaqarnirminik qaujigami
ninngaktummarialuugilluni.
When he discovered he had pups for grandchildren he became very
angry.

qimmiq nangmausiqsimalluni niqiisurmingmat
When the dog, with a pack on its back, was fetching food again

nangmautaa ujaqqanik ilulliqsuq&uniuk.
he filled its pack with rocks.

qimmiq qikiqtamut utiqpallialiraluaq&uni
As the dog was slowly returning to the island,

aqtuqsaluamut qitiqparaluaq&uni sanngiilivallialirami
he only got as far as the middle before he gradually lost strength because of the heaviness he felt.

asuilaak
And so

kivivuq.
he sank.

panialu qiturngangillu pijiksaqarunniirmata
Because his daughter and her children no longer had a provider,

ittuup agjaqsivvigivaliq&unigit nangminiq niqimik
the old man himself then started to bring food to them.

**aggilirmingmat paniata qiturngarasani uqautillunigit,
"ataatattiaqsi nunalippat**
His daughter told her many children, "When your grandfather comes ashore,

unamajunnguaqsiqturlusiuk qajanga kingmaarilaurniaqpasiuk
pretend to fawn all over him and chew his *qajaq* to pieces

apailaukalla&&armasi."
because he made you fatherless."

asuilaak ittunga tikimmingmat irngutarasangita
Well, then when their grandfather arrived, his many grandchildren

niuvviuriaraangamijjuk unamajukpakkamijjuk unamajulirivaat.
once again fawned over him, because it was their habit to fawn over him whenever they greeted him.

**unamajuksinnaq&utik qajanganik alupajuksimallutik
kingmaliramik**
They fawned over him, licking at his *qajaq* and then chewing away at it

atuqtuksaujunniiqtippaat.
until they had made it unfit for use.

ittunga qajaqarunniirami
Because their grandfather no longer had a *qajaq*,

**qikiqtamisiuqataujariaqaliq&uni
angunasugiarutiksaqarunniiq&unilu.**
he had to spend time with them on the island. He also had no hunting equipment.

qimmirlakuluit angiglivalliallutik
The little pups were gradually getting bigger

kaaqattaqtukuluungmata anaanangatta aullaqtinnasusivait.
and because the poor things often got hungry their mother prepared to send them off.

pingasuingullutik pingasuuttaq&utik aullarviginiaqtanginnut uqautivait
Dividing them into three groups of three, she told them about their destinations,

qanuiliuqattarniarajariaksaillu uqaujjuq&unigit.
and she impressed on them what they would have to do.

aullaqtirngautaujani taununga nigiup miksaanut aullaquvait
She told the first group she sent away to head down towards the south.

pisiksilijatuinnaq&utik. taakkua iqqilinnguq&utik.
They had only bows and arrows, and these became Indians.

aullaqtimmijani atungavinirmik umialiqtippait uqautillunigit
She made a boat out of an old boot-sole for the next ones she sent away, telling them,

"umiarjuakkuurlusi utirumaarivusi." taakkua qallunaannguq&utik.
"You will come back by ship." These ones became *qallunaat*.

taakkua kingulliqpaat aullanngikkaluarlutik
The last ones were not told to go away; however,

inungnut takuksauvanngituinnaquvait. taakkua ijirannguq&utik.
she told them simply that they should be unseen by people. These became *ijirait* (the unseen people who show up as caribou).

ataatagiik piqatituariilirillutik.
Once again the father and daughter were alone

ammailaak arnaq nulianiktuqtauvakkannilirilluni
and once again the woman was often courted.

suli narruvak&uni nuliaqtaarumajuugaluanik.
but she still rejected those who wanted her as a wife.

tikittuqa&&aqpuq angijuttiavaaluuqquujilluni
Then there arrived someone who appeared to be nicely big;

arnaullu angutittiavaaluuqquujigigilluniuk.
the woman also thought that he seemed to be handsome.

qisingnik annuraaqsimalluni
He was dressed in sealskin,

iggaanginnaq&unilu qajarminillu niulaurani.
he never took off his goggles

qajarminillu niulaurani.
and he never got out of his *qajaq*.

angutittiavauqquujininganugguuq uinigumasuittuup
narruginngirulutainnaqpaa.
Because he seemed to be handsome, so they say, the one-who-never-wanted-to-marry finally did not reject him.

asuilaak nuliaqtaarijaujumatillugu angirulutainnarmat
aullarujjauvuq.
And so, when she at last agreed to be taken as a wife, she was taken away.

aullaqsimaqsaliqtillugik qikiqtalinnamik uitaarijaa
quijaqturumaliqpuq.
After they had been gone for a while and they got to an island, her new husband wanted to urinate.

niupalaagaajjungmat niurlaalungik naittullaaluuk;
When he finally got around to getting out, his ugly tiny legs were disgustingly short;

amma iggaipalaagaajjungmat ijingik amikinnikumut auppatut!
and when at last he bothered to take off his goggles, his lidless eyes … how red!

sunauvvauna uitaarulua qaqulluruluk.
So there he was, her awful new husband, a wretched fulmar.

arnaq kamairrisimalluni uitaaruluni uqautivaa "usiummalu
angijuttiavaaluujutit."
The woman, in shock, said to her new husband, "But I thought you were a fine big fellow."

qaqulluruluguuq inngiqsilluni, "ikurrattiakka ahahahahaha,
So then, they say, the ugly fulmar started to sing, "My beautiful pin tail feathers, ahahahahaha,

ijaujaarjuakaa ahahahahaha."
my grand goggles, ahahahahaha."

sunauvvauna papingminik ikurraqsimannirami
angijuttiavauqquujijuviniq.
And so, because he had been propped up by his tail feathers, he had
looked to her eyes as if he was a fine big fellow.

uinigumasuittuuniku qaqullungmik uiqassuujaliq&luni
Because of her unwillingness to get married, she now had a fulmar husband, for a long time,

kipinngullakpak&unilu, ugguaqtualuugalualiq&unilu
and she was extremely lonely, and very regretful

narrutuluaqpalaurnirminik nuliaqtaarumavalauqtuugaluanik.
of her pickiness in refusing all those who had come courting.

qanganngukallaktillugu ataatanga niurrulluni paningminik
takujaqtuq&uni.
After a fairly long time, her father came all the way to visit his daughter.

pimmatuktauttianngittuqsiarigamiuk aullarutinasuliqpaa.
Because he found her to be neglected, he tried to arrange for her to leave.

ungavaqparaluaq&utik qaqulluruluk angirrarami,
When they had gone some distance, the fulmar arrived home,

nuliani aullarujjaujuqsiarigamiuk maliksaq&luni.
and realizing his wife had been taken, he followed.

anngutivalliajunniirami anuuraaliqtitaalugilluniuk taakkuak
ataatagiik maliksiuqtualuuliq&utik.
Because he couldn't catch up, he made a great wind, and the father and
daughter were caught by huge waves.

kinnguniatuinnaliramik ittuup panini singi&&uniuk imaanut.
Because they were inevitably going to capsize, the old man threw his
daughter into the water.

pania suuqaimma qajanganik pakiniksilluni.
Naturally his daughter grabbed hold of his *qajaq*.

iputiminut anaulituinnalauraluaq&uniuk savingminut aggangit
ulammaaliqpait
He hit her with his paddle, and (when that didn't work) he chopped off
her fingers.

nakapalliajut imaanuaraangamik imarmiutannguqpalliallutik.
As the parts that were chopped off fell into the water, they became the
sea mammals.

nattiqtaqaliq&unilu ugjuktaqaliq&unilu,
qilalugaqtaqaliq&unilu.
There now were seals, and square-flippers, and beluga.

arnaq kivigami imaup iqqanganirmiutauliq&uni.
When the woman sank, she became a dweller of the sea floor.

ataataa angirraqsimaliraluaq&uni atuqpaksimajaminik
Even though when her father got home

ugguarutiqaqpalliatuinnalirami nanurautiminut immusiq&uni
he was so regretful of the things he had done that, wrapping himself in
his bearskin,

ulinnirmuarami ulujjauttiliq&uni.
he went to the tide-edge and waited to be engulfed.

taakkua pingasut imaup iqqanganiittuinnauliq&utik
These three are now on the sea floor,

uinigumasuittuvinirlu ataatangalu qimmingalu
the woman who was Uinigumasuittuq, her father and her dog.

taimanngat ukpirniqtaalaunnginninginnit
Since then, until they acquired Christianity,

tuqujut inuttiavaunninngittaraangata takannaaluup ataataaluata
whenever people who had not lived well died, they found themselves

nanurautialuata iluanunii&&utik
qinukkaqsimajaalugilauqtillunigit
inside the horrible bearskin belonging to the nasty father of that ghastly
person down there, where he made them go through agonies

kisiani ullurmiunuarunnaqsitainnaqpaktuviniit
until finally they were able to go to the land of the Ullurmiut, the people
of the day.

qanuiliurluqattarningit angijualuujaraangata
akuniuniqsauvak&utik
Whenever they had done many evil things, they stayed (there) longer.

arnarli takannaaluulajauvaktuq aggaqannginirminut
But because the woman whom they called Takannaaluk (the horrible one down there) had no fingers

illairunnangimmat nujangit ilaqqajualuuliqpak&utik.
she wasn't able to (use a) comb, and so her hair became tangled.

ilaqqalualiraangat imarmiuttat nujanginni nigaviqqaliqpak&utik.
Whenever her hair got tangled, sea mammals became entangled in it.

nigaviqqajualuuliraangamik puijunnaillivak&utik puijunnaillijaraangata
Whenever they became entangled, they could no longer surface, and whenever they could no longer surface

inuit anngutaqarunnaillijaraangamik kaaktualuliqpak&utik.
people became hungry, no longer able to catch (the sea mammals).

mauliqpakkaluaq&utik kisuttuqarunnaillissuujaqsimaliraangata
Whenever they couldn't catch anything for a long time at the seal breathing-holes,

angakkurmik nakkaajuqariaqaliqpak&uni.
a shaman would have to go down to the bottom of the sea.

angakkuq takannaaluliaq&uni imaup iqqanganunngaujaraangat nakkaaniraqtauvalaurmat
Whenever a shaman went to Takannaaluk by going to the sea-floor, he was said to
"*nakkaa-*."

taqanaqtualuuninganut angakkuit nakkaajumattiaqpangninngittut
Because it was so tiring, the shamans were often reluctant to "*nakkaa-*."

nakkaaniaraangamik inuluktaat kati&&lutik iglumut atausirmut.
Whenever they were about to "*nakkaa-*" all the people would gather in one iglu.

angakkuq mattaaq&uni qilaksuqtaulluni amiup taluliarisimajuup
The bare-chested shaman was tied up, and put behind

ungataanuaqtaulluni qulliillu qattiqtaullutik.
a blind made of skin, while the seal-oil lamps were extinguished.

angakkuq inngiq&uni imaanut aqqaqpallianinganut nipinga ungasiksivallialluni.
The singing shaman would slowly descend to the bottom of the sea as his voice gradually would become distant.

angakkuq imaup iqqanganiiliraangami takannaalungmik illaiqsivak&uni
When the shaman would get to the sea-bed, he would comb Takannaaluk's hair.

kisiani illaiqtaujaraangat puijunnaqsikkannitainaqpak&utik imarmiuttat.
Only when her hair was combed would the sea-mammals be able to surface once again.

⌒ *Summit with Sedna, the Mother of Sea Beasts* ⌒
Alootook Ipellie

Alootook Ipellie (1951–2007) was an Inuit author, editor, artist, and cartoonist whose *Arctic Dreams and Nightmares* (1993) was the first published collection of short stories by an Inuit writer. Born in a small hunting camp on Baffin Island, the majority of his younger days were spent in Iqaluit, now the largest city of Nunavut. Shortly after his fifth birthday, he was diagnosed with tuberculosis and was taken from his family and placed in a sanatorium, where he was forced to learn English in order to communicate. As a teenager, Ipellie moved to Ottawa to attend high school and continued to live there for most of his adult life. In the early 1970s, he did translations between English and Inuktitut, worked as a journalist, and drew cartoons for *Inuit Monthly* (later renamed *Inuit Today*) magazine. Ipellie served as editor of *Inuit Today* from 1979 to 1982. In the 1970s, his ongoing cartoon strip "Ice Box" in *Inuit Today* provided a humorous, critical view of life for Inuit in the changing North. Another strip, "Nuna and Vut," which appeared in Iqaluit's *Nunatsiaq News* in the 1990s, continued his satiric look at a life of transition in the Arctic, leading up to the creation of Nunavut in 1999. His pen-and-ink drawings have been featured in exhibitions in Canada, Norway, and Greenland.

In "Summit with Sedna," Ipellie gives us a comic, erotic, and irreverent episode in the saga of Sedna the sea monster, a figure that populates many Inuit stories, both traditional and contemporary. In this episode of her life, Sedna is feeling sexually frustrated, and it is up to the narrator, a shaman, to band together with the other shamans to give her an "ecstatic dream" that will satisfy her. Ipellie's writing works in tandem with his visionary line drawing to tackle issues of sexuality, abuse, spirituality, and balance in the natural world. While reading, consider what sort of contribution to the narrative Ipellie's drawing makes. Does it help build an image of who Sedna is in your mind? How does Ipellie represent femininity and sexuality in ways that depart from the norm? What relationship to the rest of the world does Sedna's sexuality have?

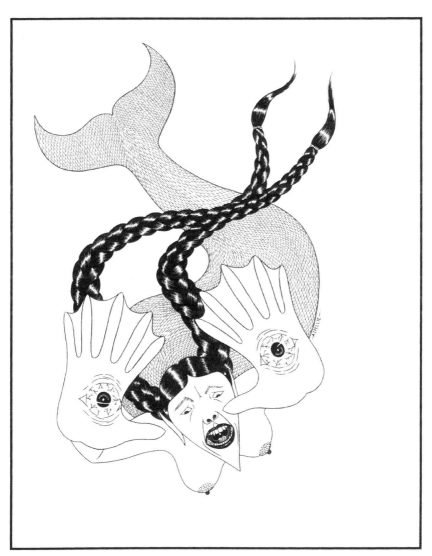

Figure 5.1 Sedna by Alootook Ipellie. From *Arctic Dreams and Nightmares*. (*Credit:* Theytus Books)

As a shaman, I had many occasions to visit Sedna, the Mother of Sea Beasts. Making spirit journeys to her home at the bottom of the sea was often perilous. But these journeys were done out of a great sense of duty to my people when hard times beset us.

One winter, a famine was affecting a number of camps in our region of the Arctic. I was curious to know if other regions were having the same problem. So I made a spirit journey in order to contact all my fellow shamans. Indeed, the great famine was not restricted to our area.

A decision was immediately made as to what we, as a collective of shamans, could do to reverse our bad fortune. This was before I found out our respective shamanic powers had greatly diminished in recent months. Sedna, in her moodiness, was directing her vengeance toward all shamans by not granting their pleas to release the sea beasts. I questioned my fellow shamans about the type of encounters they recently had with the Goddess of the Sea.

Unbelievably, what I found out from my peers could well go down in history as a sexual misconduct that had the potential to wipe out the Inuit nation from the face of the earth! It was the kind of news I could not have fathomed in my lifetime.

From the beginning of winter, Sedna had apparently been making sexual advances to the visiting spirit helpers of the shamans. Although she was well acquainted with certain sea beasts she had control over, she had never been able to have an orgasm no matter how hard she tried. In an act of desperation, she had begun to solicit sexual favours before she would release the sea beasts to the Inuit living in the Arctic world.

My peers didn't really have any choice but to feel obliged to fulfil her requests, fearing their failure to convince Sedna to release the sea beasts might brand them incapable in the eyes of their people. Being seen as a weak shaman would not only diminish their economic well-being but most certainly wipe out their hard-earned prestige among their fellow Inuit. As hard as they tried to use their sexual experience, they had all failed the ultimate test.

Sedna, feeling miserable and sexually bankrupt, had decided to withhold all the sea beasts until a shaman, any old shaman, succeeded in releasing her sexual tensions.

After having heard this unbelievable story, I spent some time trying to figure out a way to break the impasse. Our people's predicament became a desperate situation calling for a once-in-a-lifetime encounter with the Goddess of the Sea. Being one of the most powerful shamans living in the Arctic, I was selected by my peers to prepare a summit with Sedna.

It took me a week to go back and study all my shamanic rituals and taboos that had worked before. Then I had to come up with a new technique that might change the course of our misfortune.

My plan called for all shamans of the Arctic Kingdom to get together for a combined spirit journey to the bottom of the sea. Each shaman was asked to invite their respective spirit helpers which would be collectively moulded to create a giant malevolent creature, a hundred times larger than a normal human being. This new creature would possess spiritual powers equivalent to a hundred spirit souls.

From the very beginning, I knew it was quite unusual planning to confront Sedna in such an unorthodox manner. We had never before gone out of our way to try and make her submit to our demands. Our foolproof method was always to plead with her to release the sea beasts. So it was with some apprehension that we proceeded to try our luck.

Moments after darkness descended over our camp, the ecstatic journey began. I started with a song which I had composed for this particular journey in order to evoke my spirit helpers, as well as those of my peers. It was one of the most complicated seances I had ever attempted.

Finally, after having expended a vast amount of emotional energy through my songs and chants, I was successful in summoning all the spirit helpers to one location. The next step was to make the Earth open so that we could enter it and proceed to find our way to Sedna's abode. Before we ever got close to its vicinity, we had to pass through abysses, fire and ice, and then face Sedna's Sea Dogs, which always guard the entrance to her home.

After successfully passing the Sea Dogs, we got a glimpse of Sedna swimming into her huge bedroom. I motioned the spirit helpers to wait behind as planned so that I could confront Sedna one-to-one in order to find my bearings with her.

She lay there on her bed, which was well covered with seaweed. Her long, unkept hair had become quite dirty. By the look of her distraught eyes and downturned mouth, I had the inkling she was still quite sexually frustrated.

As was always the custom in my past encounters with her, I immediately started combing and then braided her hair, all the while pleading with her to release the sea beasts. She was perfectly willing to—under one condition. I wanted to know what this condition was. What I then heard was a long, drawn-out preamble to her life-long sexual history, or, more appropriately, lack of it.

It had started when she was still a little girl living in the natural world a few years before she became a Goddess of the Sea. Her father had sexually abused her many times, and when it occurred, it lasted for hours on end. It was because of this prolonged abuse that she became emotionally, mentally, and physically doomed to sexual impotency—unable to have an orgasm no matter how hard or what method she tried.

In a last-ditch effort to turn her misfortune around, she had begun to relegate her hopes on the visiting spirit helpers of the shamans from the entire

Arctic Kingdom. When an attempted bribe failed with each spirit helper, she would try again with another. This sordid affair continued for the duration of the winter. And now, she was asking me to do the unthinkable! I was perversed by her desperate words.

It was at this moment that I turned and left her bedroom as if I had given up like the other spirit helpers and was returning to the natural world. Sedna began sobbing like a little, trembling child. I understood that nothing would make her sadder than another opportunity lost for sexual fulfillment.

My only alternative was to release our version of Frankenstein to confront Sedna. Frankenstein crawled into Sedna's bedroom. Sensing the presence of unusual energy around her, Sedna sat up, moving like a cobra, and turned her head to look over her shoulder.

What she saw behind her was a giant of a monster, more fearsome than any creature she had ever encountered at the bottom of the sea. Frankenstein stood up and towered over the tiny body of Sedna. Sedna shrieked the hell out of her lungs. She begged the monster to stand back, extending her webbed hands toward the monster's eyes which were streaked with crimson and glowing like gold!

Frankenstein began doing a special chant I had composed for him. It was designed to put Sedna into a trance. This would allow her to have an ecstatic dream—a sensual trip she had never taken in her lifetime. Sedna had become, over the passing of many years, an almost senseless soul, unable to express intimacy in light of her sexual impotency.

During her forced-sensual-dream-trance, Sedna finally met her match. It was her male equivalent, Andes, a God of the Sea, who presided over all the sea beasts on the other side of the universe. In her dream of dreams, Sedna had a sexual encounter measurable in ecstatic terms only attainable in the realm of gods and goddesses.

In a state of sexual ecstasy, Sedna released a perpetual explosion of orgasmic juices. In the same instance, during her virgin joy, she released all the sea beasts, which immediately proceeded to travel with impunity to the hungry Arctic world.

It was beautiful to see the lovely beasts, swimming torpedo-like, toward the breathing holes on the Arctic sea ice. It was wonderful to experience the same excitement of unleashing bottled tension Sedna was going through for the first time in her long vocation!

It was the first time in the history of the Arctic Kingdom that all of its shamans had worked together to avert a certain threat of extinction of its people from the face of the Earth. From this day on, the Inuit were assured survival as a vibrant force in what was oft-times an inhospitable Arctic world.

And, more importantly for me, in the eyes of my people, my reputation as a powerful shaman remained perfectly intact.

⟶ *Beaded Soles* ⟵
Susan Power

Susan Power is a Standing Rock Sioux author from Chicago. Power's parents raised her to be politically and socially aware. At the age of three, she had the opportunity to meet Dr. Martin Luther King Jr.; along with her parents, Power eventually became active in the civil rights movement. Power was named Miss Indian Chicago at the age of seventeen, earned an AB degree in Psychology at Harvard/Radcliffe, and later received her Juris Doctorate from Harvard Law School. After a short career in law, she decided to become a writer, starting her career by earning an MFA from the Iowa Writer's Workshop. Her best-known works are her novel, *Grass Dancer* (1994), which won the PEN/Hemmingway Award for Best First Work of Fiction, and *Roofwalker* (2002), a collection of stories that includes "Beaded Soles."

Integral to Power's "Beaded Soles" are the concepts of memory and history, and the ways in which they leave their mark on the present. In this work of short fiction, Maxine Bullhead is the great-granddaughter of Lieutenant Henry Bullhead, the Sioux policeman responsible for the death of Sitting Bull, the political leader and warrior. The bad luck created by this egregious act has been passed down through the generations and now sits squarely with Maxine, like "the familiar weight of old sin" (222). When reading this story, pay attention to how memory and the persistence of history are important tools as well as burdens in Maxine's life. For example, how does "refusing to forget" help Maxine and Marshall survive their years at St. Joseph's Catholic Indian School? What does Power's writing suggest to you about the power of history?

I am beading moccasins for my husband, Marshall Azure. I am beading the soles so he can walk clear up to the sky. There was a fuss about letting me have a needle. They take it away at night so I can't use it as a weapon to put out someone's eye.

The Chicago Indian Center took up a collection for me to get whatever I needed, and I asked for cut beads, sinew, and buckskin so I could make a pair of death moccasins for Marshall to wear into the next world.

They're taking his body home to Fort Yates, North Dakota, on the Standing Rock Sioux Reservation. I won't be able to attend the services. It's just as well though, because I know Father Zimmer's "Sermon for a Dead Indian" by heart. He likes to call heaven "The Happy Hunting Ground," but it is an Anglo heaven Father Zimmer describes. It sounds like a great bureaucracy:

the most sophisticated filing system in the world, where all your sins and virtues are entered like tax statements to the IRS. Father Zimmer's heaven is exclusive—don't call us, we'll call you. Half the fun of being there is knowing others didn't make it.

Father's eyes change from blue to gray when he talks about heaven. His sharp overbite slices the words as they leave his mouth until he resembles a great snapping turtle rending pieces of flesh. He doesn't realize that later Herod Small War will negate him. Herod will clean Father's words from the congregation's mind. He will talk over the body of Marshall Azure in Dakota, and Father Zimmer will nod as though he understands. Herod will explain to Marshall that Indian heaven is democratic, it is home, it is the place where we shall all meet again to join in the Great Powwow which goes on well into the night. In Indian heaven the Dakota people wear moccasins with beaded soles and dance on air. Herod will tell Marshall to look for us later on, to meet us on the road when it is our turn to make the journey.

Even *I* will make it to Indian heaven, where I will dance all night with my husband, Marshall Azure, carrying our son, Jasper, in my arms.

On the reservation, memory is a sap that runs thick and deep in the blood. The community memory is long, preserving ancient jealousies, enmities, and alliances until they become traditional. In my family, memory was a soldier's navy blue tunic, stiffened on the left side with a spatter of sacred brown blood. Memory lured me into my parents' bedroom closet, where the tunic was kept on a hanger, covered by a flour sack.

My fingers unpinned the bottom of the flour sack to stroke the coarse material. I touched memory and pain in the dark back of the closet, biting the tip of my tongue and slowing my breath to its most silent. When I refolded the hem of the flour sack and repinned the garment, I wanted to leave memory behind me. My parents' bedroom closet should have been its museum. But memory's shadow pinned my own to the ground until some days I imagined I could feel God's thumb pressing on the crown of my head.

The soldier's tunic belonged to my great-grandfather, Lieutenant Henry Bullhead, an Indian policeman sent to arrest Sitting Bull. Lieutenant Bullhead was shot in the side by Catch-the-Bear—one of Sitting Bull's followers—and the lieutenant shot Sitting Bull as he fell. It was said that the soldier's wound wasn't serious, that he would have lived if Sitting Bull hadn't been fatally shot and fallen across him. The holy man's blood was enough to kill his enemy. Lieutenant Bullhead's blood washed away as Sitting Bull's blood drenched the policeman's jacket, poisoning his wound.

As it turned out, Lieutenant Bullhead got off easy. He died and his body was taken back to his family. They buried him dressed in a fresh uniform, his hands folded across his chest like a white man.

Lieutenant Bullhead left his sin behind him, scraped from his soul the way caked dirt had been knocked off his boots. The sin was left to his children.

———

My great-grandfather's sin against our own tribe came down through the generations as if it was packaged in our genes. When a Bullhead made a misstep in life people would say, "What can you expect from a Bullhead?" Our word was doubted and we were considered unlucky. This last was true.

My father owned a horse we called *Ista Sa*, Red Eyes, for the angry glowing eyes in his black face. No one could safely approach *Ista Sa* except my father, yet every morning the horse's mane and tail were plaited in tight knots, which my father spent a half hour untangling. It was said that mischievous *heyoka* spirits the size of small children played tricks on the dangerous horse to tease my father.

My mother never had success with her canning. No matter how careful she was, the chokeberry jelly would ferment and the tomatoes spoil until the mason jars exploded.

Our cabin burned to the ground in 1939, when I was nine years old, and the next year my father was killed by a bolt of lightning. He had just been paid for helping a white rancher break in a herd of wild ponies. He was found by the side of the road leading to the reservation, five silver dollars in each hand. My mother tried to give me one of the silver dollars so I would have something of my father's, but I wouldn't touch it. I imagined the scorched silver was evil.

My mother had always been generous, but after my father's death she gave away anything she considered frivolous. People trained themselves not to compliment her clothes, house, or vegetable garden because whatever they admired she would offer. I had been in Father Zimmer's catechism class long enough to believe she was doing penance. I finally asked her, when our small house was nearly empty.

"*Ina*," mother, "are we repenting?" My mother was busy altering a dress for the wife of Mr. Mitchell, the reservation agent. We didn't own a sewing machine but her stitches were neatly uniform. She looked up from a flounced skirt.

"I don't understand," she said impatiently. She needed to finish the dress, which was to be worn that evening.

"Giving everything away. The blankets even."

"You're Dakota," she scolded. "I thought I raised you to be generous."

"But almost everyone else has more than us now."

"Greedy. Do we have to be like everyone else?" She was dismissing me. "Do you think we're like everyone else?"

No, I had never thought that. But perhaps we could have been. I never forgave my mother for marrying the grandson of Lieutenant Henry Bullhead. She could have chosen wisely. She'd had her choice of any Sioux, Cheyenne, or Assiniboin. My mother was a Sioux and French beauty, one of three Arshambault sisters who specialized in collecting hearts. And here she had chosen my father, taken his name, helped him create a child in his own image. She hadn't refused him the way I'd refused the silver dollar, not wanting what my father had to give me.

My father was a tall, quiet man with a tremendously thick mustache. I secretly believed the heavy mustache was what kept him silent, making it too difficult for him to lift his upper lip.

I was an awkward version of my father, stretched to his height—nearly six feet tall—as a grown woman. People said I was like him, they called me handsome, but I felt too strong to be attractive. My hands and feet were too broad, my hair too thick. I could chop wood like a man and carry three times the load of kindling my mother carried.

People expected me to be an old maid. I had two strikes against me: being a Bullhead *and* physically powerful.

My mother tried to assure me. "Remember the Dakota War Women," she said. She reminded me about the Sioux women who chose to join their husbands in battle.

"Your grandma killed this many of the enemy," my mother would say, holding up both hands to spread ten fingers. "She was one of the best fighters and everyone wanted her for a wife. The best thing is to fight side by side."

I almost smiled. I couldn't imagine my mother riding into the dirt and blood, her face painted black like a Sioux warrior. The songs of insult flung at the enemy would never sound mocking on her sweet tongue.

"Dakota men will respect you. They will value your strength," she promised.

Maybe Dakota men had seen too many movies in Bismarck. Movies where Jean Harlow pouted, Greta Garbo was silent, Merle Oberon fainted, and Claudette Colbert's eyes widened in innocent confusion. Either that or the long shadow of memory stretched across my face like a veil so I was hidden from consideration.

I was twenty years old before Marshall Azure came looking for me. He showed up on washing day, when my sleeves were rolled up and my arms looked long, like they extended forever. He came right up to me in back of our house, hands on his hips. When he looked me in the face our eyes were level.

"You remember me?" he asked, trying to puff himself taller. I nodded, ready to crack down the middle with a huge smile.

"You're a Bullhead," he teased.

"You're a fathead." Words we had spoken before in the school yard of Saint Joseph's Catholic Indian School in Bismarck. The school had anticipated a showdown between us, the two tallest Dakotas in the third grade. Minnie, a Gros Ventre girl with a rapid tongue, spread the news when the time came. She must have seen it in our eyes.

We circled one another slowly, carefully balanced, working our toes into the ground. The first move wouldn't happen until we'd offered the words. We stood toe to toe, square-matched in height and frame like a reflection.

"You're a Bullhead," Marshall said, tapping me on the chest with a forefinger. There was a terrible pause. The children were delighted.

"You're a fathead." I spat, toed the dust so it kicked across his shins. We rolled on the ground, becoming dark earth, sometimes becoming one person. The struggle was even and lasted until Sisters Fatima and Michael pulled us apart. Blood was in Marshall's mouth, smearing his teeth. I felt a knot rising on my forehead. We smiled at one another, sudden allies.

For the rest of our school days we were conspirators. We whispered Sioux together in the halls and play yard, defiant of rules. We talked about the Sun Dance and Herod Small War, a powerful Yuwipi man. We wrote perfect essays the nuns tacked on the wall, and secret essays we passed back and forth through a great underground system of resistance. Essays on what it was to be Indian, what it was to refuse to forget.

Now Marshall Azure stood before me, a grown man. He was still restless in his own body, squirming a little in the sun. He had the pigeon-toes of a traditional dancer, and a straight Sioux nose so old-fashioned it was almost arrogant. His top lip lifted in a permanent sneer, reminding me of Kicking Bear, one of Sitting Bull's contemporaries. His skin was so even in its warm color I imagined old women had gone over it with their flat thumbs, smoothing and blending.

"I'm back," Marshall said, waiting. His silence pressed me to answer. I wanted to run my thumb across the plane of his forehead.

"Took you long enough," I answered, finally putting my arms around him in welcome.

Marshall and I went down to Mobridge, South Dakota, to get married. We went to Happy Sam's place, about twenty miles out of town. Happy Sam was a white justice of the peace who specialized in Indian weddings. At powwows he handed out brochures that were so attractive most people on the reservation had one tacked up on their cabin wall.

The cover pictured a handsome Sioux couple wrapped together in a star quilt. Their heads were bowed, the target of a pointing finger reaching down from a pulpit in the upper left-hand corner. Beneath the couple was printed:

HAS THE CHURCH RENOUNCED YOU?
DOES THE CHURCH STAND IN THE WAY OF YOUR ETERNAL BLISS?

The following pages described how Happy Sam could make dreams come true. He married all comers—no questions asked.

We left the reservation and the state of North Dakota to get married because Marshall came from an important Sioux family.

"Your blood is from the Black Hills," his mother liked to say, exaggerating its purity. His family didn't want him linking his name to mine, marrying into the long shadows. But Marshall had a mind of his own.

Happy Sam was plucking a wild turkey when we pulled up. He was pasted with blood and feathers. He dropped his work and ran up to our car before we ever made a move to get out.

"You're *sure* you're going through with it?" he asked, wiping his hands on the seat of his overalls. "*And* you got the money?" Happy Sam hadn't smiled yet the way he did on the last page of the brochure. Marshall nodded. Happy Sam smiled. "I'll go wash up then," he said.

I watched him walk back toward his clean-painted two-story house. It was a soft blue that melted into the sky. I watched him climb the steps to his porch and open the front door. Just inside I could see a narrow hallway, the floor covered with an Oriental carpet runner. Happy Sam walked right across that runner in his blood-and-feathered clothes. I'd heard that he had Oriental rugs throughout his house in rich colors like wine red and royal blue. He had real Chantilly lace curtains at every window and tatted doilies on each piece of furniture.

Happy Sam's two sons appeared from somewhere behind the house. One carried an accordion and the other a fragile guitar that looked very old. They could have been twins, both about fifteen years old, all corners in their clothes, standing on long, skinny feet. Their hair was the color of a match flame, silver white at the roots burning yellow at the tips.

They leaned against the house and stared at us, passive as two cows in a pasture. The accordion made me remember that back in the thirties Happy

Sam had toured throughout the Dakotas with Lawrence Welk's band. He must have passed the music on to his sons.

When Happy Sam returned he was dressed in a worn black suit which had a plum purple shine in the sun. He wore black-and-red striped moccasins on his feet and a warbonnet on his head with feathers trailing all the way down his back to brush against the ground.

He motioned for us to stand beside him in front of the house. I realized then that we would be married outside, like every other Indian couple he led to eternal bliss. I'd heard that when it rained or snowed he would move as far as the porch, but that an Indian had never set foot on his Oriental rugs or sat on a piece of his doily-covered furniture. Somehow I had imagined that Marshall and I would be exceptions. We were dressed so carefully and standing straight. We had combed our hair again before leaving the car.

Marshall seemed unhappy about something himself. He was cracking the knuckles of his thumbs over and over, their pop like the snapping of wishbones. He waved his hand at Happy Sam's warbonnet.

"You don't have to wear that," he said.

"You pay the full price, you get the full treatment," Happy Sam told him. He fingered the folded bills already tucked in his breast pocket.

"Where'd you get that anyway?" Marshall asked him.

"Satisfied customers," Happy Sam answered. "Satisfied customers. But you know, you don't have to worry," he told Marshall, opening a ragged pamphlet to the words he used to bind couples together. "I have respect." Happy Sam snapped his fingers at his sons, who launched into a bouncy song, something like a polka.

I want to remember the words Marshall and I gave one another, the promises we spoke into the wind, standing on a South Dakota plain. But I don't remember the vows. I don't remember saying my name, Maxine Bullhead.

Instead I see the limp turkey resting on a bench, its broken neck dangling over the side, beak dipped toward the ground. I see Happy Sam's sons in the background, their instruments slack in their hands, mouths open, eyes fixed on the grass. I see Happy Sam sweating in his suit, wetting the feathers of the warbonnet that framed his face. And I remember feeling the sudden weight of sin—tired, well-handled sin passed from hand to hand—slam against my heart.

"You're married," Happy Sam told us as I struggled to catch my breath. "It's over," he said when I didn't move. Happy Sam pulled off the warbonnet and wiped his dripping forehead on the arm of his suit jacket. He slung the warbonnet over his shoulder and walked his boys into the house.

Marshall took my hands and squeezed them too hard. "Let's get out of here," he whispered. And we did.

It was five years later that Herod Small War caught me after church. "You visit the doctor," he counseled, grinning mischievously.

I tried not to hope too hard. I tried not to let my dreams run loose. But it turned out Herod was right. Marshall and I were finally going to have a child. Between us we knew he would be a boy named Jasper. We knew what he would look like. In bed together at night we drew pictures in the air. Jasper would be a singer, his voice would cry and sing, bringing back the old days. Jasper would be eloquent like the ancestors. We would close our eyes to hear him speak. Jasper would expand our married circle, increasing the love between us. Jasper would forever seal the busy mouths of rumor weavers who strung their looms each morning with deft tongues, claiming our childlessness was proof of what marrying a Bullhead would do.

Marshall worked hard at whatever jobs he could get. He helped local farmers with harvesting and rode with ranchers to tend cattle. He threshed, branded, and butchered. He dreamed as hard as I did.

On my last visit to the Indian Health Clinic before the delivery, the doctor called the two of us into his office. He was a new doctor from somewhere in the East where people spoke too quickly. His glasses kept slipping down his nose. He looked frightened. The three of us sat in silence for long moments. Marshall shifted. We were both too large for the small, hard chairs.

Suddenly the doctor was telling us, "The baby is already dead. It happens sometimes. We can't find a heartbeat."

I wanted to offer my own. *Give Jasper mine*, I thought. *Give him something of mine to warm his blood.* The doctor's voice was pitched too high, on the verge of hysteria. I wondered why this doctor was so upset for us.

Marshall had risen. He was arguing with the doctor. I wanted to rise too, but Jasper weighed me down like an anchor. Marshall told the doctor his science wasn't the last word—it was only good up to a point. Marshall looked stronger than I'd ever seen him. He looked like he could hammer the doctor into the ground with just a few more sentences.

That's why he's upset, I realized. *He's afraid of us.* Who knew what a wild Indian would do to a white doctor from the East. Too much John Wayne. Too many Hollywood hatchets dripping stage blood. I calmly watched the doctor in his terror, purposely concentrating on him to keep my mind from slipping off sideways, running out of the clinic and scrabbling on all fours to the top of Angry Butte, where its last trace of understanding would explode into slivers of howling sound.

The baby was due that week, so the doctor told me he wouldn't induce labor for two days. It was still possible for me to deliver naturally and avoid an operation. Marshall was convinced there was hope. He worked harder than ever.

When I was alone I kept my eyes busy, off the rounded hill of my stomach rising like a burial mound. I had my mother make special moccasins for Jasper, just in case. But I wouldn't allow them in the house. The ancestors might become anxious to fit them on his feet.

Marshall took me to the Indian Health Hospital when I went into labor. The pain made me happy. The pain stretched a smile across my face. Marshall shivered in the car. His hands drifted over the steering wheel, locking and unlocking. Slim twists of prayer tobacco were spread on the dashboard, their spicy smell sweetening the air. Marshall was watching the straight, empty road.

"Don't give up," he told me. They could have been my son's words.

"No," I told my husband, "we won't." Pain was my son's voice. He was trying to be heard. I listened and listened. My body strained to hear until the whole world became the angry voice of pain and the scent of tobacco.

When we arrived at the hospital Marshall stayed with me until I was taken away to a yellow room.

"He's run off," I heard one of the nurses tell the doctor. She smiled at me and her features pinched together. "We'll get this over with as soon as possible," she said.

No. Don't give up. Voices were filling my head. My brain was swollen and tight with voices until I felt them exploding from my body: rushing from my ears, singing from my mouth, falling from my eyes, rising from my pores.

"Poor soul," the nurse was whispering, "he's probably off getting drunk and left her with this tragedy." She placed her hands on my knees and I felt the voices stab her flesh and soar to the ceiling.

"I see it time and time again," the doctor said. He didn't touch me. He was looking at his clean white hands as the voices slipped inside his jacket to lick his skin.

"It was a mistake to repeal," the nurse said. I knew what she meant. The Indian Liquor Law, prohibiting Indians from buying liquor, had been repealed only two years earlier. She was flushed and smug. She didn't notice that the voices had tipped her cap and were chewing on the nipples of her breasts.

"You're almost there," the doctor told me. "It'll be over soon."

No. Don't give up. The voices punctured his eyes.

Eventually the pain became quiet and the voices died. They scattered like petals, and the doctor and nurse crushed them underfoot. My son, Jasper, was silent in the nurse's arms.

"I want him," I told her. She shook her head, no, and moved toward the door.

I sat up and touched my feet to the cold floor. "You bring him to me right now," I told her, starting to rise.

"You'd better let her," the doctor said as he left the room.

I held my son, Jasper, in my arms. His body was light as a rag doll's, but his head was heavy. His thoughts must have petrified, layer upon layer. He was beautiful, like my mother. His lashes were very long, brushing down the rim of his cheeks. His body was perfect. It was hard to believe anything was wrong.

"*Abu*," I whispered. Sleep. "*Abu*." In the few minutes the nurse left me I let go of Jasper's spirit. I put my lips to the unfused well of his soft spot, whispering "*abu*," until it became a mother's song, and rocked him away.

———

When he returned later that same day, Marshall's hair was wet, making it spike and separate like quills on a porcupine. His face was dirty, oiled with dust, sweat, and tears. He took my face in his hands. They smelled of tobacco and were hot, as if he had just snatched them from a fire. When my tears hit his hands I expected a spitting hiss.

"It didn't work," he whispered, looking not at me but at a corner of the room where two yellow walls met in a gray shadow. "We prayed. We called on everyone we could remember, and see what happened." He was talking to himself, I thought. "See what happened," he insisted.

Marshall had driven to Herod Small War's place to pray for Jasper. Their voices had joined me from across thirty miles and held me up when I brought death into the world. The ancestors they called on for help were sleeping. The ancestors were peeking at us from behind their hands but wouldn't look and wouldn't answer.

"It's because I'm a Bullhead," I told my husband, and I moved my eyes to the same spot in the corner of the room he had watched so carefully. I thought the gray shadow moved. I thought it quivered before settling back against the yellow walls.

I had felt empty after the delivery, light and hollow, ready to float up to the ceiling except for my heavy tears. But now I felt the familiar weight of old sin. Marshall had brought it back. He had seen its shadow in the corner. Its poison was released through my body, filling up the emptiness from my toes to the cracked-bone splinters of my mind.

"I'm a Bullhead," I repeated, and Marshall nodded. He took back his hands and stuck them in his pockets. His skin had cooled and dried, and my tears had ended. The only trace of them was a fine salt dust on my face and his fingers.

———

Two months after Jasper was buried, brochures arrived from the Bureau of Indian Affairs. They were neatly folded, printed on slick white paper proclaiming: CHICAGO—THE CITY BEAUTIFUL!

The photographs of Chicago caught my eye. They pictured elegant homes with broad staircases, grand pianos in apartments, flowers on every table; sailboats drifted on Lake Michigan, skirting the skyline; well-dressed Chicagoans smiled a welcome. I collected brochures from neighbors who were settled. I liked to stand them in a semicircle on the kitchen table so that when I rested my chin on its surface the brochures rose above my head like the city itself. I surrounded myself with Chicago's promises.

"I want to go to Chicago," I told Marshall one morning. He was eating oatmeal at the kitchen table, his bowl thrust into the center of my paper city. Marshall pushed the bowl away from him, nearly destroying the delicate lakeshore I'd created.

"So, you've got Relocation fever." It wasn't a question. He had seen the paper city rise.

"I want to get out of here," I nearly cried. Marshall's silence reminded me of my father's. I wanted to fill it up with all my reasons, but I didn't, because the truest reason of all was too large for my mouth. I couldn't tell Marshall that I believed Chicago would wash me in a clean light. Chicago would never know I was a Bullhead. The ancestors and *heyoka* spirits with their long memories would never see me in Chicago. I would walk barefoot on Oak Street Beach as Maxine Azure, and the sun would be so bright on my head I wouldn't have a shadow to fall forward or behind.

"Don't you know it's just another one of their tricks?" Marshall scolded me. He took down the brochures, placing them in a neat pile. His hands played with the corners. "They figure if they move us into the cities they'll get the last bit of land."

I believed him, and I didn't care. If the government was putting one over on me, I was putting one over on the higher powers. I was young enough to turn into Maxine Azure and have children we would raise in the city.

Marshall started to reach for me, his right hand moved to cover my own. But instead it jerked back to the brochures, tapping their edges on the table to even them up. His incomplete gesture made me cold the way I'd been cold every night since Jasper was buried. Marshall and I no longer fit together at night like a married puzzle but kept to our own sides, chilled separately by the moon. Sometimes his hand reached out to rub my back, but the hand was always cold and stiff.

Marshall was watching me. He'd never stared at me like that before because we were raised to understand it was rude. I could tell he pitied me. His eyes were sad and careful.

"Whatever you want to do, Maxine, that's what we'll do." I knew he would take me to Chicago because he felt sorry for me, something I would have hated a few months earlier. But now I just wanted to get away. I imagined in Chicago I would become the real Maxine, and my husband's pity would be transformed into wild admiration.

So we moved. Our house was government property to be turned over to another Sioux family, and our relatives took the furniture. Sitting Bull had been reburied in Mobridge, South Dakota, by white businessmen hoping to attract tourist dollars, but I went to his old grave anyway to walk the sacred ground. I visited Jasper before we left, smothering him with sage and wildflowers. "You'll always be my first child," I promised him.

When Marshall and I drove away from Fort Yates, North Dakota, I felt the road was lined with eyes. It wasn't until we'd left the reservation and hit the highway that we drove unseen. I wondered if that was what I had wanted all my life: to be invisible so that the sin lodged inside me would wink out, drained of all its terrible power.

———

In Chicago, Marshall and I pretended things we were new. We went to the Field Museum and Marshall Field's Department Store. We stood beside the stone water tower. We had conversations about city life—the noise and traffic, all the different tribes we met at the Chicago Indian Center. We pretended to be angry at the BIA for fooling us, sending us pictures of the North Shore, where the wealthy lived, while we were caught in slum areas, chased from room to room by tenant cockroaches.

Mostly we worked hard. There was a lot of competition for jobs. I finally landed a waitressing job at an all-night cafe under the elevated train. All week I worked the late shift, coming home after eleven o'clock. Sometimes strange men walked closely behind me, so I took to strapping a thin knife to my forearm, just inside my sleeve. Marshall got home even later. He was the night watchman for the Indian Center. I liked having a key to the center, pretending the building was mine to be divided into large apartments for all the Indian people living in Chicago. Before I found my own job I would bring Marshall a late supper, and we'd sit for hours listening to the radio. Once I started work, I missed this chance for us to be together because we slept most of the day, and when we weren't sleeping the bright light made us shy, highlighting the fact that very little had actually changed.

Marshall's increasing silence was too much like my father's. It had a power I couldn't ignore. It could fill a room, doubling on itself, leaping from floor to wall to ceiling like a runaway flame, or it could drain the room like a sump pump, sucking at the bottom of my shoes.

I became homesick and wrote more often to my mother. One evening on my way to work I stopped by the post office just before closing to pick up a package. My mother had sent us *wasna*—a Sioux delicacy. She had packed the small round balls consisting of ground chokecherries and cornmeal, in wax paper inside a coffee can. On impulse I decided to call in sick to work and share the *wasna* with my husband.

I enjoyed the cold walk back to the Indian Center. I had never seen so many trees together as in the city, and I liked to walk on the bright leaves collecting on the ground.

I unlocked the heavy front door of the Indian Center, shutting it behind me with my hip and shoulder. The coffee can was cold from the walk and my cheeks were numb. I had no idea where Marshall would be, the building covered half a city block and was five stories high. I started down in the basement, slowly making my way to the fifth floor. Of course he was in the last place I looked, the chapel on the top floor. An Indian minister held services there every Sunday, which I liked to attend because his sermons were always on the edge of losing control. I imagined it had something to do with the setting: bloodred velvet drapes dropped from ceiling to floor, covering the four walls. The air was thick and oppressive. I had the feeling I was inside a human heart.

This time when I entered the chapel I noticed a drape had fallen from the wall. I heard voices. I don't remember walking toward the voices but I must have, because suddenly my feet trampled red velvet. Somehow the coffee can had fallen and the plastic lid popped off. Precious *wasna* rolled across the carpet. I found my husband wrapped in red velvet like a king, a woman curled to him. Marshall jumped away from her when he saw me. He wasn't careful and his movements exposed her body. Her face made no impression—it was very white and the features seemed smudged. Her black hair was thin and stringy. But her body offended me. Stretch marks on her breasts and belly marked her fertile; she had children. Her nipples were the pressed shape of a nursing mother; they had lived.

Marshall stood before me in his shorts. I realized I was still his height.

"What're you doing here?" he asked me. He looked desperate. He couldn't look me in the eye so he discovered the *wasna*. "*Wasna*," he whispered stupidly.

I had choices then. I felt one in each hand. It was the sin that decided me—my great-grandfather's original sin swelling to fill me, pushing my organs aside, displacing my heart. I became the sin that was inside me from the time of my birth, and wrestled my husband to the ground.

I pinned his legs between my own and he twisted, slippery with sweat. The chapel was silent but for our breath like two snakes spitting fear. Our hands were clasped, finally warm again as they had been when we made Jasper. We wrenched arms, rolling over and over the *wasna* until it crumbled, dusting our bodies. I pushed Marshall's face into the red velvet, my knee on his neck, but he reared and threw me off. Now he was on top, his body crushing me. For a confused moment I wondered if we would make love.

The sin saved me. It was speaking aloud, its voice echoing in the chapel. *The blade. The blade.*

Marshall was sitting on my ribcage and my arms were raised above my head.

He has no respect. He thinks you killed Jasper. The sin spoke Sioux now. *The blade.*

Marshall had relaxed for a moment. We were both tired but I was fueled by sin. In that instant I reached inside my sleeve and pulled out the knife, slim and light as a razor. I stabbed Marshall in the heart. It was a completed act.

I held Marshall in my arms as he died, and our last words were all in Dakota so the shaking white woman wouldn't understand.

"I'm sorry," he told me, his pierced breath breaking the words apart. "We should never have left."

I shook my head. It wasn't Chicago or Relocation. But I could only whisper, "I love you," and cover his body with my own to keep him warm.

When the police came I said goodbye to my husband, and I could walk in a straight line. I knew who I was. I knew as I sat in the squad car, watching the dark streets of Chicago. I was Maxine Bullhead.

———

I am beading moccasins for my husband, Marshall Azure. I am beading the soles so I will see his flashing footprints in the sky.

Marshall is teaching Jasper to dance the old way. I can see them moving together when I close my eyes. Lieutenant Bullhead is dancing with an eagle feather fan. His body shakes with joy when he bends at the waist. Sitting Bull is singing the song. His voice is high. He is smiling because they are all together.

I cry over my beadwork and prick my fingers. It is hard for me to sit up straight on the edge of my cot because sins weigh me down, heavy as cannonballs welded to my shoulders.

Sins are at the center of my headache, slicing my thoughts into wedges. The sins are a pounding fluid, ripping through my arteries with a hot fire like gunshot in the bloodstream.

⟶ *The Devil* ⟵
Zitkala-Sa (Gertrude Bonnin)

Zitkala-Sa, Sioux fiction writer, essayist, musician, composer, and political activist, was born in 1876 in the Yankton Reservation in South Dakota, where she was raised by her mother, Ellen Tate Iyohiwin. Zitkala-Sa attended a number of schools, including the Quaker missionary school in Indiana named White's Manual Labor Institute, Earlham College, and the Boston Conservatory of Music. After graduating, Zitkala-Sa taught music at Carlisle Indian Training School while writing articles for literary magazines such as *Harper's* and *Atlantic Monthly* on the side. Her articles, fiercely critical of the assimilationist education provided by Carlisle, saw her fired in the early 1900s. She is the author of two books of short stories, *Old Indian Legends* (1901) and *American Indian Stories* (1921); a political text entitled *Oklahoma's Poor Rich Indians: An Orgy of Graft and Exploitation of the Five Civilized Tribes, Legalized Robbery* (1924); numerous articles for magazines; and an opera, *Sun Dance*, which premiered in New York City shortly before her death in 1938.

"The Devil," first published in Zitkala-Sa's *American Indian Stories*, tells of a young Sioux girl who is taught about the Christian devil at an Indian boarding school. Interestingly, Zitkala-Sa begins and ends this tale with reference to the relationship between her main character and *story*. "Among the legends the old warriors used to tell me ..." begins this work of very short fiction. It ends with the young girl holding the bible. What parallels does Zitkala-Sa draw between the stories from the "old warriors" and the "white man's legend"? What differences does the writer point to? What benefits might Zitkala-Sa be suggesting in taking an active role, rather than a passive role, as reader or listener?

Among the legends the old warriors used to tell me were many stories of evil spirits. But I was taught to fear them no more than those who stalked about in material guise. I never knew there was an insolent chieftain among the bad spirits, who dared to array his forces against the Great Spirit, until I heard this white man's legend from a paleface woman.

Out of a large book she showed me a picture of the white man's devil. I looked in horror upon the strong claws that grew out of his fur-covered fingers. His feet were like his hands. Trailing at his heels was a scaly tail tipped with a serpent's open jaws. His face was a patchwork: he had bearded cheeks, like some I had seen palefaces wear; his nose was an eagle's bill, and his sharp-pointed ears were pricked up like those of a sly fox. Above them a pair of cow's horns curved upward. I trembled with awe, and my heart throbbed in my throat, as I looked at the king of evil spirits. Then I heard the paleface woman say that this terrible creature roamed loose in the world, and that little girls who disobeyed school regulations were to be tortured by him.

That night I dreamt about this evil divinity. Once again I seemed to be in my mother's cottage. An Indian woman had come to visit my mother. On opposite sides of the kitchen stove, which stood in the center of the small house, my mother and her guest were seated in straight-backed chairs. I played with a train of empty spools hitched together on a string. It was night, and the wick burned feebly. Suddenly I heard someone turn our door-knob from without.

My mother and the woman hushed their talk, and both looked toward the door. It opened gradually. I waited behind the stove. The hinges squeaked as the door was slowly, very slowly pushed inward.

Then in rushed the devil! He was tall! He looked exactly like the picture I had seen of him in the white man's papers. He did not speak to my mother, because he did not know the Indian language, but his glittering yellow eyes were fastened upon me. He took long strides around the stove, passing behind the woman's chair. I threw down my spools, and ran to my mother. He did not fear her, but followed closely after me. Then I ran round and round the stove, crying aloud for help. But my mother and the woman seemed not to know my danger. They sat still, looking quietly upon the devil's chase after me. At last I grew dizzy. My head revolved as on a hidden pivot. My knees became numb, and doubled under my weight like a pair of knife blades without a spring. Beside my mother's chair I fell in a heap. Just as the devil stooped over me with out-stretched claws my mother awoke from her quiet indifference, and lifted me on her lap. Whereupon the devil vanished, and I was awake.

On the following morning I took my revenge upon the devil. Stealing into the room where a wall of shelves was filled with books, I drew forth *The Stories of the Bible*. With a broken slate pencil I carried in my apron pocket, I began by scratching out his wicked eyes. A few moments later, when I was ready to leave the room, there was a ragged hole in the page where the picture of the devil had once been.

— *Coyote and the People Killer* —
Tania Willard

Tania Willard is a Secwepemc artist and curator. Her work explores bodies of knowledge and skills that lie at the intersection between Indigenous and other cultures. She has worked as an artist in residence with Gallery Gachet in Vancouver's Downtown East Side, the Banff Centre's visual arts residency, and was a curator in residence at the Kamloops Art Gallery and at grunt gallery in Vancouver. In 2016, she was co-curator, with Karen Duffek, of *Unceded Territories: Lawrence Paul Yuxweluptun* at the Museum of Anthropology in Vancouver.

"Coyote and the People Killer" was originally told by Tania's great-grandfather, Isaac (Ike) Willard, and was written down and published by the anthropologists, Randy Bouchard and Dorothy Kennedy, in *Shuswap Stories: Collected 1971–1975*. In her artist's statement from an exhibition of the illustrated story at an art gallery,[1] Willard writes: "I wanted to illustrate this story, told by my great-grandfather and collected by anthropologists for *Shuswap Stories*, because I have always wanted to bring these stories alive" (Willard). Bouchard and Kennedy had worked with Willard's Elders in her home community in the 1970s as part of the British Columbia Indian language project. Willard's repositioning of the published version of the story within her artist's statement and artwork is arguably a kind of repatriation of the story. As you read the story, think about the relationship between the words and the images. You will notice that one of the collages invokes the same iconic image from the Oka Crisis as Gord Hill, in his excerpt from *The Five Hundred Years of Resistance Comic Book*, included in Chapter 2. How does Willard interweave images from different contexts, and how do Willard's images influence your interpretation of the words? Is she successful in reclaiming her great-grandfather's story?

Told by Isaac Willard and transcribed by Randy Bouchard and Dorothy Kennedy.

Coyote was travelling along looking for some food for his hungry family. He lay down and told his son to go to the river and get some water. The boy did as his father requested, but as he stood on the bank of the river, he saw something floating in the water. He returned and told Coyote that he saw something that looked like a deer being tossed in the waves.

Coyote went down to the river and looked at the object in the water. It was a deer, so Coyote sent his son out to drag it to the shore. The boy swam out in the river and hauled the large deer to the shore, where Coyote then dragged it up the bank and began to skin it.

"Hold one end of the animal while I try to skin it," Coyote told his wife, Mole. While he cut up the deer, the stingy Coyote was trying to think of a way by which he could have it all to himself. He splashed some of the deer's blood on his wife.

Then he began to holler at her.

"You just sprinkled the deer's blood on me," protested Mole.

"No, my word is the truth!" insisted Coyote. "You must move away from the main camp and stay by yourself!"

Figure 5.2 Tania Willard, "Coyote and the People Killer" (detail). (*Credit:* Tania Willard. Artwork photographed by Aaron Leon)

Mole had to do as Coyote demanded so she packed her belongings and moved away from their camp.

Coyote quartered the deer and took it to the camp. After barbecuing it near the fire, he and his son ate all the cooked meat. But still Coyote was hungry. "Go tell your mother that I want some berries," he told his son.

Figure 5.3   Tania Willard, "Coyote and the People Killer" (detail). (*Credit:* Tania Willard. Artwork photographed by Aaron Leon)

The boy did as his father requested, but Mole told the boy to tell his father to get his own berries. Coyote went to the storage cache to look for some berries, but they had been chewed and were scattered in the dirt. Coyote returned empty-handed.

"Go tell your mother I want some lily roots to eat," Coyote told his boy. But when the boy told this to Mole, she told him to tell his father to get them himself. Coyote also wanted some Indian carrots. Mole wasn't about to get them for him either.

Figure 5.4   Tania Willard, "Coyote and the People Killer" (detail). (*Credit:* Tania Willard. Artwork photographed by Aaron Leon)

Coyote went to the storage cache again. All that he could find was chewed roots mixed in the dirt. "That wife of mine has done this to me," Coyote muttered to himself.

He searched for a club with which to beat his wife to death.

Mole knew what Coyote was thinking, so she made her own plans. She hummed a song, and as she hummed Mole rose higher and higher in the air. Then a wind came along and blew her away.

"Come back, come back!" pleaded Coyote, but Mole didn't pay any attention to him. Coyote tried to follow Mole. When he realized that he wasn't able to catch her, Coyote went back to the camp and lay down.

Figure 5.5   Tania Willard, "Coyote and the People Killer" (detail). (*Credit:*
Tania Willard. Artwork photographed by Aaron Leon)

Coyote became hungry again. He and his son began to walk along the
river looking for food.

Soon they heard a rattling noise. Coyote knew that it was the people-killer
who was approaching.

"Stay here and keep still," he told his young son. "That people-killer is a
horrible person!" Coyote stood in the middle of the path and waited for the
people-killer to reach him.

They met face to face.

"I have eaten all of the people west of here," said the people-killer.

Coyote looked the people-killer straight in the eye and said, "I have eaten
all the people east of here. We will each vomit what we have eaten and that
will prove who is telling the truth."

Figure 5.6 Tania Willard, "Coyote and the People Killer" (detail). (*Credit:*
Tania Willard. Artwork photographed by Aaron Leon)

They placed a mat between them. "You must close your eyes while you
vomit and I will tell you when to open them," explained Coyote.

The people-killer closed his eyes and vomited a piece of human flesh.
Coyote slapped his stomach and vomited a clump of an underwater plant.
Quickly Coyote exchanged their piles of vomit so that it appeared that the
people-killer had vomited the plant.

"Okay, let's open our eyes and see who is telling the truth," announced
Coyote. "Look what is in front of you! Nothing but a pile of underwater plants,
but in front of me there is a pile of human flesh. You, people-killer, will be
something from the past. No longer will you eat people."

Figure 5.7   Tania Willard, "Coyote and the People Killer" (detail). (*Credit:* Tania Willard. Artwork photographed by Aaron Leon)

Coyote and his son followed the river until they came to a place where a young girl was dancing on the opposite shore.

They sat down and watched the girl dance, but soon Coyote became sleepy, so the girl transformed him into a rock. His son was also transformed into a rock.

"When people come to this land, this rock will be called Ska-CHEEN," the girl said.

The rocks that are Coyote and his son can still be seen along the South Thompson River.

⟬ *Language and Literature from a Pueblo Indian Perspective* ⟭
Leslie Marmon Silko

Leslie Marmon Silko was born in Albuquerque, New Mexico, and grew up on the Laguna Pueblo Reservation, where members of her family still reside. Silko received her BA with honours from the University of New Mexico in 1969 and is the author of several novels, collections of short stories, and works of non-fiction. Among her celebrated publications are *Ceremony* (1977), *Storyteller* (1981), *Almanac of the Dead* (1991), and *Yellow Woman and a Beauty of the Spirit: Essays on Native American Life Today* (1997). In addition to writing, her career includes an association with the University of New Mexico, Albuquerque, the Navajo Community College in Tsaile, Arizona, and the University of Arizona in Tucson.

"Language and Literature from a Pueblo Indian Perspective" is a piece of writing that holds many stories and ideas within it. Just as Silko explains that Laguna Pueblo stories contain information in them, from recipes to geography to the location of different places, her essay explains aspects of Pueblo oral traditions, breaks down linguistic structures, retells two different narratives from her community, and speaks to how story can transcend even death. In doing so, Silko brilliantly demonstrates the way language and stories work in the Pueblo world view to connect all things.

Where I come from, the words most highly valued are those spoken from the heart, unpremeditated and unrehearsed. Among the Pueblo people, a written speech or statement is highly suspect because the true feelings of the speaker remain hidden as she reads words that are detached from the occasion and the audience. I have intentionally not written a formal paper because I want you to *hear* and to experience English in a structure that follows patterns from the oral tradition. For those of you accustomed to being taken from point A to point B to point C, this presentation may be somewhat difficult to follow. Pueblo expression resembles something like a spider's web—with many little threads radiating from the center, crisscrossing one another. As with the web, the structure emerges as it is made, and you must simply listen and trust, as the Pueblo people do, that meaning will be made.

My task is a formidable one: I ask you to set aside a number of basic approaches that you have been using and probably will continue to use, and, instead, to approach language from the Pueblo perspective, one that embraces the whole of creation and the whole of history and time.

What changes would Pueblo writers make to English as a language for literature? I have some examples of stories in English that I will use to address this question. At the same time, I would like to explain the importance of storytelling and how it relates to a Pueblo theory of language.

So I will begin, appropriately enough, with the Pueblo Creation story, an all-inclusive story of how life began. In this story, Tse'itsi'nako, Thought Woman, by thinking of her sisters, and together with her sisters, thought of everything that is. In this way, the world was created. Everything in this world was a part of the original Creation; the people at home understood that far away there were other human beings, also a part of this world. The Creation story even includes a prophecy that describes the origin of European and African peoples and also refers to Asians.

This story, I think, suggests something about why the Pueblo people are more concerned with story and communication and less concerned with a particular language. There are at least six, possibly seven, distinct languages among the twenty pueblos of the southwestern United States, for example, Zuñi and Hopi. And from mesa to mesa there are subtle differences in language. But the particular language being spoken isn't as important as what a speaker is trying to say, and this emphasis on the story itself stems, I believe, from a view of narrative particular to the Pueblo and other Native American peoples—that is, that language *is* story.

I will try to clarify this statement. At Laguna Pueblo, for example, many individual words have their own stories. So when one is telling a story and one is using words to tell the story, each word that one is speaking has a story of its own, too. Often the speakers, or tellers, will go into these word stories, creating an elaborate structure of stories within stories. This structure, which becomes very apparent in the actual telling of a story, informs contemporary Pueblo writing and storytelling as well as the traditional narratives. This perspective on narrative—of story within story, the idea that one story is only the beginning of many stories and the sense that stories never truly end—represents an important contribution of Native American cultures to the English language.

Many people think of storytelling as something that is done at bedtime, that it is something done for small children. But when I use the term *storytelling*, I'm talking about something much bigger than that. I'm talking about something that comes out of an experience and an understanding of that original view of Creation—that we are all part of a whole; we do not differentiate or fragment stories and experiences. In the beginning, Tse'itsi'nako, Thought Woman, thought of all things, and all of these things are held together as one holds many things together in a single thought.

So in the telling (and you will hear a few of the dimensions of this telling), first of all, as mentioned earlier, the storytelling always includes the audience, the listeners. In fact, a great deal of the story is believed to be inside the listener; the storyteller's role is to draw the story out of the listeners. The storytelling continues from generation to generation.

Basically, the origin story constructs our identity—with this story, we know who we are. We are the Lagunas. This is where we come from. We came this way. We came by this place. And so from the time we are very young, we hear these stories, so that when we go out into the world, when one asks who we are or where we are from, we immediately know: we are the people who came from the north. We are the people of these stories.

In the Creation story, Antelope says that he will help knock a hole in the Earth so that the people can come up, out into the next world. Antelope tries and tries; he uses his hooves but is unable to break through. It is then that Badger says, "Let me help you." And Badger very patiently uses his claws and digs a way through, bringing the people into the world. When the Badger clan people think of themselves, or when the Antelope people think of themselves, it is as people who are of *this* story, and this is *our* place, and we fit into the very beginning when the people first came, before we began our journey south.

Within the clans there are stories that identify the clan. One moves, then, from the idea of one's identity as a tribal person into clan identity, then to one's identity as a member of an extended family. And it is the notion of extended family that has produced a kind of story that some distinguish from other Pueblo stories, though Pueblo people do not. Anthropologists and ethnologists have, for a long time, differentiated the types of stories the Pueblos tell. They tended to elevate the old, sacred, and traditional stories and to brush aside family stories, the family's account of itself. But in Pueblo culture, these family stories are given equal recognition. There is no definite, preset pattern for the way one will hear the stories of one's own family, but it is a very critical part of one's childhood, and the storytelling continues throughout one's life. One will hear stories of importance to the family—sometimes wonderful stories—stories about the time a maternal uncle got the biggest deer that was ever seen and brought it back from the mountains. And so an individual's identity will extend from the identity constructed around the family—"I am from the family of my uncle who brought in this wonderful deer, and it was a wonderful hunt."

Family accounts include negative stories, too; perhaps an uncle did something unacceptable. It is very important that one keep track of all these stories—both positive and not so positive—about one's own family and other families. Because even when there is no way around it—old Uncle Pete *did* do a terrible thing—by knowing the stories that originate in other families, one is able to deal with terrible sorts of things that might happen within one's own family. If a member of the family does something that cannot be excused, one always knows stories about similarly inexcusable things done by a member of another family. But this knowledge is not communicated for malicious reasons. It is very important to understand this. Keeping track of all the stories within the community gives us all a certain distance, a useful perspective, that brings incidents down to a level we can deal with. If others have done it before, it cannot be so terrible. If others have endured, so can we.

The stories are always bringing us together, keeping this whole together, keeping this family together, keeping this clan together. "Don't go away, don't isolate yourself, but come here, because we have all had these kinds of experiences." And so there is this constant pulling together to resist the tendency to run or hide or separate oneself during a traumatic emotional experience. This separation not only endangers the group but the individual as well—one does not recover by oneself.

Because storytelling lies at the heart of Pueblo culture, it is absurd to attempt to fix the stories in time. "When did they tell the stories?" or "What time of day does the storytelling take place?"—these questions are nonsensical from a Pueblo perspective, because our storytelling goes on constantly: as some old grandmother puts on the shoes of a child and tells her the story of a little girl who didn't wear her shoes, for instance, or someone comes into the house for coffee to talk with a teenage boy who has just been in a lot of trouble, to reassure him that someone else's son has been in that kind of trouble, too. Storytelling is an ongoing process, working on many different levels.

Here's one story that is often told at a time of individual crisis (and I want to remind you that we make no distinctions between types of story—historical, sacred, plain gossip—because these distinctions are not useful when discussing the Pueblo *experience* of language). There was a young man who, when he came back from the war in Vietnam, had saved up his army pay and bought a beautiful red Volkswagen. He was very proud of it. One night he drove up to a place called the King's Bar, right across the reservation line. The bar is notorious for many reasons, particularly for the deep arroyo located behind it. The young man ran in to pick up a cold six-pack, but he forgot to put on his emergency brake. And his little red Volkswagen rolled back into the arroyo and was all smashed up. He felt very bad about it, but within a few days everybody had come to him with stories about other people who had lost cars and family members to that arroyo, for instance, George Day's station wagon, with his mother-in-law and kids inside. So everybody was saying, "Well, at least your mother-in-law and kids weren't in the car when it rolled in," and one can't argue with that kind of story. The story of the young man and his smashed-up Volkswagen was now joined with all the other stories of cars that fell into that arroyo.

Now I want to tell you a very beautiful little story. It is a very old story that is sometimes told to people who suffer great family or personal loss. This story was told by my Aunt Susie. She is one of the first generation of people at Laguna who began experimenting with English—who began working to make English speak for us, that is, to speak from the heart. (I come from a family intent on getting the stories told.) As you read the story, I think you will hear that. And here and there, I think, you will also hear the influence of the Indian school at Carlisle, Pennsylvania, where my Aunt Susie was sent (like being sent to prison) for six years.

This scene is set partly in Acoma, partly in Laguna. Waithea was a little girl living in Acoma and one day she said, "Mother, I would like to have some *yashtoah* to eat."

Yashtoah is the hardened crust of corn mush that curls up. *Yashtoah* literally means "curled up." She said, "I would like to have some *yashtoah*," and her mother said, "My dear little girl, I can't make you any *yashtoah* because we haven't any wood, but if you will go down off the mesa, down below, and pick up some pieces of wood and bring them home, I will make you some *yashtoah*." So Waithea was glad and ran down the precipitous cliff of Acoma mesa. Down below, just as her mother had told her, there were pieces of wood, some curled, some crooked in shape, that she was to pick up and take home. She found just such wood as these.

She brought them home in a little wicker basket. First she called to her mother as she got home, "*Nayah, deeni!* Mother, upstairs!" The Pueblo people always called "up- stairs" because long ago their homes were two, three stories, and they entered from the top. She said, "*Deeni! Upstairs!*" and her mother came. The little girl said, "I have brought the wood you wanted me to bring." And she opened her little wicker basket to lay out the pieces of wood, but here they were snakes. They were snakes instead of the crooked sticks of wood. And her mother said, "Oh my dear child, you have brought snakes instead!" She said, "Go take them back and put them back just where you got them." And the little girl ran down the mesa again, down below to the flats. And she put those snakes back just where she got them. They were snakes instead, and she was very hurt about this, and so she said, "I'm not going home. I'm going to Kawaik, the beautiful lake place Kawaik, and drown myself in that lake, *byn'yah'nah* [the 'west lake']. I will go there and drown myself."

So she started off, and as she passed by the Enchanted Mesa near Acoma, she met an old man, very aged, and he saw her running, and he said, "My dear child, where are you going?" "I'm going to Kawaik and jump into the lake there."

"Why?" "Well, because," she said, "my mother didn't want to make any *yashtoah* for me." The old man said, "Oh, no! You must not go, my child. Come with me and I will take you home." He tried to catch her, but she was very light and skipped along. And every time he would try to grab her she would skip faster away from him.

The old man was coming home with some wood strapped to his back and tied with yucca. He just let that strap go and let the wood drop. He went as fast as he could up the cliff to the little girl's home. When he got to the place where she lived, he called to her mother. "*Deeni!*" "Come on up!" And he said, "I can't. I just came to bring you a message. Your little daughter is running away. She is going to Kawaik to drown herself in the lake there." "Oh my dear little girl!" the mother said. So she busied herself with making the *yashtoah* her little girl liked so much. Corn mush curled at the top. (She must have found enough wood to boil the corn meal and make the *yashtoah*.)

While the mush was cooling off, she got the little girl's clothing, her *manta* dress and buckskin moccasins and all her other garments, and put them in a bundle—probably a yucca bag. And she started down as fast as she could on the east side of Acoma. (There used to be a trail there, you know. It's gone now, but it was accessible in those days.) She saw her daughter way at a distance and she kept calling: "Stsamaku! My daughter! Come back! I've got your *yashtoah* for you." But the little girl would not turn. She kept on ahead and she cried: "My mother, my mother, she didn't want me to have any *yashtoah*. So now I'm going to Kawaik and drown myself." Her mother heard her cry and said, "My little daughter, come back here!" "No," and she kept a distance away from her. And they came nearer and nearer to the lake. And she could see her daughter now, very plain. "Come back, my daughter! I have your *yashtoah*." But no, she kept on, and finally she reached the lake and she stood on the edge.

She had tied a little feather in her hair, which is traditional (in death they tie this feather on the head). She carried a feather, the little girl did, and she tied it in her hair with a piece of string; right on top of her head she put the feather. Just as her mother was about to reach her, she jumped into the lake. The little feather was whirling around and around in the depths below. Of course the mother was very sad. She went, grieved, back to Acoma and climbed her mesa home. She stood on the edge of the mesa and scattered her daughter's clothing, the little moccasins, the *yashtoah*. She scattered them to the east, to the west, to the north, to the south. And the pieces of clothing and the moccasins and *yashtoah* all turned into butterflies. And today they say that Acoma has more beautiful butterflies: red ones, white ones, blue ones, yellow ones. They came from this little girl's clothing.

Now this is a story anthropologists would consider very old. The version I have given you is just as Aunt Susie tells it. You can occasionally hear some English she picked up at Carlisle—words like *precipitous*. You will also notice that there is a great deal of repetition, and a little reminder about *yashtoah* and how it is made. There is a remark about the cliff trail at Acoma—that it was once there but is there no longer. This story may be told at a time of sadness or loss, but within this story many other elements are brought together. Things are not separated out and categorized; all things are brought together, so that the reminder about the *yashtoah* is valuable information that is repeated—a recipe, if you will. The information about the old trail at Acoma reveals that stories are, in a sense, maps, since even to this day there is little information or material about trails that is passed around with writing. In the structure of this story the repetitions are, of course, designed to help you remember. It is repeated again and again, and then it moves on.

There are a great many parallels between Pueblo experiences and those of African and Caribbean peoples—one is that we have all had the conqueror's language imposed on us. But our experience with English has been somewhat different in that the Bureau of Indian Affairs schools were not interested in teaching us the canon of Western classics. For instance, we never heard of Shakespeare. We were given Dick and Jane, and I can remember reading that the robins were heading south for the winter. It took me a long time to figure out what was going on. I worried for quite a while about our robins in Laguna because they didn't leave in the winter, until I finally realized that all the big textbook companies are up in Boston and *their* robins do go south in the winter. But in a way, this dreadful formal education freed us by encouraging us to maintain our narratives. Whatever literature we were exposed to at school (which was damn little), at home the storytelling, the special regard for telling and bringing together through the telling, was going on constantly.

And as the old people say, "If you can remember the stories, you will be all right. Just remember the stories." When I returned to Laguna Pueblo after attending college, I wondered how the storytelling was continuing (anthropologists say that Laguna Pueblo is one of the more acculturated pueblos), so I visited an English class at Laguna-Acoma High School. I knew the students had cassette tape recorders in their lockers and stereos at home, and that they listened to Kiss and Led Zeppelin and were well informed about culture in general. I had with me an anthology of short stories by Native American writers, *The Man to Send Rain Clouds.* One story in the book is about the killing of a state policeman in New Mexico by three Acoma Pueblo men in the early 1950s. I asked the students how many had heard this story and steeled myself for the possibility that the anthropologists were right, that the old traditions were indeed dying out and the students would be ignorant of the story. But instead, all but one or two raised their hands—they had heard the story, just as I had heard it when I was young, some in English, some in Laguna.

One of the other advantages that we Pueblos have enjoyed is that we have always been able to stay with the land. Our stories cannot be separated from their geographical locations, from actual physical places on the land. We were not relocated like so many Native American groups who were torn away from their ancestral land. And our stories are so much a part of these places that it is almost impossible for future generations to lose them—there is a story connected with every place, every object in the landscape.

Dennis Brutus has talked about the "yet unborn" as well as "those from the past," and how we are still *all* in *this* place, and language—the storytelling—is our way of passing through or being with them, of being together again. When Aunt Susie told her stories, she would tell a younger child to go open the door so that our esteemed predecessors might bring their gifts to us. "They are out there," Aunt Susie would say. "Let them come in. They're here, they're here with us *within* the stories."

A few years ago, when Aunt Susie was 106, I paid her a visit, and while I was there she said, "Well, I'll be leaving here soon. I think I'll be leaving here next week, and I will be going over to the Cliff House." She said, "It's going to be real good to get back over there." I was listening, and I was thinking that she must be talking about her house at Paguate village, just north of Laguna. And she went on, "Well, my mother's sister [and she gave her Indian name] will be there. She has been living there. She will be there and we will be over there, and I will get a chance to write down these stories I've been telling you." Now you must understand, of course, that Aunt Susie's mother's sister, a great storyteller herself, has long since passed over into the land of the dead. But then I realized, too, that Aunt Susie wasn't talking about death the way most of us do. She was talking about "going over" as a journey, a journey that perhaps we can only begin to understand through an appreciation for the boundless capacity of language that, through storytelling, brings us together, despite great distances between cultures, despite great distances in time.

CHAPTER 6

■ ■ ■ ■

COMMUNITY, SELF, TRANSFORMATION

Sherman Alexie, "The Toughest Indian in the World"

Isaías Hernández Isidro, "The Secret of the Zutz'baläm"

Richard Van Camp, "Devotion"

Sylvain Rivard, "Grandma and the Wendigo"

Michael Nicoll Yahgulanaas, excerpt from *Red: A Haida Manga*

Ellen Rice White, "The Boys Who Became a Killer Whale"

HOW DO WE UNDERSTAND the self in relation to others—not only human but those belonging to the wider living world? In these stories characters transform, reminding us to respect one another as beings that are both related and interdependent. For instance, in Ellen Rice White's "The Boys Who Became a Killer Whale," a group of young people looking to prove themselves become a killer whale in order to impress their Elders. As White describes in her own commentary, the story is, on the one hand, about the impertinence of youth and, on the other hand, a lesson for parents and grandparents in properly instructing children. Once they become the whale, however, the youth begin to lose track of their individual identities and begin to meld into one another. When the young people beg the killer whale to take them back to shore, the animal insists, "it cannot be done … We are one now. Each one of you has become one with me" (283). White's story illustrates the primary themes of this chapter: the inextricably complex relationships between individuals, communities, and nature, and the potential for characters and animals to transform, shift, and blend together. These stories demonstrate how the "self" is an open concept defined by our relationships and responsibilities to other human and non-human beings.

In these stories, animals and supernatural beings are often characters as much as humans. For example, in Isaías Hernández Isidro's story, Teófila realizes that the boy she thought she was looking after is really a "Zuzt'bälam," which translates literally as a "bat-jaguar." This creature, which has wings of a bat and the roar of a jaguar, is also a deity or supernatural creature who protects the fields. In Richard Van Camp's story, "Devotion," the white caribou is a shape-shifter who can move between human and animal forms. Michael Nicoll Yahgulanaas's "haida manga" comic, *Red*, explores transformation and human-animal characters using images and text. He illustrates the intimate connection between human and non-human worlds, suggesting that this connection is vital to the survival of the community. In many of the stories included in this chapter, transformation is simultaneously a point of cultural access and a means of exploring the self through a sense of connection and responsibility to other beings.

When reading these stories, think about how your understanding of character transforms as the stories progress. For instance, in Sherman Alexie's "The Toughest Indian in the World," the protagonist is the window through which the reader understands gender and sexuality. By framing his story around a character described as "the toughest Indian in the world," Alexie evokes certain masculine stereotypes, only to challenge the reader to question those stereotypes and push the boundaries of what a "tough Indian" might do or be. How do the authors in this chapter use the idea of character differently? How are supernatural and animal characters used to shape how we think about community and what it means to be human?

The Toughest Indian in the World
Sherman Alexie

Sherman Alexie is a Spokane/Coeur d'Alene poet, writer, and filmmaker with over twenty books and a number of significant literary awards to his name. His stories have been published in several short-story collections, including the prestigious yearly anthology, *The Best American Short Stories* (2004). *Smoke Signals*, the film he wrote and co-produced with Chris Eyre, based on his collection of stories, *The Lone Ranger and Tonto Fistfight in Heaven* (1993), received the Audience Award and Filmmakers Trophy at the 1998 Sundance Film Festival. Alexie grew up in a family of six in Wellpinit, Washington, on the Spokane Indian Reservation. Due to health problems, which restricted his participation in the games and sports of his peers, Alexie focused his attention on academics, pursuing, at one time or another, careers in both medicine and law. In the 2003 *Dictionary of Literary Biography*, literary critic Sarah A. Quirk identifies three questions prevalent across all of his works: "What does it mean to live as an Indian in this time? What does it mean to be an Indian man? Finally, what does it mean to live on an Indian reservation?" (5).

"The Toughest Indian in the World" explicitly contends with all of these questions: modernity, masculinity, and reservation life. Alexie's protagonist is a Spokane/Coeur d'Alene journalist working for a city newspaper. Travelling to do an interview for his newspaper, the protagonist picks up a Native hitchhiker. The man he picks up turns out to be a professional fighter and, after listening to his stories, the protagonist concludes he may even be "the toughest Indian in the world" (254). The narrator's desire to connect with this man, along with his own Indigenous history, is at the centre of this story. While you are reading, consider how Alexie explores the three themes Quirk identifies: How does the narrator understand himself in relation to the time and place in which he lives? What is Alexie saying about masculinity in this story and how is he challenging our predispositions? How does he view his relationship to his reservation, and how does this view change as the story progresses?

Being a Spokane Indian, I only pick up Indian hitchhikers. I learned this particular ceremony from my father, a Coeur d'Alene, who always stopped for those twentieth-century aboriginal nomads who refused to believe the salmon were gone. I don't know what they believed in exactly, but they wore hope like a bright shirt.

My father never taught me about hope. Instead, he continually told me that our salmon—our hope—would never come back, and though such lessons seemed cruel, I know enough to cover my heart in any crowd of white people.

"They'll kills you if they get the chance," my father said. "Love you or hate you, white people will shoot you in the heart. Even after all these years, they'll still smell the salmon on you, the dead salmon, and that will make white people dangerous."

All of us, Indian and white, are haunted by salmon.

When I was a boy, I leaned over the edge of one dam or another—perhaps Long Lake or Little Falls or the great gray dragon known as the Grand Coulee—and watched the ghost of the salmon rise from the water to the sky and become constellations.

For most Indians, stars are nothing more than white tombstones scattered across a dark graveyard.

But the Indian hitchhikers my father picked up refused to admit the existence of sky, let alone the possibility that salmon might be stars. They were common people who believed only in the thumb and the foot. My father envied those simple Indian hitchhikers. He wanted to change their mind about salmon; he wanted to break open their hearts and see the future in their blood. He loved them.

In 1975 or '76 or '77, driving along one highway or another, my father would point out a hitchhiker standing beside the road a mile or two in the distance.

"Indian," he said if it was an Indian, and he was never wrong, though I could never tell if the distant figure was male or female, let alone Indian or not.

If a distant figure happened to be white, my father would drive by without comment.

That was how I learned to be silent in the presence of white people.

The silence is not about hate or pain or fear. Indians just like to believe that white people will vanish, perhaps explode into smoke, if they are ignored enough times. Perhaps a thousand white families are still waiting for their sons and daughters to return home, and can't recognize them when they float back as morning fog.

"We better stop," my mother said from the passenger seat. She was one of those Spokane women who always wore a purple bandanna tied tightly around her head.

These days, her bandanna is usually red. There are reasons, motives, traditions behind the choice of color, but my mother keeps them secret.

"Make room," my father said to my siblings and me as we sat on the floor in the cavernous passenger area of our blue van. We sat on carpet samples because my father had torn out the seats in a sober rage not long after he bought the van from a crazy white man.

I have three brothers and three sisters now. Back then, I had four of each. I missed one of the funerals and cried myself sick during the other one.

"Make room," my father said again—he said everything twice—and only then did we scramble to make space for the Indian hitchhiker.

Of course, it was easy enough to make room for one hitchhiker, but Indians usually travel in packs. Once or twice, we picked up entire all-Indian basketball teams, along with their coaches, girlfriends, and cousins. Fifteen, twenty Indian strangers squeezed into the back of a blue van with nine wide-eyed Indian kids.

Back in those days, I loved the smell of Indians, and of Indian hitchhikers in particular. They were usually in some state of drunkenness, often in need of soap and a towel, and always ready to sing.

Oh, the songs! Indian blues bellowed at the highest volumes. We called them "49s," those cross-cultural songs that combined Indian lyrics and rhythms with country-and-western and blues melodies. It seemed that every Indian knew all the lyrics to every Hank Williams song ever recorded. Hank was our Jesus, Patsy was our Virgin Mary, and Freddy Fender, George Jones, Conway Twitty, Loretta Lynn, Tammy Wynette, Charley Pride, Ronnie Milsap, Tanya Tucker, Marty Robbins, Johnny Horton, Donna Fargo, and Charlie Rich were our disciples.

We all know that nostalgia is dangerous, but I remember those days with a clear conscience. Of course, we live in different days now, and there aren't as many Indian hitchhikers as there used to be.

Now, I drive my own car, a 1998 Toyota Camry, the best-selling automobile in the United States, and therefore the one most often stolen. *Consumer Reports* has named it the most reliable family sedan for sixteen years running, and I believe it.

In my Camry, I pick up three or four Indian hitchhikers a week. Mostly men. They're usually headed home, back to the reservations or somewhere close to the reservations. Indians hardly ever travel in a straight line, so a Crow Indian might hitchhike west when his reservation is back east in Montana. He has some people to see in Seattle, he might explain if I ever asked him. But I never ask Indians their reasons for hitchhiking. All that matters is this: They are Indians walking, raising their thumbs, and I am there to pick them up.

At the newspaper where I work, my fellow reporters think I'm crazy to pick up hitchhikers. They're all white and never stop to pick up anybody, let alone an Indian. After all, we're the ones who write the stories and headlines: HITCHHIKER KILLS HUSBAND AND WIFE, MISSING GIRL'S BODY FOUND, RAPIST STRIKES AGAIN. If I really tried, maybe I could explain to them why I pick up any Indian, but who wants to try? Instead, if they ask I just give them a smile and turn back to my computer. My coworkers smile back and laugh loudly. They're always laughing loudly at me, at one another, at themselves, at goofy typos in the newspaper, at the idea of hitchhikers.

I dated one of them for a few months. Cindy. She covered the local courts: speeding tickets and divorces, drunk driving and embezzlement. Cindy firmly believed in the who-what-where-when-why-and-how of journalism. In daily conversation, she talked like she was writing the lead of her latest story. Hell, she talked like that in bed.

"How does that feel?" I asked, quite possibly the only Indian man who has asked that question.

"I love it when you touch me there," she answered. "But it would help if you rubbed it about thirty percent lighter and with your thumb instead of your middle finger. And could you maybe turn the radio to a different station? KYZY would be good. I feel like soft jazz will work better for me right now. A minor chord, a C or G-flat, or something like that. Okay, honey?"

During lovemaking, I would get so exhausted by the size of her erotic vocabulary that I would fall asleep before my orgasm, continue pumping away as if I were awake, and then regain consciousness with a sudden start when I finally did come, more out of reflex than passion.

Don't get me wrong. Cindy is a good one, cute and smart, funny as hell, a good catch no matter how you define it, but she was also one of those white women who date only brown-skinned guys. Indians like me, black dudes, Mexicans, even a few Iranians. I started to feel like a trophy, or like one of those entries in a personal ad. I asked Cindy why she never dated pale boys.

"White guys bore me," she said. "All they want to talk about is their fathers."

"What do brown guys talk about?" I asked her.

"Their mothers," she said and laughed, then promptly left me for a public defender who was half Japanese and half African, a combination that left Cindy dizzy with the interracial possibilities.

Since Cindy, I haven't dated anyone. I live in my studio apartment with the ghosts of two dogs, Felix and Oscar, and a laptop computer stuffed with bad poems, the aborted halves of three novels, and some three-paragraph personality pieces I wrote for the newspaper.

I'm a features writer, and an Indian at that, so I get all the shit jobs. Not the dangerous shit jobs or the monotonous shit jobs. No. I get to write the articles designed to please the eye, ear, and heart. And there is no journalism more soul-endangering to write than journalism that aims to please.

So it was with reluctance that I climbed into my car last week and headed down Highway 2 to write some damn pleasant story about some damn pleasant people. Then I saw the Indian hitchhiker standing beside the road. He looked the way Indian hitchhikers usually look. Long, straggly black hair. Brown eyes and skin. Missing a couple of teeth. A bad complexion that use to be much worse. Crooked nose that had been broken more than once. Big, misshapen ears. A few whiskers masquerading as a moustache. Even before he climbed into my car I could tell he was tough. He had some serious muscles that threated to rip though his blue jeans and denim jacket. When he was in the car, I could see his hands up close, and they told his whole story. His fingers were twisted into weird, permanent shapes, and his knuckles were covered with layers of scar tissue.

"Jeez," I said. "You're a fighter, enit?"

I threw in the "enit," a reservation colloquialism, because I wanted the fighter to know that I had grown up on the rez, in the woods, with every Indian in the world.

The hitchhiker looked down at his hands, flexed them into fists. I could tell it hurt him to do that.

"Yeah," he said. "I'm a fighter."

I pulled back onto the highway, looking over my shoulder to check my blind spot.

"What tribe are you?" I asked him, inverting the last two words to sound as aboriginal as possible.

"Lummi," he said. "What about you?"

"Spokane."

"I know some Spokanes. Haven't seen them in a long time."

He clutched his backpack in his lap like he didn't want to let it go for anything. He reached inside a pocket and pulled out a piece of deer jerky. I recognized it by the smell.

"Want some?" he asked.

"Sure."

"It had been a long time since I'd eaten jerky. The salt, the gamy taste. I felt as Indian as Indian gets, driving down the road in a fast car, chewing on jerky, talking to an indigenous fighter.

"Where you headed?" I asked.

"Home. Back to the rez."

I nodded my head as I passed a big truck. The driver gave us a smile as we went by. I tooted the horn.

"Big truck," said the fighter.

I haven't lived on my reservation for twelve years. But I live in Spokane, which is only an hour's drive from the rez. Still, I hardly ever go home. I don't know why not. I don't think about it much, I guess, but my mom and dad still live in the same house where I grew up. My brothers and sisters, too. The ghosts of my two dead siblings share an apartment in the converted high school. It's just a local call from Spokane to the rez, so I talk to them once or twice a week. Smoke signals courtesy of U.S. West Communications. Sometimes they call me up to talk about the stories they've seen that I've written for the newspapers. Pet pigs and support groups and science fairs. Once in a while, I used to fill in for the obituaries writer when she was sick. Then she died, and I had to write her obituary.

"How far are you going?" asked the fighter, meaning how much closer was he going to get to his reservation than he was now.

"Up to Wenatchee," I said. "I've got some people to interview there."

"Interview? What for?"

"I'm a reporter. I work for the newspaper."

"No," said the fighter, looking at me like I was stupid for thinking he was stupid. "I mean, what's the story about?"

"Oh, not much. There's two sets of twins who work for the fire department. Human-interest stuff, you know?"

"Two sets of twins, enit? That's weird."

He offered me some more deer jerky, but I was too thirsty from the salty meat, so I offered him a Pepsi instead.

"Don't mind if I do," he said.

"They're in a cooler on the backseat," I said. "Grab me one, too."

He maneuvered his backpack carefully and found room enough to reach into the backseat for the soda pop. He opened my can first and handed it to me. A friendly gesture for a stranger. I took a big mouthful and hiccupped loudly.

"That always happens to me when I drink cold things," he said.

We sipped slowly after that. I kept my eyes on the road while he stared out the window into the wheat fields. We were quiet for many miles.

"Who do you fight?" I asked as we passed through another anonymous small town.

"Mostly Indians," he said. "Money fights, you know? I go from rez to rez, fighting the best they have. Winner takes all."

"Jeez, I never heard of that."

"Yeah, I guess it's illegal."

He rubbed his hands together. I could see fresh wounds. "Man," I said. "Those fights must be rough."

The fighter stared out the window. I watched him for a little too long and almost drove off the road. Car horns sounded all around us.

"Jeez," the fighter said. "Close one, enit?"

"Close enough," I said.

He hugged his backpack more tightly, using it as a barrier between his chest and the dashboard. An Indian hitchhiker's version of a passenger-side air bag.

"Who'd you fight last?" I asked, trying to concentrate on the road.

"Some Flathead," he said. "In Arlee. He was supposed to be the toughest Indian in the world."

"Was he?"

"Nah, no way. Wasn't even close. Wasn't even tougher than me."

He told me how big the Flathead kid was, way over six feet tall and two hundred and some pounds. Big buck Indian. Had hands as big as this and arms as big as that. Had a chin like a damn buffalo. The fighter told me that he hit the Flathead kid harder than he ever hit anybody before.

"I hit him like he was a white man," the fighter said. "I hit him like he was two or three white men rolled into one."

But the Flathead kid would not go down, even though his face swelled up so bad that he looked like the Elephant Man. There were no referees, no judge, no bells to signal the end of the round. The winner was the Indian still standing. Punch after punch, man, and the kid would not go down.

"I was so tired after a while," said the fighter, "that I just took a step back and watched the kid. He stood there with his arms down, swaying from side to side like some toy, you know? Head bobbing on his neck like there was no bone at all. You couldn't even see his eyes no more. He was all messed up."

"What'd you do?" I asked.

"Ah, hell, I couldn't fight him no more. That kid was planning to die before he ever went down. So I just sat on the ground while they counted me out. Dumb Flathead kid didn't even know what was happening. I just sat on the ground while they raised his hand. While all the winners collected their money and all the losers cussed me out. I just sat there, man."

"Jeez," I said. "What happened next?"

"Not much. I sat there until everybody was gone. Then I stood up and decided to head for home. I'm tired of this shit. I just want to go home for a while. I got enough money to last me a long time. I'm a rich Indian, you hear? I'm a rich Indian."

The fighter finished his Pepsi, rolled down his window, and pitched the can out. I almost protested, but decided against it. I kept my empty can wedged between my legs.

"That's a hell of a story," I said.

"Ain't no story," he said. "It's what happened."

"Jeez," I said." You would've been a warrior in the old days, enit? You would've been a killer. You would have stolen everybody's goddamn horses. That would've been you. You would've been it."

I was excited. I wanted the fighter to know how much I thought of him. He didn't even look at me.

"A killer," he said. "Sure."

We didn't talk much after that. I pulled into Wenatchee just before sundown, and the fighter seemed happy to be leaving me.

"Thanks for the ride, cousin," he said as he climbed out. Indians always call each other cousin, especially if they're strangers.

"Wait," I said.

He looked at me, waiting impatiently.

I wanted to know if he had a place to sleep that night. It was supposed to get cold. There was a mountain range between Wenatchee and his reservation. Big mountains that were dormant volcanoes, but that could all blow up at any time. We wrote about it once in the newspaper. Things can change so quickly. So many emergencies and disasters that we can barely keep track. I wanted to tell him how much I cared about my job, even if I had to write about small-town firemen. I wanted to tell the fighter that I pick up all Indian hitchhikers, young and old, men and women, and get them a little closer to home, even if

I can't get them all the way. I wanted to tell him that the night sky was a graveyard. I wanted to know if he was the toughest Indian in the world.

"It's late," I finally said. "You can crash with me, if you want."

He studied my face and then looked down the long road toward his
reservation.

"Okay," he said. "That sounds good."

We got a room at the Pony Soldier Motel, and both of us laughed at the
irony of it all. Inside the room, in a generic watercolor hanging above the bed,
the U.S. Cavalry was kicking the crap out of a band of renegade Indians.

"What tribe do you think they are?" I asked the fighter.

"All of them," he said.

The fighter crashed on the floor while I curled up in the uncomfortable
bed. I couldn't sleep for the longest time. I listened to the fighter talk in his
sleep. I stared up at the water-stained ceiling. I don't know what time it was
when I finally drifted off, and I don't know what time it was when the fighter
got into bed with me. He was naked and his penis was hard. I felt it press
against my back as he snuggled up close to me, reached inside my underwear,
and took my penis in his hand. Neither of us said a word. He continued to
stroke me as he rubbed himself against my back. That went on for a long time.
I had never been that close to another man, but the fighter's callused fingers
felt better than I would have imagined if I had ever allowed myself to imagine
such things.

"This isn't working," he whispered. "I can't come."

Without thinking, I reached around and took the fighter's penis in my
hand. He was surprisingly small.

"No," he said. "I want to be inside you."

"I don't know," I said. "I've never done this before."

"It's okay," he said. "I'll be careful. I have rubbers."

Without waiting for my answer, he released me and got up from the bed.
I turned to look at him. He was beautiful and scarred. So much brown skin
marked with bruises, badly healed wounds, and tattoos. His long black hair
was unbraided and hung down to his thin waist. My slacks and dress shirt
were folded and draped over the chair near the window. My shoes were sitting
on the table. Blue light filled the room. The fighter bent down to his pack and
searched for his condoms. For reasons I could not explain then and cannot
explain now, I kicked off my underwear and rolled over on my stomach. I could
not see him, but I could hear him breathing heavily as he found the condoms,
tore open a package, and rolled one over his penis. He crawled onto the bed,
between my legs, and slid a pillow beneath my belly.

"Are you ready?" he asked.

"I'm not gay," I said.

"Sure," he said as he pushed himself into me. He was small but it hurt more than I expected, and I knew that I would be sore for days afterward. But I wanted him to save me. He didn't say anything. He just pumped into me for a few minutes, came with a loud sigh, and then pulled out. I quickly rolled off the bed and went into the bathroom. I locked the door behind me and stood there in the dark. I smelled like salmon.

"Hey," the fighter said through the door. "Are you okay?"

"Yes," I said. "I'm fine."

A long silence.

"Hey," he said. "Would you mind if I slept in the bed with you?"

I had no answer for that.

"Listen," I said. "That Flathead boy you fought? You know, the one you really beat up? The one who wouldn't fall down?"

In my mind, I could see the fighter pummeling that boy. Punch after punch. The boy too beaten to fight back, but too strong to fall down.

"Yeah, what about him?" asked the fighter.

"What was his name?"

"His name?"

"Yeah, his name."

"Elmer something or other."

"Did he have an Indian name?"

"I have no idea. How the hell would I know that?"

I stood there in the dark for a long time. I was chilled. I wanted to get into bed and fall asleep.

"Hey," I said. "I think maybe—well, I think you should leave now."

"Yeah," said the fighter, not surprised. I heard him softly singing as he dressed and stuffed all of his belongings into his pack. I wanted to know what he was singing, so I opened the bathroom door just as he was opening the door to leave. He stopped, looked at me, and smiled.

"Hey, tough guy," he said. "You were good."

The fighter walked out the door, left it open, and walked away. I stood in the doorway and watched him continue his walk down the highway, past the city limits. I watched him rise from earth to sky and become a new constellation. I closed the door and wondered what was going to happen next. Feeling uncomfortable and cold, I went back into the bathroom. I ran the shower with the hottest water possible. I stared at myself in the mirror. Steam quickly filled the room. I threw a few shadow punches. Feeling stronger, I stepped into the shower and searched my body for changes. A middle-aged man needs to look for tumors. I dried myself with a towel too small for the job. Then I crawled naked into bed. I wondered if I was a warrior in this life and if I had been a warrior in a previous life. Lonely and laughing, I fell asleep. I didn't dream at all, not one bit. Or perhaps I dreamed but remembered none of it. Instead, I woke early the next morning, before sunrise, and went out into the world. I walked past my car. I stepped onto the pavement, still warm from the previous day's sun. I started walking. In bare feet, I traveled upriver toward the place where I was born and will someday die. At that moment, if you had broken open my heart you could have looked inside and seen the thin white skeletons of one thousand salmon.

⟶ The Secret of the Zutz'baläm[1] ⟵
Isaías Hernández Isidro

Isaías Hernández Isidro is a Chontal author, translator, and teacher born in the village of Mazateupa, in Nacajuca, a major hub of the Chontal Maya population in the state of Tabasco, in Mexico. He is a founding member of the Indigenous Language Writers Incorporation and an active participant in the Gathering of Indigenous Language Writers. He is the author of a number of texts, including *La gatita enamorada* (The Enamoured Kitten), and the co-author of *Relatos Chontales* (Chontal stories) and *Cuentistas jóvenes* (young short-story writers).

"The Secret of the Zuzt'bälam" tells the story of Teófila, a mother who has been exiled from her home by her children because she can no longer work. Wandering the countryside looking for food, Teófila comes across a mother and her strange and powerful son. Teófila is taken in by her new family and soon discovers that the boy she is now caring for is a Zuzt'bälam, a supernatural creature who protects the fields. Ultimately, however, the tensions between self, community, and the supernatural become impossible to bear, as Teófila fatally weighs her commitment to the Zuzt'bälam against her increasingly compromised relationship to her community. When reading this story, think about the relationships between self, family, and community that Hernández Isidro constructs and consider how the Zuzt'bälam contributes to (or takes away from) these relationships. What is the significance of the "secret" in this story? And how does Teófila's point of view contribute to our understanding of the supernatural?

Translated from the Tabasco Chontal (Yokot'an) language[2]

Teófila's children ran her off because she could no longer work. Thereafter, she would go from house to house looking for something to do in exchange for a mouthful to survive the day. One morning she crossed a river and went to another town. After much walking, she found herself in front of an abandoned-looking house. A chill ran through her body.

"Come in, we were expecting you," a voice called to her.

Nervous, she did not see who was speaking to her since the room was very dark. A large figure fell from the ceiling; the ground shook.

"Do not be afraid, Señora,[3] this is your house. My mother is in the fields; I have already notified her that you are here."

"It is so dark. Are you not you afraid? It is dangerous for you to be alone. The evil ones do not care about their victims' size."

The child laughed. Teófila could not make out his face in the darkness.

"Do not be afraid; I like the darkness," replied the child.

From the kitchen appeared a short, elderly, robust woman with a happy face and the gaze of an eagle.

"Mamá, this is the woman I told you about. She has no place to live because her children threw her out on the street."

There was Teófila, sitting on a tree trunk next to the grinding board in the kitchen, with her gaze riveted to the ground: confused, frightened, without words, unable to comprehend how a child could know her name and her background without ever having seen her. The women ate *pijije*[4] soup, and when Teófila was about to bring the child a plate of food, the old woman stopped her.

"He eats at night."

When it became dark, the old woman ordered Teófila to bring a turkey from the pen. Both women hung it from a beam in the kitchen. The child's mother took a knife and cut off its head, and Teófila collected the blood in a clay dish. The old woman asked her to take all of that food to her son. Within the house, there was an altar made of *jaguacte*[5] with two incense burners that spread the aroma of *estoraque*.[6] There, atop a *toj*[7] leaf, she placed the child's food.

At dawn, as they were working in the kitchen, the mother observed Teófila, who was pensive: "You are very quiet, woman. Are you not happy here with us? You look very sad."

"I do not know what is wrong with me. It is as if I do not know where I am, or whom I am with. Your son lives in the darkness; I do not know what he is like. I do not know him."

"Look, Teófila, a Zutz'baläm lives here; he is still small, but when he turns twelve years of age he will leave. He made you come here to take care of him while I work in the fields. I strongly recommend to you that no one else learn of this. Zutz'baläms are cruel with traitors and the unfaithful."

Once, when the old woman had to go far away, Teófila took charge of the house. At nightfall, the child came out onto the patio and began to dance. She spied on him through a crack in the kitchen wall. The little one extended his arms and, along with them, huge bat wings. The child rose up into the air, and his jaguar roar shook the house. A strong wind began to blow, and clouds began to build. The sky became threatening, and just as the old woman arrived, it began to rain. A storm ensued that lasted several days; the fields were destroyed. Several nights later, the child came out and ran circles all around the patio in the downpour; the trees bent over as he passed. At dawn the storm had disappeared.

One early morning, a whistle was heard near the house, and it clearly felt like something had landed on the roof. Frightened, Teófila woke the old woman, who said to her in an annoyed tone: "No matter what you hear at night, do not be afraid and do not think about getting up. It is only my son arriving."

Teófila gradually became accustomed to the old woman and the small Zutz'baläm. Her sadness faded since she now had another family. One morning, while they were grinding corn for tortillas, Teófila said: "At times, when you arrive late from the fields, your child goes out to dance in the night. He runs and even flies. He is so powerful, it seems that the air he stirs is going to knock the house down."

"When that happens, he is warning us that something terrible will happen. If it is a storm, he dances furiously; if it is a drought, he runs until he is out of breath; if it is to be a big crop, he runs, laughs, and whistles softly."

The woman suddenly became serious: "Everything you have seen here you must keep secret. If you ever tell about this without the Zutz'baläms' permission, they will punish you; you might die."

One day Teófila climbed up into the house's storage loft to get some corn, and she saw a gourd with money in it. She ran to tell her mistress.

"Do not touch that money because my son brings it on Mondays.[8] Thanks to him, there is food in this house."

That year marked the worst drought they had lived through in many years. The heat was unbearable. The animals were choking, and the earth cracked open. There was no water. The trees appeared dead, and the crops were practically lost. The child came running out onto the patio, and he threw himself upon the ground. He squirmed about as if he were in great pain. It seemed as if he were dying.

"No, it cannot be!" said the old woman, concerned. "Tomorrow the fields will go up in flames since the earth is so dry. We must save the crops."

They went out at dawn. They harvested the corn and in the middle of the field piled up the ears and covered them with *chäk to'*.[9] They had barely finished when the grass began to burn. The entire savannah burned, and only ash remained. The birds and the animals suffered from lack of food for several months; nevertheless, Teófila and her patrons did not perish.

The years went by, and one day the child Zutz'baläm called the two women together: "I am happy that Teófila has helped us so much. Tomorrow I turn twelve years of age and must go to my proper place."

He looked at his mother: "It saddens me that you will remain alone. Today Teófila will return to her children, who anxiously await her. All this time they have thought about their ingratitude, so she must return to them."

Teófila attempted to speak, but the little one stopped her: "I know what you are going to say, but you have completed your task. Mother, give her some money and make sure she leaves before nightfall. Do not be sad, Teófila. When you are under a great burden at home, do not be afraid; I will bring you some money."

She began her return. She became lost along unfamiliar pathways. It had been so long! A fisherman who was passing by immediately recognized her. They sat down in the shade of a *guayabo*[10] tree, and the good man filled her in on what had gone on in town during her absence.

"No one knew what had happened to you."

He accompanied her to her house. Her children, happy to see her, organized a big fiesta and invited the whole town. They served a lot of *guarapo*.[11] They roasted numerous turkeys in the town square. People gathered around the celebrated woman, wanting to hear of her adventures, but as they could not get her to tell them anything, they served her so much alcohol that she got drunk.

She then told them the story of the Zutz'baläm and how, when he danced and flew, he predicted storms, droughts, and the fires that char the fields. She also said that he promised to bring her money every Monday. After talking for hours in her drunken state, she realized she had betrayed the trust of her friends because she had failed to keep their secret. A terrible wind rose up. A spark from the cooking fires fell upon Teófila's clothing, setting it aflame. No one could extinguish the flames, and she did not even protest her punishment. Her children gathered up her ashes and took them to the cemetery. They built an offering to placate the ire of the young Zutz'baläm. They begged him to pardon Teófila and themselves for their carelessness.

⟶ *Devotion* ⟵

Richard Van Camp

Richard Van Camp is an internationally renowned storyteller and best-selling author. He is a member of the Dogrib (Tlicho) Nation from Fort Smith, Northwest Territories, Canada. A graduate of the En'owkin International School of Writing, the University of Victoria's Creative Writing BFA Program, and the MFA in Creative Writing at the

University of British Columbia, Van Camp is a prolific artist who works in a variety of genres and disciplines, including short stories, novels, graphic novels, illustrated children's books, film, and storytelling performance. His critically acclaimed novel, *The Lesser Blessed* (1996), became a movie with First Generation Films, premiering in September 2012 at the Toronto International Film Festival. He is also the author of several collections of short stories, including *Angel Wing Splash Pattern* (2002), *The Moon of Letting Go* (2009), *Godless but Loyal to Heaven* (2012), and *Night Moves* (2015).

The story "Devotion," which was originally published in *Godless but Loyal to Heaven*, is a complex, multilayered narrative: a story within a story. The narrative frame is provided by an unnamed narrator speaking to an unnamed audience (although who this audience is becomes clearer as we read). She relays a story about the white caribou, a story told to her by an ex-boyfriend, Charlie, many years ago. In Inuit orature, which Van Camp draws on here, the white caribou are shape-shifters and can transform between human and animal. In Van Camp's account, the white caribou poses as a human in order to discover where humans will be hunting that year, thus allowing the caribou to escape death. In relaying a traditional story through a narrator who is herself telling a story that has been passed on to her, Van Camp is encouraging us as readers to think about how stories are told, to whom, and for what purpose. As a Tlicho writer retelling an Inuit story, the cross-cultural relationships between teller and audience are of key importance. When reading this story think carefully about the ways in which Van Camp frames the narrative. Who is the narrator telling the story to and why is she telling it? How does her perspective influence what we can and cannot know about Charlie's own narrative? Also consider the nature of transformation and community in "Devotion." Who, in your mind, is the white caribou? How are animal and human communities interrelated here and to what effect?

I know I've … I know I've never been one to borrow from grace before, but the day Charlie went missing, a raven came to me outside my window and tried telling me something. It clucked its beak and started to chatter, and I waved it away, prayed it away. I spoke English; I spoke Dogrib. I even spoke Cree: "*Awas! Awas!*"

Then it gripped its claws on the branch and swung upside down. Looking at me. Clucking. It would not stop trying to tell me something. And that's when I knew: It was Charlie. His spirit, asking for help.

When I was with Charlie we laughed all the time. When I went with him … it was the best time of my life. The way we were. How people loved him. He brightened every room he walked into. People still ask me about him, even after all these years.

When that raven came to me, I had a feeling. Just like when Dad died. I had a feeling. They say many things about the spirit world and here's what I want to say to you. I am going to write this down so you know I know about you, and I'm going to tell you how I figured you out. All of you.

Charlie told me a story one night. It was late. We'd gone dancing. He got into his whiskey. Just a touch. That's what he'd say: just a touch. And he told me a story. Well, it was a secret. I had been after him for weeks to tell me a secret he'd never told anyone before, and I remember when he started to tell it to me it was because he knew we would be together forever, and that this was the biggest secret of his life.

It went like this. Charlie said a long time ago he was up in the eastern Arctic. "The artic," he used to call it, and you know how his mother is Eskimo, right? Inuit? He could speak Inuktitut. He could also speak Dogrib. He loved languages. I always meant to ask him what language he dreamt in, but maybe you can for me. You know, Charlie was never the same person after he told me this story.

This happened before he knew me. Charlie said that he was skidooing, going to a hunter's camp. It was a beautiful day on Baffin Island. He was making his way and he noticed a camp to his left. The tents were canvas with hides. He passed by and was so excited to go hunting. He had been home for a while with his mom and he was aching for muktuk with soya sauce. Oh he loved to smack his lips when he talked about muktuk and soya sauce. I tried it once with him, and I swear my hair was shiny for a month. It's ever greasy. Oh our kisses were gross after. He loved it. But me, I'll pass….

Anyhow, as he was a mile or so past the camp, the belt broke on his skidoo and he came to a stop. Most hunters have extra fan belts, and the man he borrowed the machine from was known for many things, but an extra of anything was not one of them.

Charlie was stuck. As nice of a day as it was, he knew he was the last hunter to make his way to the camp, and he was losing the light. As hard as he tried, he could not think of anything that would work. Then he remembered the camp.

So he decided to walk. It took a long time to get there and he used his skidoo trail as a path. He knew not to run, not to overheat. He took his time. Oh, I miss his walk. He was so handsome and he looked so relaxed all the time.

He made his way to the camp and knocked once before opening the tent flap to go in. Inside were several Inuit hunters. There was tea, he said. Pilot biscuits. No muktuk, but they had broth from seals.

He said hello and the hunters said hello back. Charlie explained his situation and the hunters listened to his Inuktitut.

The leader invited him in. "Eat," he said. And they served him. The hunters all had their guns and their harpoons. They had a little lamp of stone that they burned seal oil on. Charlie ate. It was so good to be home. Strangely, all of the men used *ulus*, the curved knife of the Inuit that looks like a quarter moon. Mom said the *ulu* was only for women and boys with girls' names.

"How do you know our language?" the leader asked him. "You have an accent."

"Oh," Charlie explained. He told them who his mother was and how he spent time in the west with his father. He apologized for speaking lnuktitut like a *kalunat*. A white man. And they all laughed.

"We do not know your mother," one of the hunters said.

"No?" Charlie asked. "She's a leader. She's helping get Nunavut off the ground. You must have heard of her."

The hunters all looked at each other. "No," they said. "Where are you going?"

Charlie gave them the name of a great hunter who was expecting him. He was surprised when the hunters all said they did not know of him or who he was. The man he was to join was famous for leading many community hunts and for fighting for the rights of hunters.

"Where have you come from?" they asked. "Have you seen any caribou?" He had come from Lypa's, his mom's boyfriend. He'd come right from the airport to Lypa's to get his gear, gun and skidoo and directions to the camp.

"We don't know him either," the leader said.

"Lypa?" Charlie said. "Everyone knows Lypa. He's a great carver. He's one of the trainers for the Canadian military with the Rangers."

Again, the hunters all looked at one another. "We do not know him either."

Charlie told me he had had a bad feeling, that he was a stranger to these people and that he had better leave. He explained to the hunters that the day was losing its light and that perhaps he'd better get back to his machine. He asked them if any of them had an extra belt, but they all said no.

"Then I'd better get going," he said. And he stood up to leave. He told me how he wished he'd had his gun then. It was the strangest feeling to think this amongst hunters, but he had it loud in his head to leave right away. That was when the leader touched his own rifle by his side and told him to sit down and keep talking.

"Why?" Charlie asked. "I am sorry, but it seems I have offended you somehow and I apologize. I am sorry you don't know my mother or the hunter who I am seeking or my mother's boyfriend."

"Keep talking," another hunter said who touched his rifle. Charlie stood again and the hunters all told him to sit.

"What is it?" Charlie said. "What have I done? I do not understand why you're treating me this way."

The leader held his hand up and motioned for Charlie to sit. "Keep talking," he ordered. "Prove to us you are not a white caribou."

Oh no! Charlie thought. He had heard for years about the white caribou. They are beings who pretend to be human and steal into camps pretending to be visitors, only to learn where the men are going to hunt the caribou. When they leave, they leave nothing but bad luck and afterwards the caribou are never where they're supposed to be.

"Prove to us you are human," the eldest hunter said. "Keep talking."

My Charlie sat, and he told me he spoke for what seemed like days. Days and days. They fed him and watched him. They questioned him over and over, the stories he told. He told them everything he could think of about his life and they listened carefully. When he was tired, they would let him sleep. When he had to use the bathroom, they went out with him. Sometimes it was day; sometimes it was night. It was then that he realized they had no dog teams, nor did they have skidoos. When he tried asking them questions, he was bullied to keep answering, to keep talking. Finally, after he burst into tears from exhaustion and after they'd all run out of food, the hunters let him go. He said he ran all the way back in the direction of town where the Rangers were looking for him.

My Charlie told that secret to me only because I nagged him and only because he loved me. I want you to know this.

And you know, I think it was that story that broke us. After that, everything fell apart. Bad luck found our home. Worse luck found our love. Charlie hurt his back; he couldn't work. He got mean. He was jealous when I came home happy. He told me he could not taste his food. We tried all we could to make things last, but I lost him. You know I lost him.

They say we live many lives in this one and we have to give thanks for our exes. I think about him more and more. Yes, I'm with Hank. Yes, our kids have grown. Yes, I have a home filled with memories of feasts and laughter. But then I heard that Charlie had gone missing. I heard he was training with the Rangers and that they were jogging and he vanished like he did—his footprints vanished—I knew because it was a raven who came to him the day his mother died. She had returned as a raven to say goodbye. That raven outside my window was Charlie telling me something I figured out some time ago.

The more I think about that story ... I figured it out. I figured you out. You see, that camp he described—there were no dogs. No skidoos. "Men" using *ulus*. And those hunters. How they treated him. How *you* treated him.

I think *they* were the white caribou. I think you are the white caribou. I think you were getting ready to split up and go after the camps and learn the plans of the hunters. I think he surprised you and that you made him earn his freedom as a human.

You know, he used to hold me in his sleep like a vice. Sometimes he'd shiver and yell out, "They're coming for me! They are, Susan. They're coming!"

I believe you came back for him. All of you. I believe you let him and his glorious heart go so he could live a few years and that you'd come for him so you could steal him back. I believe you missed him just as much as I do … all these years later. I think you know I know now. I think you know he told one person on this earth the story of all of you.

They say my family has medicine. It's true my grandmother saved her cousin from having his leg cut off due to diabetes using beaver castors. Ehtsi cured my styes using skunk juice. It's true she knows how to cure asthma. And she trained me how.

I was the one who told Charlie how to gather medicine under the full moon: to always work in fours; to always offer tobacco first; to talk to the earth and sky and spirit of the leaf, root or tree about why you were taking what you were from them. I tried passing this on to my kids and my husband but it never took. So I'm willing to pass it on to you. All I know. For your people.

I think you should come back and take me. When I think of how hard Charlie's life has been. When I think of his good heart, even when he was drinking. It wasn't his fault he told me the story about you. I was the one who figured this story out.

I've lived a good life. My kids are grown. My husband is a good man but he'll move on….

I have only been in love once in my life. I will tell you that. When I light this letter on fire and give it back to the spirit world … give my words back to the Creator and to you, I know you will see this letter and wish from the other side.

I will never tell anyone about you, and I have learned where the hunters are coming this month to find you. I've made my rounds in my own quiet way, and I will tell you everything. This is a good trade. I want you to consider my offer. I want you to consider this—

⤙ *Grandma and the Wendigo* ⤚
Sylvain Rivard

Born in Montréal, Sylvain Rivard (a.k.a Vainvard) is a multidisciplinary artist of French-Canadian and Abenaki origins. He is the author and illustrator of *Contes du trou d'cul* (2010), *Moz en cinq temps* (2011), *Skok en sept temps* (2012), *Pmola en quatre temps* (2013), and *The Arrow Sash* (2014). He is also the author of an essay on the Abenaki chief, *Joseph Laurent* (2009). "Grandma and the Wendigo" was originally written in French and was translated into English for this volume.

Rivard's story references a cycle of traditional Cree stories relating to the "Wendigo," also written as Weetigo or Wetigo, a cannibalistic monster that also appears in

Tomson Highway's *Kiss of the Fur Queen*, Steven Keewatin Sanderson's *Darkness Calls*, and Paul Seesequasis's "The Republic of Tricksterism" (see Chapter 4). In Highway's story the hero Weesageechak, in the form of a weasel, enters the beast by his anus and destroys him by chewing his intestines "to smithereens" (164). In Sanderson's comic, on the other hand, it is up to the protagonist Kyle, to defy the Wetigo in the epic battle between Wîsahkêcâhk and Wetigo (168). In Rivard's telling, the narrator's grandmother, who is described simply as "Indian," covers the shoulders of the "very tall, very thin man" with a blanket and gives him a warm drink. The grandmother refuses to give any explanation the following morning as she mops up a large puddle on the floor, "the only trace of his melted heart, which had run out of his body and through the anus of the beast" (268). What similarities or differences do you notice between these three stories that reference Wetigo?

Translated by Kristin Talbot Neel and Sylvain Rivard

> *I have seen colonists settle fifty leagues from here, on the Lièvre River, with a humble sled or a simple cart. The land is so fertile in that country that they don't hesitate to brave the difficulties of the road, the length of the journey and the great distance from other populated areas....*
> —Curé Antoine Labelle (1888)

He was damn right, Father Labelle, when he wrote those lines about the Laurentides, lands of the up-country. Every summer when I was a kid I made the trip from Montréal to Mont-Laurier, taking the old highway in my grandfather's big, beige Chrysler. The highway hadn't been built yet, just route 117 the whole way up. A never-ending Holy Procession that paraded through cities, towns and villages: Sainte-Thérèse, Saint-Jérôme, Saint-Sauveur-des-Monts, Sainte-Adèle, Sainte-Agathe-des-Monts, Saint-Jovite, La Conception, L'Annonciation, Sainte-Véronique, Lac-Saint-Paul, pray for us! A long asphalt trail running between two hedges of pine, birch and spruce where the colonists, guided by God, carefully chose where to settle their houses, farms, businesses and churches.

Perceived as the crowning moment of the year, we inevitably headed up to the Hautes-Laurentides to my maternal grandparents' summer cabin on Lac-Saint-Paul, near Ferme-Neuve. "We" were my grandparents, one of my three sisters, my brother and myself.

"How long 'til we get there, Grandpa?"

No answer, or a tirade from Grandma on the history of the Oratory of Saint-Joseph and Brother André. It should be mentioned that my grandparents were that type of ignorant Christian married couple, obedient and pious, living close to nature and in the fear of God. My grandfather collected animal hides and worked the land, my grandmother gathered berries and made pies. This was how my ancestors lived their peaceful, mixed-blood, everyday lives. For me, at that age, the Oratory was just a little house in yellow plastic, about six or seven inches high, that my grandparents kept on a table in their living room and that I always wanted to play with. As for Brother André, he was the missing figurine.

All along this Way of the Cross, this long ascent up to the countryside, there were certain stops that had to be made. The first one, and the worst of all, was the museum dedicated to Aurore, the martyred child, in Labelle. What a horror! Damn, was I scared of all those realistic and macabre displays of Aurore eating soap, Aurore with her hands on the woodstove, Aurore all beat up, curled up on the floor, etc. How stupid do you have to be to show all that to a kid?! That place and the Midgets' Palace on Rachel Street in Montréal, I just don't get it. It must be a generational thing.

At the second station, in L'Annonciation, was the promise of a paper bag full of greasy fries at Pierrette's. What could be more comforting than fries out of a fry house on the side of the road? My favourites were the little ones, kind of burned, at the bottom of the bag. My grandfather said that the place was named after my mother, whose name was also Pierrette. But my grandfather was kind of full of it.

"Are we there yet, Grandpa?"

No answer, or a joke about cows.

Once we got off route 117, after driving down another long road, this time in dirt, we would get to Lac-Saint-Paul. Right after the big farm with the red metal roof. It wasn't a big place, Lac-Saint-Paul. Two, maybe three roads that ran alongside Lake Moreau. Because of course the lake couldn't be called Saint-Paul, it had to have its own name, Moreau. How stupid is that? Just one more thing to confuse a small child.

Next stop the General Store, where I remember the sliced bread being displayed on a shelf right next to the fishing lures. And where the little toys for sale were either so old or from a distributor so obscure that I had never seen anything like them, not even at Eaton's, the pharmacy or the corner store. Every time I just had to have one, and I always got one. Grandma and Grandpa picked up the basics and then, off we went! Straight on to the cabin, which wasn't very far away.

A brick-red log cabin perched on a sandy slope awaited us. Enthroned in the centre was a big woodstove. One room at the front served as kitchen, dining room and living room, while two tiny bedrooms were tucked in behind each side of the woodstove. A big porch ran along the side that faced Lac-Saint-Paul, or Moreau, with, of course, no electricity or running water, so the well and the outhouse were outside. It was the kind of lack of luxury that could either completely discourage you or fulfill you, depending on your predisposition.

One tranquil evening, a few minutes after the sunset and its accompanying light show, as we were eating one of my grandmother's memorable strawberry-rhubarb pies, my grandfather said:

"Flora, you see what I see out that window?"

"'Course I see it Léo. It's been looking in at us a while now."

Before we could even look out the window our grandfather sent us into our room. I witnessed the rest of the story in the manner of a Chinese shadow theatre; a curtain served as the door into our room so as to let the heat from the woodstove pass through easily during the night.

Once we were in our room, all three of us piled into one bed, my grandfather turned up the oil lamp and said to my grandmother:

"Okay you're the Indian woman here, so you get rid of that beast now, hear?"

"'Course, Léo, sure will."

Then he went into the other room.

My brother and my sister, the oldest of the three of us and also the most fearful, thought it was a bear. I was just hoping it wasn't the Boogeyman. We had heard enough stories to be scared to death of him.

Grandma Flora calmly put on her light wool cardigan, opened the door and let in a very tall, very thin man. We could tell how tall he was because he had to lower his head and his shoulders to pass through the doorway. "Oh my God, this is it. It's the Boogeyman and he's gonna get us," I said to myself. She sat him down next to the woodstove and he curled himself quietly into a ball. Next, she put an old blanket over his shoulders and gave him something warm to drink. He was right next to the curtain leading into our room and we were scared as hell. Soon I noticed an odour like a wet animal and I thought to myself, "It can't be the Boogeyman. No one ever said the Boogeyman smelled like wet dog. He also looks like he has no clothes on and the Boogeyman is supposed to be wearing a big cloak and hat, and he carries a big bag on his back. So then who the hell is this guy?"

I stared at his shadow all night long, absolutely petrified that all of a sudden he would move aside the curtain and come into our room, until I fell into the arms of Morpheus.

The next morning I woke up to the smell of burned toast and coffee. I got up and hesitated a moment before pulling back the curtain to our room. I slowly snuck my head through the gap and, surprise! There was no mysterious figure on the floor next to the woodstove, just a big, dark puddle of water that Grandma, on all fours, was sponging up. She absolutely refused to tell my brother and me who the tall, smelly man was and what had happened to him. It was my sister who, coming back from picking raspberries with Grandma the following summer, told us that our grandmother had confronted a Wendigo. A cannibalistic monster that she had healed by melting his heart with one of her herbal concoctions. The puddle I had seen in the morning was the only trace of his melted heart, which had run out of his body and through the anus of the beast. My sister added that Grandma had been lucky to have not come across a female Wendigo, because they are even more unpredictable, aggressive and voracious than the males.

— Excerpt from *Red: A Haida Manga* —
Michael Nicoll Yahgulanaas

Haida artist and author Michael Nicoll Yahgulanaas was born in 1954 in Masset, Haida Gwaii, and is a descendant of the master carver Charles Edenshaw. His award-winning artwork is exhibited across the globe in public spaces, museums, galleries, and private collections. He has written and illustrated two graphic novels that became national bestsellers, *Flight of the Hummingbird* (2008) and *Red: A Haida Manga* (2009). Yahgulanaas became a full-time artist after many decades working for the Haida Nation in its successful campaign to protect its forest and its biocultural diversity. In the late 1990s, he learned Chinese brush techniques under the guidance of Cantonese master Cai Ben Kwon, and began developing his self-taught practice, "Haida Manga," which blends North Pacific Indigenous iconographies and formlines with the graphic dynamism of Asian manga.

Red brings together manga, North American comics, a private family story, and the use of formline typically featured in traditional Haida art. Yahgulanaas began by painting a giant mural that encompasses the entire story before cutting the pages out to create a graphic novel that follows a sequence from left to right. The story features two orphans, Red and his big sister Jaada, who live together in their village. Disaster strikes when invaders arrive and, even though Red calls an alarm and alerts the village, Jaada is kidnapped. In the subsequent years Red shows leadership; however, against the advice of his Elders, he is consumed with thoughts of revenge. He flouts the rules of his community, works with a newcomer to manufacture a submarine in the shape of a whale, and then uses his invention to pursue someone he thinks is Jaada's kidnapper, not realizing it is Jaada's husband and his own brother-in-law. In the excerpt we have included here, the formline (which doubles as the panels' contours) is strained by Red's single-minded pursuit of revenge, eventually snapping. Literary critic Miriam Brown-Spiers argues that the shattering of the formline is a sign that Red is not monitoring his own actions, leading to his disrespect of his human community and the land itself (Brown-Spiers 48). As he fixates on his individual pain, he upsets fragile social, ecological, and familial balances and damages himself and his community.

Figure 6.1   Michael Nicoll Yahgulanaas, from *Red: A Haida Manga*. (*Credit:* Douglas and McIntyre Press)

Figure 6.2   Michael Nicoll Yahgulanaas, from *Red: A Haida Manga*. (*Credit:* Douglas and McIntyre Press)

Figure 6.3   Michael Nicoll Yahgulanaas, from *Red: A Haida Manga*. (*Credit:* Douglas and McIntyre Press)

Figure 6.4   Michael Nicoll Yahgulanaas, from *Red: A Haida Manga*. (*Credit:* Douglas and McIntyre Press)

The Boys Who Became a Killer Whale
Ellen Rice White

Ellen Rice White is a Snuneymuxw Elder, storyteller, and writer of *Legends and Teachings of Xeel's the Creator* (2006). The stories she shares have been handed down to her from her grandparents and her ancestors. White lives in the Snuneymuxw Nation of Nanaimo on the eastern shore of Vancouver Island and has worked for decades as a teacher, storyteller, dancer, drummer, healer, and political activist. She has also served as Resident Elder at Vancouver Island University.

"The Boys Who Became a Killer Whale" tells the story of a group of young people who wish to learn new skills from their parents and other family members, but these adults are too busy and impatient to take the time to teach the youth how to do things properly. The young people resolve to prove to their Elders that they are mature enough to take on adult responsibilities. Drawing on knowledge they have overheard from their Elders, but lacking the guidance they still need, the youth "make" a killer whale using a skin they find drying on the beach. After they have created the whale, however, they find that they have less control over the animal than they had assumed. As White points out in her own commentary on this story, "The Boys Who Became a Killer Whale" is not simply a cautionary tale for brash children. It is a story about the relationships that constitute a community and the responsibilities that youth and Elders have to one another.

A group of young people was gathered at a private meeting place far away from their village. It was a special place where they went when they had concerns that they didn't want the Elders to hear. These young people, who had not quite reached the age of puberty, were upset that they were not included with their older brothers and sisters during the teaching time and felt they were missing out on the sacred teachings.

A boy named Shuyulh, which means "the older one," led the group. Shuyulh and his three younger brothers were always first to arrive at their special meeting place, and they made a fire. No one spoke until they were all gathered. They knew how to conduct themselves as they sat around the fire. They waited until everyone arrived and then the older one looked up and nodded to them.

The younger ones who did not know what they were meeting about thought, "This is very, very serious." As young as they were, they knew the difference between the time to talk and the time to be quiet. They all felt the heaviness and waited for direction.

Shuyulh looked at them and said, "We are all gathered here today because of the way we have been treated. We are not babies anymore. Our parents and the Elders ask us to get wood, look for pitch in the woods to start their fires, search for special types of wood for barbequing, gather special rocks for pit cooking, and do other things such as getting water or berry juice for the Elders. They do not have to tell us how to do these jobs because we already know how. They have taught us these things many times."

"But why is it when they address problems or teachings we are sent away? When we are learning how to soften the inner cedar bark and we are doing it the right way we are included, but if we do anything wrong we are told to go away."

One of the young cousins spoke next, saying, "One time I cried for a long time after being yelled at and I fell asleep behind our bighouse. One of my older sisters found me and brought me inside and told everyone how she had found me.

"An Elder questioned me and I told him I was just tired and had fallen asleep. The Elder asked, 'But why are your eyes swollen? Why have you been crying?' I told him I had made a mistake and broken the inner cedar bark while I was preparing it for rope. I offered to do it again and make another one. I said I would keep it soaked so it would be pliable and not break, but my uncle took all the inner cedar bark away from me and said, 'Just go away. Stay away from here.'"

The young cousin continued. "Then we all heard a big voice from up in the sky say, 'Have you forgotten the teachings of the Father?' The Elders said this was the voice of the Creator. One of the Elders then told my uncle, 'You have to watch what the children are doing. You must teach them. They have to learn how to do it right.'

"But my uncle didn't offer to show me how to do it right so I asked my grandmother and she said, 'You have to go and ask the adults. It is their job to teach you. I can't help you right now, but if the adults tell you to come to me then I will help you.' The adults were working on the bighouse and I went to them even though I was afraid, but they still told me to go away."

Another cousin agreed. "I couldn't swallow my food for two days when I thought about what happened to me. Why do we think about these things while we are eating? I can't swallow my food when I think about them.

"I was one of the people making rope. When we finished the rope, we tied the planks with it and hauled the planks up to the roof of the bighouse, but the rope snapped. The planks came tumbling down and we scrambled away. One of my cousins wasn't fast enough and a plank hit him. He was crying and I wanted to cry with him.

"One of my uncles said, 'You children go away from here. Don't offer to help anymore until you learn to do it properly.' We said, 'Tell us how to do it

properly, then.' My uncle replied, 'You don't speak to the rope, you don't honour it. You are just playing. That is why the rope got angry and broke.' What
did he mean? Why did he say the rope gets angry? I would like to talk to the
rope but I don't know how."

Then a girl shared a similar experience. "While we were helping to make
baskets one day the adults told us to wash and separate the inner cedar bark
and to make long strands from the roots of the stinging nettles. We didn't
know we should make both long pieces and shorter pieces, so the longer and
shorter pieces can be twisted together into one. The long pieces kept breaking
and separating and we just let them break. When we gave our older cousins the
rope to finish the basket, they said, 'This is too short. Why is it so short?' They
didn't tell us how to make the long and the short strings so it would be strong.
When they used the basket to haul rocks up to the roof of the bighouse, the
rocks came tumbling down on us because the fibres were weak. They blamed
us and told us to go away. We came here that day and we dug up some roots,
some fern roots, and that is all we ate all day. When we went home we could
hear them teaching our older sisters and brothers. We crept closer and closer
and when they saw us they told us to go to the far end of the bighouse. Then
we couldn't hear what was said."

Shuyulh spoke next. "My three brothers and I were talking about this and
I was selected to crawl under the steps of the *leyl'we's* (seating place). I was able
to stay there for a long time listening. My older brother is only a year older
than me but he was allowed to be there. My eyes became accustomed to the
darkness and then I saw other eyes and recognized *Ĉuĉiq'un*, Mink. Mink just
stared at me but I was too busy listening to pay attention, until I realized Mink
was also listening. Was he curious or did he want to learn, like I did?

"The Elders were talking about the importance of 'speaking' to the mate-
rials you are working with. It is important to talk to the trees when they are
standing, and to the bark when you are separating it from the tree. It is important to honour the trees.

"The Elders also talked about *tumulh* (red ochre), which they put on their
faces when they dance, as a way to honour the tree. They talked about how
they use *qa'* (water) and about the different uses of fresh water and salt water.
They discussed how you can make water do what you want it to do—to help
you make things.

"Why didn't they tell us this when we were making ropes and when the
girls were making baskets? Why didn't they teach us how to make them strong
in our minds? You don't actually have to say it out loud. You can say it in your
mind and you can think it and it will happen. That is what I heard."

A young girl spoke up. "When my granny wants things to be done I hear
her ask for help. When she wants a skin to help her she speaks to it and asks

it to help her. But how can we do that? How can we make a skin come alive? That is what I heard her saying but I don't know what kind of skins she meant."

Shuyulh looked at the others and said, "Remember the skin that is soaking in front of the canoe?"

"Oh," one of them said, "Do you mean the grey whale skin?"

"Yes, the one we dragged down to the beach, the one we weighed down with rocks the girls had gathered so it wouldn't drift away."

Shuyulh's younger brother said, "Do you mean we can make it do what we want it to do?"

"That is what I learned while I was listening to the Elders," Shuyulh said. "That is what they do."

"How can they do that?"

The boys and girls talked for a long time and they came up with a plan: they would make a killer whale.

"During the night, we will go down to the beach and drag the skin around the point to this place," Shuyulh said. "The girls will be the look-outs."

One of the younger boys worried. "It will take us all night," he said.

"Do they ever check on us when we sleep?" Shuyulh asked. "The only time they come is to wake us up. We will be all right as long as we are in bed when they come in the morning. We will bring the skin to our diving place and anchor it there until we use it."

Some of the girls were afraid because they thought the Elders would find out. Shuyulh said, "We will wait for a few days and we will go behind the bighouses where they have thrown away some of the spoiled wood. The wood is still good. The Elders have already spoken to those planks so we won't have to talk to them much ourselves. We will get some of the rocks that have been spoken to and these rocks will weigh the skin down." One of the boys was directed to do this, since his grandfather is the one who speaks to the rocks.

Shuyulh said to the girls, "Your grandmothers talk to the ropes while they are making them. Get some of those ropes to tie the poles with. We need poles double our length so we can make the skin become a killer whale."

The children were scared but they were very excited as well. One of the girls said, "I can see the grey whale skin from here. How are we going to make it into a killer whale?"

"That is where you come in," Shuyulh answered. "At night you will start taking some of the black paint and the white paint that is hidden under your mothers' beds. You will also get some from your aunties." Three of them had already learned to prepare paint so they knew what they were doing.

"Also, get as much *tumulh* (red ochre) as you can from the baskets under the platforms in the bighouse. We must have everything ready. We can't just take a little bit at a time or we won't be able to do it." Some of the younger ones were afraid and Shuyulh said, "If any of you are afraid, do not follow us but do not say anything to spoil our plan."

"Why are we doing this? Why are we making a killer whale?" one of the younger boys asked.

Shuyulh said, "How many of you have hidden in the evening or early morning just to listen to a little bit of the sacred lessons the Elders are giving to the older ones? If we do this and it becomes real then we will prove that we are like our older brothers and sisters."

"What if something happens?" one of the boys said.

"No, it will work," another one answered. "If we learn to do it the right way then we will be just like our older brothers and sisters. The adults won't tell us to go away anymore."

"We aren't just children anymore," said Shuyulh, "and we have proven that by working. We will talk to the rocks and they will become part of us. We will talk to *Smuyuth* (deer) and make it do what we want it to do. Nobody can do that unless they are knowledgeable. If we are thrown out of the village after we do this we will go and make another village somewhere where we can use fish to do our work for us. We can use Deer to run and be the watcher of our Village. We can use Mink to be our Elders because they know everything. Mink become like us sometimes—like people—because they watch and listen to our old masters, our grandfathers. We can do that."

The young people crept back into the village and went to sleep. Early the next morning before the sun came up, the boys and girls did their chores. They brought in the wood for the morning fire and water to make the herb teas and boil the dried fish.

One of the old ladies said, "Something is going on with these children. I can feel it."

"You are just getting old," her husband said. "All children become very active at this age. They don't listen to what we say anymore."

"This is different. I can feel it."

The children watched and waited and continued to help. They had signals now. Shuyulh taught them signals and body language. They could send a message by the way they threw their heads back and how they moved their eyes. One of them said, "I hear your voice telling me what to do even when you are not looking at me."

"It's good that you hear thoughts because that is what we will be doing when we are inside the skin," Shuyulh said.

The young people became so in tune with each other that each knew what the others were thinking at all times.

They gathered everything they needed and made all the preparations. One of the boys dug deep down in the sand to get old clamshells. The clamshells were ground up and used to make white paint. Only special clamshells could be used and only a few of the old ladies knew how to talk to them. The boys carried some of the fine split cedar, and while they were packing it, they talked to it and asked it to become light.

While they were working, they could feel the energy of the air and the trees. They said to the air and the trees, "Are you helping us? Do you feel sorry for us because we are being shunned by the others in the village?" Now they really felt they were being helped by the energies.

"I can feel them. I feel they are helping us," Shuyulh said. "They are going to help us do what we want them to do. The energy of the air, of Mother Earth, of the rocks, and the trees will help us. The water is bubbling and yes, it will help us also." They were so excited now. "Tonight we will all go to the beach to start preparing. The older boys are going to help me. Some of the girls will have to stay home and listen. Who do you hear in your mind?" Shuyulh asked them. "Who do you talk to when they are not in sight?"

One of the girls said, "I talk to my cousin."

"Then your cousin will stay home and you will stand guard at our meeting place." Shuyulh asked the boys, "Who do you speak to when they are not in sight?"

One of the boys said, "I speak to my younger cousin."

"All right, he will stay home and you will send messages to each other."

Everything was ready and they all had their partners.

"We will meet at the beach but we will call you one by one—we will contact you with our minds," Shuyulh said. "No torches will be used but you will know where we are even in the dark. We will go when the tide is coming in. I have spoken to our grandfather *Qa'*. The message I received is, 'We are waiting for you.' I've spoken to our grandfather the tide and asked him to put the little fish and the fluorescence in the water to sleep so no one will know we are in the water."

That evening all the boys and girls gathered at their meeting place. Some went ahead to the hidden bay where they would take the skin. The others took the skin of the grey whale, *Qwunus*, into the water. Some of the children were carrying the special rocks that they had left there. Some of them got underneath the skin, some of them got inside the skin, and some of them cut holes in the skin and laced the timbers through the holes. They talked to the skin constantly, pleading with it, praising it. And they could almost feel the skin swimming. When they were hungry, the children talked to themselves and they were no longer hungry, and when they were thirsty, they talked to themselves and they stopped being thirsty.

When the boys and girls went around the point, the tide started to change and the children quickened their pace. They were hurrying, hurrying. They pleaded with the skin to be safe so it would not be harmed or damaged. They spoke to the skin as if it were alive, saying, "If you are tired, we will stop" but the skin said, "No, keep going. I will help you." This made the children very happy. They were all listening to the skin now and understanding it. As they came around the rough and rocky point, they didn't even feel the rocks. It was almost as if they were walking on water.

The boys and girls reached the bay where the rest of the young people had made a little fire on the beach to guide the whale. As they saw it approach, they thanked the skin.

Everyone gathered together and ate some dried fish and deer meat and put some of the food underneath the skin to feed it. The skin was very happy. Then the young people weighed down the skin with the rocks. They remembered that they must speak to the four corners of the skin because of the four winds in the universe: north, south, east, and west. They talked to the winds as they worked, especially *Stuywut*, the north wind. The children begged and pleaded with the wind to help them, as all the winds were their grandfathers. The west wind is *Tun'weqw'*, meaning lots of water. If you are lost at sea, the water will look after you. They pleaded with *Tun'weqw'* to look after the skin.

As the young people spoke to the winds, they asked that the skin and the boys who would enter it become one. They asked *Sotuts*, the south wind, to support and help them with its power. The east wind, *Tun?tsa?luqw*, is so far up in the mountains that they had to holler so their voices would reach this grandfather. When they were finished speaking to these winds they heard the eerie response, "Mmmmmmmm."

Some of the children were afraid but Shuyulh said, "*Hychqa, hychqa* (thank you, thank you)," to the four winds.

Their work was done for the day and they snuck back home and slept until they heard the old ladies get up. Shuyulh woke his brother and said, "Our *Se'la* (grandmother) is up. We must get water for her."

The two boys weren't sleepy now because they knew they had a job to do. They grabbed the *shkwe'em* (water baskets) and ran down to the water hole, filling the baskets as fast as they could. Then they went further out to the shoreline and jumped in the ocean. They knew they must not go to fresh water now. They must go to the salt water to honour it. They rubbed themselves with sand and then rubbed on the rocks. The rocks answered and said *hychqa* to the boys for leaving some of their aroma on the rocks. The rocks would feed on this and become their helpers. Then they brought the water and firewood to their *Se'la*.

When they passed the enclosed area where some of the girls were sleeping the boys called, "Are you awake? *Umut* (get up)." The girls got up and ran over to the next house to wake the other girls. They didn't have to go inside; they just went to the place where the girls slept and nodded and the girls woke up. The girls inside knew their cousins were telling them to get up.

Shuyulh and his brother sent a different kind of energy to the girls who lived on the edge of the village. These girls were sleeping in the woods because their families had disowned them and they were being punished. Although these girls were separated from their families, they always had enough food because they collected roots. The roots of the skunk cabbage and the roots of ferns were especially good when cooked.

When the boys had finished their chores they asked their *Se'la* if they could have some dried fish and dried clams to take with them while they collected more wood in the hills. Their *Se'la* told them to take as much as they needed. *Se'la* watched the boys and thought they didn't look the same anymore. When Shuyulh was leaving, he heard his *Se'la* saying that he looked so different that she must speak to his grandfather about starting to teach him because he was becoming a young man. "Even his smell is different," she was thinking. "He smells like the fresh wood that is brought down from the hills, yet he also smells like very wet, warm sand."

Shuyulh smiled to himself; he could hear what she was thinking.

"Yes, I can hear you also, my grandson," she said, surprising him. "Be happy this day, my grandson."

He was very happy now and he ran to join the others at their hiding place. The young people sat in a circle, not talking, but each one was praying. This is how they had been taught to pray. Each person prays in his or her own way, using their own energy first and then listening to others praying for them.

Once they were all together, Shuyulh prayed for everyone and told them what he had heard his grandmother say. "We must remember these words from her. She is sending us forth; she knows we are grown, that we are not children anymore. You girls are not children anymore; you are becoming women. If they do not accept you back in the village after this day you must look after one another. When it is time for you to live with a man you must look for that person in another village—it must not be one of your relatives." He sounded like a little old man, like an ancient man who was dying.

"You are not going to die, are you?" one of the girls asked.

"I am going to live forever."

The boys and girls began their work. They laid out the long, "spoken-to" cedar sticks they had brought along. The longest one became the fin of *Q'ull-hanamatsun*, the killer whale. "This is the only way we are going to use this skin," Shuyulh said. "Our Elders have wanted a killer whale but no killer whale has come. Only *Qwunus*, the grey whale, has come. We are going to stretch the skin on the rocks."

The rocks were honoured and said *hych' qa*. The young people stretched the skin over the biggest rock and Shuyulh marked where the lines would be. He marked the top black, the bottom white, and the fins with little white tips. The *sqe'uq*—youngest boy—would be in the front holding the fire bag. The fire bag was used at other times to take fire with them when they journeyed far into the hills. Tonight they were going to use the fire bag to make smoke. When the whale surfaced they would blow smoke through the blowhole. They used the large kelp, cutting the bulb in half so it was like a funnel to take smoke from the fire pouch to the blowhole.

They talked to the kelp, pleading with it to honour them by becoming part of the blowhole. They knew that the kelp might not like the heat from the smoke, as it was not used to this. They explained, "It is very important that we have this smoke, which is part of our breath, to make the skin become alive with us in it."

The children had gathered black paint, white paint, and red ochre. "Why do we need the red ochre?" one of the younger girls asked.

"Red ochre represents blood," Shuyulh said. "Red ochre is a special gift from Mother Earth. It is very powerful."

The children had also collected clamshells. The girls put their mouths on the clamshells to give them life, and then they put white markings along the blowhole and along the eyes with the white clamshells. The clamshells on the beach were making noises and the eldest clam said "Shhh" and they became quiet.

"This is our work too," said the eldest clam. "All of you, all of us. We don't want the grandfathers and grandmothers to know we are here helping or we might get into trouble." Some of the clam Elders were very kind and willing to teach them but some of them were mean and refused to help.

The girls were mixing the *tumulh* (red ochre) in great big clamshells. The clamshells said "Oohhhhh" when they felt the red liquid in their pores and "*Hych'qa*" when they were nourished by the *tumulh*. They had been buried for so long and now they were dripping red ochre from the bottom of their porous shells and their little tongues were licking it up. The girls were laughing and petting the little clamshells.

Then the girls and boys crawled inside the skin to paint it with the red ochre, and it went into all the crevices. The skin lapped it up, making appreciative noises. Some of the boys were painting red ochre on the long sticks, saying, "Breathe, my little brothers and my big brothers." The sticks ate it up and became pliable, loving it.

The girls took long ropes made from stinging nettle to sew the skin together. The skin said, "I am going to be whole again. I am going to be me again."

Everyone was very excited. It was almost like the skin was blowing up as they moved it; it was like a huge bubble on the beach. The skin was buoyant and floating. They were putting the long sticks inside to become the ribs and pushing the clamshells and sticks into the tail. Then they squeezed a very small boy into the tail and he giggled and giggled. Next they pushed the smallest boy into the nose, as it wasn't a very long nose.

The mouth was very big; it took its shape from the bodies of several young boys. One boy crouched down inside; he was the holder of the fire. They inserted the *Ts'e?we?* (clamshells) into the eye sockets, making the whale's white eyes. Next to the little one who was the fire holder was another short boy who would steer the skin. The oldest boy, Shuyulh, held the longest pole, now the whale's fin.

The skin had become *Q'ullhanamatsun*, the killer whale. The boys inside the skin were painted with red ochre. They asked their bodies to become the body and the flesh of the whale. The girls made little holes on the bottom of the skin for the boys' feet. They lined up special rocks along the belly of the whale—rocks painted with red ochre and white paint. Now everyone was in place. The firekeeper was in his place, the one who moved the eyes was crouched inside, the small one inside the tail was ready, and all those in the middle section were ready.

The girls started to sew the belly closed. Everything was covered in red ochre. They started to blow inside the skin and the skin started to fill out.

The boys inside the whale skin were moving in the water now. The children on the beach were "ohhhhing" and "ahhhhhing" as they looked at it. It actually looked like *Q'ullhanamatsun*—the one that didn't come around anymore. Some of them were scared and yet they were also excited and happy. They knew that they must be happy for the whale before it would work and they knew that it heard them. The whale said, "I am here, I am with you" as the children pushed it into the ocean.

The whale went out into the ocean and then it dove down. When it came up to the surface, it was shiny and wet and it blew smoke out with water, just like real whales do. It started to swim towards the point. The girls and boys started to run along the point, hollering and encouraging the whale and praising it. They ran to the village hollering, "There is a great whale out there. It is the killer whale, *Q'ullhanamatsun*, not *Qwunus*."

Grandfather wanted a killer whale for its skin, but he didn't bother to look because the children were always lying. One of the women looked up and said, "There is a funny-looking whale out there. It is the one that rarely comes our way."

The boys inside the skin stayed close to shore so their feet could run on the sand but then one of the little boys said, "My feet are inside. The skin is moving by itself. It is swimming on its own!"

The boys just wanted to show the village that they were there, to show the adults what they could do. They didn't want this to happen, for the skin to swim by itself, out of their control. They asked the skin to help them, but they received no answer.

The old grandfather went down to the shore, running slowly, since he was very old. Some young fellows ran alongside him, held him underneath his arms, and ran with him, in the way it was done long ago. Grandfather called the whale to come close. He said, "It is going away, it is going out to sea. Get your canoes and spears. I want that whale." The young men went to a special canoe that was already loaded; everything was ready in the canoe. They even had water and food in the canoe in case the whale took them out to sea.

By this time, Shuyulh knew they were becoming one with the whale. He said to his brother, "See if you can move."

His brother said, "I can't move on my own. It is like I am part of you now."

The firekeeper also knew he was no longer blowing the smoke, yet every time the whale surfaced the smoke blew out on its own. The boy who was steering said, "The whale is telling me to hang on. It is telling me there is a canoe coming our way and the spearsmen are standing up. Can you see them? No? But the eyes are telling me. I can see through the eyes. Our uncle is there and our father is holding a spear."

"This cannot be," Shuyulh said. "Get close to shore."

"I can't! I can't seem to push the skin close to shore! I can't feel my feet! I can't feel the rocks beneath my feet!"

Shuyulh said to the skin, "My brothers are getting afraid. Please release us and let us drop to the sand."

"It cannot be done," the whale said. "We are one now. Each one of you has become one with me."

They were all thinking to themselves, "We are one. We are one."

By this time the grandfather was at the water's edge and he heard the sound of Xeel's, the Creator in the heavens. Many of the others heard the voice of Xeel's as well.

"You have forgotten the teachings of the old ways," spoke Xeel's. "You must teach the children as they grow. You must start teaching them when they first start to walk and continue teaching them as they grow. Do not neglect the teachings." The Creator was very sad, because he felt it was too late.

Now the grandfather was yelling at the men with spears. "Stop! There is something wrong with that whale. The whale—it is not what it seems to be."

But it was too late. The spear spiralled in the air for a long time and then went straight for the whale.

The firekeeper yelled, "My brother has a spear in him. And we are receiving messages from outside, from our grandfather."

They all heard it. The grandfather knelt down by the water's edge and put his head right in the water. The young men were trying to hold him back, but the old ladies told the boys to let him be.

"He can't communicate if you touch him. He has to have his own energy." Grandfather was in the water, with his head underwater. They were afraid he would drown but he was speaking in the water.

"Are you my grandsons?"

"Yes, we are, Grandfather," Shuyulh said. "We are your grandsons but we are now one with the whale. I am now one with my younger brothers and my younger cousins. We have become one with my brother in the tail and we have all become the head and the brain as well. One of our brothers is dead but he is still alive inside of us. He has a spear in him; somebody is pulling the spear out now.

The grandfather said, "It is the energy of the water. You are one with the water now."

"Grandfather, we are very sorry for what we have done," Shuyulh said. "We were angry that you didn't want to share the sacred teachings with us. We heard some of the teachings but we didn't know the right words or the right way to do it and this is what happened to us. We used the skin of *Qwunus* to become *Q'ulhanamatsun*, the killer whale."

The grandfather was crying now. He surfaced and told his older grandsons—the ones who had received the teachings—what had happened.

"Tell them we are very sorry for shunning them and chasing them away," the older grandsons said.

"It is our fault. It is my fault," the grandfather said. "I will carry this into the next world. The next generations will know better. The teachings will go on but in a different way. There will be fewer teachings for the younger ones, but the teachings will increase as the young ones grow. Nothing will be held back. In this way our people will live a long time and in harmony."

Then the grandfather spoke directly to those who had become the whale. "Forgive us and forgive me, my children. We want to thank you for the teachings you have given us. How else would we have known what words can do to make a skin come alive again, but sacrificing yourselves is a very hard and sorrowful way to find out. We will call the other children, we will heal them, and we will work with them in their healing, remembering the loss of you."

The grandfather paused a moment, then said, "I can see in my mind that there is a whale pod around the point. Go join them. I am asking them to honour you and accept you. I am asking them not to be afraid of the smell of *Qwunus* on your skin. But perhaps by the time you reach there the aroma of *Qwunus* will have changed into the aroma of *Q'ullhanamatsun*, the killer whale."

By this time the spear was out of the whale and it was drifting away. Shu-yulh's father picked up the spear as they stood and waved and sang a mournful song to the young men who had become a killer whale. He said, "This will be an honoured place. Even after I am gone it will still be an honoured place and we will honour the lives of all killer whales. They are our brothers, fathers, grandfathers, healers, and educators in the ways of the water."

The people began to walk back to the village and the old man sent forth the fathers and mothers of the children banished to the woods and told them to bring the children home. "We have a lot of healing to do," he said.

Ellen Rice White Speaks about "The Boys Who Became a Killer Whale"

This is a story of alienated youth, about young people just entering puberty who feel angry and rebellious. They are trying to prove their independence and worth, and at the same time they are questioning authority. The story shows how young people can suffer harsh consequences because of their behaviour. The adults and Elders in the story learn a hard lesson, too, about their responsibilities to their children's education. They come to realize that their role in training their children is vital and that they must not neglect it. They also realize that the *way* you teach a child can be just as important as *what* you teach a child. It is still true today, that young people must learn the basic skills of daily living before they proceed to more advanced teachings. The story reminds us that teaching basic life skills is vital to the survival of humankind and that spiritual teachings must not be forgotten.

The story begins with a group of young people, angry at the adults of their community who treated them like babies, or so they thought. They were eager to know all the teachings, but they were not included at teaching time. Their cousins and siblings weren't much older, yet they were included. When they wanted to help, or even remedy a difficult situation they may have caused, they were not given explanations but were yelled at and told to go away. So now they were determined to make their own decisions and plans so they could prove their worth to the community.

These young people didn't understand that the community was following a set path for their training, and that they needed to pass through each stage of development in the proper order. They were impatient, leaping ahead, thinking of what more they could learn. They felt they had been at their present stage for many winters and many summers, and they had had enough.

The adults in the story did not understand the importance of setting the stage for learning and creating a positive learning environment. For example, one important lesson the young people felt they were missing out on was how to "speak to the rope" and "honour the rope" so that it would not break. The thirst for knowledge was clear, but they found it difficult to approach the adults with their questions—and the adults were not helping the situation by becoming angry and refusing to explain.

The adults were missing an opportunity to perhaps lay the young people's concerns to rest. They could have given a brief explanation in order to lay the groundwork for future teachings, such as giving a very basic lesson about "speaking to" objects and "honouring" objects. This opening might also have allowed them to introduce the idea of learning certain things first before they move on to the next ones, and to reassure the young people that all the teachings would come to them in good time.

Xeel's teaches the importance of respecting all things, both living and non-living. The people were taught to "speak to" the tree and honour it, if they were going to take bark from it or cut it down to make a canoe. Animate and inanimate things exist together in the universal energy and support each other. The importance of this belief was shown in the story by the use of *tumulh* (red ochre), which comes from deep within Mother Earth. It is taught that when water hits certain kinds of dirt or minerals, it becomes different in substance, "two in one," or maybe more than two. *Tumulh* was used so much because it united many different forms of energy into one.

CHAPTER 7

■ ■ ■ ■

SHIFTING PERSPECTIVES

Sandra Cisneros, "Never Marry a Mexican"

Gordon Robinson, "Weegit Discovers Halibut Hooks"

Joe Panipakuttuk, "The Many Lives of Anakajuttuq"

Walter K. Scott, excerpt from *Wendy*

Leslie Marmon Silko, "Lullaby"

Jo-Ann Episkenew, "Notes on Leslie Marmon Silko's 'Lullaby': Socially
Responsible Criticism"

THIS CHAPTER, ON "SHIFTING PERSPECTIVES," asks the reader to consider the role of point of view in filtering perceptions and shaping judgments. For example, in Sandra Cisneros's "Never Marry a Mexican," the protagonist Clemencia defiantly rejects the points of view of her society, her mother, and her lover, all of whom pressure her to adopt restrictive gendered and culturally stereotypical roles. The stakes are high in her attempt to discover her own point of view: her lover, Drew, used to call her "my Malinche," thereby invoking the historical figure of Malinche, an Aztec woman who was abducted from her family and who became the translator for Cortez, the Spanish explorer. Malinche is often represented in historical and popular accounts as a traitor of her people who aided in Cortez's efforts to claim Mexico as a colony for Spain. Yet Clemencia makes her own choices, affirming her own (and by extension Malinche's) point of view. Shifts in perspective compel the reader to acknowledge that how we see and interpret events is determined by our experiences and world view.

As Jo-Ann Episkenew argues in her essay in this chapter, too often students and scholars of literature are trained to identify and analyze how ideology functions within literary texts, but these readers sometimes overlook the ideologies that they themselves bring to the texts—the personal experiences and world views that profoundly affect the way they read. The stories in this section deliberately challenge us to consider more carefully how our own ideologies as readers influence our point of view. Episkenew further argues that

Indigenous stories often demand that we learn something about the cultural and social contexts in which the stories are situated in order to better appreciate the perspectives embedded within them. For example, the conclusion of Silko's story "Lullaby," as Episkenew points out, might be interpreted tragically if we don't take into consideration the characters' profound knowledge of and familiarity with the land and climate in the Pueblo people's territories in the southwestern United States. Similarly, the extraordinary transformations that the narrator in Joe Panipakuttuk's "The Many Lives of Anakajuttuq" undergoes may be difficult to decode without acknowledging the cultural contexts of the story and its engagement with Inuit traditions of shamanistic power.

"Weegit Discovers Halibut Hooks" by Gordon Robinson (the uncle of Eden Robinson, whose story "Terminal Avenue" is included in Chapter 8), implies that readers or listeners should not jump to conclusions about how characters may behave or how stories may end. In "Weegit Discovers Halibut Hooks," the question of who is being "trapped" or "hooked" can be answered in multiple ways. "Hooks" are also what give stories power, and encourage us to read them or listen to them many times over. Taken together, the stories in this chapter suggest that part of our work as readers is to examine the ideological baggage that shapes our own perspectives and appreciate how and why the stories experiment with multiple perspective shifts.

⟶ *Never Marry a Mexican* ⟵
Sandra Cisneros

Sandra Cisneros was born in 1954 to a Mexican father and a Mexican American mother. With her six brothers, she grew up in Chicago, travelling frequently with her family to Mexico City for several weeks or months at a time. Along with Ana Castillo, Denise Chavez, and Gloria Anzaldúa, Cisneros was among the first Chicana writers to publish work in the 1980s. Her stories revolve around Chicana/o characters with Mexican, pre-Columbian, mestizo and southwestern roots, straddling two or three cultures, languages, and mythologies. She is best known for her critically acclaimed novel, *A House on Mango Street* (1984), which received the Before Columbus American Book Award in 1985. She also won a Lannan Foundation Literary Award for *Woman Hollering Creek and Other Stories* (1991), a collection that includes the story we have chosen for this reader.

In "Never Marry a Mexican," the main character Clemencia rejects the confining roles of mother or wife, ignoring her mother's advice to "never marry a Mexican," and choosing instead to marry no one at all. She is haunted in equal parts by her mother, whom she cannot forgive for having remarried after her father's death; by her father, who died painfully and alone in hospital; and by her memories of her love affair with her art teacher Drew, an older white man, years ago. She is now sleeping with Drew's son, who is in his twenties. She remembers Drew calling her "[m]y Malinalli, Malinche, my courtesan" (293), as if attempting to collapse her identity with the historical figure of the Aztec woman, Malinche, who is often misunderstood in historical and popular discourses as a traitor of her people, and his identity with Cortez, who claimed Mexico as a colony for Spain. Yet Clemencia, memorably describing herself as "amphibious," as "a person who doesn't belong to any class," affirms her own as well as Malinche's choices, and asks the reader to reconsider the repercussions of this self-affirmation into the present day.

Never marry a Mexican, my ma said once and always. She said this because of my father. She said this though she was Mexican too. But she was born here in the U.S., and he was born there, and it's *not* the same, you know.

I'll *never* marry. Not any man. I've known men too intimately. I've witnessed their infidelities, and I've helped them to it. Unzipped and unhooked and agreed to clandestine maneuvers. I've been accomplice, committed premeditated crimes. I'm guilty of having caused deliberate pain to other women. I'm vindictive and cruel, and I'm capable of anything.

I admit, there was a time when all I wanted was to belong to a man. To wear that gold band on my left hand and be worn on his arm like an expensive jewel brilliant in the light of day. Not the sneaking around I did in different bars that all looked the same, red carpets with a black grillwork design, flocked wallpaper, wooden wagon-wheel light fixtures with hurricane lampshades a sick amber color like the drinking glasses you get for free at gas stations.

Dark bars, dark restaurants then. And if not—my apartment, with his toothbrush firmly planted in the toothbrush holder like a flag on the North Pole. The bed so big because he never stayed the whole night. Of course not.

Borrowed. That's how I've had my men. Just the cream skimmed off the top. Just the sweetest part of the fruit, without the bitter skin that daily living with a spouse can rend. They've come to me when they wanted the sweet meat then.

So, no. I've never married and never will. Not because I couldn't, but because I'm too romantic for marriage. Marriage has failed me, you could say. Not a man exists who hasn't disappointed me, whom I could trust to love the way I've loved. It's because I believe too much in marriage that I don't. Better to not marry than live a lie.

Mexican men, forget it. For a long time the men clearing off the tables or chopping meat behind the butcher counter or driving the bus I rode to school every day, those weren't men. Not men I considered as potential lovers.

Mexican, Puerto Rican, Cuban, Chilean, Colombian, Panamanian, Salvadorean, Bolivian, Honduran, Argentine, Dominican, Venezuelan, Guatemalan, Ecuadorean, Nicaraguan, Peruvian, Costa Rican, Paraguayan, Uruguayan, I don't care. I never saw them. My mother did this to me.

I guess she did it to spare me and Ximena the pain she went through. Having married a Mexican man at seventeen. Having had to put up with all the grief a Mexican family can put on a girl because she was from *el otro lado*, the other side, and my father had married down by marrying her. If he had married a white woman from *el otro lado*, that would've been different. That would've been marrying up, even if the white girl was poor. But what could be more ridiculous than a Mexican girl who couldn't even speak Spanish, who didn't know enough to set a separate plate for each course at dinner, nor how to fold cloth napkins, nor how to set the silverware.

In my ma's house the plates were always stacked in the center of the table, the knives and forks and spoons standing in a jar, help yourself. All the dishes chipped or cracked and nothing matched. And no tablecloth, ever. And newspapers set on the table whenever my grandpa sliced watermelons, and how embarrassed she would be when her boyfriend, my father, would come over and there were newspapers all over the kitchen floor and table. And my grandpa, big hardworking Mexican man, saying Come, come and eat, and slicing a big wedge of those dark green watermelons, a big slice, he wasn't stingy with food. Never, even during the Depression. Come, come and eat, to whoever came knocking on the back door. Hobos sitting at the dinner table and the children staring and staring. Because my grandfather always made sure they never went without. Flour and rice, by the barrel and by the sack. Potatoes. Big bags of pinto beans. And watermelons, bought three or four at a time, rolled under his bed and brought out when you least expected. My grandpa had survived three wars, one Mexican, two American, and he knew what living without meant. He knew.

My father, on the other hand, did not. True, when he first came to this country he had worked shelling clams, washing dishes, planting hedges, sat on the back of the bus in Little Rock and had the bus driver shout, You—sit up here, and my father had shrugged sheepishly and said, No speak English.

But he was no economic refugee, no immigrant fleeing a war. My father ran away from home because he was afraid of facing his father after his first-year grades at the university proved he'd spent more time fooling around than studying. He left behind a house in Mexico City that was neither poor nor rich, but thought itself better than both. A boy who would get off a bus when he saw a girl he knew board if he didn't have the money to pay her fare. That was the world my father left behind.

I imagine my father in his *fanfarrón* clothes, because that's what he was, a *fanfarrón*. That's what my mother thought the moment she turned around to the voice that was asking her to dance. A big show-off, she'd say years later. Nothing but a big show-off. But she never said why she married him. My father in his shark-blue suits with the starched handkerchief in the breast pocket, his felt fedora, his tweed topcoat with the big shoulders, and heavy British wing tips with the pin-hole design on the heel and toe. Clothes that cost a lot. Expensive. That's what my father's things said. *Calidad.* Quality.

My father must've found the U.S. Mexicans very strange, so foreign from what he knew at home in Mexico City where the servant served watermelon on a plate with silverware and a cloth napkin, or mangos with their own special prongs. Not like this, eating with your legs wide open in the yard, or in the kitchen hunkered over newspapers. *Come, come and eat.* No, never like this.

How I make my living depends. Sometimes I work as a translator. Sometimes I get paid by the word and sometimes by the hour, depending on the job. I do this in the day, and at night I paint. I'd do anything in the day just so I can keep on painting.

I work as a substitute teacher, too, for the San Antonio Independent School District. And that's worse than translating those travel brochures with their tiny print, believe me. I can't stand kids. Not any age. But it pays the rent.

Any way you look at it, what I do to make a living is a form of prostitution. People say, "A painter? How nice," and want to invite me to their parties, have me decorate the lawn like an exotic orchid for hire. But do they buy art?

I'm amphibious. I'm a person who doesn't belong to any class. The rich like to have me around because they envy my creativity; they know they can't buy that. The poor don't mind if I live in their neighborhood because they know I'm poor like they are, even if my education and the way I dress keeps us worlds apart. I don't belong to any class. Not to the poor, whose neighborhood I share. Not to the rich, who come to my exhibitions and buy my work. Not to the middle class from which my sister Ximena and I fled.

When I was young, when I first left home and rented that apartment with my sister and her kids right after her husband left, I thought it would be glamorous to be an artist. I wanted to be like Frida or Tina. I was ready to suffer with my camera and my paint brushes in that awful apartment we rented for $150 each because it had high ceilings and those wonderful glass skylights that convinced us we had to have it. Never mind there was no sink in the bathroom, and a tub that looked like a sarcophagus, and floorboards that didn't meet, and a hallway to scare away the dead. But fourteen-foot ceilings was enough for us to write a check for the deposit right then and there. We thought it all romantic. You know the place, the one on Zarzamora on top of the barber shop with the Casasola prints of the Mexican Revolution. Neon BIRRIA TEPATITLÁN sign round the corner, two goats knocking their heads together, and all those Mexican bakeries, Las Brisas for *huevos rancheros* and *carnitas* and *barbacoa* on Sundays, and fresh fruit milk shakes, and mango *paletas*, and more signs in Spanish than in English. We thought it was great, great. The barrio looked cute in the daytime, like Sesame Street. Kids hopscotching on the sidewalk, blessed little boogers. And hardware stores that still sold ostrich-feather dusters, and whole families marching out of Our Lady of Guadalupe Church on Sundays, girls in their swirly-whirly dresses and patent-leather shoes, boys in their dress Stacys and shiny shirts.

But nights, that was nothing like what we knew up on the north side. Pistols going off like the wild, wild West, and me and Ximena and the kids huddled in one bed with the lights off listening to it all, saying, Go to sleep, babies, it's just firecrackers. But we knew better. Ximena would say, Clemencia, maybe we should go home. And I'd say, Shit! Because she knew as well as I did there was no home to go home to. Not with our mother. Not with that man she married. After Daddy died, it was like we didn't matter. Like Ma was so busy feeling sorry for herself, I don't know. I'm not like Ximena. I still haven't worked it out after all this time, even though our mother's dead now. My half brothers living in that house that should've been ours, me and Ximena's. But that's—how do you say it?—water under the damn? I can't ever get the sayings right even though I was born in this country. We didn't say shit like that in our house.

Once Daddy was gone, it was like my ma didn't exist, like if she died, too. I used to have a little finch, twisted one of its tiny red legs between the bars of the cage once, who knows how. The leg just dried up and fell off. My bird lived a long time without it, just a little red stump of a leg. He was fine, really. My mother's memory is like that, like if something already dead dried up and fell off, and I stopped missing where she used to be. Like if I never had a mother. And I'm not ashamed to say it either. When she married that white man, and he and his boys moved into my father's house, it was as if she stopped being my mother. Like I never even had one.

Ma always sick and too busy worrying about her own life, she would've sold us to the Devil if she could. "Because I married so young, *mi'ja*," she'd say. "Because your father, he was so much older than me, and I never had a chance to be young. Honey, try to understand…." Then I'd stop listening.

That man she met at work, Owen Lambert, the foreman at the photo-finishing plant, who she was seeing even while my father was sick. Even then. That's what I can't forgive.

When my father was coughing up blood and phlegm in the hospital, half his face frozen, and his tongue so fat he couldn't talk, he looked so small with all those tubes and plastic sacks dangling around him. But what I remember most is the smell, like death was already sitting on his chest. And I remember the doctor scraping the phlegm out of my father's mouth with a white washcloth, and my daddy gagging and I wanted to yell, Stop, you stop that, he's my daddy. Goddamn you. Make him live. Daddy, don't. Not yet, not yet, not yet. And how I couldn't hold myself up, I couldn't hold myself up. Like if they'd beaten me, or pulled my insides out through my nostrils, like if they'd stuffed me with cinnamon and cloves, and I just stood there dry-eyed next to Ximena and my mother, Ximena between us because I wouldn't let her stand next to me. Everyone repeating over and over the Ave Marías and Padre Nues-tros. The priest sprinkling holy water, *mundo sin fin*, *amén*.

Drew, remember when you used to call me your Malinalli? It was a joke, a private game between us, because you looked like a Cortez with that beard of yours. My skin dark against yours. Beautiful, you said. You said I was beautiful, and when you said it, Drew, I was.

My Malinalli, Malinche, my courtesan, you said, and yanked my head back by the braid. Calling me that name in between little gulps of breath and the raw kisses you gave, laughing from that black beard of yours.

Before daybreak, you'd be gone, same as always, before I even knew it. And it was as if I'd imagined you, only the teeth marks on my belly and nipples proving me wrong.

Your skin pale, but your hair blacker than a pirate's. Malinalli, you called me, remember? *Mi doradita*. I liked when you spoke to me in my language. I could love myself and think myself worth loving.

Your son. Does he know how much I had to do with his birth? I was the one who convinced you to let him be born. Did you tell him, while his mother lay on her back laboring his birth, I lay in his mother's bed making love to you.

You're nothing without me. I created you from spit and red dust. And I can snuff you between my finger and thumb if I want to. Blow you to kingdom come. You're just a smudge of paint I chose to birth on canvas. And when I made you over, you were no longer a part of her, you were all mine. The landscape of your body taut as a drum. The heart beneath that hide thrumming and thrumming. Not an inch did I give back.

I paint and repaint you the way I see fit, even now. After all these years. Did you know that? Little fool. You think I went hobbling along with my life, whimpering and whining like some twangy country-and-western when you went back to her. But I've been waiting. Making the world look at you from my eyes. And if that's not power, what is?

Nights I light all the candles in the house, the ones to La Virgen de Guadalupe, the ones to El Niño Fidencio, Don Pedrito Jaramillo, Santo Niño de Atocha, Nuestra Señora de San Juan de los Lagos, and especially, Santa Lucía, with her beautiful eyes on a plate.

Your eyes are beautiful, you said. You said they were the darkest eyes you'd ever seen and kissed each one as if they were capable of miracles. And after you left, I wanted to scoop them out with a spoon, place them on a plate under these blue blue skies, food for the blackbirds.

The boy, your son. The one with the face of that redheaded woman who is your wife. The boy red-freckled like fish food floating on the skin of water. That boy.

I've been waiting patient as a spider all these years, since I was nineteen and he was just an idea hovering in his mother's head, and I'm the one that gave him permission and made it happen, see.

Because your father wanted to leave your mother and live with me. Your mother whining for a child, at least that. And he kept saying, Later, we'll see, later. But all along it was me he wanted to be with, it was me, he said.

I want to tell you this evening when you come to see me. When you're full of talk about what kind of clothes you're going to buy, and what you used to be like when you started high school and what you're like now that you're almost finished. And how everyone knows you as a rocker, and your band, and your new red guitar that you just got because your mother gave you a choice, a guitar or a car, but you don't need a car, do you, because I drive you everywhere. You could be my son if you weren't so light-skinned.

This happened. A long time ago. Before you were born. When you were a moth inside your mother's heart, I was your father's student, yes, just like you're mine now. And your father painted and painted me, because he said, I was his *doradita*, all golden and sun-baked, and that's the kind of woman he likes best, the ones brown as river sand, yes. And he took me under his wing and in his bed, this man, this teacher, your father. I was honored that he'd done me the favor. I was that young.

All I know is I was sleeping with your father the night you were born. In the same bed where you were conceived. I was sleeping with your father and didn't give a damn about that woman, your mother. If she was a brown woman like me, I might've had a harder time living with myself, but since she's not, I don't care. I was there first, always. I've always been there, in the mirror, under his skin, in the blood, before you were born. And he's been here in my heart before I even knew him. Understand? He's always been here. Always.

Dissolving like a hibiscus flower, exploding like a rope into dust. I don't care what's right anymore. I don't care about his wife. She's not *my* sister.

And it's not the last time I've slept with a man the night his wife is birthing a baby. Why do I do that, I wonder? Sleep with a man when his wife is giving life, being suckled by a thing with its eyes still shut. Why do that? It's always given me a bit of crazy joy to be able to kill those women like that, without their knowing it. To know I've had their husbands when they were anchored in blue hospital rooms, their guts yanked inside out, the baby sucking their breasts while their husband sucked mine. All this while their ass stitches were still hurting.

Once, drunk on margaritas, I telephoned your father at four in the morning, woke the bitch up. Hello, she chirped. I want to talk to Drew. Just a moment, she said in her most polite drawing-room English. Just a moment. I laughed about that for weeks. What a stupid ass to pass the phone over to the lug asleep beside her. Excuse me, honey, it's for you. When Drew mumbled hello I was laughing so hard I could hardly talk. Drew? That dumb bitch of a wife of yours, I said, and that's all I could manage. That stupid stupid stupid. No Mexican woman would react like that. Excuse me, honey. It cracked me up.

He's got the same kind of skin, the boy. All the blue veins pale and clear just like his mama. Skin like roses in December. Pretty boy. Little clone. Little cells split into you and you and you. Tell me, baby, which part of you is your mother. I try to imagine her lips, her jaw, her long long legs that wrapped themselves around this father who took me to his bed.

This happened. I'm asleep. Or pretend to be. You're watching me, Drew. I feel your weight when you sit on the corner of the bed, dressed and ready to go, but now you're just watching me sleep. Nothing. Not a word. Not a kiss. Just sitting. You're taking me in, under inspection. What do you think already?

I haven't stopped dreaming you. Did you know that? Do you think it's strange? I never tell, though. I keep it to myself like I do all the thoughts I think of you.

After all these years.

I don't want you looking at me. I don't want you taking me in while I'm asleep. I'll open my eyes and frighten you away.

There. What did I tell you? *Drew? What is it?* Nothing. I knew you'd say that.

Let's not talk. We're no good at it. With you I'm useless with words. As if somehow I had to learn to speak all over again, as if the words I needed haven't been invented yet. We're cowards. Come back to bed. At least there I feel I have you for a little. For a moment. For a catch of the breath. You let go. You ache and tug. You rip my skin.

You're almost not a man without your clothes. How do I explain it? You're so much a child in my bed. Nothing but a big boy who needs to be held. I won't let anyone hurt you. My pirate. My slender boy of a man.

After all these years.

I didn't imagine it, did I? A Ganges, an eye of the storm. For a little. When we forgot ourselves, you tugged me, I leapt inside you and split you like an apple. Opened for the other to look and not give back. Something wrenched itself loose. Your body doesn't lie. It's not silent like you.

You're nude as a pearl. You've lost your train of smoke. You're tender as rain. If I'd put you in my mouth you'd dissolve like snow.

You were ashamed to be so naked. Pulled back. But I saw you for what you are, when you opened yourself for me. When you were careless and let yourself through. I caught that catch of the breath. I'm not crazy.

When you slept, you tugged me toward you. You sought me in the dark. I didn't sleep. Every cell, every follicle, every nerve, alert. Watching you sigh and roll and turn and hug me closer to you. I didn't sleep. I was taking *you* in that time.

Your mother? Only once. Years after your father and I stopped seeing each other. At an art exhibition. A show on the photographs of Eugene Atget. Those images, I could look at them for hours. I'd taken a group of students with me.

It was your father I saw first. And in that instant I felt as if everyone in the room, all the sepia-toned photographs, my students, the men in business suits, the high-heeled women, the security guards, everyone, could see me for what I was. I had to scurry out, lead my kids to another gallery, but some things destiny has cut out for you.

He caught up with us in the coat-check area, arm in arm with a redheaded Barbie doll in a fur coat. One of those scary Dallas types, hair yanked into a ponytail, big shiny face like the women behind the cosmetic counters at Neiman's. That's what I remember. She must've been with him all along, only I swear I never saw her until that second.

You could tell from a slight hesitancy, only slight because he's too suave to hesitate, that he was nervous. Then he's walking toward me, and I didn't know what to do, just stood there dazed like those animals crossing the road at night when the headlights stun them.

And I don't know why, but all of a sudden I looked at my shoes and felt ashamed at how old they looked. And he comes up to me, my love, your father, in that way of his with that grin that makes me want to beat him, makes me want to make love to him, and he says in the most sincere voice you ever heard, "Ah, Clemencia! *This* is Megan." No introduction could've been meaner. *This* is Megan. Just like that.

I grinned like an idiot and held out my paw—"Hello, Megan"—and smiled too much the way you do when you can't stand someone. Then I got the hell out of there, chattering like a monkey all the ride back with my kids. When I got home I had to lie down with a cold washcloth on my forehead and the TV on. All I could hear throbbing under the washcloth in that deep part behind my eyes: *This* is Megan.

And that's how I fell asleep, with the TV on and every light in the house burning. When I woke up it was something like three in the morning. I shut the lights and TV and went to get some aspirin, and the cats, who'd been asleep with me on the couch, got up too and followed me into the bathroom as if they knew what's what. And then they followed me into bed, where they aren't allowed, but this time I just let them, fleas and all.

———

This happened, too. I swear I'm not making this up. It's all true. It was the last time I was going to be with your father. We had agreed. All for the best. Surely I could see that, couldn't I? My own good. A good sport. A young girl like me. Hadn't I understood … responsibilities. Besides, he could *never* marry *me*. You didn't think…? *Never marry a Mexican. Never marry a Mexican.…* No, of course not. I see. I see.

We had the house to ourselves for a few days, who knows how. You and your mother had gone somewhere. Was it Christmas? I don't remember.

I remember the leaded-glass lamp with the milk glass above the dining-room table. I made a mental inventory of everything. The Egyptian lotus design on the hinges of the doors. The narrow, dark hall where your father and I had made love once. The four-clawed tub where he had washed my hair and rinsed it with a tin bowl. This window. That counter. The bedroom with its light in the morning, incredibly soft, like the light from a polished dime.

The house was immaculate, as always, not a stray hair anywhere, not a flake of dandruff or a crumpled towel. Even the roses on the dining-room table held their breath. A kind of airless cleanliness that always made me want to sneeze.

Why was I so curious about this woman he lived with? Every time I went to the bathroom, I found myself opening the medicine cabinet, looking at all the things that were hers. Her Estée Lauder lipsticks. Corals and pinks, of course. Her nail polishes—mauve was as brave as she could wear. Her cotton balls and blond hairpins. A pair of bone-colored sheepskin slippers, as clean as the day she'd bought them. On the door hook—a white robe with a MADE IN ITALY label, and a silky nightshirt with pearl buttons. I touched the fabrics. *Calidad.* Quality.

I don't know how to explain what I did next. While your father was busy in the kitchen, I went over to where I'd left my backpack, and took out a bag of gummy bears I'd bought. And while he was banging pots, I went around the house and left a trail of them in places I was sure *she* would find them. One in her lucite makeup organizer. One stuffed inside each bottle of nail polish. I untwisted the expensive lipsticks to their full length and smushed a bear on the top before recapping them. I even put a gummy bear in her diaphragm case in the very center of that luminescent rubber moon.

Why bother? Drew could take the blame. Or he could say it was the cleaning woman's Mexican voodoo. I knew that, too. It didn't matter. I got a strange satisfaction wandering about the house leaving them in places only she would look.

And just as Drew was shouting, "Dinner!" I saw it on the desk. One of those wooden babushka dolls Drew had brought her from his trip to Russia. I know. He'd bought one just like it for me.

I just did what I did, uncapped the doll inside a doll inside a doll, until I got to the very center, the tiniest baby inside all the others, and this I replaced with a gummy bear. And then I put the dolls back, just like I'd found them, one inside the other, inside the other. Except for the baby, which I put inside my pocket. All through dinner I kept reaching in the pocket of my jean jacket. When I touched it, it made me feel good.

On the way home, on the bridge over the *arroyo* on Guadalupe Street, I stopped the car, switched on the emergency blinkers, got out, and dropped the wooden toy into that muddy creek where winos piss and rats swim. The Barbie doll's toy stewing there in that muck. It gave me a feeling like nothing before and since.

Then I drove home and slept like the dead.

These mornings, I fix coffee for me, milk for the boy. I think of that woman, and I can't see a trace of my lover in this boy, as if she conceived him by immaculate conception.

I sleep with this boy, their son. To make the boy love me the way I love his father. To make him want me, hunger, twist in his sleep, as if he'd swallowed glass. I put him in my mouth. Here, little piece of my *corazón*. Boy with hard thighs and just a bit of down and a small hard downy ass like his father's, and that back like a valentine. Come here, mi *cariñito*. Come to *mamita*. Here's a bit of toast.

I can tell from the way he looks at me, I have him in my power. Come, sparrow. I have the patience of eternity. Come to *mamita*. My stupid little bird. I don't move. I don't startle him. I let him nibble. All, all for you. Rub his belly. Stroke him. Before I snap my teeth.

What is it inside me that makes me so crazy at 2 A.M.? I can't blame it on alcohol in my blood when there isn't any. It's something worse. Something that poisons the blood and tips me when the night swells and I feel as if the whole sky were leaning against my brain.

And if I killed someone on a night like this? And if it was *me* I killed instead, I'd be guilty of getting in the line of crossfire, innocent bystander, isn't it a shame. I'd be walking with my head full of images and my back to the guilty. Suicide? I couldn't say. I didn't see it.

Except it's not me who I want to kill. When the gravity of the planets is just right, it all tilts and upsets the visible balance. And that's when it wants out from my eyes. That's when I get on the telephone, dangerous as a terrorist. There's nothing to do but let it come.

So. What do you think? Are you convinced now I'm as crazy as a tulip or a taxi? As vagrant as a cloud?

Sometimes the sky is so big and I feel so little at night. That's the problem with being a cloud. The sky is so terribly big. Why is it worse at night, when I have such an urge to communicate and no language with which to form the words? Only colors. Pictures. And you know what I have to say isn't always pleasant.

Oh, love, there. I've gone and done it. What good is it? Good or bad, I've done what I had to do and needed to. And you've answered the phone, and startled me away like a bird. And now you're probably swearing under your breath and going back to sleep, with that wife beside you, warm, radiating her own heat, alive under the flannel and down and smelling a bit like milk and hand cream, and that smell familiar and dear to you, oh.

Human beings pass me on the street, and I want to reach out and strum them as if they were guitars. Sometimes all humanity strikes me as lovely. I just want to reach out and stroke someone, and say There, there, it's all right, honey. There, there, there.

⟶ *Weegit Discovers Halibut Hooks* ⟵
Gordon Robinson

Gordon Robinson was born in 1918 in Kitamaat Village, B.C., part of the territories of his people, the Haisla Nation. Kitamaat, meaning "People of the Snow," refers to the heavy snowfall in the area. Robinson completed public school at Kitamaat and then attended Coqualeetza Residential School in Sardis, B.C. He obtained a teaching diploma at Surpass College in Vancouver. In 1949, he became Assistant Superintendent of the Kwakiutl Indian Agency at Alert Bay and served as Chief Councillor of Kitamaat Village from 1950 to 1954. He published *Tales of Kitamaat*, a collection of traditional Haisla stories illustrated by Vincent Haddelsey, in 1956. This book is a significant accomplishment given the difficulties Indigenous authors faced in the 1950s to publish their work under their own name (rather than under the name of an editor). Before publishing his stories as a collection, Robinson's work appeared in the *Kitimat Northern Sentinel*. Eden Robinson, his niece, told *Quill & Quire* in 2000 that "he wrote down stories he didn't want people to forget but he got some flack for it. He was told, 'You're not supposed to write them down.' All our stories are oral. Other than that book, you're not going to find any books about the Haisla" ("Spirits" par. 18).

"Weegit Discovers Halibut Hooks" centres on Weegit, or Raven (a recurring figure not only in Robinson's collection but in Northwest Coast First Nations stories more generally), who is hungry and looking for something good to eat. He schemes to take advantage of Kwa-ga-noo, a fisher who alone knows the secret of catching halibut. Though Weegit is successful in taking possession of Kwa-ga-noo's fishing hooks, it is Kwa-ga-noo who has the last laugh. As you read this story, think about the many possible meanings of "hooks" in both fishing and storytelling, and how a skilful raconteur can reel in listeners and readers … by hook or by crook.

Weegit, the raven, went from one person to the other asking the same question—"Do you know where Kwa-ga-noo lives?" No one seemed to be able to answer his question and Weegit was now getting quite desperate for he had had nothing to eat these past few days. His only hope for getting food was to find the man named Kwa-ga-noo, for it was said that he alone knew the secret of catching halibut. "If no one can help me then I shall have to help myself," thought Weegit to himself as he spread his black wings and started flying.

"Halibut love deep water," he reasoned, "Therefore I may expect to find Kwa-ga-noo where the water is deep and that would be far out at sea." So he set his wings and flew higher and higher and farther out to sea. After much time had passed and he had reached the place where the sky meets the sea he saw in the distance a thin column of smoke. After more time passed he saw that the smoke came from a little house which was built on some logs floating on the ocean. To this house he flew and sat on the logs and rested. He then opened the door and went inside and there sat a man beside an opening in the floor. The man had a rope in his hand and this rope dangled in the sea. He did not appear to notice Weegit and he sat there motionless a long time until finally something gave a strong jerk on the rope in his hand. He quickly hauled in the line and there on a hook attached to the line was a halibut. Weegit carefully noted that the hook was made of a spruce root in the shape of the letter "U" with a sharp bone tied on one prong and pointed a little inward and toward the opposite prong. A piece of bait was tied on the bone barb and it was on this bone barb that the halibut was caught.

"So this is the man called Kwa-ga-noo," thought Weegit. "And this is his secret way of catching halibut. So far—so good, but now to get the hook."

Weegit softly cleared his throat then said: "I have come to tell you that our poor father has just died, brother Kwa-ga-noo; and that it was his last wish that you should be at his funeral." At this point Weegit squeezed his eyes tightly together and let fall a few tears.

"I don't recall having a brother and I certainly don't know whether or not my father is living," replied Kwa-ga-noo.

Weegit blew his nose, rubbed his eyes (or rather stuck his fingers into his eyes to bring more tears) then continued in a shaky voice, "Oh yes; many is the time that our dear departed father told me of the painful time when you were lost while still a small child and it was at his insistence that I have spent half a lifetime looking for you. But now that I have at last found you it is too late to end his grief over your loss, for at this very moment his poor, wasted body now lies cold and stiff at home awaiting only your arrival to be buried in the unfeeling ground." And Weegit started bawling loudly and the tears which streamed out of his eyes were quite real, for his fingernails were so dirty that his eyes were smarting and watering profusely due to the dirt he had introduced into them.

Touched by the sight of Weegit's tears, Kwa-ga-noo put his arms around his long lost brother's neck, and he too started weeping and bawling, and the louder he bawled—the louder were the laments of his newly found brother.

When they finally stopped their wailing, Kwa-ga-noo asked: "Tell me brother, how can I go quickly to our father's house?"

"Merely climb onto my back," replied Weegit, "and I shall take you there at once."

So Kwa-ga-noo climbed on his back and Weegit flew away, only he flew farther out to sea. Higher and higher and higher flew Weegit, then all of a sudden he flipped himself right over and flew momentarily upside down in the characteristic raven habit.

Poor Kwa-ga-noo just managed to hang on to Weegit's neck. "Don't do that again, brother Weegit," pleaded Kwa-ga-noo. "You almost threw me off."

"I could not help that, dear brother," replied Weegit. "It's just that I hiccoughed."

Farther and farther Weegit flew until Kwa-ga-noo relaxed his hold on Weegit's neck, then suddenly he again flipped himself over on his back and this time Kwa-ga-noo could not hold on and he fell head over heels down into the sea, where he landed with a mighty splash.

At once and with all speed Weegit returned to the house on the float there to find the halibut hook and line. "At last," said Weegit to himself, "I have my late brother's secret but I must try it out before taking it home." So he lowered the hook through the opening in the floor and into the sea as Kwa-ga-noo had done, and sat waiting impatiently.

Presently he felt a tug on the line and he hauled it in as quickly as he could. When he thought that the hook was close he looked down into the water to see what he had caught. Just then an arm reached up, grabbed him by the neck, pulled him into the water and held him there until poor Weegit almost drowned.

Kwa-ga-noo, for it was he, tossed poor Weegit's limp body onto the float logs where he slowly recovered his breath.

When Weegit had recovered, Kwa-ga-noo told him to leave at once and Weegit did not need to be told twice.

He flew back home, made a copy of Kwa-ga-noo's hook and this he loaned to his friends for he did not dare to use it himself for fear Kwa-ga-noo would surely drown him if he had another chance.

⤙ *The Many Lives of Anakajuttuq* ⤚
Joe Panipakuttuk

Joe Panipakuttuk[1] was born at Igarjuaq, a few miles to the east of Pond Inlet on 16 June 1914. His mother was Panikpak and his father Uirngut. In 1944, Panipakuttuk and his family were hired to accompany the RCMP schooner, *St. Roch*, when it voyaged through the Northwest Passage—the first time in history a ship completed the passage in a single season. Panipakuttuk worked as both a guide and a hunter on the journey, and for this service he received a Polar Medal in 1975. "The Many Lives of Anakajuttuq" was first published in the journal *North/nord* in 1969, and was later republished in *Paper Stays Put: A Collection of Inuit Writing* (1982), edited by Robin Gedalof.

"The Many Lives of Anakajuttuq" describes the multiple transformations that a man named Anakajuttuq undergoes, from cloud to caribou to wolf to seal to spirit, finally joining a human community near the end of the story. Not only does Anakajuttuq move between species, but he also dies numerous times, coming back to life in different forms. The story's conception of the dynamic interrelationships between life and death, spirit and embodiment, human and other life forms, offers a glimpse of life as a spiritually trained person who lives in a world that is deeply interconnected. Jo-Ann Episkenew, in the essay from this chapter, argues that it is important to consider the context of both text and readers in interpreting stories. This caution is applicable to Panipakuttuk's story, which asks you as a reader not only to research and learn something about traditional Inuit storytelling and the role of shamans in Inuit cosmology, but also to acknowledge the horizon of your own ideological formation in crafting an interpretation of the story.

First Anakajuttuq was a cloud but since a cloud will not stand up, he soon became tired of being a cloud and turned into a caribou. He ate black soil and became very thin.

The rest of the caribou were fat, so one day he asked, "What do you eat to keep fat? I eat a lot but I am thin."

He showed the other caribou what he ate and they said, "Eat caribou moss. You see the moss we are talking about is yellowish. Also eat a bit of the moss that forms on the rocks."

So Anakajuttuq started to eat caribou moss and became fat. He was now happy about his appearance, but when the other caribou played games in racing, he was always last. Again he asked, "How do you run to be so fast?"

They said, "Take long steps and try to keep your hair straight." So he did what he was told. When the caribou were playing games he joined in and kept up with no trouble.

Soon the migrating season came and the caribou were on their way to where they would spend the winter. They came to a lake and stopped to feed near it. While they were eating, one of the caribou saw hunters far away. They ran to the lake with all their might, but there was enough daylight left and the hunters killed many caribou.

Anakajuttuq was afraid to go into the water. He kept walking back and forth along the lake and the hunters were coming closer to him all the time. Finally another caribou told him to go in and cross the lake. He was swimming as hard as he could to survive, but the hunters were gaining on him. Finally one caught up with him and thrust down his harpoon. He tried not to think about the pain there would be when the harpoon went into him, but it was nothing but an itchy feeling and everything he could see became black.

When he regained consciousness he was a wolf. He chased caribou, but he could never keep up. He would catch up with the pack when the caribou was all eaten. Again he became thin when the rest of the wolves were fat. One day when the wolves were again chasing caribou, Anakajuttuq (knowing he would be last) shouted to the rest "Leave some meat for me when you get your catch."

He caught up and ate the left overs. Then he asked the eldest of the pack, "How do you run fast to catch a caribou?"

The old wolf said, "When you're running, try to kick the sky."

He tried kicking on the next chase and it worked. He kept up with the rest and ate with them. In a little while he was able to catch caribou alone and he became fat and happy.

One day, he came to a large igloo. The door was not closed and there was no one inside. At the back, there was a piece of meat and when he saw it he became hungry. He walked up to it, took it in his jaws and headed for the door. Suddenly the doorway closed, and then he heard a noise outside on top of the igloo. Something was trying to make a hole in the ceiling. He was frightened and thought he smelled smoke, but it was really the scent of a man. So the man made the hole in the ceiling and held up his spear. Anakajuttuq could not bear to think of the pain so he closed his eyes. The man speared him and he died again.

Later in his existence he became a seal. He was thin until the other seals told him to eat sea worms.

Winter came and each seal had a breathing hole. Above they could hear sounds of hunters looking for seals. They went to their breathing holes and above they could see people looking down with no sign of a smile on their face and making no sound. Anakajuttuq went to his breathing hole and when the man was about to harpoon him he swam away. He noticed that some of the seal holes were dark and some were light. The dark seal holes were where the poor hunters waited and the bright ones were where the good hunters waited out of sight.

Anakajuttuq couldn't hold his breath any longer so he went up and he saw the face of the hunter who harpooned him. He tried to break the hair (harpoon line) that was attached to him, but with no success. The next thing he knew he was being cut up. One piece of his flesh was taken home by a woman to her igloo. This woman did not go out early in the morning and she did not comb her hair early. He did not feel at home in this igloo, so his spirit left and went to another igloo. The next woman he lived with was much different. She went out early in the morning and combed her hair. He felt at home and stayed with her. At times he saw different faces peeking in, searching for a wife.

The igloo in which he stayed was very small and uncomfortable and after a while he started to go out. The air outside was cold. When he felt the cold, he tried to say how cold it was but he could only make the crying sound of an infant. No matter how hard he tried to speak, the only sound he made was the sound of a baby crying.

Later in life, when he grew up, he had a song that went like this:

> Although I tried hard to speak,
> the only sound I could make was Ungaa.
> Although I tried hard to say I am cold,
> I only cried.

— Excerpt from *Wendy* —
Walter K. Scott

Walter Kaheró:ton Scott is a Mohawk artist whose practice includes writing, video, performance, comics, and sculpture. He grew up on the Kanien'kehá:ka territory of Kahnawà:ke and has performed and exhibited across Canada and internationally. Scott's ongoing comic book series, *Wendy*, follows the fictional narrative of a young woman living in an urban centre, whose dreams of contemporary art stardom are "perpetually derailed by the temptations of punk music, drugs, alcohol, parties, and boys" (Langdon). As an artist, Scott himself works across media, and leaves the details of Wendy's art practice ambiguous: "Her practice is hard to pin down, so it keeps the focus on the personal" (Langdon). Having begun as a self-published zine, *Wendy* has since been serialized on the digital magazine *Hazlitt* and published as a full-length book by Koyama Press.

In a 2013 interview with *BODY*, Scott says that he sometimes feels like he is the "alternate universe Wendy," and that each of his characters reflects some part of himself (Langdon). Wendy is supported—in her failures and successes, outfits and hangovers—by her good friend and collaborator, Winona. In the scene immediately preceding this excerpt, Winona and Wendy's collaborative performance draws the pair acclaim and attention, but this success strains Wendy's ability to keep sight of what's important to her. In spite of the initially warm reception, Wendy's boyfriend, Byron, publishes a harshly negative review in an art magazine. Hurt by criticism, Wendy storms out and meets Winona in the studio, who has just read the same review. Wendy takes her offence and anger out on Winona, using as an emotional weapon the stereotypes she holds about Indigenous peoples.

Figure 7.1   Walter K. Scott, from *Wendy*. (*Credit*: Koyama Press)

Figure 7.2   Walter K. Scott, from *Wendy*. (*Credit:* Koyama Press)

Figure 7.3   Walter K. Scott, from *Wendy*. (*Credit:* Koyama Press)

Figure 7.4   Walter K. Scott, from *Wendy*. (*Credit*: Koyama Press)

⟶ *Lullaby* ⟵
Leslie Marmon Silko

Leslie Marmon Silko was born in Albuquerque, New Mexico, and grew up on the Laguna Pueblo Reservation. She received her BA (with honours) from the University of New Mexico in 1969. In addition to writing, her career includes an association with the University of New Mexico, Albuquerque; Navajo Community College in Tsaile, Arizona; and she was professor of English at the University of Arizona–Tucson. Her best-known works, which include fiction, poetry, and textualized oral narrative, are *Ceremony* (1977), *Storyteller* (1981), and *Almanac of the Dead* (1991).

The story "Lullaby" confronts one of the most painful aspects of colonial history in North America: the removal of Indigenous children from their families. The medical officers suspect that the children, Danny and Ella, have tuberculosis, and so take them for treatment to a sanatorium far from their home. Although the ostensible reason for removing Danny and Ella is to ensure their health, the breakup of Indigenous families, the suppression of language and cultural practices, and the alienation of the younger generation from their families and territories may ultimately have a greater negative impact in reinforcing governmental policies of assimilation and cultural genocide. In spite of the tremendous losses that this story invokes, as Jo-Ann Episkenew argues in her essay in this chapter, the grandparents Ayah and Chato are survivors who assert their deep, ongoing connections to the land and the cultural ties embedded within it. As you read, think about the different possible interpretations of the story's ending that Episkenew reviews in recalling her experiences as an undergraduate student studying this story many years ago. Are the meanings of stories entirely open-ended, or should readers aim to pay closer attention to context in order to craft a more convincing interpretation of a story?

The sun had gone down but the snow in the wind gave off its own light. It came in thick tufts like new wool—washed before the weaver spins it. Ayah reached out for it like her own babies had, and she smiled when she remembered how she had laughed at them. She was an old woman now, and her life had become memories. She sat down with her back against the wide cottonwood tree, feeling the rough bark on her back bones; she faced east and listened to the wind and snow sing a high-pitched Yeibechei song. Out of the wind she felt warmer, and she could watch the wide fluffy snow fill in her tracks, steadily, until the direction she had come from was gone. By the light of the snow she could see the dark outline of the big arroyo a few feet away. She was sitting on the edge of Cebolleta Creek, where in the springtime the thin cows would graze on a grass already chewed flat to the ground. In the wide deep creek bed where only a trickle of water flowed in the summer, the skinny cows would wander, looking for new grass along winding paths splashed with manure.

Ayah pulled the old Army blanket over her head like a shawl. Jimmie's blanket—the one he had sent to her. That was long time ago and the green wool was faded, and it was unraveling on the edges. She did not want to think about Jimmie. So she thought about the weaving and the way her mother had done it. On the tall wooden loom set into the sand under a tamarack tree for shade. She could see it clearly. She had been only a little girl when her grandma gave her the wooden combs to pull the twigs and burrs from the raw, freshly washed wool. And while she combed the wool, her grandma sat beside her, spinning a silvery strand of yarn around the smooth cedar spindle. Her mother worked at the loom with yarns dyed bright yellow and red and gold. She watched them dye the yarn in boiling black pots full of beeweed petals, juniper berries, and sage. The blankets her mother made were soft and woven so tight that rain rolled off them like birds' feathers. Ayah remembered sleeping warm on cold windy nights, wrapped in her mother's blankets on the hogan's sandy floor.

The snow drifted now, with the northwest wind hurling it in gusts. It drifted up around her black overshoes—old ones with little metal buckles. She smiled at the snow which was trying to cover her little by little. She could remember when they had no black rubber overshoes; only the high buckskin leggings that they wrapped over their elkhide moccasins. If the snow was dry or frozen, a person could walk all day and not get wet; and in the evenings the beams of the ceiling would hang with lengths of pale buckskin leggings, drying out slowly.

She felt peaceful remembering. She didn't feel cold any more. Jimmie's blanket seemed warmer than it had ever been. And she could remember the morning he was born. She could remember whispering to her mother, who was sleeping on the other side of the hogan, to tell her it was time now. She did not want to wake the others. The second time she called to her, her mother stood up and pulled on her shoes; she knew. They walked to the old stone hogan together, Ayah walking a step behind her mother. She waited alone, learning the rhythms of the pains while her mother went to call the old woman to help them. The morning was already warm even before dawn and Ayah smelled the bee flowers blooming and the young willow growing at the springs. She could remember that so clearly, but his birth merged into the births of the other children and to her it became all the same birth. They named him for the summer morning and in English they called him Jimmie.

It wasn't like Jimmie died. He just never came back, and one day a dark blue sedan with white writing on its doors pulled up in front of the box-car shack where the rancher let the Indians live. A man in a khaki uniform trimmed in gold gave them a yellow piece of paper and told them that Jimmie was dead. He said the Army would try to get the body back and then it would be shipped to them; but it wasn't likely because the helicopter had burned after it crashed. All of this was told to Chato because he could understand English. She stood inside the doorway holding the baby while Chato listened. Chato spoke English like a white man and he spoke Spanish too. He was taller than the white man and he stood straighter too. Chato didn't explain why; he just told the military man they could keep the body if they found it. The white man looked bewildered; he nodded his head and he left. Then Chato looked at her and shook his head, and then he told her, "Jimmie isn't coming home anymore," and when he spoke, he used the words to speak of the dead. She didn't cry then, but she hurt inside with anger. And she mourned him as the years passed, when a horse fell with Chato and broke his leg, and the white rancher told them he wouldn't pay Chato until he could work again. She mourned Jimmie because he would have worked for his father then; he would have saddled the big bay horse and ridden the fence lines each day, with wire cutters and heavy gloves, fixing the breaks in the barbed wire and putting the stray cattle back inside again.

She mourned him after the white doctors came to take Danny and Ella away. She was at the shack alone that day they came. It was back in the days before they hired Navajo women to go with them as interpreters. She recognized one of the doctors. She had seen him at the children's clinic at Cañoncito about a month ago. They were wearing khaki uniforms and they waved papers at her and a black ball-point pen, trying to make her understand their English words. She was frightened by the way they looked at the children, like the lizard watches the fly. Danny was swinging on the tire swing on the elm tree behind the rancher's house, and Ella was toddling around the front door, dragging the broomstick horse Chato made for her. Ayah could see they wanted her to sign the papers, and Chato had taught her to sign her name. It was something she was proud of. She only wanted them to go, and to take their eyes away from her children.

She took the pen from the man without looking at his face and she signed the papers in three different places he pointed to. She stared at the ground by their feet and waited for them to leave. But they stood there and began to point and gesture at the children. Danny stopped swinging. Ayah could see his fear. She moved suddenly and grabbed Ella into her arms; the child squirmed, trying to get back to her toys. Ayah ran with the baby toward Danny; she screamed for him to run and then she grabbed him around his chest and carried him too. She ran south into the foothills of juniper trees and black lava rock. Behind her she heard the doctors running, but they had been taken by surprise, and as the hills became steeper and the cholla cactus were thicker, they stopped. When she reached the top of the hill, she stopped to listen in case they were circling around her. But in a few minutes she heard a car engine start and they drove away. The children had been too surprised to cry while she ran with them. Danny was shaking and Ella's little fingers were gripping Ayah's blouse.

She stayed up in the hills for the rest of the day, sitting on a black lava boulder in the sunshine where she could see for miles all around her. The sky was light blue and cloudless, and it was warm for late April. The sun warmth relaxed her and took the fear and anger away. She lay back on the rock and watched the sky. It seemed to her that she could walk into the sky, stepping through clouds endlessly. Danny played with little pebbles and stones, pretending they were birds' eggs and then little rabbits. Ella sat at her feet and dropped fistfuls of dirt into the breeze, watching the dust and particles of sand intently. Ayah watched a hawk soar high above them, dark wings gliding; hunting or only watching, she did not know. The hawk was patient and he circled all afternoon before he disappeared around the high volcanic peak the Mexicans called Guadalupe.

Late in the afternoon, Ayah looked down at the gray boxcar shack with the paint all peeled from the wood; the stove pipe on the roof was rusted and crooked. The fire she had built that morning in the oil drum stove had burned out. Ella was asleep in her lap now and Danny sat close to her, complaining that he was hungry; he asked when they would go to the house. "We will stay up here until your father comes," she told him, "because those white men were chasing us." The boy remembered then and he nodded at her silently.

If Jimmie had been there he could have read those papers and explained to her what they said. Ayah would have known then, never to sign them. The doctors came back the next day and they brought a BIA policeman with them. They told Chato they had her signature and that was all they needed. Except for the kids. She listened to Chato sullenly; she hated him when he told her it was the old woman who died in the winter, spitting blood; it was her old grandma who had given the children this disease. "They don't spit blood," she said coldly. "The whites lie." She held Ella and Danny close to her, ready to run to the hills again. "I want a medicine man first," she said to Chato, not looking at him. He shook his head. "It's too late now. The policeman is with them. You signed the paper." His voice was gentle.

It was worse than if they had died: to lose the children and to know that somewhere, in a place called Colorado, in a place full of sick and dying strangers, her children were without her. There had been babies that died soon after they were born, and one that died before he could walk. She had carried them herself, up to the boulders and great pieces of the cliff that long ago crashed down from Long Mesa; she laid them in the crevices of sandstone and buried them in fine brown sand with round quartz pebbles that washed down the hills in the rain. She had endured it because they had been with her. But she could not bear this pain. She did not sleep for a long time after they took her children. She stayed on the hill where they had fled the first time, and she slept rolled up in the blanket Jimmie had sent her. She carried the pain in her belly and it was fed by everything she saw: the blue sky of their last day together and the dust and pebbles they played with; the swing in the elm tree and broom stick horse choked life from her. The pain filled her stomach and there was no room for food or for her lungs to fill with air. The air and the food would have been theirs.

She hated Chato, not because he let the policeman and doctors put the screaming children in the government car, but because he had taught her to sign her name. Because it was like the old ones always told her about learning their language or any of their ways: it endangered you. She slept alone on the hill until the middle of November when the first snows came. Then she made a bed for herself where the children had slept. She did not lie down beside Chato again until many years later, when he was sick and shivering and only her body could keep him warm. The illness came after the white rancher told Chato he was too old to work for him anymore, and Chato and his old woman should be out of the shack by the next afternoon because the rancher had hired new people to work there. That had satisfied her. To see how the white man repaid Chato's years of loyalty and work. All of Chato's fine-sounding English talk didn't change things.

—---—

It snowed steadily and the luminous light from the snow gradually diminished into the darkness. Somewhere in Cebolleta a dog barked and other village dogs joined with it. Ayah looked in the direction she had come, from the bar where Chato was buying the wine. Sometimes he told her to go on ahead and wait; and then he never came. And when she finally went back looking for him, she would find him passed out at the bottom of the wooden steps at Azzie's Bar. All the wine would be gone and most of the money too, from the pale blue check that came to them once a month in a government envelope. It was then that she would look at his face and his hands, scarred by ropes and the barbed wire of all those years, and she would think, this man is a stranger; for forty years she had smiled at him and cooked his food, but he remained a stranger. She stood up again, with the snow almost to her knees, and she walked back to find Chato.

It was hard to walk in the deep snow and she felt the air burn in her lungs. She stopped a short distance from the bar to rest and readjust the blanket. But this time he wasn't waiting for her on the bottom step with his old Stetson hat pulled down and his shoulders hunched up in his long wool overcoat.

She was careful not to slip on the wooden steps. When she pushed the door open, warm air and cigarette smoke hit her face. She looked around slowly and deliberately, in every corner, in every dark place that the old man might find to sleep. The bar owner didn't like Indians in there, especially Navajos, but he let Chato come in because he could talk Spanish like he was one of them. The men at the bar stared at her, and the bartender saw that she left the door open wide. Snowflakes were flying inside like moths and melting into a puddle on the oiled wood floor. He motioned to her to close the door, but she did not see him. She held herself straight and walked across the room slowly, searching the room with every step. The snow in her hair melted and she could feel it on her forehead. At the far corner of the room, she saw red flames at the mica window of the old stove door; she looked behind the stove just to make sure. The bar got quiet except for the Spanish polka music playing on the jukebox. She stood by the stove and shook the snow from her blanket and held it near the stove to dry. The wet wool smell reminded her of newborn goats in early March, brought inside to warm near the fire. She felt calm.

In past years they would have told her to get out. But her hair was white now and her faced was wrinkled. They looked at her like she was a spider crawling slowly across the room. They were afraid; she could feel the fear. She looked at their faces steadily. They reminded her of the first time the white people brought her children back to her that winter. Danny had been shy and hid behind the thin white woman who brought them. And the baby had not known her until Ayah took her into her arms, and then Ella had nuzzled close to her as she had when she was nursing. The blonde woman was nervous and kept looking at a dainty gold watch on her wrist. She sat on the bench near the small window and watched the dark snow clouds gather around the mountains; she was worrying about the unpaved road. She was frightened by what she saw inside too: the strips of venison drying on a rope across the ceiling and the children jabbering excitedly in a language she did not know. So they stayed for only a few hours. Ayah watched the government car disappear down the road and she knew they were already being weaned from these lava hills and from this sky. The last time they came was in early June, and Ella stared at her the way the men in the bar were now staring. Ayah did not try to pick her up; she smiled at her instead and spoke cheerfully to Danny. When he tried to answer her, he could not seem to remember and he spoke English words with the Navajo. But he gave her a scrap of paper that he had found somewhere and carried in his pocket; it was folded in half, and he shyly looked up at her and said it was a bird. She asked Chato if they were home for good this time.

He spoke to the white woman and she shook her head. "How much longer?" he asked, and she said she didn't know; but Chato saw how she stared at the boxcar shack. Ayah turned away then. She did not say good-bye.

She felt satisfied that the men in the bar feared her. Maybe it was her face and the way she held her mouth with teeth clenched tight, like there was nothing anyone could do to her now. She walked north down the road, searching for the old man. She did this because she had the blanket, and there would be no place for him except with her and the blanket in the old adobe barn near the arroyo. They always slept there when they came to Cebolleta. If the money and the wine were gone, she would be relieved because then they could go home again; back to the old hogan with a dirt roof and rock walls where she herself had been born. And the next day the old man could go back to the few sheep they still had, to follow along behind them, guiding them, into dry sandy arroyos where sparse grass grew. She knew he did not like walking behind old ewes when for so many years he rode big quarter horses and worked with cattle. But she wasn't sorry for him; he should have known all along what would happen.

There had not been enough rain for their garden in five years; and that was when Chato finally hitched a ride into the town and brought back brown boxes of rice and sugar and big tin cans of welfare peaches. After that, at the first of the month they went to Cebolleta to ask the postmaster for the check; and then Chato would go to the bar and cash it. They did this as they planted the garden every May, not because anything would survive the summer dust, but because it was time to do this. The journey passed the days that smelled silent and dry like the caves above the canyon with yellow painted buffaloes on their walls.

He was walking along the pavement when she found him. He did not stop or turn around when he heard her behind him. She walked beside him and she noticed how slowly he moved now. He smelled strong of woodsmoke and urine. Lately he had been forgetting. Sometimes he called her by his sister's name and she had been gone for a long time. Once she had found him wandering on the road to the white man's ranch, and she asked him why he was going that way; he laughed at her and said, "You know they can't run that ranch without me," and he walked on determined, limping on the leg that had been crushed many years before. Now he looked at her curiously, as if for the first time, but he kept shuffling along, moving slowly along the side of the highway.

His gray hair had grown long and spread out on the shoulders of the long over-coat. He wore the old felt hat pulled down over his ears. His boots were worn out at the toes and he had stuffed pieces of an old red shirt in the holes. The rags made his feet look like little animals up to their ears in snow. She laughed at his feet; the snow muffled the sound of her laugh. He stopped and looked at her again. The wind had quit blowing and the snow was falling straight down; the southeast sky was beginning to clear and Ayah could see a star.

"Let's rest awhile," she said to him. They walked away from the road and up the slope to the giant boulders that had tumbled down from the red sand-rock mesa throughout the centuries of rainstorms and earth tremors. In a place where the boulders shut out the wind, they sat down with their backs against the rock. She offered half of the blanket to him and they sat wrapped together.

The storm passed swiftly. The clouds moved east. They were massive and full, crowding together across the sky. She watched them with the feeling of horses—steely blue-gray horses startled across the sky. The powerful haunches pushed into the distances and the tail hairs streamed white mist behind them. The sky cleared. Ayah saw that there was nothing between her and the stars. The light was crystalline. There was no shimmer, no distortion through earth haze. She breathed the clarity of the night sky; she smelled the purity of the half moon and the stars. He was lying on his side with his knees pulled up near his belly for warmth. His eyes were closed now, and in the light from the stars and the moon, he looked young again.

She could see it descend out of the night sky: an icy stillness from the edge of the thin moon. She recognized the freezing. It came gradually, sinking snowflake by snowflake until the crust was heavy and deep. It had the strength of the stars in Orion, and its journey was endless. Ayah knew that with the wine he would sleep. He would not feel it. She tucked the blanket around him, remembering how it was when Ella had been with her; and she felt the rush so big inside her heart for the babies. And she sang the only song she knew to sing for babies. She could not remember if she had ever sung it to her children, but she knew that her grandmother had sung it and her mother had sung it:

> The earth is your mother,
>   she holds you.
> The sky is your father,
>   he protects you.
> Sleep,
> sleep.
> Rainbow is your sister,
>   she loves you.

The winds are your brothers,
     they sing to you.
Sleep,
sleep.
We are together always.
We are together always.
There never was a time
when this
was not so.

"Notes on Leslie Marmon Silko's 'Lullaby': Socially Responsible Criticism"
Jo-Ann Episkenew

Métis scholar Jo-Ann Episkenew was born in Manitoba but lived most of her adult life in Saskatchewan. She was a professor of English at the First Nations University of Canada before she served as Director of the Indigenous Peoples' Health Research Centre from 2010 until 2016, when she died unexpectedly at the age of sixty-three. As an English professor working in the area of health research, she applied literary analysis skills—close readings of texts—to study the connection between story and healing in her work with Indigenous youth. She was the author of many articles in the fields of health and literary and cultural criticism, as well as the award-winning book *Taking Back Our Spirits: Indigenous Literature, Public Policy, and Healing* (2009). In 2015, she was the recipient of a Lifetime Achievement Award from the Women of Distinction YWCA Regina; in 2016, she received the nationally broadcast Inspire Award for Education.

In her essay Episkenew argues that too often, scholars and students focus on analyzing the ideologies within a text without acknowledging how the ideologies they themselves bring to the page shape their interpretations profoundly. She writes: "When analyzing literary works, most scholars are very conscious that ideology is embedded in the text; what they often forget is the ideology that they bring to their reading." Episkenew's challenge to the reader is to develop more self-reflexive strategies of reading and to meaningfully acknowledge how social positioning and personal experiences influence how we interpret texts.

During my most cynical moments I believe that the literary canon—that collection of "great" works of literature—is merely a creation of academics looking for teachable works of literature, and publishers looking for the profits that are likely to ensue if their texts are taught in university English classes. Works of literature, then, become incorporated into the canon when a substantial number of academics teach them. At some point in our development, most burgeoning academics infer—or are told—that we must have a specialization, we must claim our "turf" if you will, that area in which we will become experts. Our future tenure and promotion depend on it. As a result, we look for some area of study that piques our interest and, with luck, has enough room to enable us to carve out an intellectual space for ourselves. If Shakespeare is our passion, our challenge is a large one; after all, it is hard to make a space for one's self in such an occupied area. Clearly it is easier to find a space in an area that is new and unoccupied, one like the area of Canadian Indigenous Literature. That choice, however, brings with it its own challenges.

Unlike its relative south of the border, writing by Canadian Indigenous authors still occupies the literary margins of the canon. While the works of Native American authors, such as Leslie Marmon Silko, N. Scott Momaday, and Louise Erdrich, appear in every new anthology of modern American literature, the works of Canadian Indigenous writers, especially early writers, such as George Clutesi, Maria Campbell, and Beatrice Culleton Mosionier, are absent. In the U.S., the canonized Native American writers are well educated in a western sense and are often academics themselves. Although their works include many allusions to Native American epistemology, they are complex in a way with which literary scholars are comfortable. We can find a reason for the differences between Canadian and U.S. Indigenous literatures when we examine the social and political context from which they came into being.

Although governments on both sides of the forty-ninth parallel used education as a weapon of colonization, they wielded this weapon in different manners. Both colonial governments chose to use residential schools, or boarding schools as they were called in the U.S., as a strategy to assimilate the Indians; however, in the U.S., many Native Americans[1] were encouraged to obtain further education—usually in the trades—after finishing boarding school. To further its goal of assimilation, the U.S. Government passed the Indian Relocation Act in 1956 to gain access to resource-rich reservations. As a result, relocated Native Americans were educated in mainstream schools, and eventually many found their way into universities. In Canada, attitudes were much different, and First Nations people were sent back to their reserves when their tenure at residential school was complete. Smaller and rarely rich in natural resources, reserve land was not coveted to the same extent. It was valued more as a place to confine First Nations people. First Nations people were typically discouraged from attempting to gain access to higher education, and Métis people were often denied access to any education at all.[2] In the unlikely event that they did gain access to a university, status Indians could lose their legal status as Indians if they received a university degree.[3] Métis and non-Status Indians' access to education was inconsistent. They were allowed to attend residential schools if there were vacancies, but forced to leave when the schools became full of status Indians.[4] If living near town, they found themselves at the mercy of the white property owners who could deny their children access to school, which they often did, especially if the Métis families did not own property.[5] Canadian Indigenous literature reflects this history. Most early writers, therefore, were not well educated and could not be expected to be familiar with the language of academia. Later writers, although more educated, are cognizant that many of their people are not, and so they write in a way that their works are accessible to a variety of educational levels and not solely for an academic audience.

Today many literary scholars choose to teach Canadian Indigenous literature as witnessed by the growing number of "Native Lit" sessions at mainstream academic conferences. It is only a matter of time before works of Indigenous literature begin to appear regularly in anthologies of Canadian literature. Canadian Indigenous literature is knocking on the door of the Canadian literary canon, and scholars are already publishing articles about this new area. The challenge scholars face is finding something to say about these works of literature when their context is often alien to them.

Even before works of Canadian Indigenous literature begin to make regular appearances in anthologies of Canadian literature, articles about them have begun to form a canon of interpretations. Although scholars write ostensibly to analyze works of literature to make them better understood, we also write to refute or augment the ideas presented in the critical writings that precede ours. And so, critical works beget more critical works, and often the literary works that are their subjects become mere examples illustrating the critical thoughts of the academics who create them. I see this happening with Canadian Indigenous literature, and as an Indigenous academic it concerns me.

When analyzing literary works, most scholars are very conscious that ideology is embedded in the text; what they often forget is the ideology that they bring to their reading. I use the term "ideology" to refer to those ideas and beliefs that we take so for granted that we do not hold them up for critical examination and consider them to be "just the way it is." Interpretations are grounded in this kind of ideology. It is important to note that almost all of the scholars who create these interpretations are not Indigenous people. Most are members of settler culture and, therefore, cannot possibly share the same ideology as Indigenous people, whether they are the authors who create the literature, the people about whom they write, or the few Indigenous students in their classes. Let me give you an example from my own experience.[6]

As an undergraduate student majoring in English, I registered in a class in literary analysis based on New Criticism. The assigned text was an anthology entitled *Literature: An Introduction to Reading and Writing*, 2nd edition (1989), which included Leslie Marmon Silko's story "Lullaby" (1981). "Lullaby" was the topic of the first writing assignment the professor gave the class. Although I cannot remember the topic of the assignment, I can remember my grade. I received a D+/C-, which I remember vividly because it hurt my pride. At the end of the essay the professor left a note explaining that my low mark resulted from my not addressing the suicide at the end of the story. I was dumbfounded because in my interpretation there was no suicide. I asked my professor to explain. My professor, a Montreal anglophone, pointed out that, at the end of the story, the central character Ayah, an older Dine (Navajo) woman, wraps herself and her drunken husband, Chato, in a blanket, curls up beside a rock, and prepares to go to sleep. Because this happens on a freezing night, she is, therefore, committing suicide. The text, he said, clearly reveals that the old woman, unable to bear the weight of her tragic life, chooses death for herself and her husband. I suspected that he had heard stories of old Native people who, weary of life, walk out into the wilderness to die. If one is analyzing only the text of "Lullaby," this is a plausible interpretation. What is missing, however, is the context of both text and readers.

It is important to consider the context of "Lullaby," in that both Silko and her characters are Indigenous to the American Southwest. The land that seemed so frightening and dangerous to my professor is their home. Ayah and Chato live in a hogan, a structure made out of rocks, earth, and wood, which is as much a part of the land as the cluster of rocks beside which they spent the night. It is not suicidal for them to take shelter beside these rocks and cover themselves with their blankets; indeed, they carry blankets along with them for just such an occasion. They are old people, and despite their tragic lives, they have survived. To an Indigenous reader, "Lullaby" is not a story of suicide; it is one of survival, albeit filled with references to the suffering that results from a lifetime of colonization and oppression.

As a reader, my context differs radically from that of my professor. Although I too spent my early years in a large urban centre, I moved to northern Saskatchewan as a teenager. What is a cold winter night in Arizona, would likely be a nice day in late autumn in Saskatchewan. I have lived with trappers who regularly go out on foot to check their trap lines regardless of the weather. Sometimes they sleep out in the bush—albeit by a fire—wrapped in blankets in temperatures falling below -20°C. This is how Indigenous people who live on the land exist; this is how we have always lived. My husband grew up on a reserve near Fort Qu'Appelle in southern Saskatchewan. He tells a story of how he walked from Fort Qu'Appelle to Muscowepetung Reserve, a distance of about forty kilometers, one cold winter night. When he found that he was too tired to go on, he made a shelter in a farmer's field by piling bales of hay around himself. He slept there for the night and finished walking to the reserve in the morning. My brothers-in-law found it necessary to do the same thing from time to time. This land is our home, and Indigenous people have learned to do what they must to survive. I didn't tell this to my professor, however. Somehow, at the time, I felt embarrassed to reveal that I—and my people—still live this way at the end of the twentieth century. Somehow my husband's story smacked of poverty and social problems and all the things that I was sure that my professors associated with Indigenous people. Even worse, what if I told him and he didn't believe me? What if he accused me of telling or believing tall tales? His was the voice of authority. How could I convince him that my voice contained authority, too? So I silenced my voice, kept my knowledge to myself, and tried to always be cognizant that my professors knew nothing of Indigenous realities. I followed the rules, tried to anticipate their objections, and wrote "objective" literary analyses that did not reflect my community context.

Over the last few years, I have become increasingly aware that many interpretations of the works of Canadian Indigenous literature lack a fundamental understanding of the ideological context in which the works were written. Worse yet, because the authors of these interpretations are educated people with academic positions at prestigious universities, the general public deems their voices to be ones of authority. However, these interpretations are grounded in the ideology of the colonizer culture, not the ideology of the colonized people who are the authors and subjects of the texts being interpreted. It is important to remember that colonization is not only militaristic, economic, and political; it is also psychological, social, and spiritual.[7] No matter how well intended, interpretations that lack a fundamental understanding of Indigenous people as survivors of colonization can inadvertently become weapons of colonization themselves because their authors' voices become the voices of authority that could easily overpower the voices of Indigenous people. That is not to say that only Indigenous people should be interpreting and critiquing Indigenous literature. What I am saying is that non-Indigenous scholars need to be cognizant of the authority that society accords their voices. It is inevitable, then, that their literary interpretations will have an effect not only on the perceptions that settler Canadians have of Indigenous society but that Indigenous people have of ourselves. It is important that scholars examine the ideological baggage they bring to their readings and counter it by looking outside the texts into the contexts in which they were written to glean some kind of understanding of the ideology of the people whose works they interpret. It is not acceptable to remain secure in the ivory towers writing objective critical articles because these articles, imbued with the voice of authority, have an effect on the social situation of the Indigenous people who are their subjects.

As I said earlier, choosing Canadian Indigenous literature as a field of study has its own challenges, especially when Indigenous people are able to write back.

Scholars are not unfamiliar with the requirement to provide students with an understanding of the social, political, and cultural context out of which the texts that they teach arise. Indeed, any class on Shakespeare would not be complete without a comprehensive examination of the political and religious situation in Elizabethan England, no doubt comprised of information that the instructor has gathered from books in the library. These scholars need not worry that there just might be an Elizabethan enrolled in his or her class and that Elizabethan student just might dispute the information given in the lecture. However, this might very well occur in a class on contemporary Indigenous literature. And, to further complicate things, the instructor cannot always count on the information on the context of Indigenous literature that she or he has found in the library. At best it is likely to be incomplete and at worst inaccurate. Nevertheless, if one examines the *text* of works of Indigenous literature without examining the *context* from which it is written, Indigenous people become abstractions, metaphors that signify whatever the critic is able to prove they signify. However, to write in this way shows a lack of social responsibility because it has an effect on the living people who are the subjects of Indigenous literature. To really understand the context of the literature, then, scholars must leave the ivory tower and talk to Indigenous people. This must be done with care and respect.

CHAPTER 8

▰ ▰ ▰ ▰

INDIGENOUS FANTASY AND SF

Daniel Heath Justice, "Tatterborn"

Simon Ortiz, "Men on the Moon"

Stephen Graham Jones, "Father, Son, Holy Rabbit"

Eden Robinson, "Terminal Avenue"

Allison Hedge Coke, "On Drowning Pond"

L. Catherine Cornum, "The Space NDN's Star Map"

GENRE FICTION IS OFTEN BUILT out of colonial tropes. Take, for instance, the Indian Burial Ground, a trope deeply embedded in contemporary horror. The Indian Burial Ground trope is fuelled by the imagining of a disturbed bed of Indigenous spirits that take their vengeance on settlers who build their homes in sacred places. "Haunting" in this sense is thus inextricably linked to the violence of colonialism and the unacknowledged ghosts of settler histories. As this section illustrates, Indigenous authors are taking up the genre from very different perspectives. Simon Ortiz's story, "Men on the Moon," invokes many of the colonial tropes of science fiction, but it does so from an Elder's living room, shifting the viewpoint away from that of an explorer to that of an Indigenous man rooted in his home. "Men on the Moon" thus becomes a critique of the colonial drive to discover, to "boldly go where no man has gone before," to invoke the original Star Trek series. Allison Hedge Coke's beautifully written "On Drowning Pond" has the resonances of a ghost story, but the ways in which the narrator takes up the position of investigator also locate it within the boundaries of Noir, a genre driven by cynical, fast-talking detectives with unique views on urban landscapes. Hedge Coke's Noir, however, investigates violence against Indigenous women, drawing the "private-eye" to an issue too often overlooked by mainstream society and media coverage.

Like any group of writers, Indigenous authors have composed stories in any number of genres, including (but not limited to) fantasy, science fiction, erotica, and horror. Indigenous writers such as Hedge Coke, Daniel Heath Justice, Eden Robinson, and Stephen Graham Jones are shaping, adapting, and indigenizing well-known literary genres to create some of the most innovative, provocative, and fun-to-read short fiction available. As Grace Dillon points out in her 2012 essay, "Global Indigenous Science Fiction," "many Indigenous cultures do not classify discourse genres, making 'storytelling' the singular means of passing all knowledge from generation to generation" (377). For instance, a story might be humorous, but also record an important historical moment or pass on important skills and knowledge. A "horror" story can similarly entertain and captivate audiences while expressing important lessons or warnings. In this sense, genre is secondary to the transmission of knowledge. As such, a strict application of genre categories is not always relevant to Indigenous writing. In fact, an uncritical genre application risks mirroring colonialism: assigning top-down categorization instead of recognizing the author's own unique forms of storytelling.

That being said, there are a number of Indigenous authors who are inspired by genre fiction and what it can do in terms of reaching wider audiences and bringing about cultural change. For instance Justice, who was heavily influenced by J. R. R. Tolkien's *Lord of the Rings*, uses the fantasy genre to explode assumptions about sexuality and settler–Indigenous relationships. Reading Indigenous narrative texts through the lens of genre can illuminate and give new resonance to issues of place, sovereignty, and self-determination—key issues that many of the Indigenous writers included in this anthology return to again and again.

Justice's "Tatterborn," published for the first time in this anthology, illuminates the colonial structure of the world of Oz, illustrating how the tropes of L. Frank Baum's *The Wizard of Oz* (first published in 1900) are indicative of a larger colonial framework. As "Tatterborn" imagines, the iconic yellow brick road is more than just a colourful path for Dorothy to follow; it is also an expressway for the extraction and transportation of natural resources, taken from that world's forests and its Indigenous peoples. The road, of course, leads to the city of Oz, where the wizard, the colonial ruler and ideologue of the fictional world, lives and conducts his business. "Tatterborn" uncovers the colonial conceits structuring this classical fantasy. Indeed, many examples of science fiction and fantasy (also known as speculative fiction, or SF) rely heavily on metaphors of colonization, Indigeneity, and the myth of *terra nullius*—the erroneous idea that uncolonized land was uninhabited before settlers arrived. As in colonization, in order for new planets to be "discovered," space must first be imagined to be empty, or, at best, inhabited by "savages." In this sense, to "indigenize" genre is not only to read Indigenous stories alongside genre-specific tropes, but also to identify the ways in which the stories themselves contribute to and shape these tropes.

⤙ Tatterborn ⤚
Daniel Heath Justice

Daniel Heath Justice is a Colorado-born Canadian citizen of the Cherokee Nation and Canada Research Chair in Indigenous Literature and Expressive Culture at the University of British Columbia, on the traditional, ancestral, and unceded territories of the Musqueam people. He is an avowed fan of J. R. R. Tolkien and his Indigenous epic fantasy novel, *The Way of Thorn and Thunder: The Kynship Chronicles*, is an intertext with Tolkien's *Lord of the Rings* (2011). He is also the author and editor of a diverse selection of academic books and articles, including *Our Fire Survives the Storm: A Cherokee Literary History* (2006), *The Oxford Handbook of Indigenous American Literature* (2014), and *Badger* (2015), a cultural history of badgers. His current work includes a new dark fantasy series, a study of kinship in Indigenous literature, and a manifesto, *Why Indigenous Literatures Matter*, forthcoming from Wilfrid Laurier University Press.

"Tatterborn" showcases Justice's talent as a speculative fiction (SF) author and critical Indigenous studies scholar, employing the fictional world of L. Frank Baum's *Wizard of Oz* to rearticulate the impacts of colonialism on Indigenous peoples. "Tatterborn," framed as a prequel to Baum's famous story, is told from the perspective of the Scarecrow. Far from the bumbling fool we find in Baum's account, however, Justice's Scarecrow was once a Firekeeper for his people and the one who carries the story of Oz's colonization. "Tatterborn" is a heartbreaking account of the love and betrayal that occurs between Nic (or the Tin Man) and the Scarecrow, set against a landscape of resource extraction and colonial greed. Justice's reimagining of this iconic world draws into sharp relief the colonial tropes that often frame popular fantasy, while illustrating the strength of the communities and individuals who are written into its margins.

It is cold here in the City tonight. It is cold here every night.

There is much I do not remember these days. It is better when I am alone, for other voices crowd out the thoughts from the past, of the home I knew and lost, the memories that make sense of this strange new world I inhabit. But even then, much of the past remains unclear, or confused. It has been that way for a very long time.

But some things I have not forgotten. I remember the mocking laughter of crows and monkeys. I recall glistening skin in the moonlight, fields ready for harvest, a cruel storm, an old woman's dying scream. I remember Fire.

Of all my muddled memories, Fire burns brightest. She was what gave meaning to my life. She was who I was, and how I served.

And she reminds me of all I lost for love.

While some have claimed otherwise, it was the Old Women who started the War. They feared the Smiling Man more than they hated one another. But conflict was not their first choice. They tried for years to build good relations with the visitor, to share of the bounty of the land and weave him and his ways into our own. They reminded him that the land and the People had existed long before his storm-wracked arrival, that they all wanted friendship, that there was plenty for all, but that all in the fair Four Lands had responsibilities and not simply privileges.

Their guidance was rejected. The Smiling Man no longer smiled when the Old Women came to visit. He dismissed every overture for council and sowed seeds of dissent against them. He called himself a wonder-worker, a marvel-maker, a wizard of extraordinary power. He drew the prairie folk into his service, at first with smooth promises and later with cruel deeds, and as their hearts hardened and their desires grew, they helped him build his hungry City. And the greater and grander the City became, the greater his fame, and the deeper into the Four Lands his minions went. And their Roads came with them, making way for swifter transport of goods and the City's soldiers. Their roads drove deep into the northern mountains for iron ore and precious metals. They went westward, to the great fields for the grain and wild herds that fed their ever-growing numbers. The City claimed the southern rivers and lakes as its own, and the waters soon ran foul and poisonous.

And then, after the War began, when the Old Women began striking back through means both mundane and marvelous, the City-folk and their road came at last to our deep forests in the east, where the ringing of axe blades and the roar of crashing trees echoed across the valleys day and night, and the cries of birds and beasts were lost in the din.

I was Firekeeper when the first Choppers came to the East, to the Blue Forest, new to my task but faithful in my duty. I tended the council-fire when our headmen met with their chief, a brash, beautiful, broad-shouldered woodsman who assured them that they would leave the settlements unmolested. He smiled and cupped his chest over his heart, insisting that their only interest was easing transport between the City and the larger towns of the Four Lands. Sparks leaped from the firepit as he spoke, and it was all I could do to keep the Fire from flaring to the timbered ceiling.

It is only one Road, he said. *This will be good for your people. A brick path linking all the Four Lands. Think of the possibilities. Think of your future. Wealth untold. You will join the City in a prosperous future. And think: what will happen when your neighbours grow rich and you have nothing? The future is not with forests and fields. It is with swift thinking, quick action, clockwork and progress. Structure. Order. Certainty. These are the ways of the City. These can be yours, too.*

He asked for nothing more than the right to pass unmolested through our lands, and the right to the timber felled on each side of their road. When he left, the headmen withdrew to consider the proposal. I remained in the greathouse to tend my obligations, but the Fire would not be calmed—she quivered and raged in ways I had never seen. Cinders popped, ash billowed upward, choking the light from the smoke-hole above.

As I tried to soothe her, I heard a noise from the doorway. I looked up to see a hunched old woman in midnight blue standing nearby, her dark eyes fixed on the far door, behind which the headmen continued their deliberations.

"Fools," she muttered in a low, mocking voice, and at that moment I knew who she was, and I began to shake. As if aware of my thoughts, she turned her glittering gaze on me, and then she was at my side, her knobbed and gnarled hands clenching my shoulders with a fierce grip.

"They forget the land," she said, her unblinking gaze never wavering from my own. "They forget their duty. They think this road will be their freedom, but they wrap the snare firmly around their own throats." She grinned then, and a groan escaped my trembling lips as I looked upon row after row of sliver-sharp teeth, moon-bright in a mouth that stretched too wide for her face.

I wanted to turn away, but her eyes and hands held me tightly, and I felt her mind move into my own, unravelling all my secrets, fears, and desires, even those I had long hidden from myself. And when she had unravelled all, she laughed again. "Did you think yourself so clever that you could hide these things from me?" she purred as she released me, and I fell sobbing to the plank floor. I lay there for some time with eyes squeezed shut. When at last I remembered my duty and risked a glance, Old Blue Woman was gone.

That night, the headmen made their decision. The Smiling Man would have his road. The Choppers would have a clear path. And I would be Fire-keeper to their bold young leader, to teach him respect for the forests he came to fell, to serve as the headmen's eyes and voice when the cutting ceased and the men rested for the night.

I should have been honoured. I should have been warned. But all I could think about was the old woman's terrible, knowing smile.

His name was Nic. He carried the axe like a lover, and wielded it like it was made of his own flesh and bone. It shone as sun-bright as his broad smile, and there were times I turned away, heart pounding, dazzled by the brilliance of the sweat on his muscled chest. He seemed to enjoy my discomfort, but he was always kind, and he always thanked me for his food each night as we sat together by the Fire.

He had set his men at camps along the planned roadway. Every day they would work together in long lines through the woods, and the axes rang and the trees crashed from dawn until dusk. Every night, the men would return to their camps, where others waited with food. And every night, he returned to his simple cabin where only the two of us lingered. He asked me of the forest, of my people, of my dreams. He told me little of his life in the City, of his family, of his clan. But never seemed to lack interest in the ways of my world and the People.

Every day he drove his men deeper into the trees, but every night, he returned to my fireside, and the nights were ours alone. He seemed to fear the darkness; he shuddered at the wood-lion's roars. He took comfort from the Fire, and, at last, from me.

Late one sweltering night, when at last he reached out, my body burned with another fire, one so fierce I thought I would never be quenched again. I surrendered to these flames. I held him tightly and felt his heartbeat melt into mine. We rolled together into the grass with ravenous kisses, seeking sustenance no food could provide. There was nothing our fingers and lips did not touch, no soft secret places left unexplored and untasted. When at last he pulled me close and thrust deep, he whispered words I did not understand, words that sounded to my unknowing ears like love. And as he quivered and gasped and I wept for the beauty of the moment, I glanced to the sky and saw the moon gazing back at me, grinning wide like a hungry tiger. I shivered then, but the heat had suddenly chilled, for I had seen that bright-toothed smile before.

Each day the forest diminished, and each night our passions flared. *Nimmee ammee,* he called me—beloved one in the language of the City. And I believed him. I believed everything he said, never once thinking about what his words meant, even when everything I saw around me told otherwise. Perhaps I did not want to know, for knowledge meant accountability, and I was increasingly failing my people, the land, myself. I forgot my duty to my headmen and to my clan. Even the Fire suffered, for I was too distracted to harvest the best deadfall and chose still-green wood that smoked and sputtered as it struggled to bright life. All that mattered was enduring the long shadows of the endless daytime until Nic was back beside the flames and back in my arms. The Fire never burned so fiercely.

Old Blue Woman warned the headmen that a storm was coming, that they were foolishly squandering the land and her blessings, but beautiful goods began to make their way from the City, and the People were soon dressed in false finery they had never known before. These glittering baubles and colourful fabrics seemed an endless stream, and the People gasped with oohs and awes at each new wagonload from their generous new friend, the Smiling Man.

But after the Choppers came the Pavers, and eventually the gifts came to a halt. The great golden Road stretched long through the Blue Forest to the endless sands at our eastern borders.

It was harvest-time. The cornfields had grown tall, and the crows were fearless. Even our best scarecrows did little to frighten them away; the birds knew we were distracted by larger worries than a missing corncob or two.

The Road was not what we had anticipated. It came too near to the greater settlements, too close to our autumn fields and winter storehouses. Even someone as love-besotted as I was could see that its strange, meandering path was no accident. More than anyone else, I knew that route, for it had been built along the path of stories I had shared over the days, weeks, and months I lay beside Nic in the darkness of the cabin I now called home. He had so many questions, and I had answered them all. And now, at last, I understood.

I had been too generous, too blind, too foolish. It was as Old Blue Woman had said. This was not a road built for trade. It was a road built for War.

Their kindness turned sour. Their numbers swelled, and they needed more food than we could give. When our headmen at last refused their unending demands, telling them that our children were going hungry and that our folk needed care, too, the Choppers and Pavers took it themselves, shaming our headmen and the speaker-women. Our fields were diminished, and even the crows were incensed by their arrogance.

And having lived among us the longest and benefited of our generosity the most, the mockery of the Choppers cut deepest. They knew that we were the People of the Blue Maize, the descendants of Maizemother and the Deerman, born from the marriage of the earth and the first four-legged folk of the forest. But the City-men laughed and called us cob-biters, tassel-twirlers, the sad and silly little munch-corns. They raided our storehouses, burned our fields, killed our dogs, and at last drove the People into the deep woods to starve among the fierce and ravenous beasts.

The People at last heard the Old Blue Woman of the East: the Road was the cause of our misery, so the Road must go. And our fighting men struck suddenly from the forest, and under their protection the strong women came with long pikes and shovels. The City-men did not expect the attacks. And they did not understand our strength, or our fury. The little munch-corns sent them fleeing.

The bricks were torn up, the workers' cabins set aflame and their bodies bloodied and bruised. Terrible great beasts stalked the darkness at Old Blue Woman's bidding. Some Choppers and Pavers fled, but others remained true to their duty, and they met each attack with swift, merciless force.

And their numbers grew. Fattened on our crops, they were stronger than we were. Their axes now cleaved flesh, and the Blue Forest burned.

I knew what he had done, what he continued to do. I hated it all, but at that time I thought him courageous. I was ashamed, but I loved him, and mingled love and shame made me want him more now than ever. I wanted to believe that he did not understand what he was doing, that love would clear the veil from his eyes. We did not speak of his work, but we both knew, and we said nothing.

And every new day brought some fresh news of another stretch of the Road that was destroyed, and Nic grew fearful, and some nights he remained at one of the other camps with his fellows, and I was left to tend the Fire alone. And every day there was something new in his eyes when he looked at me. Some nights when he did come back, he refused to touch me. Other times, he was brutal. There was a desperate rage as he took me, as though my love-hungry flesh could contain all his fear and frustration. I wept when it was over. Sometimes he would comfort me. But sometimes he would curse me and leave me alone to nurse my wounds and remember when the flame had been a cleansing one. Now it was all ashes and smoke, only the barest flicker remaining.

But I still reached out; I still wanted him. For there was no one else. The headmen had cast me out for my failure and my treachery. They did not understand my love; all they knew was that I had chosen to remain to tend his Fire, and that was enough. There were none to speak for me, for the land was ravaged, my family was scattered, our house burned, the town at last abandoned. I did not know where they were. Nic was my only protection now.

The War ended when the People surrendered, but the Road remained broken, for the Smiling Man had other Roads through other lands, and he had tired of the little munch-corns in the woods. We had been a distraction, but he had greater concerns. Old Blue Woman had some few lions and tigers and bears at her command, but she had proven less formidable than her fierce sister, Old Yellow Woman of the West, whose winged army proved a true threat, not just to his Road-makers, but to his very City itself. So he called his forces back, and they prepared to return to the City, and to begin their campaign against the lands of the dying sun.

———

"No heart!" I wept when he told me. "You have no heart!" I had found him on the edge of what had once been my clan's greathouse, now charred cinders and wind-tossed ash. All that endured were the ragged remnants of a picked-over cornfield and a mocking scarecrow hanging limply from a rough gibbet nearby. "What will happen to me now?"

"I do not know," he said. There was no fire in his eyes. He looked at me as if I were a stranger.

"Take me with you," I begged, aching to touch him but not daring to reach out. "I can keep your fire, feed you, care for you. Please let me come with you."

Now his cold eyes burned. "I have no need of your help. You belong here, with the rest of your kind."

"But I am your *nimmee ammee*," I whispered.

"Be silent," he hissed and grabbed my arms, glancing over his shoulders to the broken Road and quivering with fearful rage. Sudden awareness dawned on me: his fellows did not know what we had shared. "Never say those words again. You were a convenience, nothing more."

A convenience. All those months of love and sacrifice; all I had given up, all the betrayals unknown and willing. Now I was angry, too. I had surrendered myself to him, abandoned reason and clear thinking, betrayed the People and the land to which we belonged—and for what? I had given everything for him, and *he* was ashamed of *me*? What a brainless fool I had been. Now I saw what he truly was. He was no longer the brave man I had once believed him to be. He was a coward who roared his lion's fury but fled mewling at the slightest threat.

He was frightened, but I was not. I turned down the Road and began shouting every tender word he had whispered, every passionate act we had shared, every base desire I had sated. I would let his City-folk know just what kind of man led them. Nic Chopper was a heartless coward, cheap metal that once gleamed gold, a hollow man without honour. He grabbed me, but I broke free and ran back toward the field, weeping and cursing him and his kind, screaming the truth as loudly as my broken voice could manage. The Fire was dead, reduced to brittle ash. All that remained was cold, relentless truth, which I shouted to the blood-streaked sky and the dark crows that circled above.

I did not see him grab his axe. I turned only when I heard the whistle of the blade. There was a blinding silver light, searing pain, and then, nothing.

———

Death whistled at my side, and with it came Old Blue Woman. "All things come at a cost," she said, stroking my cooling cheek. This time she did not smile. She looked worn beyond the count of years.

"You gave much for false love, foolish Fire-Boy. But your fate is not yet finished; great things await you, if you are brave enough to risk them. I can hold
you here for a few moments longer. Great things incur great debts—you must
give something precious now, if you would stay. But it must be your choice."

I did not understand. I knew only that I did not want to go. So I said yes.

A freed spirit needs a home, lest it scatter like a breath in the breeze. She
glanced over to the scarecrow hanging in the dying field. She cupped her hands
and carried me to it, gently, as if I were a fragile moth. "This will be your home
now, brainless one." Then she looked at my torn clothes and sack-cloth face,
and gave me a new name in recognition of my new birth. "Tatterborn. That
suits you well, a good name for a new man in what has become this patchwork
world of ours."

She told the crows to keep me company and to teach me once again what
it was to be a Maize Person. I had forgotten, but I could remember. She said
that she would not return, that I was their responsibility now, for she had other
work to attend to. As she limped toward the dark tree-line, she turned and
winked at me, and the smile she gave was a promise.

She had failed to stop the Smiling Man; she had diminished, now little
more than a scorned witch, not the great Power she had once been before the
days of the City and its Roads and its hunger for trees and gold and obedi-
ence. But she was still the Old Blue Woman; she was still one of the fierce and
fearsome mothers of the Four Lands. The People had abandoned her, but she
had not abandoned us.

I knew her destination. And in spite of all that had happened, for a brief
moment, I pitied Nic Chopper.

My voice was strange, but I could speak. But there was no one who shared my
language. My family, my clan, all were gone. Old Blue Woman was gone. Nic,
too, was gone. And the fire was long dead. The crows spoke to me, but I did
not understand them, not for a very long time.

The Choppers and Pavers were gone, too, but brigands roamed what
remained of the Road, looting and burning as they went. And then I learned
the price of my new existence. Fire was no longer my friend. She, too, had
abandoned me. It was the least that I deserved.

Over time, the crows taught me their speech, and others. I was an eager
student, and I learned of ways and worlds I had never before dreamed of. And
I learned that others had known loves like mine, but many had flourished,

making the hearts and minds of those who shared honestly and gently even greater than they had been before. Mine had been a selfish love, done in service to another's greed and need. It was not a gift shared and accepted with generosity. For a time I wanted more of those stories, but they soon came to torment me, and I asked them to share other news. I wanted no more tales of great, good love, for they reminded me too much of my failure.

So the crows told me of the fierce War in the far West, where Old Yellow Woman had driven the Smiling Man's forces from her land. She now made her way toward the City, where she intended to put an end to the Smiling Man's ambitions one way or another, with or without help from her sisters.

And they told me of Nic's grief, of his flight into the forest after he killed me, and of the old woman in robes of midnight blue who visited his cabin that very night. There were stranger stories, too, of a strange statue that now stood at his doorway, a man made of metal but with no heart in his chest, an empty man who wept all day and night.

The crows suspected that the Smiling Man learned to command storms from the Old Red Woman of the South, who never did much like her sisters. In spite of everything, Old Blue Woman took care of her own, but for all her wisdom even she was taken by surprise by the storm.

We all felt her death, and we grieved, though I no longer had tears to weep. So I spoke to the crows and to the clouds and told them of the life I had been given and the things I had learned. I no longer feared rain or darkness; I never quailed when the hunted lion slunk past my pole in the twilight, or when the winds whipped the treetops to a frenzy.

There was little I missed about the life I had lost, but once, in the distance, a woodman's campfire sparked to life, and I remembered flames, and heat, and the welcome warmth of bodies glistening and shimmering in the darkness. And in those memories, I walked boldly on the earth among the People, and I belonged to them. But that fire had long ago gone cold. I no longer spoke to the crows, and they left me. I was alone.

The Girl was a very queer creature, all elbows and ankles in a too-big dress, but she spoke kindly to me, and I was lonely. I remembered very little, but as she talked I remembered the Smiling Man, and the Fire. I would never know the warmth of the flames again, or dance to her light, or sing those songs with others, the ones that kept us strong for so long until we abandoned them for the chiming clockwork trinkets of the City.

I joined the Girl and her little dog on the Road. It was in the forest that we found what Nic had become. He did not know me then, but he still grieved my death. So I forgave him.

The rest of the story is known, though the details change with the teller: the addition of a sullen, sickly beast to our strange company, the quest to the Old Yellow Woman's stronghold and her unintended death, the unmasking of the Smiling Man for the cringing charlatan he was, the end of the Western War, the Girl's return to her homeland, my elevation to the seat of the City and, now, Old Red Woman's supremacy. She smiles more than her sisters ever did, and she is far more dangerous, for the People love her but they do not fear her. It is a blind, selfish love, one that burns too quickly, one never reflected in her smile. It will be their undoing.

Nic knows me now. He swears his eternal love, but now I, too, am heartless. It does not grieve me as it does him. I gave to him what I loved the most. And he reduced it to ashes. So we sit alone, together, in this City of greed and lies, and wait for Old Red Woman to reveal herself. Perhaps we will stop her. Perhaps.

Life is colder now than it was, but there is clarity there, too. No fog of warmth, no mist of passion. No heat to be given, none received. Always I remain apart from the memories: memories of Fire, forests, fields. Family. They are all far, far away, in a world I once knew and served well. That world endures, but I am no longer part of it. I gave it up, but I no longer remember why. And although I now live in this glittering, glamourous City of jewels and always smiling people, I find that I am still a stranger here, always.

And deep in the darkness of night, when the people and the animals are sleeping and Nic has left me to my silent reverie, when I stand at the balcony and watch campfires flare in the distance, I wonder at Old Blue Woman's last words to me. I wonder about this place, and this world, and this body of burlap and oats and straw and stained cloth, all reduced to ash with the kiss of a single spark. Is there no place that is home? Is there nothing that endures? Smoke rises to the stars. But where does it go then?

It is cold here in the City tonight; it is cold *every* night. But of all my muddled memories, I remember Fire.

And that is the memory that makes me smile.

～ *Men on the Moon* ～
Simon Ortiz

Born and raised near Albuquerque, New Mexico, Acoma Pueblo author Simon Ortiz grew up speaking the Acoma language, which he credits with shaping the thinking behind his work. His deep engagement with the language and landscape of his home makes him one of the most respected and widely read Indigenous writers on Turtle Island. Ortiz is a prolific writer, publishing children's books, memoirs, non-fiction, short stories, and a number of books of poetry, including *Song, Poetry, and Language* (1978), *Woven Stone* (1992), and *Men on the Moon: Collected Short Stories* (1999). His literary career began in 1968, when he received a fellowship for writing in the International Writers Program at the University of Iowa. In 1993, he received a Lifetime Achievement Award from the *Returning the Gift* Festival of Native Writers and the Native Writers' Circle of the Americas.

Originally published in *Howbah Indians* (1978), "Men on the Moon" tells the story of the *Apollo 11* astronauts' journey to the moon through the eyes of an old man who, like so many other "Mericanos," watches the events live on television. Ortiz provides the story's insight and humour by interrupting the excitement that accompanied the event. While history remembers and records *Apollo 11* as one of America's greatest achievements—and one of its most widely viewed television events—the old man's incredulous response to the first great space mission highlights the colonial desire that propelled it. When his grandson tells him that the men are journeying there for knowledge, he wonders whether "they have run out of places to look for knowledge on the earth" (339). Don't let the setting of this story fool you. In shifting the narrative action away from the heroic explorer, "Men on the Moon" asks the reader to question the ideologies and desires that support science fiction, while recasting the action of that genre within local, land-based frameworks.

I

Joselita brought her father, Faustin, the TV on Father's Day. She brought it over after Sunday mass, and she had her son hook up the antenna. She plugged the TV cord into the wall socket.

Faustin sat on a worn couch. He was covered with an old coat. He had worn that coat for twenty years.

It's ready. Turn it on and I'll adjust the antenna, Amarosho told his mother. The TV warmed up and then the screen flickered into dull light. It was snowing. Amarosho tuned it a bit. It snowed less and then a picture formed.

Look, Naishtiya, Joselita said. She touched her father's hand and pointed at the TV.

I'll turn the antenna a bit and you tell me when the picture is clear, Amarosho said. He climbed on the roof again.

After a while the picture turned clearer. It's better! his mother shouted. There was only the tiniest bit of snow falling.

That's about the best it can get, I guess, Amarosho said. Maybe it'll clear up on the other channels. He turned the selector. It was clearer on another channel.

There were two men struggling mightily with each other. Wrestling, Amarosho said.

Do you want to watch wrestling? Two men are fighting, Nana. One of them is Apache Red. Chisheh tsah, he told his grandfather.

The old man stirred. He had been staring intently into the TV. He wondered why there was so much snow at first. Now there were two men fighting. One of them was a Chisheh—an Apache—and the other was a Mericano. There were people shouting excitedly and clapping hands within the TV.

The two men backed away from each other for a moment and then they clenched again. They wheeled mightily and suddenly one threw the other. The old man smiled. He wondered why they were fighting.

Something else showed on the TV screen. A bottle of wine was being poured. The old man liked the pouring sound and he moved his mouth and lips. Someone was selling wine.

The two fighting men came back on the TV. They struggled with each other, and after a while one of them didn't get up. And then another man came and held up the hand of the Apache, who was dancing around in a feathered headdress.

It's over, Amarosho announced. Apache Red won the fight, Nana.

The Chisheh won. Faustin stared at the other fighter, a light-haired man who looked totally exhausted and angry with himself. The old man didn't like the Apache too much. He wanted them to fight again.

After a few minutes, something else appeared on the TV.

What is that? Faustin asked. In the TV picture was an object with smoke coming from it. It was standing upright.

Men are going to the moon, Nana, Amarosho said. That's *Apollo*. It's going to fly three men to the moon.

That thing is going to fly to the moon?

Yes, Nana, his grandson said.

What is it called again? Faustin asked.

Apollo, a spaceship rocket, Joselita told her father.

The *Apollo* spaceship stood on the ground, emitting clouds of something, something that looked like smoke.

A man was talking, telling about the plans for the flight, what would happen, that it was almost time. Faustin could not understand the man very well because he didn't know many words in the language of the Mericano.

He must be talking about that thing flying in the air? he said.

Yes. It's about ready to fly away to the moon.

Faustin remembered that the evening before he had looked at the sky and seen that the moon was almost in the middle phase. He wondered if it was important that the men get to the moon.

Are those men looking for something on the moon, Nana? he asked his grandson.

They're trying to find out what's on the moon, Nana. What kind of dirt and rocks there are and to see if there's any water. Scientist men don't believe there is any life on the moon. The men are looking for knowledge, Amarosho said to Faustin.

Faustin wondered if the men had run out of places to look for knowledge on the earth. Do they know if they'll find knowledge? he asked.

They have some already. They've gone before and come back. They're going again.

Did they bring any back?

They brought back some rocks, Amarosho said.

Rocks. Faustin laughed quietly. The American scientist men went to search for knowledge on the moon and they brought back rocks. He kind of thought that perhaps Amarosho was joking with him. His grandson had gone to Indian School for a number of years, and sometimes he would tell his grandfather some strange and funny things.

The old man was suspicious. Sometimes they joked around. Rocks. You sure that's all they brought back? he said. Rocks!

That's right, Nana, only rocks and some dirt and pictures they made of what it looks like on the moon.

The TV picture was filled with the rocket spaceship close-up now. Men were sitting and standing and moving around some machinery, and the TV voice had become more urgent. The old man watched the activity in the picture intently but with a slight smile on his face.

Suddenly it became very quiet, and the TV voice was firm and commanding and curiously pleading. Ten, nine, eight, seven, six, five, four, three, two, one, liftoff. The white smoke became furious, and a muted rumble shook through the TV. The rocket was trembling and the voice was trembling.

It was really happening, the old man marveled. Somewhere inside of that cylinder with a point at its top and long slender wings were three men who were flying to the moon.

The rocket rose from the ground. There were enormous clouds of smoke and the picture shook. Even the old man became tense, and he grasped the edge of the couch. The rocket spaceship rose and rose.

There's fire coming out of the rocket, Amarosho explained. That's what makes it fly.

Fire. Faustin had wondered what made it fly. He had seen pictures of other flying machines. They had long wings, and someone had explained to him that there was machinery inside which spun metal blades that made the machines fly. He had wondered what made this thing fly. He hoped his grandson wasn't joking him.

After a while there was nothing but the sky. The rocket *Apollo* had disappeared. It hadn't taken very long, and the voice on the TV wasn't excited anymore. In fact, the voice was very calm and almost bored.

I have to go now, Naishtiya, Joselita told her father. I have things to do.

Me too, Amarosho said.

Wait, the old man said, wait. What shall I do with this thing? What do you call it?

TV, his daughter said. You watch it. You turn it on and you watch it.

I mean how do you stop it? Does it stop like the radio, like the mahkina? It stops?

This way, Nana, Amarosho said and showed his grandfather. He turned a round knob on the TV and the picture went away.

He turned the knob again, and the picture flickered on again. Were you afraid this one-eye would be looking at you all the time? Amarosho laughed and gently patted the old man's shoulder.

Faustin was relieved. Joselita and her son left. Faustin watched the TV picture for a while. A lot of activity was going on, a lot of men were moving among machinery, and a couple of men were talking. And then the spaceship rocket was shown again.

The old man watched it rise and fly away again. It disappeared again. There was nothing but the sky. He turned the knob and the picture died away. He turned it on and the picture came on again. He turned it off. He went outside and to a fence a short distance from his home. When he finished peeing, he zipped up his pants and studied the sky for a while.

II

That night, he dreamed.

Flintwing Boy was watching a Skquuyuh mahkina come down a hill. The mahkina made a humming noise. It was walking. It shone in the sunlight. Flintwing Boy moved to a better position to see. The mahkina kept on moving toward him.

The Skquuyuh mahkina drew closer. Its metal legs stepped upon trees and crushed growing flowers and grass. A deer bounded away frightened. Tsushki came running to Flintwing Boy.

Anahweh, Tsushki cried, trying to catch his breath.

What is it, Anahweh?

You've been running, Flintwing Boy said.

The coyote was staring at the thing, which was coming toward them. There was wild fear in his eyes.

What is that, Anahweh? What is that thing? Tsushki gasped.

It looks like a mahkina, but I've never seen one quite like it before. It must be some kind of Skquuyuh mahkina, Anahweh, Flintwing Boy said. When he saw that Tsushki was trembling with fear, he said, Sit down, Anahweh. Rest yourself. We'll find out soon enough.

The Skquuyuh mahkina was undeterred. It walked over and through everything. It splashed through a stream of clear water. The water boiled and streaks of oil flowed downstream. It split a juniper tree in half with a terrible crash. It crushed a boulder into dust with a sound of heavy metal. Nothing stopped the Skquuyuh mahkina. It hummed.

Anahweh, Tsushki cried, what can we do?

Flintwing Boy reached into the bag hanging at his side. He took out an object. It was a flint arrowhead. He took out some cornfood.

Come over here, Anahweh. Come over here. Be calm, he motioned to the frightened coyote. He touched the coyote in several places on his body with the arrowhead and put cornfood in the palm of his hand.

This way, Flintwing Boy said. He closed Tsushki's fingers over the cornfood. They stood facing east. Flintwing Boy said, We humble ourselves again. We look in your direction for guidance. We ask for your protection. We humble our poor bodies and spirits because only you are the power and the source and the knowledge. Help us, then. That is all we ask.

Flintwing Boy and Tsushki breathed on the cornfood, then took in the breath of all directions and gave the cornfood unto the ground.

Now the ground trembled with the awesome power of the Skquuyuh mahkina. Its humming vibrated against everything.

Flintwing Boy reached over his shoulder and took several arrows from his quiver. He inspected them carefully and without any rush he fit one to his bowstring.

And now, Anahweh, Flintwing Boy said, you must go and tell everyone. Describe what you have seen. The people must talk among themselves and learn what this is about, and decide what they will do. You must hurry, but you must not alarm the people. Tell them I am here to meet the Skquuyuh mahkina. Later I will give them my report.

Tsushki turned and began to run. He stopped several yards away. Hahtrudzaimeh! he called to Flintwing Boy. Like a man of courage, Anah-weh, like our people.

The old man stirred in his sleep. A dog was barking. He awoke fully and got out of his bed and went outside. The moon was past the midpoint, and it would be daylight in a few hours.

III

Later, the spaceship reached the moon.

Amarosho was with his grandfather Faustin. They watched a TV replay of two men walking on the moon.

So that's the men on the moon, Faustin said.

Yes, Nana, there they are, Amarosho said.

There were two men inside of heavy clothing, and they carried heavy-look-ing equipment on their backs.

The TV picture showed a closeup of one of them and indeed there was a man's face inside of glass. The face moved its mouth and smiled and spoke, but the voice seemed to be separate from the face.

It must be cold, Faustin said. They have on heavy clothing.

It's supposed to be very cold and very hot on the moon. They wear special clothes and other things for protection from the cold and heat, Amarosho said.

The men on the moon were moving slowly. One of them skipped like a boy, and he floated alongside the other.

The old man wondered if they were underwater. They seem to be able to float, he said.

The information I have heard is that a man weighs less on the moon than he does on earth, Amarosho said to his grandfather. Much less, and he floats. And there is no air on the moon for them to breathe, so those boxes on their backs carry air for them to breathe.

A man weighs less on the moon, the old man thought. And there is no air on the moon except for the boxes on their backs. He looked at Amarosho, but his grandson did not seem to be joking with him.

The land on the moon looked very dry. It looked like it had not rained for a long, long time. There were no trees, no plants, no grass. Nothing but dirt and rocks, a desert.

Amarosho had told him that men on earth—scientists—believed there was no life on the moon. Yet those men were trying to find knowledge on the moon. Faustin wondered if perhaps they had special tools with which they could find knowledge even if they believed there was no life on the moon.

The mahkina sat on the desert. It didn't make a sound. Its metal feet were planted flat on the ground. It looked somewhat awkward. Faustin searched around the mahkina, but there didn't seem to be anything except the dry land on the TV. He couldn't figure out the mahkina. He wasn't sure whether it moved and could cause harm. He didn't want to ask his grandson that question.

After a while, one of the bulky men was digging in the ground. He carried a long, thin tool with which he scooped up dirt and put it into a container. He did this for a while.

Is he going to bring the dirt back to earth too? Faustin asked. I think he is, Nana, Amarosho said. Maybe he'll get some rocks too. Watch.

Indeed, several minutes later, the man lumbered over to a pile of rocks and gathered several handsized ones. He held them out proudly. They looked just like rocks from around anyplace. The voice on the TV seemed to be excited about the rocks.

They will study the rocks, too, for knowledge?

Yes, Nana.

What will they use the knowledge for, Nana?

They say they will use it to better mankind, Nana. I've heard that. And to learn more about the universe in which we live. Also, some of the scientists say the knowledge will be useful in finding out where everything began a long time ago and how everything was made in the beginning.

Faustin looked with a smile at his grandson. He said, You are telling me the true facts, aren't you?

Why, yes, Nana. That's what they say. I'm not just making it up, Amarosho said.

Well then, do they say why they need to know where and how everything began? Hasn't anyone ever told them?

I think other people have tried to tell them but they want to find out for themselves, and also they claim they don't know enough and need to know more and for certain, Amarosho said.

The man in the bulky suit had a small pickax in his hand. He was striking at a boulder. The breathing of the man could be heard clearly. He seemed to be working very hard and was very tired.

Faustin had once watched a work crew of Mericano drilling for water. They had brought a tall mahkina with a loud motor. The mahkina would raise a limb at its center to its very top and then drop it with a heavy and loud metal clang. The mahkina and its men sat at one spot for several days, and finally they found water.

The water had bubbled out weakly, gray-looking, and did not look drinkable at all. And then the Mericano workmen lowered the mahkina, put their equipment away, and drove away. The water stopped flowing. After a couple of days, Faustin went and checked out the place.

There was nothing there except a pile of gray dirt and an indentation in the ground. The ground was already dry, and there were dark spots of oil-soaked dirt.

Faustin decided to tell Amarosho about the dream he had had.

After the old man finished, Amarosho said, Old man, you're telling me the truth now, aren't you? You know that you've become somewhat of a liar. He was teasing his grandfather.

Yes, Nana. I have told you the truth as it occurred to me that night. Everything happened like that except I might not have recalled everything about it.

That's some story, Nana, but it's a dream.

It's a dream, but it's the truth, Faustin said.

I believe you, Nana, his grandson said.

IV

Some time after that the spacemen returned to earth. Amarosho told his grandfather they had splashed down in the ocean.

Are they alright? Faustin asked.

Yes, Amarosho said. They have devices to keep them safe. Are they in their homes now?

No, I think they have to be someplace where they can't contaminate anything. If they brought back something from the moon that they weren't supposed to, they won't pass it on to someone else, Amarosho said to his grandfather.

What would that something be?

Something harmful, Nana.

In that dry desert land of the moon there might be something harmful, the old man said. I didn't see any strange insects or trees or even cactus. What would that harmful thing be, Nana?

Disease which might harm people on earth, Amarosho said.

You said there was the belief by the men that there is no life on the moon. Is there life after all? Faustin asked.

There might be the tiniest bit of life.

Yes, I see now, Nana. If the men find even the tiniest bit of life on the moon, then they will believe, the old man said.

Yes. Something like that.

Faustin figured it out now. The Mericano men had taken that trip in a spaceship rocket to the moon to find even the tiniest bit of life. And when they found even the tiniest bit of life, even if it was harmful, they would believe that they had found knowledge. Yes, that must be the way it was.

He remembered his dream clearly now. The old man was relieved.

When are those two men fighting again, Nana? he asked Amarosho.

What two men?

Those two men who were fighting with each other the day those Mericano spaceship men were flying to the moon.

Oh, those men. I don't know, Nana. Maybe next Sunday. You like them?

Yes. I think the next time I will be cheering for the Chisheh. He'll win again. He'll beat the Mericano again, Faustin said.

➤ Father, Son, Holy Rabbit ➤
Stephen Graham Jones

Blackfeet author Stephen Graham Jones is a prolific genre fiction author, with five collections of short fiction and fifteen novels to date. Jones has written crime fiction, science fiction, and experimental fiction, but he is best known as a writer of horror. He has been a finalist for the Bram Stoker Award (named after the author of *Dracula*), the Black Quill Award, and the International Horror Guild Award. His short-story collection, *After the People Lights Have Gone Off* (2014), was selected by the web-based organization, *This is Horror*, for the Short Story Collection of the Year. Jones was born in West Texas and has a PhD from the University of Florida, which he completed in just two years. He is a professor of English at the University of Colorado–Boulder.

"Father, Son, Holy Rabbit" was originally published as the opening story in Jones's collection, *The Ones That Got Away* (2010). The story is loosely based on the author's own experience hunting—and getting lost—on a reservation and is told from the perspective of a young boy whose understanding of the situation is limited and partial. That the perspective is restricted to the unnamed boy is integral to the story's suspense and horror, which erupts as a chilling reveal in the final pages. While certainly unsettling, "Father, Son, Holy Rabbit" is not "just" a horror story. It is also a survival tale, speaking to the deep love between a father and a son, and the lengths to which a parent will go to protect their child. On yet another level, "Father, Son, Holy Rabbit" is a retelling of the Catholic sacrament of transubstantiation. Substituting "Holy Rabbit" for "Holy Ghost," Jones connects the Holy Trinity to land and the natural environment, casting a different light on the sacred and divine. From whatever perspective you read it, Jones's story is a deeply captivating and evocative read.

By the third day they were eating snow. Years later it would come to the boy again, rush up to him at a job interview: his father spitting out pieces of seed or pine needle into his hand. Whatever had been in the snow. The boy had looked at the brown flecks in his father's palm, then up to his father, who finally nodded, put them back in his mouth, turned his face away to swallow.

Instead of sleeping, they thumped each other in the face to stay awake.

The place they'd found under the tree wasn't out of the wind, but it was dry.

They had no idea where the camp was, or how to find the truck from there, or the highway after that. They didn't even have a gun, just the knife the boy's father kept strapped to his right hip.

The first two days, the father had shrugged and told the boy not to worry, that the storm couldn't last.

The whole third day, he'd sat watching the snow fall like ash.

The boy didn't say anything, not even inside, not even a prayer. One of the times he drifted off, though, waking not to the slap of his father's fingernail on his cheek but the sound of it, there was a picture he brought up with him from sleep. A rabbit.

He told his father about it and his father nodded, pulled his lower lip into his mouth, and smiled like the boy had just told a joke.

That night they fell asleep.

This time the boy woke to his father rubbing him all over, trying to make his blood flow. The boy's father was crying, so the boy told him about the rabbit, how it wasn't even white like it should be, but brown, lost like them.

His father hugged his knees to his chest and bounced up and down, stared out at all the white past their tree.

"A rabbit?" he said.

The boy shrugged.

Sometime later that day he woke again, wasn't sure where he was at first. His father wasn't there. The boy moved his mouth up and down, didn't know what to say. Rounded off in the crust of the snow were the dragging holes his father had made, walking away. The boy put his hand in the first, then the second, then stood from the tree into the real cold. He followed the tracks until they became confused. He tried to follow them back to the tree but the light was different now. Finally he started running, falling down, getting up, his chest on fire.

His father found him sometime that night, pulled him close.

They lowered themselves under another tree.

"Where were you?" the boy asked.

"That rabbit," the father said, stroking the boy's hair down.

"You saw it?"

Instead of answering, the father just stared.

This tree wasn't as good as the last. The next morning they looked for another, and another, and stumbled onto their first one.

"Home again home again," the father said, guiding the boy under then gripping onto the back of his jacket, stopping him.

There were tracks coming up out of the dirt, onto the snow. Double tracks, like the split hoof of an elk, except bigger.

"Your rabbit," the father said.

The boy smiled.

That night his father carved their initials into the trunk of the tree with his knife. Later he broke a dead branch off, tried sharpening it. The boy watched, fascinated, hungry.

"Will it work?" he asked.

His father thumped him in the face, woke him. He asked it again, with his mouth this time.

The father shrugged. His lips were cracked, lined with blood, his beard pushing up through his skin.

"Where do you think it is right now?" he said to the boy.

"The—the rabbit?"

The father nodded.

The boy closed his eyes, turned his head, then opened his eyes again, used them to point the way he was facing. The father used his sharp stick as a cane, stood with it, and walked in that direction, folded himself into the blowing snow.

The boy knew this was going to work.

In the hours his father was gone, he studied their names in the tree. While the boy had been asleep, his father had carved the boy's mother's name into the bark as well. The boy ran the pads of his fingers over the grooves, brought the taste to his tongue.

The next thing he knew was ice. It was falling down on him in layers.

His father had returned, had collapsed into the side of the tree.

The boy rolled him in, rubbed his back and face and neck, and then saw what his father was balled around, what he'd been protecting for miles, maybe: the rabbit. It was brown at the tips of its coat, the rest white.

With his knife, the father opened the rabbit in a line down the stomach, poured the meat out. It steamed.

Over it, the father looked at the son, nodded.

They scooped every bit of red out that the rabbit had, swallowed it in chunks because if they chewed they tasted what they were doing. All that was left was the skin. The father scraped it with the blade of his knife, gave those scrapings to the boy.

"Glad your mom's not here to see this," he said.

The boy smiled, wiped his mouth.

Later, he threw up in his sleep, then looked at it soaking into the loose dirt, then turned to see if his father had seen what he'd done, how he'd betrayed him.

His father was sleeping. The boy lay back down, forced the rabbit back into his mouth then angled his arm over his lips, so he wouldn't lose his food again.

The next day, no helicopters came for them, no men on horseback, following dogs, no skiers poling their way home. For a few hours around what should have been lunch, the sun shone down, but all that did was make their dry spot under the tree wet. Then the wind started again.

"Where's that stick?" the boy asked.

The father narrowed his eyes as if he hadn't thought of that. "Your rabbit," he said after a few minutes.

The boy nodded, said, almost to himself, "It'll come back."

When he looked around to his father, his father was already looking at him. Studying him.

The rabbit's skin was out in the snow, just past the tree. Buried hours ago.

The father nodded like this could maybe be true. That the rabbit would come back. Because they needed it to.

The next day he went out again, with a new stick, and came back with his lips blue, one of his legs frozen wet from stepping through some ice into a creek. No rabbit. What he said about the creek was that it was a good sign. You could usually follow water one way or another, to people.

The boy didn't ask which way.

"His name is Slaney," he said.

"The rabbit?"

The boy nodded. Slaney. Things that had names were real.

That night they slept, then woke somehow at the same time, the boy under his father's heavy, jacketed arm. They were both looking the same direction, their faces even with the crust of snow past their tree. Twenty feet out, its nose tasting the air, was Slaney.

The boy felt his father's breath deepen.

"Don't … don't …" his father said, low, then exploded over the boy, crashed off into the day without his stick, even.

He came back an hour later with nothing slung over his shoulder, nothing balled against his stomach. No blood on his hands.

This time the son prayed, inside. Promised not to throw any of the meat up again. With the tip of his knife, his father carved a cartoon rabbit into the trunk of their tree. It looked like a frog with horse ears.

"Slaney," the boy said.

The father carved that in a line under the rabbit's feet, then circled the boy's mother's name over and over, until the boy thought that piece of the bark was going to come off like a plaque.

The next time the boy woke, he was already sitting up.

"What?" the father said.

The boy nodded the direction he was facing.

The father watched his eyes, nodded, then got his stick.

This time he didn't come back for nearly a day. The boy, afraid, climbed up into the tree, then higher, as high as he could, until the wind could reach him.

His father reached up with his stick, tapped him awake.

Like a football in the crook of his arm was the rabbit. It was bloody and wonderful, already cut open.

"You ate the guts," the boy said, his mouth full.

His father reached into the rabbit, came out with a long sliver of meat. The muscle that runs along the spine, maybe.

The boy ate and ate and then, when they were done, trying not to throw up, he placed the rabbit skin in the same spot he'd placed the last one. The coat was just the same—white underneath, brown at the tips.

"It'll come back, " he told his father.

His father rubbed the side of his face. His hand was crusted with blood.

The next day there were no walkie-talkies crackling through the woods, no four-wheelers or snowmobiles churning through the snow. And the rabbit skin was gone.

"Hungry?" the boy's father said, smiling, leaning on his stick just to stand, and the boy smiled with him.

Four hours later, his father came back with the rabbit again. He was wet to the hips this time.

"The creek?" the boy said.

"It's a good sign," the father said back.

Again, the father had fingered the guts into his mouth on the way back, left most of the stringy meat for the boy.

"Slaney," the father said, watching the boy eat.

The boy nodded, closed his eyes to swallow.

Because of his frozen pants—the creek—the father had to sit with his legs straight out. "A good sign," the boy said after the father was asleep.

The next morning his father pulled another dead branch down, so he had two sticks now, like a skier.

The boy watched him walk off into the bright snow, feeling ahead of himself with the sticks. It made him look like a ragged, four-legged animal, one long since extinct, or made only of fear and suspicion in the first place. The boy palmed some snow into his mouth and held it there until it melted.

This time his father was only gone thirty minutes. He'd had to cross the creek again. Slaney was cradled against his body.

"He was just standing there," the father said, pouring the meat out for the boy. "Like he was waiting for me."

"He knows we need him," the boy said.

One thing he no longer had to do was dab the blood off the meat before eating it. Another was swallow before chewing.

That night his father staggered out into the snow and threw up, then fell down into it. The boy pretended not to see, held his eyes closed when his father came back.

The following morning he told his father not to go out again, not today.

"But Slaney," his father said.

"I'm not hungry," the boy lied.

The day after that he was, though. It was the day the storm broke. The woods were perfectly still. Birds were even moving from tree to tree again, talking to each other.

In his head, the boy told Slaney not to keep being on the other side of the creek, but he was; the boy's father came back wet to the hip again. His whole frontside was bloodstained now, from hunting, and eating.

The boy scooped the meat into his mouth, watched his father try to sit in one place. Finally he couldn't, fell over on his side. The boy finished eating and curled up against him, only woke when he heard voices, like on a radio.

He sat up and the voices went away.

On the crust of snow, now, since no more had fallen, was Slaney's skin. The boy crawled out to it, studied it, wasn't sure how Slaney could be out there already, reforming, all its muscle growing back, and be here too. But maybe it only worked if you didn't watch.

The boy scooped snow onto the blood-matted coat, curled up by his father again. All that day, his father didn't wake, but he wasn't really sleeping either.

That night, when the snow was melting more, running into their dry spot under the tree, the boy saw little pads of ice out past Slaney. They were footprints, places where the snow had packed down under a boot, into a column. Now that column wasn't melting as fast as the rest.

Instead of going in a line to the creek, these tracks cut straight across.

The boy squatted over them, looked in the direction they were maybe going.

When he stood, there was a tearing sound. The seat of his pants had stuck to his calf while he'd been squatting. It was blood. The boy shook his head no, fell back, pulled his pants down to see if it had come from him.

When it hadn't, he looked back to his father, then just sat in the snow again, his arms around his knees, rocking back and forth.

"Slaney, Slaney," he chanted. Not to eat him again, but just to hold him.

Sometime that night—it was clear, soundless—a flashlight found him, pinned him to the ground.

"Slaney?" he said, looking up into the yellow beam.

The man in the flannel was breathing too hard to talk into his radio the right way. He lifted the boy up, and the boy said it again: "Slaney."

"What?" the man asked.

The boy didn't say anything then.

The other men found the boy's father curled under the tree. When they cut his pants away to understand where the blood was coming from, the boy looked away, the lower lids of his eyes pushing up into his field of vision. Over the years it would come to be one of his mannerisms, a stare that might suggest thoughtfulness to a potential employer, but right then, sitting with a blanket and his first cup of coffee, waiting for a helicopter, it had just been a way of blurring the tree his father was still sleeping under.

Watching like that—both holding his breath and trying not to focus— when the boy's father finally stood, he was an unsteady smear against the evergreen. And then the boy had to look.

Somehow, using his sticks as crutches, the boy's father was walking, his head slung low between his shoulders, his sticks reaching out before him like feelers.

When he lurched out from the under the tree, the boy drew his breath in.

The father's pants were tatters, now, and his legs too, where he'd been carving off the rabbit meat, stuffing it into the same skin again and again. He pulled his lower lip into his mouth, nodded once to the boy, then stuck one of his sticks into the ground before him, pulled himself towards it, then repeated the complicated process, pulling himself deeper into the woods.

"Where's he going?" one of the men asked.

The boy nodded, understood, his father retreating into the trees for the last time, having to move his legs from the hip now, like things, and the boy answered—*hunting*—then ran back from the helicopter forty minutes later, to dig in the snow just past their tree, but there was nothing there. Just coldness. His own numb fingers.

"What's he saying?" one of the men asked.

The boy stopped, closed his eyes, tried to hear it too, his own voice, then just let the men pull him out of the snow, into the world of houses and bank loans and, finally, job interviews. Because they were wearing gloves, though, or because it was cold and their fingers were numb too, they weren't able to pull all of him from the woods that day. Couldn't tell that an important part of him was still there, sitting under a blanket, watching his father move across the snow, the poles just extensions of his arms, the boy holding his lips tight against each other. Because it would have been a betrayal, he hadn't let himself throw up what his father had given him, not then, and not years later—seconds ago—when the man across the desk palms a handful of sunflower seeds into his mouth all at once, then holds his hand there to make sure none get away, leans forward a bit for the boy to explain what he's written for a name here on this application.

Slade?

Slake?

Slather, slavery?

What the boy does here, what he's just now realizing he should have been doing all along, is reach across, delicately thump the man's cheek, and then pretend not to see past the office, out the window, to the small brown rabbit in the flowers, watching.

Soon enough it'll be white.

The boy smiles.

Some woods, they're big enough you never find your way out.

➤ *Terminal Avenue* ➤
Eden Robinson

Eden Robinson was born in 1968 and grew up in Kitamaat, a Haisla village near the mostly white community of Kitimat, located east of Haida Gwaii on the coast of mainland British Columbia, Canada. Her father's ancestry is Haisla while her mother's is Heiltsuk. Her uncle is Gordon Robinson, whose short story, "Weegit Discovers Hooks," is included in Chapter 7. Eden Robinson worked in a variety of jobs, such as a mail clerk, dry cleaner, and receptionist, before she enrolled in the creative writing program at the University of British Columbia. In 1996, she published *Traplines*, a critically acclaimed collection of four short stories that she wrote in four months while at UBC. Her first novel, *Monkey Beach* (2000), won the Ethel Wilson Fiction Prize, was nominated for the Giller Prize, and was shortlisted for the IMPAC Dublin Literary Award. In her second novel, *Blood Sports* (2006), the influence of one of her favourite authors, Stephen King, is strongly felt in the story's suspense, twisted violence, and horror. Her third novel, *Son of a Trickster* (2017), the first in a trilogy, is a coming-of-age story that brings together pop culture, traditional Haisla teachings, comedy, and the legacy of violent colonial histories in unexpected, scathing ways.

Robinson has made a name for herself as an author of the dark and disquieting. Her birthday falls on the same day as Edgar Allen Poe. "Terminal Avenue" captures the essence of Robinson's dark sensibility while showcasing her skill in the economy and impact of the short-story form. Originally published in the science fiction anthology, *So Long Been Dreaming* (2004), "Terminal Avenue" casts an Indigenous protagonist into a futuristic and dystopic Vancouver, in which Indigenous communities are under increased threat of extinction as a result of oppressive government policy. The main character makes his living as a sex worker serving the fetishistic desires of a white clientele. The narrative takes place on at least two different levels: one describing the protagonist's current situation, and the other reflecting on the experiences that led him there. Through the interlocking narrative, we come to learn how the protagonist and his family have struggled to maintain their Indigenous identities in the face of an oppressive state order. "Terminal Avenue" is fast, punchy, and exciting storytelling that will change how you think about the future and the representation of Indigenous peoples within it.

His brother once held a peeled orange slice up against the sun. When the light shone through it, the slice became a brilliant amber: the setting sun is this colour, ripe orange.

The uniforms of the five advancing Peace Officers are robin's egg blue, but the slanting light catches their visors and sets their faces aflame.

In his memory, the water of the Douglas Channel is a hard blue, baked to a glassy translucence by the August sun. The mountains in the distance form a crown; *Gabiswa*, the mountain in the centre, is the same shade of blue as his lover's veins.

She raises her arms to sweep her hair from her face. Her breasts lift. In the cool morning air, her nipples harden to knobby raspberries. Her eyes are widening in indignation: he once saw that shade of blue in a dragonfly's wing, but this is another thing he will keep secret.

Say nothing, his mother said, without moving her lips, careful not to attract attention. They waited in their car in silence after that. His father and mother were in the front seat, stiff.

Blood plastered his father's hair to his skull; blood leaked down his father's blank face. In the flashing lights of the patrol car, the blood looked black and moved like honey.

A rocket has entered the event horizon of a black hole. To an observer who is watching this from a safe distance, the rocket trapped here, in the black hole's inescapable halo of gravity, will appear to stop.

To an astronaut in the rocket, however, gravity is a rack that stretches his body like taffy, thinner and thinner, until there is nothing left but x-rays.

———

In full body-armour, the five Peace Officers are sexless and anonymous. With their visors down, they look like old-fashioned astronauts. The landscape they move across is the rapid transit line, the Surreycentral Skytrain station, but if they remove their body-armour, it may as well be the moon.

The Peace Officers begin to match strides until they move like a machine. This is an intimidation tactic that works, is working on him even though he knows what it is. He finds himself frozen. He can't move, even as they roll towards him, a train on invisible tracks.

———

Once, when his brother dared him, he jumped off the high diving tower. He wasn't really scared until he stepped away from the platform. In that moment, he realized he couldn't change his mind.

You stupid shit, his brother said when he surfaced.

In his dreams, everything is the same, except there is no water in the swimming pool and he crashes into the concrete like a dropped pumpkin.

———

He thinks of his brother, who is so perfect he wasn't born, but chiselled from stone. There is nothing he can do against that brown Apollo's face, nothing he can say that will justify his inaction. Kevin would know what to do, with doom coming towards him in formation.

But Kevin is dead. He walked through their mother's door one day, wearing the robin's egg blue uniform of the great enemy, and his mother struck him down. She summoned the ghost of their father and put him in the room, sat him beside her, bloody and stunned. Against this Kevin said, I can stop it, Mom. I have the power to change things now.

She turned away, then the family turned away. Kevin looked at him, pleading, before he left her house and never came back, disappeared. Wil closed his eyes, a dark, secret joy welling in him, to watch his brother fall: Kevin never made the little mistakes in his life, never so much as sprouted a pimple. He made up for it though by doing the unforgivable.

Wil wonders if his brother knows what is happening. If, in fact, he isn't one of the Peace Officers, filled himself with secret joy.

———

His lover will wait for him tonight. Ironically, she will be wearing a complete Peace Officer's uniform, bought at great expense on the black market, and very, very illegal. She will wait at the door of her club, Terminal Avenue, and she will frisk clients that she knows will enjoy it. She will have the playroom ready, with its great wooden beams stuck through with hooks and cages, with its expensive equipment built for the exclusive purpose of causing pain. On a steel cart, her toys will be spread out as neatly as surgical instruments.

When he walks through the door, she likes to have her bouncers, also dressed as Peace Officers, hurl him against the wall. They let him struggle before they handcuff him. Their uniforms are slippery as rubber. He can't get a grip on them. The uniforms are padded with the latest in wonderfabric so no matter how hard he punches them, he can't hurt them. They will drag him into the back and strip-search him in front of clients who pay for the privilege of watching. He stands under a spotlight that shines an impersonal cone of light from the ceiling. The rest of the room is darkened. He can see reflections of glasses, red-eyed cigarettes, the glint of ice clinking against glass, shadows shifting. He can hear zippers coming undone, low moans; he can smell the cum when he's beaten into passivity.

Once, he wanted to cut his hair, but she wouldn't let him, said she'd never speak to him again if he did. She likes it when the bouncers grab him by his hair and drag him to the exploratory table in the centre of the room. She says she likes the way it veils his face when he's kneeling.

In the playroom though, she changes. He can't hurt her the way she wants him to; she is tiring of him. He whips her half-heartedly until she tells the bouncer to do it properly.

A man walked in, one day, in a robin's egg blue uniform, and Wil froze. When he could breathe again, when he could think, he found her watching him, thoughtful.

She borrowed the man's uniform and lay on the table, her face blank and smooth and round as a basketball under the visor. He put a painstick against the left nipple. It darkened and bruised. Her screams were muffled by the helmet. Her bouncers whispered things to her as they pinned her to the table, and he hurt her. When she begged him to stop, he moved the painstick to her right nipple.

He kept going until he was shaking so hard he had to stop.

That's enough for tonight, she said, breathless, wrapping her arms around him, telling the bouncers to leave when he started to cry. My poor virgin. It's not pain so much as it is a cleansing.

Is it, he asked her, one of those whiteguilt things?

She laughed, kissed him. Rocked him and forgave him, on the evening he discovered that it wasn't just easy to do terrible things to another person: it could give pleasure. It could give power.

She said she'd kill him if he told anyone what happened in the playroom. She has a reputation and is vaguely ashamed of her secret weakness. He wouldn't tell, not ever. He is addicted to her pain.

To distinguish it from real uniforms, hers has an inverted black triangle on the left side, just over her heart: asocialism, she says with a laugh, and he doesn't get it. She won't explain it, her blue eyes black with desire as her pupils widened suddenly like a cat's.

The uniforms advancing on him, however, are clean and pure and real.

———

Wil wanted to be an astronaut. He bought the books, he watched the movies and he dreamed. He did well in Physics, Math, and Sciences, and his mother bragged, He's got my brains.

He was so dedicated, he would test himself, just like the astronauts on TV. He locked himself in his closet once with nothing but a bag of potato chips and a bottle of pop. He wanted to see if he could spend time in a small space, alone and deprived. It was July and they had no air conditioning. He fainted in the heat, dreamed that he was floating over the Earth on his way to Mars, weightless.

Kevin found him, dragged him from the closet, and laughed at him.

You stupid shit, he said. Don't you know anything?

When his father slid off the hood leaving a snail's trail of blood, Kevin ran out of the car.

Stop it! Kevin screamed, his face contorted in the headlight's beam. Shadows loomed over him, but he was undaunted. Stop it!

Kevin threw himself on their dad and saved his life.

Wil stayed with their father in the hospital, never left his side. He was there when the Peace Officers came and took their father's statement. When they closed the door in his face and he heard his father screaming. The nurses took him away and he let them. Wil watched his father withdraw into himself after that, never quite healing.

He knew the names of all the constellations, the distance of the stars, the equations that would launch a ship to reach them. He knew how to stay alive in any conditions, except when someone didn't want to stay alive.

No one was surprised when his father shot himself.

At the funeral potlatch, his mother split his father's ceremonial regalia between Wil and Kevin. She gave Kevin his father's frontlet. He placed it immediately on his head and danced. The room became still, the family shocked at his lack of tact. When Kevin stopped dancing, she gave Wil his father's button blanket. The dark wool held his smell. Wil knew then that he would never be an astronaut. He didn't have a backup dream and drifted through school, coasting on a reputation of Brain he'd stopped trying to earn.

Kevin, on the other hand, ran away and joined the Mohawk Warriors. He was at Oka on August 16 when the bombs rained down and the last Canadian reserve was Adjusted.

Wil expected him to come back broken. He was ready with patience, with forgiveness. Kevin came back a Peace Officer.

Why? his aunts, his uncles, cousins, and friends asked.

How could you? his mother asked.

Wil said nothing. When his brother looked up, Wil knew the truth, even if Kevin didn't. There were things that adjusted to rapid change—pigeons, dogs, rats, cockroaches. Then there were things that didn't—panda bears, whales, flamingos, Atlantic cod, salmon, owls.

Kevin would survive the Adjustment. Kevin had found a way to come through it and be better for it. He instinctively felt the changes coming and adapted. I, on the other hand, he thought, am going the way of the dodo bird.

There are rumours in the neighbourhood. No one from the Vancouver Urban Reserve #2 can get into Terminal Avenue. They don't have the money or the connections. Whispers follow him, anyway, but no one will ask him to his face. He suspects that his mother suspects. He has been careful, but he sees the questions in her eyes when he leaves for work. Someday she'll ask him what he really does and he'll lie to her.

To allay suspicion, he smuggles cigarettes and sweetgrass from the downtown core to Surreycentral. This is useful, makes him friends, adds a kick to his evening train ride. He finds that he needs these kicks. Has a morbid fear of becoming dead like his father, talking and breathing and eating, but frightened into vacancy, a living blankness.

His identity card that gets him to the downtown core says *Occupation: Waiter.* He pins it to his jacket so that no one will mistake him for a terrorist and shoot him.

He is not really alive until he steps past the industrial black doors of his lover's club. Until that moment, he is living inside his head, lost in memories. He knows that he is a novelty item, a real living Indian: that is why his prices are so inflated. He knows there will come a time when he is yesterday's condom.

He walks past the club's façade, the elegant dining rooms filled with the glittering people who watch the screens or dance across the dimly-lit ballroom-sized floor. He descends the stairs where his lover waits for him with her games and her toys, where they do things that aren't sanctioned by the Purity laws, where he gets hurt and gives hurt.

He is greeted by his high priestess. He enters her temple of discipline and submits. When the pain becomes too much, he hallucinates. There is no preparing for that moment when reality shifts and he is free.

They have formed a circle around him. Another standard intimidation tactic. The Peace Officer facing him is waiting for him to talk. He stares up at it. This will be different from the club. He is about to become an example.

Wilson Wilson? the Officer says. The voice sounds male but is altered by computers so it won't be recognizable.

He smiles. The name is one of his mother's little jokes, a little defiance. He has hated her for it all his life, but now he doesn't mind. He is in a forgiving mood. *Yes, that's me.*

In the silence that stretches, Wil realizes that he always believed this moment would come. That he has been preparing himself for it. The smiling-faced lies from the TV haven't fooled him, or anyone else. After the Uprisings, it was only a matter of time before someone decided to solve the Indian problem once and for all.

The Peace Officer raises his club and brings it down.

His father held a potlatch before they left Kitamaat, before they came to Vancouver to earn a living, after the aluminum smelter closed.

They had to hold it in secret, so they hired three large seiners for the family and rode to Monkey Beach. They left in their old beat-up speedboat, early in the morning, when the Douglas Channel was calm and flat, before the winds blew in from the ocean, turning the water choppy. The seine boats fell far behind them, heavy with people. Kevin begged and begged to steer and his father laughingly gave in.

Wil knelt on the bow and held his arms open, wishing he could take off his lifejacket. In four hours they will land on Monkey Beach and will set up for the potlatch where they will dance and sing and say goodbye. His father will cook salmon around fires, roasted the old-fashioned way: split down the centre and splayed open like butterflies, thin sticks of cedar woven through the skin to hold the fish open, the sticks planted in the sand; as the flesh darkens, the juice runs down and hisses on the fire. The smell will permeate the beach. Camouflage nets will be set up all over the beach so they won't be spotted by planes. Family will lounge under them as if they were beach umbrellas. The more daring of the family will dash into the water, which is still glacier-cold and shocking.

This will happen when they land in four hours, but Wil chooses to remember the boat ride with his mother resting in his father's arm when Wil comes back from the bow and sits down beside them. She is wearing a blue scarf and black sunglasses and red lipstick. She can't stop smiling even though they are going to leave home soon. She looks like a movie star. His father has his hair slicked back, and it makes him look like an otter. He kisses her, and she kisses him back.

Kevin is so excited that he raises one arm and makes the Mohawk salute they see on TV all the time. He loses control of the boat, and they swerve violently. His father cuffs Kevin and takes the wheel.

The sun rises as they pass Costi Island, and the water sparkles and shifts. The sky hardens into a deep summer blue.

The wind and the noise of the engine prevent them from talking. His father begins to sing. Wil doesn't understand the words, couldn't pronounce them if he tried. He can see that his father is happy. Maybe he's drunk on the excitement of the day, on the way that his wife touches him, tenderly. He gives Wil the wheel.

His father puts on his button blanket, rests it solemnly on his shoulders. He balances on the boat with the ease of someone who's spent all his life on the water. He does a twirl, when he reaches the bow of the speedboat and the button blanket opens, a navy lotus. The abalone buttons sparkle when they catch the light. She's laughing as he poses. He dances, suddenly inspired, exuberant.

Later he will understand what his father is doing, the rules he is breaking, the risks he is taking, and the price he will pay on a deserted road, when the siren goes off and the lights flash and they are pulled over.

At the time, though, Wil is white-knuckled, afraid to move the boat in a wrong way and toss his father overboard. He is also embarrassed, wishing his father were more reserved. Wishing he was being normal instead of dancing, a whirling shadow against the sun, blocking his view of the Channel.

This is the moment he chooses to be in, the place he goes to when the club flattens him to the Surreycentral tiles. He holds himself there, in the boat with his brother, his father, his mother. The sun on the water makes pale northern lights flicker against everyone's faces, and the smell of the water is clean and salty, and the boat's spray is cool against his skin.

～ *On Drowning Pond* ～
Allison Hedge Coke

Allison Hedge Coke is of Huron, Cherokee, French Canadian, Portuguese, Irish, and Scottish heritage and was raised in North Carolina, spending time also in Texas, Canada, and the Great Plains. As a young person, she worked in tobacco fields, later in factories, and wrote about her experiences in her memoir, *Rock, Ghost, Willow, Deer* (2014). Hedge Coke is an accomplished poet and short-story author, as well as a musician, film director, and teacher. Her 1997 poetry collection, *Dog Road Woman*, won the American Book Award, and she received the Writer of the Year Award for Poetry from the Wordcraft Circle of Native Writers and Storytellers for both *Blood Run* (2008) and *Off-Season City Pipe* (2005). She has held teaching appointments at Naropa University, the University of California–Riverside, and the University of Central Oklahoma, and served as Distinguished Writer in Residence at the University of Hawaiʻi–Mānoa.

"On Drowning Pond" was originally published in *Indian Country Noir*, a collection of fiction aimed at highlighting Indigenous contexts in the United States. Noir is a sub-genre of the Hardboiled form, defined by tough-guy protagonists (usually detectives), who bear witness to the crime and violence that lurk beneath the city. Hedge Coke borrows from some of the major tropes of the Hardboiled but tells the story through the eyes of a victim, or bystander, as opposed to a detective. Throughout the story, the unnamed protagonist tells the tragic story of Jolene and Jimmy, remembering the latter's beauty and strength, while also gesturing toward the vulnerability of Indigenous women in a colonial landscape. "On Drowning Pond" is haunting and poetic, bringing together the aesthetics of Noir with the settings of "Indian Country" to illustrate the structural violence that lurks beneath urban centres—threatening, most particularly, the lives of Indigenous women.

I saw Jimmy earlier this week. Just before the discovery of yet another fallen victim to the drowning way. He was still the same Jimmy, drunk—wasted. Crouched on the curb across from the market with a half-dozen longtime cronies and their women. Women who have been on the down edge so long their bodies have masculinized and hunched with the depression of life lost to drink, hard sex, smoke.

I saw him and I remembered Jolene, her beautiful smiling face, shining hair. Thought of her unrelinquished love for a man who'd only one wife in his heart. Thought of this bottle he'd fully committed to, of his smell, his ways. How she must have longed for him. Leaving her there the way he did, looking down on her maybe, thinking he was quite the man for taking the young passionate breath she'd had, in his making over of her brown body. Thought of his sudden losses of memory, and willingness to go on in life so soon and in such close proximity to her passing, and I wondered if he ever as much as poured a drink on the ground in her memory, or if he held that drink so precious to himself even a gulp would be too much to spare.

I saw him and I watched the walkers, those who've taken to carrying signs and speaking out against the assailants they believe they'll recognize once they stay the vigil until another passing. And I remembered how Jolene was always a private woman and doubted she would show her smiling face in a crowd this immense—especially among the sober living. The waters may look still today, but each time I glance across the creek, use my peripheral vision, for a moment her easy presence forms here, waiting. It's here I leave some hope for her, a few presents now and then, and ask her to go easy on us—the living. Here, too, I vow to follow him, take him down to the water one night, bring her Southern Comfort.

Jolene came to mind just this morning, how the light illuminated the walking bridge rail above her resplendent body. The shining of her deep black hair, under the water, on the morning they found her two dozen years ago. Right here in the thick of Brooklyn Alley. Just west/northwest from the Double Door Inn and over from the Broken Bank, Marshall Park. I remember how she always smiled when asking for "just a few quarters to get by."

It was spring. Jolene, though barely grown, had already been married and separated twice. She had a young child, but her parents had taken custody in the recognition of her spirit gone to drink. She had lived among the other ghosts, friends still walking the Earth along Independence, panhandling, selling themselves, huddling together for warmth and for desire of the strange flesh necessary to endure the jaundiced and rotting skin they themselves wore. Those who had lost lives here already, and yet still breathed, still continued this walk among the living. The ones whose blood no longer held hemoglobin, red, nor white leukocyte to speak of, yet flowed with a powerful wine-red fire-rush of alcohol-permeated heat. Those whose tears bore no salt, yet swelled each time a lost love was mentioned in conversation. Worse still if one actually passed by, nonchalant, unknowing, a member of the living world still. Those who fill the deep underworld here, though the white-collars cannot see them.

Jolene had found a lover. A great man, great in size and truly experienced among these parts. His residency here dated back a good decade or more, since his mom was chain gang in South Carolina. Heard she died there. I knew him holding his own guts in his hands. Knew him to be unstoppable. He walked with a certainty. A macho strut. He was certain—of himself, of the drink he made vows with. Everybody knew him. This familiarity, this personal community knowledge, allowed her protection from the perpetrators who infiltrated the Brooklyn-side Charlotte streets on weekends, summers, and holidays. Those who came to prey on the already forgotten but not quite gone. Those who justified rolling drunks as "teaching them a lesson." Or roughing lobs to "make them understand." Ethnic cleansers. I despise them.

It was in the month of the eclipsed moon, that time of reddened sky, after a fresh rain and hail pummeling along the curb. Jolene and her man. They were along the newly constructed revision bank when the storm broke. They had gone into the bar to avoid the wetness and to engage some draws from the deep tap-well, at least until the panhandled earnings were exhausted.

They say when the lovers went back down the construction path, Jolene was so taken by the deepening colors of the flora around them, she swelled with passion in the green and purpled midst and they lay together in the wet grasses along the bank, experiencing the fullness of newborn spring. They say she slept there. Fell asleep during, some say. When they found her she was naked from the waist down, as brown as a summer doe, lying half-in and half-out of water. The half-in was the upper part of Jolene. They dragged her out by the bare heels poking up through the wild violets blooming.

You know, she smiled even in death and her heavy hair flowed far past her physical body, much as the water flowed behind her. Jimmy was questioned but never arrested in her passing. He suffered from blackouts and seizures, and couldn't recall the last he saw her the night before. He was so sure she had returned to the bar with him. So were a few other regulars. They were all certain they saw her at least two hours after the coroner determined her expiration. They recounted Jolene hanging onto Jimmy's arm and smelling his breath and neck as if it were something scintillating. No one remembered her speaking, though Willie Notches said she tried to steal a cigarette right from his brother Tyrone's pocket but was so intoxicated she couldn't grab hold of it. Said his cousin Punchy Blackknees walked by and put a cigarette into her hand and she thought he was handing her a grasshopper since the clumsy numb-ness made the end shake up and down. Willie still laughed at the recollection. Others said they had seen her swimming near the city center at dawn, where elders and children were allowed to fish before the conversion of the city into cosmopolis. Said they averted their eyes to avoid embarrassing her obvious bathing. The city more concerned with gentrification than the fallen, then and now. Nothing was done. No follow-up, just over and buried, they say. They still claim such. Amazing.

Years passed. Winos would sometimes claim they saw a beautiful woman, underwater, facing up and smiling in the now white-collar park enclave. Back then, they'd leaned over and fallen in trying to get a better look at her before the shock of cold water woke them from drunken stupor. Then there was Tyrone. The creek-bum who hadn't seen a sober day in so many years his skin had grayed beyond redemption. Tyrone drank with Jimmy, for years they say, drank with Jolene once or twice in the living time. It was Tyrone whose death bristled my attention. Tyrone had claimed it was Jolene in the waters. Claimed she reached right out of the water for the Marlboro in his shirt and held him a moment, puckering wet lips and beckoning him with her muddy eyes. He said he'd shaken her off twice before and was afraid she would come for him again. He told Jimmy he believed her jealous of the woman Tyrone had introduced to Jimmy while he should have still been mourning her. As if the ones who lived on this bordering world were capable of remaining celibate for a year's time to mourn anyone. He drowned four years after they found Jolene. He surfaced around Freedom Park, no explaining it, the pocket completely ripped from his shirt and his trousers torn through the crotch, one entire pant leg missing.

Then there was that one up from the Catawba River for the Frontier Days rodeo. They said he looked and walked a lot like Jimmy and that he had drunk in the Double Door three days straight before going to "get some sleep" by the pond path. They said his breath had the strong smell of Peppermint Schnapps or Hot Damn over bad beer and cheap wine. Said the peppermint was the only thing kept him from getting picked up P.I. by Officer Wall on his lot patrol at the market. He surfaced exactly four years after Tyrone. After him, they came up more often.

A few full-bloods floated facedown after being lost for two or three days. They were strong men, well built, with the exception of the distended gut from too much drinking. All were known to have frequented the park and the Indian bar nearby. All were going through hard times and break-ups. Then two half-bloods rose from the bottom. One with his woman just twenty yards away, still sleeping after having relations. For a week she told the story of his sweetest day, their closest time together—ever. This day he had drowned. Then she took up with a guy who stayed over nearer the park and they poured wine on the ground for her man every time they took to drink together.

Once they found a drowned stranger, a sort-of stranger, a guy from another tribe who was a known exhibitionist and molested the street women, often paying them in cigarettes after he was finished with them. One had to be hospitalized—he had been so brutal in his business. When they pulled him from the water, his man-thing had been sheared by what appeared to be a sharp branch. They said he'd tried to bribe Jimmy for a turn at Jolene years ago.

Once, or twice maybe, a white man came floating and I began to believe Jolene had given up on Indian guys altogether. I've considered it myself, but can't stand the never-ending explaining you have to do to date outside. One came up so fast they found him minutes after he'd swallowed waters, yet no effort was made to clear his lungs by the followers or the police. I figure she shamed herself in seducing the historical enemy and wanted no part of being affiliated with him after the fact.

I saw Jimmy earlier this week. Maybe I'll follow him, take him down to the water tonight, bring her comfort. Soothe the blue-black night waters welling with Jolene. Soothe them.

— *The Space NDN's Star Map* —
L. Catherine Cornum

L. Catherine Cornum is a queer diasporic Diné writer and Indigenous futurist who grew up in various towns and cities across Arizona, before moving to New York City at the age of eighteen. Cornum currently lives in Brooklyn and studies in the English PhD program at the City University of New York Graduate Center. They are an avid fan of science fiction and a believer in the transformative power of futurist thinking for Indigenous decolonization movements. Cornum's writing has been featured in *The New Inquiry*, *Lies: A Journal of Materialist Feminism*, *Kimiwan* 'zine and the e-fagia *Voz-à-Voz* publication.

"The Space NDN's Star Map" focuses on how Indigenous writers have challenged the colonial and gender assumptions inherent in the conventions of science fiction. Not only have Indigenous writers deconstructed the Star Trek–inspired emphasis on exploration, discovery, and frontier-making; they have also re-appropriated the genre of SF and fantasy and made it their own. Cornum asks: "why can't we as Indigenous peoples also project ourselves among the stars?" (366). Re-appropriation also motivates Cornum's use of the term "NDN," a spelling that simultaneously critiques the misnomer "Indian" and yet acknowledges that it is nevertheless a term "we NDNs use to describe ourselves" (365). Another important aspect of this essay is its demonstration of an ongoing dialogue between Indigenous, Black, and Afro-Indigenous SF authors, who have mutually influenced one another's narratives and cultural productions, and whose histories of displacement through the Black Atlantic and the colonial frontier are more closely linked than often assumed.

THE CREATION STORY IS A SPACESHIP
The first time I saw a space NDN was in *The 6th World*, a short film by Diné director Nanobah Becker that extends the Diné creation story into outer space, where humanity's future is made possible through ancestral corn crops on Mars. The space NDN is a figure of Indigenous Futurism, describing (in part)

an Indigenous person either residing or traveling through space. I have also used the phrase to capture the long-standing traditions of studying the cosmos across Indigenous cultures as well as modern experience of alienation common to many NDNs living in conditions of ongoing colonialism. I utilize the typographical innovation developed online in recent years, "NDN," to highlight the digital space where I first encountered the discourse of Indigenous Futurism and because I am drawn to the ways in which this spelling further estranges the inappropriate term Indian we NDNs use to describe ourselves. *The 6th World* and its vision of a Diné space NDN was released in 2012, the same year that editor Grace L. Dillon published *Walking the Clouds: An Anthology of Indigenous Science Fiction*, the first-ever anthology of its kind. This was the official inauguration of Indigenous futurism, which has since become a term not only for science fiction (SF) but also a descriptor for a wide breadth of artistic, cultural and academic projects. The movement is in part about speaking back to the SF genre, which has long used Indigenous subjects as the foils to stories of white space explorers hungry to conquer new worlds. Given these continuously re-hashed narratives of "the final frontier," it is no coincidence that western science fiction developed during a time of imperial and capitalist expansion.

Science/speculative fiction author Nalo Hopkinson, known for her use of creole languages and Caribbean oral stories in her works, writes that people of colour engaging with SF "take the meme of colonizing the natives and, from the experience of the colonizee, critique it, pervert it, fuck with it, with irony, with anger, with humor and also, with love and respect for the genre of science fiction that makes it possible to think about new ways of doing things" (Hopkinson and Mehan iv). Perhaps because science fiction is so prone to reproducing colonial desires it has become seductive to the "colonizee" to find pleasure and power in reversing the telescope's gaze and to reassess who is exploring whom. This reversal is no mere trick, though. It is a profound deconstruction of how we imagine time, progress, and value. In particular, this strategy of reversing the gaze asks the reader to question who is considered worthy of writing the future.

Following in the rocket trails of black authors such as Hopkinson, the space NDN is also in a long tradition of NDN interstellar exploration, using technologies such as creation stories and ceremony as her means of travel. For some, she is a startling and unsettling figure. As Philip Deloria argues in *Indians in Unexpected Places*, settlers often become upset and confused when the seemingly contrasting symbolic systems of Indigeneity and high-tech modernity are put in dialogue, as demonstrated in the shocked reactions to a 1904 photograph of Geronimo in a Cadillac. This estrangement arises from "a long tradition that has tended to separate Indian people from the contemporary world and from recognition of the possibility of Indian autonomy in the world" (143). In the colonial imaginary, Indigenous life is not only separate from the present time but also out of place in the future, a time defined by the progress of distinctively western technology. If colonial society cannot accept Geronimo in a Cadillac, it can hardly conceive of him in a space ship.

The Indian in space seeks to feel at home, to undo her perceived strangeness by asking: why can't we as Indigenous peoples also project ourselves among the stars? Might our collective visions of the cosmos forge better relationships here on earth and in the present than colonial visions of a final frontier? Many of the ideas deemed strange or new-fangled in Western science fiction come naturally to the space NDN—for example, the all-pervasive "force" or the super-brain connecting all beings; the animism and agency of cyborgs, AI systems, and other non-human people; alternate dimensions and understandings of non-linear time. These are things the space NDN knows intuitively. This is not the future but historical knowledge. The future is reclaiming these technologies not for domination but for imagining better worlds structured around a different ethics of contact and relation. I am reminded of Octavia Butler's words, "There is nothing new under the sun, but there are new suns" (qtd. in Canavan). Instead of imaging a future in bleak cities made from steel and glass teeming with alienated white masses shuffling under an inescapable electronic glow, Indigenous futurists think of earthen space crafts helmed by black and brown women with advanced knowledge of land, plants, and language.

Indigenous futurism seeks to challenge notions of what constitutes advanced technology and consequently advanced civilizations. As settler colonial governments continue to demand more and more from the Earth, Indigenous peoples seek sovereign spaces and freedom to heal from these apocalyptic processes. Extractive and exploitative endeavours are just one mark of the settler death drive, which Indigenous futurism seeks to overcome by imagining different ways of relating to notions of progress and civilization. Advanced technologies are not finely tuned mechanisms of endless destruction. Advanced technologies should foster and improve human relationships with the non-human world. In many Indigenous science fiction tales of the future, technology is shown to be in dialogue with, rather than overcoming, long traditions of the past.

In the recent iteration of the constantly re-packaged tale of white men planting flags in space, *Interstellar*'s all-American space boy, Matthew McConaughey, stares into the distance and announces, "We are explorers, pioneers, not caretakers." As if one cannot be both an explorer and a caretaker. For the space NDN the two roles are intertwined. The advanced technology of the space NDN does not separate technical from natural knowledge. Technology is not divorced from or forced upon land but develops in relation to lands and the many beings that the land supports.

The space NDN's disavowal of western progress makes clear the difference between Indigenous futurism and early 20th century forms of futurism, which were compatible with the interests of fascist and oppressive governments. Unlike those futurists, who were in an antagonistic relation with their literary and cultural predecessors, Indigenous futurism is centered on bringing traditions to distant, future locations, rather than abandoning them as relics. Indigenous futurism does not care for speed so much as sustainability, not so much for progress as balance, and not for claiming power over beings, but rather for sustaining relationships between beings.

GOD IS THE RED PLANET

For many the image of the Indian in space is jarring not just because of the settler perception of Indigeneity as antithetical to high tech modernity, but because Indian identity is tied so directly to specific earthly territories. What happens to Indigeneity when the Indigenous subject is no longer in the location that has defined them? This is not just a question of outer space. Already the majority of Native people in the U.S. and Canada live in cities away from their traditional territories. Of course at one point these places would also have been viewed as Indigenous territories, and indeed they still are. While many nations have worked very hard to dispel the notion of nomadic Indian tribes, there is a history of movement among many of our peoples. Colonial forms such as reserves, reservations, nation-states and borders have made these traditions of movement nearly impossible. The need to defend our rights to live on our lands without harassment has created the political necessity of claiming our land-based political and cultural identities.

But land-based does not have to mean landlocked. This insistence on Indigenous people having to always be located on or closely connected to one particular area also erases those who are unable to return to their traditional territories. This was the case for many Indigenous women in Canada who, before the passing of bill C-31 in 1985, were deprived of their Indian Status for marrying non-Status men, and, as a result, often forced to live off-reserve. And it continues to be the case for Afro-Indigenous people who were stolen from their lands and sold as chattel. There is also the simple fact that NDNs may want to move around. I sometimes describe myself as a diasporic Diné in order to bring the often disparate ideas of Indigeneity and movement into closer proximity. Those we consider diasporic are often violently robbed of their Indigeneity and those we consider Indigenous are often on the move. The space NDN looks into the void and knows who they are.

Nanobah Becker shot part of *The 6th World* in Monument Valley, one of the sacred territories of the Diné. The red rock canyons and cliffs make a convincing backdrop for the Mars scenes in her film. They also offer a symbol of dynamic sacredness. These distant lands are connected. Just because the Diné have not lived on Mars since time immemorial, it does not mean our plants and teachings cannot take root there. I am reminded of the time before a ceremony on a college campus when we washed our hands in a drinking fountain. Like Betonie, the medicine man who makes medicine bundles from trash heaps in Leslie Marmon Silko's novel *Ceremony*, we carve out sacred space and objects where we can—which might be anywhere. I think of semi-conductors adorning pow-wow regalia and the descendants of slaves telling and re-telling their stories on new, bloodied ground. Finding ourselves in new contexts, we are always adapting, always surviving. This is the seed of many Indigenous technologies: the ability to continue and sustain ourselves against all odds.

The challenge of the space NDN is how to apply knowledge of the worlds toward non-destructive ends. Any form of travel or exploration comes with the dangers of exploitation and upheaval. Nobody knows this better than the inhabitants of those places constantly divvied up between colonial nation-states. The figure of the space NDN is not an attempt to simply put an Indigenous face on the outer space colonizer. Indigenous futurist narratives try to enact contact differently. Not all encounters with the other must end in conquest, genocide or violence. The space NDN seeks new models of interaction. We do not travel to the distant reaches of space in order to plant our flags or act under the assumption that every planet in our sights is *terra nullius*, or "empty land," waiting for the first human footprint to mark its surface. Maori poet Robert Sullivan's epic work *Star Waka* captures the complexities of Indigenous space travel. Waka is the Maori term for a canoe and Sullivan's epic poem relates the journey of this star waka to outer planets to find new homes for the Maori people. The crew of the ship wonder how their prayers will work in the cold vastness of the stars and how they can approach these distant worlds in a good way. The Indian in space does not abandon their home, their people, or their teachings. Dynamic traditions, themselves a type of advanced technology, help the space NDN to understand how to foster the kind of relationships that make futures possible.

ALL OUR INTERSTELLAR RELATIONS

For Indigenous futurism, technology is inextricable from the social. Human societies are part of a network of wider relationships with objects, animals, geological formations and so on. To grasp our relationship with the non-human world here on Earth, we must also extend our understanding of how Earth relates to the entirety of the cosmos. We live on just one among millions of planets, each an intricate and delicate system within a larger, increasing complex structure. The endeavour of the Indigenous futurist is to strive to understand the ever-multiplying connections linking us to the beginning of the universe. The constant expansion of the universe also entails unraveling the intricate relations that make up our Earthly existence.

Zainab Amadahy, who identifies as a person of mixed black, Cherokee and European ancestry, grounds her writing practice in illuminating and understanding networks of relationships: "I aspire to write in a way that views possible alternatives through the lens of a relationship framework, where I can demonstrate our connectivity to and interdependence with each other and the rest of our Relations" (qtd. in Dillon 172). Her 1992 novel *The Moons of Palmares* examines the relationships, both harmful and collaborative, between Indigenous peoples and descendants of slaves in an outer space setting that merges histories of the Black Atlantic with the colonial frontier. In a provocative bit of plotting, she casts an Indigenous character, Major Eaglefeather, as an oppressive foreign force in the lives of an outer space labour population that has shaped its society in remembrance of black slave resistance in North/South America and the Caribbean.

The story follows Major Eaglefeather's decision to reject his ties with the settler colonial nation and its corporate interests, and instead to support a rebel group of labourers. The name Palmares is taken from a real-world settlement founded by escaped slaves in 17th-century Brazil, which is also known to have incorporated Indigenous peoples and some poor, disenfranchised whites. In a chronicle written in the late 17th century and collected in Robert Edgar's *Children of God's Fire: A Documentary History of Black Slavery in Brazil*, these *quilombos* are described as networks of settlements that lived off the land and were supplemented by raids on the slave plantations where the inhabitants were formerly held. It is said that in Palmares the king was called Gangasuma, a hybrid term meaning "great lord" composed of the Angolan or Bandu word *ganga* and the Tupi word *assu*. The word succinctly captures the mixture of cultures that banded together in Palmares to live together on the margins of a colonialist, slave-holding society. While Palmares was eventually destroyed in a military campaign, it lives on as a legend of slave rebellion and utopian possibility that Amadahy finds well-suited for her outer space story about collaborative resistance to State power and harmful resource extraction processes.

Outer space, perhaps because of its appeal to our sense of endless possibility, has become the imaginative site for re-envisioning how black, Indigenous and other oppressed people can relate to one another outside of or in spite of the colonial gaze. Amadahy's work is crucial for a critical understanding of the space NDN. The space NDN cannot allow him or herself to fall into the patterns of domination and hierarchy that have for too long prevailed here on Earth as well as speculative narratives of outer space. Afro-futurists have looked to space as the site for black separatism and liberation. If the space NDN is truly committed to being responsible to the wide breadth of peoples and other-than-human beings she interacts with, it is imperative for our futurist vision to be in solidarity with our fellow Afro-futurist space travelers. Our collective refusal of colonial "progress" (which is more aptly understood as our destruction) means we must chart other ways to the future that lead us and other oppressed peoples to the worlds we deserve.

The Moons of Palmares works toward this end by revealing the strong connections between Indigenous and black histories, narratives and ways of living. Indigenous futurism is indebted to Afro-futurism: Both forms of futurism explore spaces and times outside the control of colonial powers and white supremacy. These alternative conceptions of time reject the notion that all tradition is regressive by narrating futures intimately connected to the past. SF and specifically the site of outer space give writers and thinkers the imaginative room to envision political and cultural relationships that might nourish future decolonizing movements. This focus on relationships, especially as posited by Amadahy, connects together Indigenous peoples who have been stolen from their lands with those whose lands have been stolen from them.

As the writer Sydette Harry recently tweeted, "Black people are displaced indigenous people"; and yet because of forced relocation, slavery and continuing anti-black racism, black people are often denied claims to Indigeneity. There is also a pernicious erasure of black NDNs in America and Canada. In exploring outer space, black authors are also able to assert their own relationship to land both on Earth and in the cosmos. The Black Land Project (BLP), while not an explicitly futurist organization, fosters the kind of relationships to land on Earth that futurist authors and thinkers envision in outer space. In a recent podcast, *Blacktracking through Afrofuturism*, BLP founder and director Mistinguette Smith discusses how walking over the routes of the Underground Railroad brought forth alternate dimensions and understandings of time outside the settler paradigm of ownership. These are aspects of relating to land that the Afro-futurist and the space NDN (identities which can exist in the same person) bring with them on their travels.

This focus on relationships rather than on a strict idea of location speaks to the ways in which the space NDN can remain secure in their Indigenous identity even while rocketing through dark skies far from their origins. This is not to demean the work of land protectors and defenders who risk serious repercussions for resisting corporate and state encroachments on Indigenous territories. The space NDN supports those who are able and choose to remain on the land, while also hoping to broaden understandings of Indigeneity outside of a simplistic notion of location. Locations are never simple. It is the settler who wishes to flatten the relation between place and people by claiming land through ownership. Projecting themselves forward into faraway lands and times, the space NDN reveals the myriad ways of relating to land beyond property.

NOTES

NOTES TO CHAPTER 1

Paula Gunn Allen, "Deer Woman"

1 A slang term that means cruising to pick up women.
2 "Skins" is slang for "redskins," which is slang for Indians.
3 The stomp dance originated with the Creek (Muscogee) people, but became a part of Western Cherokee cultural practice after the Trail of Tears and arrival in Oklahoma. At this time, the Cherokee Green Corn Ceremony has been replaced by the stomp dance, which is usually held during late August and early September.
4 In Cherokee lore, Long Man is a spirit being who controls rivers and streams.
5 49s are social songs and dances associated with courting.
6 The Cherokee "Little People" (or *Yunwi Tsundi*) are very small (about knee-high) spiritual beings, similar to European fairies, but with long hair reaching to the ground. They live in caves or woods and spend a great deal of time making music (drumming) and dancing. They are usually good-hearted and helpful. They are invisible to humans unless they choose to be seen.
7 Deer Woman, a familiar figure among the Native people of the southeastern United States, is a spiritual being who takes the shape of a beautiful woman, renowned for luring men away from family and community.
8 BART stands for the Bay Area Rapid Transit, a train in the San Francisco Bay Area.

NOTES TO CHAPTER 2

Kimberly Blaeser, "Like Some Old Story"

1 In the Anishinaabe language, *boozhoo* means "hello."

M. E. Wakamatsu, "Rita Hayworth Mexicana"

1 Totoaba: A type of sea bass now on the Endangered Species list. Cahuama: Sea turtle, also on the Endangered Species list.
2 La linea: The border (slang).
3 El otro lado: The U.S. side (slang).
4 Mica: Term used to refer to a Permanent Resident card (slang).
5 Papeles: Proof of citizenship.
6 Pinchi: Mean.
7 Nisei: Japanese born in a country other than Japan

NOTES TO CHAPTER 3

Sixto Canul, "The Son Who Came Back from the United States"

1 "All right. Yes" is meant as a pun. "Yes" said with a Spanish/Maya accent sounds remark-ably like *diez*, the number ten. "All right" can be understood as *Ahora*, or "Now," but could also be a pun for the Maya, "I say eat greedily."

Joel Torres Sánchez, "I'm Not a Witch, I'm a Healer!"

1 For a long time the Purépecha language was erroneously called "Tarasco." This language's origins and linguistic family remain unknown. As in the case of Euskera, the language of the Basques in Spain, Purépecha is a linguistic island on the continent. At the end of the twentieth century there were more than 204,000 speakers of Purépecha, living primarily in the state of Michoacán.
2 Apocopated form of the Old Spanish *enaguas*, a woman's exterior garment that hangs from the waist. From the Taino *naguas*, "cotton skirt."
3 Traditional white cotton blouse adorned with embroidered flower motifs.
4 A woman's exterior garment used to cover the shoulders and upper torso; a shawl.
5 Purépecha town where high-quality *rebozos* are produced.
6 A rustic house or hut.
7 A Purépecha title of respect reserved for older women who have borne children.
8 A reference to those living in the elevated and non-elevated zones of the region.
9 A Spanish title used to refer to or address married women.
10 A Purépecha form of addressing both men and women with the highest level of respect and prestige; similar to "thou" in Old English or *vuestra merced* in Old Spanish.
11 "Thou, Mother Delfina."
12 *Jurhenani*, in Purépecha: to "prepare oneself" or "be initiated into knowledge." The author translated this ambiguous concept into Spanish as *don*, "talent" or "gift."
13 A Purépecha title of respect reserved for older men.
14 From the Nahuatl *petlatl*, a weaving of palm or reeds used as a mat for sitting or sleeping or as a funerary wrap.
15 From the Nahuatl *tecolotl*, "owl." The Purépecha word is *tukuru*, closer to the Mayan *tunkuruchu*.

Jeannette Armstrong, "Land Speaking"

1 *Reinventing the Enemy's Language* is also the title of a well-known collection of Indigenous women's writing, edited by Gloria Bird and Joy Harjo.

NOTES TO CHAPTER 4

Harold Cardinal, Excerpt from "Einew Kis-Kee-Tum-Awin (Indigenous People's Knowledge)"

1 This excerpt is from the script Dr. Cardinal prepared to give in a lecture in Vancouver in 2005; it was not prepared for publication. Out of respect for his work, we have not altered any of his words but have only completed minor editing of punctuation.
2 The transcripts of this lecture were entrusted to Métis scholar and Director of the University of British Columbia's First Nations House of Learning, Madeline McIvor; she then deposited them into the X̱wi7x̱wa library, a collection at the University of British Columbia dedicated to Indigenous texts.

NOTE TO CHAPTER 5

Tania Willard, "Coyote and the People Killer"

1 Willard's images were originally created for an exhibition at the Burnaby Art Gallery in British Columbia, "First Nations Now," curated by Peter Morin in partnership with Redwire Native Youth Media Society (October 2004).

NOTE TO CHAPTER 6

Isaías Hernández Isidro, "The Secret of the Zutz'baläm"

1 Literally, "bat-jaguar": a deity.
2 The Chontal language in the state of Tabasco is known by its speakers as Yokot'an. By extension, this term also refers to any Indigenous language, possibly because *yoco* means "native" and *t'an*, "language," "regional form of speech." At the end of the twentieth century there were 72,000 Tabasco Chontal speakers.
3 A title used to address married women ("Mrs." or "ma'am").
4 *Dendrocygna autumnalis*, a web-footed, edible fowl of the Anatidae family, similar to a duck, though smaller. It is easily domesticated and is prized as a guardian, since it emits a long squawk when it sees strangers.
5 *Bactris baculifera*, a spiny palm that produces a spherical red fruit and reaches heights of up to eighteen feet. Its wood is very hard and is good for making canes. It is common in the states of Tabasco and Chiapas.
6 *Styrax argenteus*, a tree that reaches heights of up to 60 feet; its trunk produces an aromatic resin that is used as incense. The name *estoraque* is also used in reference to *Liquidambar styraciflua*, which produces another type of aromatic resin.
7 From the Mayan *to'*, "to wrap." *Calathea grandifolia*, known in Spanish also as "bijagua" or "hojablanca."
8 Day on which offerings are placed for the Zutz'baläm, to obtain something in return.
9 *Calathea lutea*, known in Tabasco as *popal* leaf; that is, pertaining to a lagoon or marsh (this is the literal meaning of the Ch'ontal expression *chäk to'*). Since these leaves are generally used to wrap foods, other authors suggest that the word *to'* comes from Yucatec Mayan, where it means "to wrap."
10 *Psidium guajava*, a tree belonging to the Mirteaceae family. Its bark is reddish, smooth, and scaly; its edible fruit is aromatic and pyriform or oval in shape.
11 Fermented sugar cane juice.

NOTES TO CHAPTER 7

Joe Panipakuttuk, "The Many Lives of Anakajuttuq"

1 The editors would like to thank Kenn Harper, historian, for some of the information provided in this biographical note.

Jo-Ann Episkenew, "Notes on Leslie Marmon Silko's 'Lullaby': Socially Responsible Criticism"

1 In the United States, "Native Americans" is a commonly used term to describe the Indigenous peoples of that country. Under the Constitution of Canada (1982), the term "Aboriginal" refers to registered Indians, as defined by the Indian Act, Métis, and Inuit. "First Nations" is a term now in common usage referring to members of Canada's First Nations, in other words Indians defined by the Indian Act. I choose, however, to use the term "Indigenous" rather than "Aboriginal." Many people use the term "Indigenous" because it is more accepted internationally, and others believe that the prefix *ab-* has negative

connotations, for example in "abnormal." My reasons began with a story I've heard via the moccasin telegraph. The story goes that the people who negotiated our inclusion in the constitution argued for the use of the term "Indigenous." The Government of Canada would not agree and insisted on the term "Aboriginal." Because of my own contrary nature, I choose to use the term "Indigenous."

2 Sherry Farrell Racette points out that in Saskatchewan, Métis children had no legal right to education until 1944, when the provincial government assumed responsibility for Métis education after a decades-long stalemate with the federal government over jurisdiction ("Métis Education.")

3 Prof. William Asikinack of the Saskatchewan Indian Federated College was stripped of his Indian status and membership to the Walpole Island First Nation in the 1960s after receiving his BEd.

4 Although born on the Cowessess Indian Reserve, my former mother-in-law, Mathilda Lavallie Bunnie, was by law a non-Status Indian, her father having applied for and been granted enfranchisement. In the early 1920s, she attended Marieval Indian Residential School until grade two when all Métis and non-Status students were required to discontinue, which put an end to her aspirations of receiving an education.

5 Isadore Pelletier, an Elder at the Saskatchewan Indian Federated College, had a similar experience. Also a non-Status Indian, Pelletier lived in Lestock, Saskatchewan, where he attended the town school until grade three. At that time the townspeople decided to expel all Métis and non-Status Indian children from the school on the basis that they were squatters and, therefore, did not pay taxes. Although Pelletier's family owned land, he was expelled along with the others.

6 I remember and appreciate Terry Goldie's cautions that the inclusion of personal reflections in academic writing has the potential to become "self-indulgent" (Congress, Edmonton 2000).

7 See the interview of Winona Stevenson in Evelyn Poitras's documentary film, *To Colonize a People: The File Hills Indian Farm Colony*.

WORKS CITED

Alexie, Sherman. "The Toughest Indian in the World." *The Toughest Indian in the World*. New York: Grove/Atlantic, 2000. 21-34. Print.

Amadahy, Zainab. *The Moons of Palmares*. Toronto: Sister Vision, 1997. Print.

Anzaldúa, Gloria. "Ghost Trap." *New Chicana/Chicano Writing*. Ed. Charles Tatum. Tucson: U of Arizona P, 1992. 40-42. Rpt. in *The Gloria Anzaldúa Reader*. Durham: Duke UP, 2009. 157-61. Print.

Armstrong, Jeannette. *Breath Tracks*. Penticton: Theytus, 1991. Print.

———. "Frogs Singing." *Durable Breath: Contemporary Native American Poetry*. Ed. John E. Smelcer and D. L. Birchfield. Anchorage: Salmon Run, 1994. 8-9. Print.

———. "Land Speaking." *Speaking for the Generations: Native Writers on Writing*. Ed. Louis Ortiz. Tucson: U of Arizona P, 1998. 174-95. Print.

———. Personal communication with Sophie McCall and Deanna Reder. Vancouver. 29 June 2016.

———. *Slash*. Penticton: Theytus, 1985. Print.

———. "This Is a Story." *All My Relations: An Anthology of Contemporary Canadian Native Fiction*. Ed. Thomas King. Toronto: McClelland & Stewart, 1990. 129-35. Print.

Baum, L. Frank. *The Wizard of Oz*. 1900. New York: Holt, Rinehart and Winston, 1982. Print.

Bird, Gloria, and Joy Harjo, eds. *Reinventing the Enemy's Language: Contemporary Native Women's Writings of North America*. New York: W. W. Norton, 1998. Print.

Bird-Wilson, Lisa. "Delivery." *Just Pretending*. Saskatoon: Coteau, 2013. 175-83. Print.

Blaeser, Kimberly. "Like Some Old Story." 2002. *Reckoning: Contemporary Short Fiction by Native American Women*. Ed. Hertha D. Sweet Wong, Lauren Stuart Muller, and Jana Sequoya Magdaleno. New York: Oxford UP, 2008. 247-51. Print.

Bloomfield, Leonard. *Sacred Stories of the Sweet Grass Cree*. Ottawa: National Museum of Canada, 1930. Print.

Bouchard, Randy, and Dorothy Kennedy. *Shuswap Stories: Collected 1971-1975*. Vancouver: CommCept, 1979. Print.

Brown-Spiers, Miriam. "Creating a Haida Manga: The Formline of Social Responsibility in *Red*." *Studies in American Indian Literatures* 26.3 (Fall 2014): 41-61. Print.

Canavan, Gerry. "'There's Nothing New / Under The Sun, / But There Are New Suns': Recovering Octavia E. Butler's Lost Parables." *Los Angeles Review of*

Books. 9 June 2014. Web. 2 Mar. 2016. <www.lareviewofbooks.org/article/theres-nothing-new-sun-new-suns-recovering-octavia-e-butlers-lost-parables>.

Canul, Sixto. "The Son Who Came Back from the United States." Orig. published in Spanish in *Relatos del centro del mundo.* Ed. Sylvia Terán and Christian H. Rasmussen. Yucatán: Mérida, 1992. English translation by Alejandra García Quintanilla. *In the Language of Kings: An Anthology of Mesoamerican Literature, pre-Columbian to the Present.* Ed. Miguel León-Portilla, Earl Shorris, and Sylvia S. Shorris. New York: W. W. Norton, 2001. 604. Print.

Cardinal, Harold. "Einew Kis-Kee-Tum-Awin (Indigenous People's Knowledge)." Unpublished lecture. X̱wi7x̱wa library, University of British Columbia, 2005. TS.

———. *The Unjust Society: The Tragedy of Canada's Indians.* Edmonton: M. G. Hurtig, 1969. Print.

Cariou, Warren. "An Athabasca Story." *Lake* 7 (2012): 71-75. Print.

Castellano, Marlene Brant. "Ethics of Aboriginal Research." *Journal of Aboriginal Health* 1.1 (2004): 98-114. Print.

Cisneros, Sandra. "Never Marry a Mexican." *Woman Hollering Creek and Other Stories.* New York: Vintage, 1992. 116-29. Print.

Coleman, Daniel, in conversation with Marie Battiste, Sákéj Henderson, Isobel M. Findlay, and Len Findlay. "Different Knowings and the Indigenous Humanities." *English Studies in Canada* 38.1 (2012): 141-59. Print.

Cornum, L. Catherine. "The Space NDN's Star Map." *The New Inquiry* (26 Jan. 2016). Web. <www.thenewinquiry.com/essays/the-space-ndns-star-map/>. 25 Mar. 2016. (Revised for *Read, Listen, Tell.*)

Deloria, Philip. *Indians in Unexpected Places.* Lawrence: U of Kansas P, 2004. Print.

Dillon, Grace L. "Global Indigenous Science Fiction." Symposium on Science Fiction and Globalization. *Science Fiction Studies* 39.3 (2012): 377-79. Print.

———, ed. *Walking the Clouds: An Anthology of Indigenous Science Fiction.* Tucson: U of Arizona P, 2012. Print.

Dumont, Dawn. "The Way of the Sword." *Nobody Cries at Bingo.* Saskatoon: Thistledown, 2011. 218-40. Print.

———. "Dawn Dumont." *Thistledown Press.* Web. 9 February 2017. <www.thistledown press.com/html/search/Authors/Dawn_Dumont/index.cfm>.

Episkenew, Jo-Ann. "Notes on Leslie Marmon Silko's 'Lullaby': Socially Responsible Criticism." Rev. version of "Socially Responsible Criticism: Aboriginal Literature, Ideology, and the Literary Canon." *Creating Community: A Roundtable on Canadian Aboriginal Literature.* Ed. Renate Eigenbrod and Jo-Ann Episkenew. Penticton: Theytus, 2002. 51-68. Print.

Fee, Margery. "Aboriginal Writing in Canada and the Anthology as Commodity." *Native North America: Critical and Cultural Perspectives.* Toronto: ECW, 1999. 135-55. Print.

Gatherings, Vol. III: *Mother Earth Perspectives: Preservation Through Words.* Ed. Greg Younging. Penticton: Theytus, 1992. Print.

Gatherings, Vol. IV: *Regeneration: Expanding the Web to Claim Our Future.* Ed. Don Fiddler. Penticton: Theytus, 1994. Print.

Glancy, Diane. "Aunt Parnetta's Electric Blisters." *Trigger Dance.* Boulder: U of Colorado and Fiction Collective Two, 1990. 11-18. Print.

Gunn Allen, Paula. "Deer Woman." *Grandmothers of the Light: A Medicine Woman's Sourcebook.* Boston: Beacon Press, 1991. 184-94. Print.

Halfe, Louise Bernice. "Rolling Head's Grave Yard." Rev. version of "Keynote Address: The Rolling Head's 'Grave' Yard." *Studies in Canadian Literature* 31.1 (2006): 65-73. Print.

Harjo, Joy. "Threads of Blood and Spirit." *A Map to the Next World.* New York: W. W. Norton, 2001. 118-19. Print.

Harry, Sydette (@blackamazon). "Black people are displaced indigenous people." 2014. Tweet. 16 Jan. 2016.

Hedge Coke, Allison. "On Drowning Pond." *Indian Country Noir.* Ed. Sarah Cortez and Liz Martinez. New York: Akashic Books, 2010. 103-10. Print.

Hernández Isidro, Isaías. "The Secret of the Zutz'baläm." 1997, trans. 2004. *Words of the True Peoples: Palabras de los Seres Verdaderos.* Ed. Carlos Montemayor and Donald Frischmann. Austin: U of Texas P, 2004. 94-96. Print.

Highway, Tomson. Ch. 14 from *Kiss of the Fur Queen.* Toronto: Doubleday, 1998. 113-21. Print.

Hill, Gord. "The 'Oka Crisis.'" *The Five Hundred Years of Resistance Comic Book.* Vancouver: Arsenal Pulp, 2010. 71-74.

Hopkinson, Nalo, and Uppinder Mehan, eds. *So Long Been Dreaming: Postcolonial Science Fiction and Fantasy.* Vancouver: Arsenal, 2004. Print.

Interstellar. Dir. Christopher Nolan. Paramount Pictures, 2014. Film.

Ipellie, Alootook. "Summit with Sedna, the Mother of Sea Beasts." *Arctic Dreams and Nightmares.* Penticton: Theytus Books, 1993. 35-44. Print.

Johnson, Emily Pauline. "As It Was in the Beginning." 1899. *E. Pauline Johnson, Tekahionwake: Collected Poems and Selected Prose.* Ed. Carole Gerson and Veronica Strong-Boag. Toronto: U of Toronto P, 2002. 205-213. Print.

Jones, Stephen Graham. "Father, Son, Holy Rabbit." *The Ones That Got Away.* Germantown: Prime Books, 2010. 15-22. Print.

Justice, Daniel Heath. "Tatterborn." Orig. publication in *Read, Listen, Tell.* Ed. Sophie McCall, Deanna Reder, David Gaertner, and Gabrielle L'Hirondelle Hill. Waterloo: Wilfrid Laurier UP, 2017. 327-36. Print.

King, Thomas. "Borders." *One Good Story, That One.* Toronto: Harper Perennial, 1993. 131-45. Print.

———. "'You'll Never Believe What Happened' Is Always a Great Way to Start." *The Truth about Stories.* Toronto: Anansi, 2003. 1-30. Print.

Kublu, Alexina. "Uinigumasuittuq / She Who Never Wants to Get Married." *Interviewing Inuit Elders.* Vol. 1. Ed. Jarich Oosten and Frédéric Laugrand. Iqaluit: Nunavut Arctic College, 1999. 152-61. Print.

Langdon, Graeme. "Interview with Walter Scott, Creator of the 'Wendy' Comics." *BODY: Poetry, Prose, Word.* 27 November 2013. Web. 18 February 2017. <www.bodyliterature.com/2013/11/>.

Lapatin, Kenneth. *Mysteries of the Snake Goddess.* Cambridge: Da Capo, 2002. Print.

Maracle, Lee. "Goodbye, Snauq." *Our Story: Aboriginal Voices on Canada's Past.* Toronto: Doubleday, 2004. 201-20. Print.

McLeod, Neal. "Coming Home through Stories." *(Ad)dressing Our Words: Aboriginal Perspectives on Aboriginal Literatures.* Ed. Armand Garnet Ruffo. Penticton: Theytus Books, 2001. 17-36. Print.

Montemayor, Carlos, and Donald Frischmann, eds. *Words of the True Peoples/Palabras de los Seres Verdaderos.* Austin: U of Texas P, 2007. Print.

"Nadia Myre: Indian Act." 1999-2002. The Medicine Project. Curated by Dana Claxton and Skeena Reece. Vancouver: grunt gallery. Web. 9 Feb. 2015. <www.themedicine project.com/nadia-myre.html>.

Ortiz, Simon. "Men on the Moon." 1978. *Men on the Moon: Collected Short Stories*. Tucson: U of Arizona P, 1999. 2-14. Print.

Panipakuttuk, Joe. "The Many Lives of Anakajuttuq." *North/nord* 16.5 (Sept.1969). Rpt. in *Paper Stays Put: A Collection of Inuit Writing*. Ed. Robin Gedalof and Alootook Ipellie. Seattle: U of Washington P, 1982. 152-55. Print.

Poitras, Evelyn, dir. *To Colonize a People: The File Hills Indian Farm Colony*. Regina: Blue Thunderbird Productions, 2000.

Power, Susan. "Beaded Soles." 1997. *Roofwalker*. Minneapolis: Milkweed, 2002. 84-110. Print.

Quirk, Sarah A. "Sherman Alexie." *Dictionary of Literary Biography Volume 278: American Novelists since World War II*. Ed. James R. Giles and Wanda H. Giles. 5th ed. Detroit: Thomson Gale, 2003. 3-10. Print.

Racette, Sherry Farrell. "Métis Education." *The Encyclopedia of Saskatchewan*. Regina: Canadian Plains Research Center, 2006. Web. 28 July 2015. <www.esask.uregina.ca/entry/metis_education.html>.

Ratt, Solomon. "I'm Not an Indian." *Wawiyatacimowinisa: Funny Little Stories*. Ed. Arok Wolvengrey. Regina: Canadian Plains Research Center, 2007. 41-45. Print.

Reder, Deanna, and Linda Morra, eds. *Learn, Teach, Challenge: Approaching Indigenous Literatures*. Waterloo: Wilfrid Laurier UP, 2016. Print.

Rivard, Sylvain. "Grandma and the Wendigo." Trans. Kristin Talbot Neel and Sylvain Rivard. Orig. published in French, "Mémère et le Windigo" from *Contes du trou d'cul*. Montreal: Cornac, 2000. Print.

Robinson, Eden. "Terminal Avenue." *So Long Been Dreaming: Postcolonial Science Fiction and Fantasy*. Ed. Nalo Hopkinson and Uppinder Mehan. Vancouver: Arsenal Pulp, 2004. 64-69. Print.

Robinson, Gordon. "Weegit Discovers Halibut Hooks." *Tales of Kitimaat*. Kitimat: Northern Sentinel, 1956. 3-5. Print.

Sanderson, Steven Keewatin. *Darkness Calls*. Vancouver: Healthy Aboriginal Network, 2004. Print.

Scott, Walter K. *Wendy*. Toronto: Koyama, 2014. Print.

Seesequasis, Paul. "The Republic of Tricksterism." 1998. *An Anthology of Canadian Native Literature in English*. Ed. Daniel David Moses, Terry Goldie, and Armand Ruffo. 4th ed. Toronto: Oxford UP, 2013. 468-74. Print.

Silko, Leslie Marmon. *Ceremony*. New York: Penguin, 1977. Print.

———. "Language and Literature from a Pueblo Indian Perspective." *English Literature: Opening up the Canon*. Ed. Leslie Fiedler and Houston A. Baker Jr. Baltimore: Johns Hopkins UP, 1981. 54-72. Rpt. in *Yellow Woman and a Beauty of the Spirit: Essays on Native American Life Today*. New York: Simon & Schuster, 1996. 48-59. Print.

———. "Lullaby." *Chicago Review* 26.1 (1974): 10-17. Rpt. in *Storyteller*. New York: Viking, 1981. 43-55. Print.

"Spirits in the Material World: Haisla Culture Takes Strange Shape in Eden Robinson's *Monkey Beach*." *Quill & Quire* 1 (2000): par. 1-24. Web. 30 July 2016. <www.quill andquire.com/authors/spirits-in-the-material-world/>.

Stevens, James R., and Carl Ray. *Sacred Legends of the Sandy Lake Cree*. Toronto: McClelland and Stewart, 1971. Print.

Sullivan, Robert. *Star Waka*. Auckland: Auckland UP, 1999. Print.

Suzuki, David, with Amanda McConnell. *The Sacred Balance: Rediscovering Our Place in Nature*. 1997. Vancouver: Douglas and McIntyre, 2002. Print.

Terán, Sylvia, and Christian H. Rasmussen, eds. and comps. *Relatos del centro del mundo/U Tsikbalo'obi Chuumuk Lu'um*. Vol. I, II, III. Yucatán: Mérida, 1992. Print.

———. *Tales of the Center of the World*. Trans. Pedro Pablo Chuc Pech. Unpublished English-language MS of *Relatos del centro del mundo/U Tsikbalo'obi Chuumuk Lu'um*, 1992. Personal communication (email), 1 Nov. 2016.

Torres Sánchez, Joel. "I'm Not a Witch, I'm a Healer!" 1998, trans. 2007. *Words of the True Peoples/Palabras de los Seres Verdaderos*. Ed. Carlos Montemayor and Donald Frischmann. Austin: U of Texas P, 2007. 179-82. Print.

Van Camp, Richard. "Devotion." *Godless but Loyal to Heaven*. Winnipeg: Enfield and Wizenty, 2012. 75-80. Print.

Wakamatsu, M. E. "Rita Hayworth Mexicana." *Cantos al sexto sol: An Anthology of Aztlanahuae Writings*. Ed. Cecilio Garcia-Camarillo, Roberto Rodriguez, and Patrisia Gonzales. San Antonio: Wings, 2002. 251-53. Print.

White, Ellen Rice. "The Boys Who Became a Killer Whale." *Legends and Teachings of Xeel's, The Creator*. Vancouver: Pacific Educational, 2006. 25-38. Print.

Willard, Tania. *Coyote and the People Killer*. Told by Isaac Willard. Illustrations by Tania Willard. Translated English text from *Shuswap Stories: Collected 1971-1975*, 38-41. Ed. Randy Bouchard and Dorothy Kennedy. Vancouver: CommCept, 1979. Burnaby: Burnaby Art Gallery, 2004. Print.

Wolfart, H. C. "Cree Literature." *Encyclopedia of Canadian Literature*. Ed. William H. New. Toronto: U of Toronto P, 2002. 243-47. Print.

———. *Plains Cree: A Grammatical Study*. Philadelphia: American Philosophical Society, 1973. Print.

Womack, Craig. "King of the Tie-snakes." *Drowning in Fire*. Tucson: U of Arizona P, 2001. 10-31. Print.

———. *Red on Red: Native American Literary Separatism*. Minneapolis: U of Minnesota P, 1999. Print.

Yahgulanaas, Michael Nicoll. *Red: A Haida Manga*. Vancouver: Douglas and McIntyre, 2009. 80-83. Print.

Zitkala-Sa. "The Devil." *American Indian Stories*. 1921. Foreword by Dexter Fisher. Lincoln: U of Nebraska P, 1985. 62-64. Print.

ABOUT THE EDITORS

As editors we have modelled self-positioning for our readers, coming as we do from a variety of perspectives on Indigenous literatures, with a question posed by Welsh, Irish, and Métis scholar Natalie Clark: "Who are you and why do you care?" Clark devised this question for herself as a foundation for her own engagement with Indigenous youth. We use it here as a means to identify ourselves in relation to *Read, Listen, Tell,* and we pass it on to you as a point of entry into the stories collected here. It is not a rhetorical question and we ask it, as Clark does, with warmth and generosity. Take a moment and ask yourself the question: *Who are you and why do you care*? If you are an instructor, ask it of your students; if you are a student, ask it of your instructor. You may want to write your replies down and come back to them after you read the text. Did your answers change?

This is who we are and why we care:

Born in Kampala, Uganda, where her father taught in the Philosophy department at Makerere University, **SOPHIE McCALL** was raised with stories about the necessity of decolonizing lands, minds, and communities; yet this consciousness was not always applied to the forms of colonialism at work in Canada. She grew up in Montreal, Quebec, where her Scottish-descended anglophone family on her father's side has lived for five generations, and where she remembers being taught in both grade school and secondary school that Montreal used to be called Hochelaga. No further explanation of this apparently inevitable transition was offered, reflecting how living in a settler colonial society requires a continuous reinscription of the denial of land takeover and of the marginalization of Indigenous peoples. Sophie has focused both her scholarship and her teaching on un-learning the violent suppressions and absences that this legacy of settler colonialism has created. She feels tremendously lucky that she has been able to participate as an ally in the current groundswell of change that is occurring at universities, with opportunities to work closely with Indigenous students, colleagues, and writers who are transforming the institution through their paradigm-shifting research. Probably the most important reason that Sophie cares about this work resides in her role as the mother of mixed-race children, whose ancestry connects to four of the world's continents, and whose need to find stories that reflect their experiences and their histories is palpable in their many urgent questions about where they come from, and how to make a difference in this world.

When **DEANNA REDER** was a child, she explained to others that she was part Cree, since that is the language her mother spoke; part German, since that was the language her father spoke; and part English, since this was the language they spoke together. It was only as she grew that she realized that her mother's family was a mix of Métis and Status Cree people from LaRonge, Saskatchewan; that her father's family had arrived in Beausejour, Manitoba after the First World War from Poland and Russia; and that both preferred that she speak English. Because her mother only went to grade nine and her father to grade six, her love of school and of English literature was hard to explain, even to herself. It was only when she stumbled on Indigenous writers in the early 1990s that she understood how important it was to read stories with contexts that reflected the experiences of her family. As she began teaching she saw that same recognition and validation among her Indigenous students, when reading, hearing, and discussing Indigenous stories. Likewise, she saw the same transformative reactions by non-Indigenous students who were provoked to reconsider what they understand to be the history of Canada. Her hope is that this reader will help teachers and all readers in this challenging work.

DAVID GAERTNER is a settler scholar of German descent on both his mother and his father's sides of the family. His father was born on a farm in Tisdale, Saskatchewan, and his mother was born on an army base in Tsawwassen, British Columbia. When locating himself in classrooms, he sometimes jokes with students that his lineage branches from the two centre poles of settler colonialism: agriculture and warfare. David grew up on Semyome (Semiahmoo) territory in what is now known as South Surrey, British Columbia, and he now lives and works on the traditional, ancestral, and unceded territory of the hən̓q̓əmin̓əm̓-speaking Musqueam people where he teaches and researches Indigenous new media in the First Nations and Indigenous Studies Program at the University of British Columbia. In hən̓q̓əmin̓əm̓ David is a *xʷənitəm*, a non-Indigenous person of Caucasian descent. David researches and teaches Indigenous literature because as an undergraduate student he realized that he knew very little about the Indigenous histories of the places that he grew up in and studied and he wanted to be more accountable to those communities and lands. As he started to learn more, David realized that Indigenous studies was where the action is: that the literature and literary theory being written by Indigenous scholars was and is challenging the very way we think of reading and writing. He wanted to be a part of this work in some small way and this book is a realization of his desire to support the field and to help it grow.

GABRIELLE L'HIRONDELLE HILL is an artist and writer descended from Cree, Métis, and English lineages. Born in K̓ómoks territory, Gabrielle moved with her family in the mid-1980s to the unceded Musqueam land so that her mother could attend the Native Indian Teacher Education Program at UBC. Gabrielle and her siblings had the privilege of being raised on Indigenous literature. From leafing through her mother's school books as a child—by authors including Chrystos, Emma LaRoque, and Gloria Anzaldúa—to passing around the novels by Sherman Alexie, Louise Erdrich, and Thomas King she and her brothers got for Christmas, Gabrielle formed a sense of who she was in a large part through that literature. To this day, Gabrielle believes in the transformative potential of stories that help readers see themselves as powerful, as part of an intellectual and artistic community, and that communicate and develop ideas about who we are and how we came to be here in the contexts of colonialism, capitalism, and resistance.

COPYRIGHT ACKNOWLEDGEMENTS

M. E. Wakamatsu. "Rita Hayworth Mexicana." From *Cantos al sexto sol: An Anthology of Aztlanahuae Writings*, edited by Cecilio Garcia-Camarillo, Roberto Rodriguez, and Patrisia Gonzales (Wings Press, 2002). Reprinted by permission of the author.

Ellen Rice White. "The Boys Who Became a Killer Whale," from *Legends and Teachings of Xeel's, The Creator* (Pacific Educational Press, 2006). Reprinted by permission of the author.

Tania Willard. *Coyote and the People Killer*. Told by Isaac Willard. Illustrations by Tania Willard. Translated English text from Randy Bouchard and Dorothy Kennedy, editors, *Shuswap Stories* (CommCept 1979, pp. 38–41). Text reprinted by permission of the British Columbia Indian Language Project; illustrations reprinted by permission of Tania Willard; photography of artwork reprinted by permission of Aaron Leon.

Craig S. Womack. "King of the Tie-snakes." From *Drowning in Fire* by Craig Womack. © 2001 Craig S. Womack. Reprinted by permission of the University of Arizona Press.

Michael Nicoll Yahgulanaas. Excerpt from *Red: A Haida Manga* by Michael Nicoll Yahgulanaas, 2014, Douglas and McIntyre. Reprinted by permission of the publisher.

Books in the Indigenous Studies Series
Published by Wilfrid Laurier University Press

Blockades and Resistance: Studies in Actions of Peace and the Temagami Blockades of 1988–89 / Bruce W. Hodgins, Ute Lischke, and David T. McNab, editors / 2003 / xi + 276 pp. / illus. / ISBN 0-88920-381-4

Indian Country: Essays on Contemporary Native Culture / Gail Guthrie Valaskakis / 2005 / x + 293 pp. / illus. / ISBN 0-88920-479-9

Walking a Tightrope: Aboriginal People and Their Representations / Ute Lischke and David T. McNab, editors / 2005 / xix + 377 pp. / illus. / ISBN 978-0-88920-484-3

The Long Journey of a Forgotten People: Métis Identities and Family Histories / Ute Lischke and David T. McNab, editors / 2007 / viii + 386 pp. / illus. / ISBN 978-0-88920-523-9

Words of the Huron / John L. Steckley / 2007 / xvii + 259 pp. / ISBN 978-0-88920-516-1

Essential Song: Three Decades of Northern Cree Music / Lynn Whidden / 2007 / xvi + 176 pp. / illus., musical examples, audio CD / ISBN 978-0-88920-459-1

From the Iron House: Imprisonment in First Nations Writing / Deena Rymhs / 2008 / ix + 147 pp. / ISBN 978-1-55458-021-7

Lines Drawn upon the Water: First Nations and the Great Lakes Borders and Borderlands / Karl S. Hele, editor / 2008 / xxiii + 351 pp. / illus. / ISBN 978-1-55458-004-0

Troubling Tricksters: Revisioning Critical Conversations / Linda M. Morra and Deanna Reder, editors / 2009 / xii+ 336 pp. / illus. / ISBN 978-1-55458-181-8

Aboriginal Peoples in Canadian Cities: Transformations and Continuities / Heather A. Howard and Craig Proulx, editors / 2011 / viii + 256 pp. / illus. / ISBN 978-1-055458-260-0

Bridging Two Peoples: Chief Peter E. Jones, 1843–1909 / Allan Sherwin / 2012 / xxiv + 246 pp. / illus. / ISBN 978-1-55458-633-2

The Nature of Empires and the Empires of Nature: Indigenous Peoples and the Great Lakes Environment / Karl S. Hele, editor / 2013 / xxii + 350 / illus. / ISBN 978-1-55458-328-7

The Eighteenth-Century Wyandot: A Clan-Based Study / John L. Steckley / 2014 / x + 306 pp. / ISBN 978-1-55458-956-2

Indigenous Poetics in Canada / Neal McLeod, editor / 2014 / xii + 404 pp. / ISBN 978-1-55458-982-1

Literary Land Claims: The "Indian Land Question" from Pontiac's War to Attawapiskat / Margery Fee / 2015 / x + 318 pp. / illus. / ISBN 978-1-77112-119-4

Arts of Engagement: Taking Aesthetic Action In and Beyond Canada's Truth and Reconciliation Commission / Dylan Robinson and Keavy Martin, editors / 2016 / viii + 376 pp. / illus. / ISBN 978-1-77112-169-9

Learn, Teach, Challenge: Approaching Indigenous Literature / Deanna Reder and Linda M. Morra, editors / 2016 / xii + 580 pp. / ISBN 978-1-77112-185-9

Read, Listen, Tell: Indigenous Stories from Turtle Island / Sophie McCall, Deanna Reder, David Gaertner, and Gabrielle L'Hirondelle Hill, editors / 2017 / xviii + 392 pp. / ISBN 978-1-77112-300-6